MONARCH
RISING

MONARCH RISING

HARPER GLENN

Library of Congress Cataloging-in-Publication Data available

ISBN 978-1-338-74145-2

1 2022

Printed in the U.S.A. 23

First edition, October 2022

Book design by Omou Barry

For Hattie, who said:

". . . everybody thinks they know what they'd do with
the world until they get it."

Here's one version of the world, Grandma.

"Nothing makes a man so adventurous as an empty pocket."

—Victor Hugo

PROLOGUE

The pistol's hammer went *Click! Click! Click!*, echoing in Moats Alley. "Shhhhh . . . slow moves, girl. Slow, slow moves," a voice from behind whispered.

My black sketchbook slid down clammy fingers, splattered in the puddle at my feet. Mud water splashed the green dumpster to my left, wet dirt sprayed my stiff neck and quivering chin, and I stood semi-motionless. Eyes to wet pavement, I glanced at the clear bag of rotten chicken in my hand.

"What's your name?" It was a woman. A jig. Words trembling, she sniffed— was high. And smelled like smack. "Speak, now! Name!"

I stuttered. "Jo, ma'am. Jo . . . Josephine Monarch."

"Age?"

"Ma'am?"

"Age!"

"Nine just last week, ma'am."

"Turn 'round." She coughed, spat.

I obeyed, turned, faced her. She pressed the pistol against the center of my forehead. My eyes turned upward at the gun, then forward, staring at the woman's blistered skin peeling away from swollen lips. Her mouth opened, moved raggedly over gritty yellow teeth as she begged for chicken clutched inside my left fist. Shivering junkie said she'd had a rough life—said chicken'd make her feel better. Said she was hungry, starved for food and warm drink. Yelled she didn't wanna do drugs no more; said she wanted her old life back.

Teary-eyed jig coughed, swallowed mucus, ran shaky fingers through unkempt dreads. "So, what of it, girl? Gimme the chicken," she said, eyeballs full of red lines, inner corners of her eyes saturated in crunchy beige crust.

I stared at the butt of the pistol wobbling erratically at the end of her wrist. I trembled, sweaty in cold weather, but I didn't give her the chicken. Told her, "No. The meat's worthless, sick with Radius. It'll kill yuh."

The jig said, "I don't care. Life ain't worth living anymore. If Radius takes my life in three days, it's God's will and no use running from him." She pushed the gun deeper into my skin, so deep that if she didn't kill me, an impression of the barrel would sit between my eyes.

Sirens erupted behind me. I told her if she left now, she'd escape—that I wouldn't tell cops what she'd done. I gave her my daily toke, told her to take it, use the money to buy fresh water, bread, and fish slices from the Fresh Food Bus. Assured her it closed in an hour, and if she hurried, took the back way around the broke amusement park, over by the trash heap, she'd make it there on time, unseen by cops.

Index finger over bloody lips, she shushed me, snatched my toke, said, "Close both eyes and count to ten." I obeyed. Closed eyes, counted to ten, opened my eyes. She was gone.

Once home, I told Aunt Vye and Cousin Neal what'd happened. Vye grabbed me, held on tight, said everything'd be alright.

Neal laughed. "That's freaking badassery," he'd said. "Shoulda gave her the chicken."

"She would've died," I'd said.

Neal scoffed, shrugged shoulders, and said, "So?"

Later that night, outside, Vye kissed my forehead and said one day I'd make it out of here, but I couldn't do it without stars. Hands in pants pockets, I stared at the sky, smirked at the stars, and smiled into the moon. Back then stars were great, but the moon was peaceful—it calmed me, always did. It's this enormous lightning bug, perfecting the night sky. Most girls wished on stars. Not me; I was a moon girl. And one day, I'd follow the moon all the way to New Georgia, away from rotted chicken and jigs with guns. And when I got there, I'd pull the moon down from the clouds with rope till it reached my nose, and when it sat there, I was gunna kiss it.

Part I
THORNS

"... and we are a nation of thorn-ridden paths. May we enter dawn untainted by our turbulent past. Those born into ashes shall have opportunity to rise from dust."

—New United States of America Constitutional Peace Doctrine

1

JOSEPHINE

A cockroach flutters ferociously to the ceiling.

I can't see it with closed eyes, but I hear it, sense its extended brown wings relax against its spine as flapping comes to a swift halt. Roaches aren't uncommon in the Ashes. Here, across the mountains from New Georgia, it's flooded with the long-winged creepy-crawlies. Before dawn, when the sun's tucked away like it is now, you can't blink or think without spotting their thumb-sized narrow frames slithering.

I open my eyes, watch the roach glide to the floor. It's three inches away, headed toward the flat sheet covering Aunt Vye's piss-stained floor mattress. The sheet's an ugly green, doused in bleach and other tangy chemicals. But no one complains; when a sheet's used properly, it does what it should: shields limbs and extremities from Radius-infected rats.

Last night, I had the nightmare again, the one about the jig with dreads. It felt real, like it was happening all over. And there, in the sleeping place of real-life terrors, I wasn't seventeen. I was nine again, shivering before her in Moats Alley.

The roach hisses, brings me back to present. Vye can't feel it, but were she to open her brown eyes, she'd catch the cockroach travel up her brown fingers, skim her black coarse hair, and skitter across her neck just before it flaps russet wings, and settles inside my cousin Neal's red sneakers.

I close my eyes tight. Tighter. Wishing I was anywhere but here.

Sweat beads cover my forehead, trickle into wild brows and long black lashes.

Despite the nightmare, the familiar cockroach, the odor, I remind myself: Today's a good day. *The* day, the day of the Lineup. The day I could be picked to leave all this behind, for good. Lingering unease from the nightmare transforms into anxiety about today. I twirl my triangular white Lineup card between index finger and thumb, rub the raised red letters on the card that read: LINEUP ALLOWED. Everyone who passes exams gets one. I exhale deep, trying to breathe out the panic about lining up with other kids, hoping New Georgia Reps pick us to leave the Ashes, to trade this place for a life of luxury across the mountain.

The cockroach climbs out of Neal's shoe. I gotta catch it. If I don't, tonight it'll be under Vye's sheets, waiting for legs to creep up. It crawls over Vye's frayed black dress and disappears. I freeze. Don't move. It's there. In my hair. It crawls between my roots, skitters across my forehead. I grab it—feel it jitter in my palm like a moth in a mason jar. I stick my arm out the window beside my bed—release it, watch it coast into opaque sewer fog.

With my head sticking out the open window, I watch Ashfolk prepare kin for Lineup. Parents outside tattered shacks comb naps out of kids' heads; fathers sit behind offspring on stools brushing kids' hair. Grandparents lick the tips of their thumbs to clean dirty spots on grandkids' faces. My cheeks sit high, smiling, but inside, my heart gulps for air as if thrown into a bottomless ocean. Oceans, fresh air. If I make it past the Lineup and move to New Georgia, I'll never look outside this cutout window again. No more catching flying roaches. In New Georgia, colorful butterflies'll dance on the tips of my fingers.

I release a heavy sigh. Butterfly dances come at a cost. I'll never look out this window, see these people, my people, again.

I fold my lips into my mouth, exhale, and watch a group of Ashfolk walk toward Town Center.

John Ready's speaking today. He spends most his time traveling, rallying other borderlands for justice, but returns home every year, the day of the Lineup, to perform his infamous speech about the old Revolt War and unity. John's speech never changes, so anyone over age ten knows it by heart.

John was just a kid during Revolt 2030—Vye too, for that matter. She grew up across the mountains, with money. Horror stories she'd tell Neal and I flash before me like a looking glass. I can almost see them, the poor folks back then who called themselves Revolt Rebels, or RR's. How RR's raided government buildings in huge numbers across all fifty-one states. How they ambushed elected officials as they slept, held them in cages barely big enough to hold their bodies. Acts committed to take back the country they loved, freedoms they'd been denied, and meager voices silenced by violence.

Blinking bloody thoughts away, I pull my head in from the window, stretch, peering around the house. Well, it's not really a house at all. It's a dilapidated old shed with three chain-saw-made windows; torn sheets cover the open space like black shades. We each have our own window; plastic navy shower curtains separate my space from Aunt Vye's part—a flat green sheet cuts Vye's area off from Neal's. This room's so small, there's no scent you can't smell. And I smell Neal—he's bare chested, golden frame splayed across his brown cot, gripping his pocketknife.

"Ugh." I hold a scrunched nose. Neal's side is junky—always is. Consumed with foul socks, and red-clay-covered red boots shedding wasteland manure—wastelands where he and most boys in the Ashes collect bones of dead animals to carve rings, necklaces, and other jewelry tradable for clothes, shoes, food, and round currency called tokes. Schlocky is Neal's middle name. And still, there's no girl in the Ashes unwilling to accept him as is.

I pass the bathroom with the body-sized mirror nailed to its door—it's so small in there, walls hug you scooching on and off the compost toilet. Splintered wood covers narrow hallways like skin tags layer Vye's high cheeks. And kitchen space's so tight Vye calls it a hole-in-a-wall.

In the kitchen, I flip the switch for kicks, knowing full well no lights'll come on. Electric doesn't exist here. After the war, Revolt Rebels left behind the tattered shacks and warehouses they lived in, minus the technology behind the switches to keep homes lit. Then forced the defeated rich folks to take their place. Vye's lived right here ever since. I light a candle. Inhale smoke lit wick creates. Open the wood-burning stove, light it, place a pot of water on top, watch it sizzle. Growls escape my stomach. I stare at the pie on the small wooden slab on the floor—the one we eat on. No use rubbing my belly; I can't eat it—it's already sold. In our house, we earn tokes best we can, and Vye's pies keep us fed.

Nose to pie, I sniff it, inhale smashed pecans and cinnamon—the only goods grown here, then traded with rich folks on the other side of the mountains. But some things grown here barely make it out alive—like animals. No one bothers keeping pets. And if they do, you'll see two- or three-legged cats and dogs hopping around their house, because someone boiled and fried their limbs for dinner, but kept them alive 'cause they couldn't bear to kill 'em straight out.

When water boils and pops like hot grits, I take the pot off the range, pour water in the iron washbowl on my scruffy dresser. Once water cools, I splash my face, watch clear liquid drip down my chin in the cracked mirror before me. I look at my small head, and thick braids growing out my skull. It's been a few months since Vye helped plait it—it's due for a touch-up. But sometimes, I like my hair wild, strands of kinky hair peeking beyond loose braids.

I turn around, plop down on my mattress, stare at my flat pillow—the only photos I have of my parents peek beneath it. I pull the photos out. They're in bad shape. Edges worn, torn, battling mold. But I don't care. It's what's left of them. I stare at their faces; they're so happy it's hard imagining the absence of money made them fall out of love and take their lives. Aunt Vye assures they weren't always unhappy. Says when reminding's needed, look at their photo, focus on their smiling eyes.

And it works. Their photos make me crave love—and sometimes, I want it so bad it feels like a part of my DNA. If I close my eyes tight, I see tadpole-like strands of deoxyribonucleic acid swimming inside my nuclei, exchanging forehead kisses. Kids wanting a better life avoid love in the Ashes. We bide our broke time waiting for the year we can line up and hope for love in New Georgia. Finding love in the Ashes is possible but risky. I don't wanna connect here, fall in and out of love, struggle, and kill myself over money.

Vye stirs, yawns—half-asleep, she says check the small closet near the front of the house, instructs me to bring what's in it to her. I obey. At the base of the closet, next to Vye's red flats, I spot a cardboard box wrapped in thorny tweed. I kneel, dust fresh rat poop off the top, lift it off the floor, tuck it under my arm. I wash my hands before handing the box to Vye.

"Open it." Vye grins ear to ear.

Inside is a long muslin rose-gold skirt, a silk spaghetti-strap blouse, and matching two-inch heels. Vye says she bought the outfit off Bootleg Jules last night—traded the skirt, top, and shoes for lemonade moonshine and her famous pecan-cinnamon pie. Says the trio was perfect, just my size, and the regulated color for the Gala.

I close the box. I'm not selfish. Besides, I know—"We can't afford this. Must've cost six tokes."

Vye smiles. "Hush, child. Let me worry about tokes. Made enough pies this month, sold 'em too."

Biggest hurdle is getting the Rep to pick you from the Lineup so you can get decked out in rose-gold clothes and attend the Gala—the next step toward Reps

11

choosing you for a lifetime of luxury and comfort. But after Lineup, some chosen kids don't board the AerTrain—they decide not to go the Gala at all. No one knows why. They return sad-faced without words in clothes their parents went broke for. Don't want Vye wasting tokes, because what if it's hard to leave the Ashes? And more so . . . "What if the Rep doesn't like me . . . if I'm not picked? I'll never go to the Gala and you'd've spent all this . . . for nothing."

Vye waves her hand, shushing. "Yuh passed the exam. Have yuh seen yuh? Met yuh?"

Pupils pinned to cracked floors, I shrug. Vye's right, yeah, sure, I passed the exams, but I can't help wondering, what if she's wrong? What if it's not enough, I'm not enough? I suck in my bottom lip, stressing over how it's not just about good grades, we gotta be liked too. Liked, and wear smiley faces to impress New Georgia Reps—a Rep with the rights to crush dreams and tell us no at the end of all that impressing. But what do I know? What does anyone know if they ain't a Rep. Years ago, I'd place bets on who'd make it through—stupid bets with zero tokes to gamble when I was often dead wrong. Most Ashfolk are.

Vye lifts my chin; our eyes meet. "Don'tcha know how special yuh are? Yuh ma'd be proud. Dad, too."

I exhale, smirk, and tremble beneath my skin. I think of my parents. Wish I remembered their faces outside of tarnished photos. Wish someone had bottled their skin, so when I felt confused inside mine, I could melt into theirs.

With narrow eyes, Vye smiles and says, "Go on in dat bathroom. Try duh clothes on."

I take the box into the bathroom, set it on the toilet, undress, and dress before the cracked mirror. No holes or stains in the fabric. It's perfect.

"Does it fit?" Vye says on the other side of the door.

"Yes," I lie. The top and skirt fit perfectly, but the rose-gold shoes are too big.

I've never worn heels before, but it shouldn't be an issue. Based on letters written home and bitter whispers from rejected Hopefuls from past Galas—more specifically, girls who don't get picked at the end of the night and return to gray lives back in the Ashes—wiggle room in dancing shoes is better than too tight.

Ignoring the largeness of these shoes, I pretend I'm one of the rich folks. Poised, refined, classy, strutting around New Georgia with a purse full of money. I think of how smash it'd be not wearing red shoes every day. And then I hear the only voice inside my head that grounds me: my best friend, Boah. His daily rants on what Revolt Rebels did to our ancestors brings guilt. Makes me feel bad wishing this place away. I take the clothes off, return them to the box, shut it, slide night clothes back on.

In my room, Neal's gone. And Vye cooks pecan pancakes in the kitchen. I twist ragged braids into a bun on top my head, pull the white paper with my test results from under my Lineup card. It's not the best, but it's a good score. I've waited my whole life for today. But I'm not alone. Everyone who took the exam feels the same—well, those who passed.

We're tested in biology, reading, math, science, and writing. Failers don't get second chances and live the rest of their lives here depressed, heads low, and still poor. Last year, my friend Tessa scored an 87, within the 80–100 passing range. Tessa couldn't wait to line up. In preparation, she studied the *Expectation*: the weekly magazine written in New Georgia, printed in the Mill here, and distributed in the Ashes. Before each year's Lineup, there's an article about that year's Lineup Rep. Plus, there's information on rich boys and girls in New Georgia. I imagine Tessa standing in front of our cracked mirror, cheek pressed against photos of cute boys, fantasizing, prepping for her chance to impress all those people at the Gala. Whenever I asked who I'd look cute with, Tessa'd laugh and say his first name starts with a *B*, ends with an *H*.

Wonder if Boah's half excited as I am? There was a time Boah couldn't wait to leave this place. He'd talk about our life in New Georgia with starry eyes; said in the Ashes we're best friends 'cause we're poor. And one day, if we made it past the Lineup, we'd shoot our shot in New Georgia. That was years ago. Boah's different—now it seems he looks for excuses to stay.

Dragonflies swarm inside my belly. I wonder who's this year's Rep. Bet Boah knows; he worked the Mill last night—he'll have already read the latest issue of the *Expectation*. I feel my smile flip upside down. Tessa worked the Mill too. Were she here, she'd have told me who the Rep is. Then we'd get ready together, line up together, and hope we'd make it through the Gala. But that'll never happen. Nine months ago, while she was sleeping, a rat bit Tessa's thumb. Forty-eight hours later, her mom buried her body in wastelands.

John Ready's Tessa's uncle. When he spoke at her funeral, he reminded us why we should fight. He waved a hand toward the raging crowd, silencing it, then said, "We were once rich, famous. We're immigrants now. Ashfolk. Begging for scraps . . . metal and wood shacks to protect from storms. Working ten hours a day, over yonder at the Mill, printing their *Expectation* magazines for one measly copper toke. Flaunting our proud youth in ego-infused 'expectations,' bragging over rags-to-riches transformation headlines in aristocratic New Georgia society."

John means well, but it isn't all bad. Each season, via AerTrain, New Georgia Reps deliver cots for sleeping, textbooks for homeschooling, and lava rocks and matches to keep warm during winter. Scratches, cuts, and minor sprains we patch ourselves. But when we're severely sick, Reps offer free medical care. Sometimes I'm glad I live here, and not over there. The Ashes is all I know. And besides, it'd be hard going from rich to poor like all the OldTimers did after Revolt 2030. When you're born with nothing, you don't waste time missing what you never had. But it never hurts to dream and hope; hope for the chance to be picked, the chance to try for something better than this—a chance to leave, escape.

That chance'll happen soon. Lineup begins at nine a.m. I glance at the tattered watch around my wrist. It's six. I touch my cheeks; they're warm from smiling. I lift my chin to the holey roof. The moon's out, but soon, the sun'll rise. If I don't get a move on, I'll be late for Boah. I grab my sketchbook and charcoal stick from the foot of my mattress. Dash out the house in brown cargos, a torn white T-shirt, and red boots, head to the broke amusement park.

When I reach Town Center, the crowd is cheering, clapping, anticipating John's powerful words. It's nerve-racking because, I don't know, it feels strange. John gives this speech every year, but this year something's changed. It's more than this finally being my year. Faces are red, foreheads wrinkled. I hear teeth-sucking and lip-smacking—see eyes speaking without blinking. After last year's Lineup, Boah said there's talk in the Ashes about forming a new generation of rebels.

John opens his speech saying, "Two lives exist in New America: one of poverty, one of riches. One only need glance tuh see which we're in. Poor place. Land of forgotten people. High crime; kids get shot pulling gum out pockets."

No one's shocked when John says this. Usually right after those words leave his instigating-thin lips, the crowd's full of plain faces because they know unwarranted murder is just . . . life. Cops shoot to kill without hesitation. And why shouldn't they? They're never punished—the law is what the bullet in their barrel hits. In the Ashes, protesting is illegal. So, we suck it up and take it—no voice can change it.

Next John points to green peaks in the distance and says, "They don't fool me over there. They foolin' you? No. We know what the Lineup's about. Promises of riches, but only if they like you. If you're smart enough, charming enough, kind enough, clean enough in clothes inferior to theirs." Then, like a prayer, John places both hands in front of his lips and says, "They could stop it all, this . . . the poverty. They've enough money to make us all rich, but they won't. Greed ain't the reason. Their reasons run deeper. It's revenge. Our rich ancestors watched their poor kin suffer. Look around, folks. This land . . . is revenge."

Whenever John says "revenge," I shrug it off. John's what we call in the Ashes an OldTimer. Rich folks born and raised in New Georgia, when it was just Georgia, before Revolt 2030 forced them here. And like most OldTimers I know, he's stuck in the past, afraid to seek the future. But I don't know. Hate to admit it, but maybe truth lives inside John's vengeful words.

As I walk to the front of the roaring crowd, I watch John unfasten a button, the one closest to his neck. "Let our young folk tell us how the Ashes was formed. Volunteers?"

A round white boy with cornrows stands beside John. I only know him as Rald, the boy who eats buggers. He spouts the history of our people, fingers fidgeting. He says after Revolt 2030, Revolt Rebels became lawmakers known as Reps. Reps kicked rich folks out the city. Moved them here, to what's become the Ashes—a see-how-you-like-being-poor stance, trapping their oppressors in the lifestyle they'd endured—forcing them, and every generation of their offspring, to live in poverty forever. Rald glances at John Ready, then turns to the crowd with a rebellious grin and says, "Reps can't be that bad, though, right? They giving us a chance; it's what Lineup is for. We've got a way out."

When Rald's done talking, John shakes his head, disappointed, and takes the spotlight again—places one hand in pants pocket, while the other hand points to morning moon. Then he stares into the crowd, looks at me, and says, "Young folks participating in today's Lineup, I urge you, reconsider. Be unrepressed! Nothing's across that mountain you can't find here."

2

JOSEPHINE

John ready's stern eyes are fixed on me, unsmiling. Straight-faced, I turn around, back away from John's stare. I'm hot inside. Starting to think Vye's right about John Ready—he's a hypocrite. It's pretty messed up he's anti-Lineup. Because when John was my age, he lined up, got chosen by Reps and educated in Saven, New Georgia. Guilt made him come back home. His mother died of Radius while he chased rich dreams across the mountain. I can't read John's mind, but I bet he still feels bad about missing his momma's burial.

Voices from John's crowd melt into nothing when I reach Moats Alley. Entrance feels violent. Things happen down this alley no one whispers about. I'd skip it, jump it, fly over it if I could, but I can't. It's the only way to get to the roller coaster to meet Boah. No, I'm lying, there's another way, but it'd take twice as long. And I don't wanna miss sunrise with Boah.

I enter Moats Alley watchful, avoiding eye contact with jigs, don't want 'em thinking I got stones to heat, needles to give. If Moats's walls weren't draped with addicts, it'd be amazing. Wall to cobbled street, Moats is layered with vintage stones, and old doors that lead to Victorian apartments that were beautiful—a cruel reminder that once upon a time, the Ashes was a well-off part of old Georgia. Rich folks once lived here, partied here, loved here. Story goes, when Revolt Rebels won the war, they took our Georgian citizenship away. Coined us Ashfolk after the ashes burned books, buildings, and bodies left behind.

Distrustful, I swallow hard, walk slow, slower; my fingers make two fists, short nails pressed into palm skin. I think of better times, days OldTimers speak of the closer Lineup gets. When the richest rich folks lived here, these dirty cobbled stones were the color of pearls—now they're rusty like copper, spoons and blown matches haunting corners. Back then, fancy welcome mats and tall plants rested at the base of every door, where jigs rest now. It's nice imagining the before, a time unlike now. For some Hopefuls, hearing tales of the old days is what inspires them to take the exam and line up. But for me, no matter its glamorous history, Moats Alley reminds me of the jig with the gun.

Sweaty palms against pants, I stand next to the dumpster where I first met her. My heart races, fingers shake. Her smell comes back to me, like cat piss and rotten eggs. I recall her eyes—expanded pupils, inner corners crusted. And her mouth; even as she pressed the gun into my forehead, I couldn't stop staring at her blistery skin peeling away from swollen lips.

Never wanna be like her—slurring faint words, dead eyes uncontrollably blinking.

Loud coughs erupt behind me, bring me back to the present. Chin over shoulder, I run faster and faster toward the end of the murky tunnel, sweating. I blink through the past. Sprint out of Moats Alley, away from a future where I end up like the woman with dreads. On the other side of the tunnel, moonlight shines over my hunched back. Palms over knees, I wheeze, staring into the darkness I've just escaped, catching sharp, quick breaths.

When I reach the park, I raise eager eyes to the top of the old roller coaster—the rusty, winding ride has the best view of sunrise. Sun's colossal up there—feels tangible, like if I reach up, try to touch it, the rims of my nails could caress its tangerine skin. I climb the lifeless machine, inspecting steps, calculating my weight on the rungs, ascending to its peak. A silver rod beneath my feet wiggles. I freeze, steady toes, look down from whence I came, think of concussions and blood-ridden broken bones. It's uncertain how secure this giant roller coaster is, but after last year's accident, anyone who hikes it does so with Curtis in mind.

Last year, spring 2069, Curtis Flan and his sister, Kyra, climbed this ride. Kyra cleared the top, but Curtis mounted the wrong bar rising, broke his neck in two places—crushed his spine severely enough to lose his lower legs. He lives in a wheelchair now, surgically scarred stubbles drooping over his elastic gray seat. He's lucky he didn't die—though sometimes, late at night, he rolls in the middle of the street, yelling that he wishes the fall had killed him.

At the top of the trestle, I sit on a large iron slate with room for two. I'm cross-legged, close to the edge, eyes closed. I raise my chest, root palms against cold steel, lift chin to fading constellations. I feel the moon smiling. I flip lids open, and smile back. She's illuminating—a circular, massive light bulb cradled in thick clouds, glowing down on candleless shacks, eroded sulfur-cloudy streets, and jigs heating silver spoons.

In the distance, thousand-year-old trees pierce hazy dark skies, blue mountains piggyback monstrous foothills, and silver fog hides Saven lights from view. I remember being little, wishing on this moon, wanting to grab it and kiss it. Not much's changed since then. I still wanna kiss it. But now I'm old enough to know the moon needs help granting wishes. I sigh and hope I'll see bright New Georgia lights up close real soon.

If selected, I will. The Rep'll be here in a bit. Whoever it is'll line us up, inspect us, decide who'll attend the Gala in New Georgia tonight.

I think back to what Vye murmured last night. How I only need one person to like me to be chosen. Vye's voice is in my head, whispering, "You're special." Reassuring I have what it takes, I know, but so does every Hopeful. Every kid grows up with New Georgia on their lips; it's the place we'd metaphorically kill for. But sometimes I wonder, with as bad as the Ashes is . . . if murder really was the skeleton key that unlocked New Georgia, would some kids steal the key to open the lock?

A whistle blows a few hundred feet below. I lean over my knees, glance down.

Officer Jessup stands on the massive sundial, holding a loudspeaker to his mouth. "Be safe up there, Jo." I wave at him. Jessup continues. "Heading over dah Vye's. See you later, Gaedah."

I wave again, giving Jessup smiles he can't see. "After while, Dile," I say, knowing he can't hear me this far up. I'm thankful for Jessup. He keeps Neal out of trouble, treats Vye like a queen, and taught me to drive—oh, he also got me hooked on old episodes of twentieth-century *Doctor Who*. Vye deserves someone good like Jessup. He's a good cop. I give him another wave, watch his patrol car drive away and turn down Moats Alley.

Sketchbook in hand, charcoal between middle fingers, I sketch the jig. I draw her lips first, always do. I sketch her hooked nose, thinking about how time moves us away from memories, and how one phrase teleports us back. I outline her eyes, sigh. They're not right. And getting 'em right feels important. I shade her cheekbones, hear her words in my ear. "Gimme the chicken."

"Whatcha drawing?" a voice says from behind.

I shut my sketchbook, hide the jig's charcoaled face. And wonder how Boah gets up this rusty roller coaster with quiet feet. I tuck braids behind my ears. "The future."

I turn. Boah smirks. "Oh yeah? Am I in it? Love me that much?"

I wanna tell Boah there's no future without him in it. That besides Vye, Neal, and Jessup, there's no one else who gets me, who I feel close to. But I don't. And I can't tell him I love him, 'cause whatever I feel for him, I don't want it to be love. Not now—not here. In the Ashes, we'd only fight over things we don't have 'cause we can't afford them and forget reasons we liked each other in the first place. But maybe that'll change soon. Boah and I'll line up, be chosen, get rich quick in New Georgia, and then, I don't know . . . we'll see what happens.

Boah sits beside me, flings legs over the edge, shoes kicking stale air. He's wearing what he always wears: gray khakis with holes in both knees, a black T-shirt, and beat-up red Chucks. I can tell he just got off, worked the graveyard at the Mill—spent night till morning boxing this month's *Expectation*. Boah adjusts his position on the trestle—straightens his spine, slumps over his knees, peels paper dust off his nails. He rubs the inked buffalo on his forearm. Boah says the tattoo makes him proud of his Siksika ancestral bloodline, what other folks call Blackfeet. Says in his culture, buffalo teaches resilience, courage, and freedom; that whenever he looks at his black iinii tattoo, he's reminded his freedom can't be taken 'cause it lives inside him. Whenever someone asks Boah why he won't cut his long black hair, he says he doesn't cut it because long ago, before the old world was new, the government cut his people's hair by force, so there's freedom in his hair, too.

In Boah's right pants pocket, I see it—the current issue of the *Expectation*. He's got that look on his face, the one where his smirk deepens the imprint of his one dimple—he's up to something, being sneaky. I wanna poke his cheek but won't. My cheeks rise, and I turn my head, hide my grin, then turn back around straight-faced.

Boah pulls the magazine out of his pocket. He fans it back and forth across his chest. I reach for the *Expectation*. Boah extends his arm, holds it above his head, shakes it midair.

"Who's the Rep this year? Is it a she, he, or they?" I tickle him.

Boah jerks, head back in laughter. "Cut it out, Jo! It's high up here. Keep playing, you'll make us both fall." His laugh is heavy like an engine turning, but the tone of it is cool and calm, like smoke swirling away from blown matches.

"Then let me see it!"

Boah shrugs; he's annoying sometimes. I tug his ear. His head tilts my direction. Our eyes meet. I gaze at his top lip, then his bottom lip. I release his ear, look away.

"'Elenore Wells, this year's Lineup Rep . . .'" Boah reads.

I turn back around to listen, but I don't look at his face. Too afraid my eyes'll show what I'm thinking. Boah continues to read the article, says Elenore is the heir to the Wells fortune, the richest family in New Georgian society. That she has two teenage kids. Says Elenore collects butterflies and books, and her favorite color is white.

"Elenore is especially excited about this year's Lineup. In her own words, 'Helping those less fortunate experience connections is a passion project I take very seriously. The Lineup and Gala do just that. Offers those poor kids prosperity—a chance at a better life—a key to the pursuit of happiness.'"

Those poor kids.

Elenore likes butterflies, so maybe she'll like me instantly because my last name is Monarch. But the phrase she used, *those poor kids* . . . makes me feel unseen. Like being surrounded by family and friends you've known your whole life, but everyone ignores you. Like being invisible.

"Wish they had a photo of her."

I exhale. "Yeah . . . they don't do that anymore."

"Yeah, not since that one kid who didn't get picked attacked the next year's Rep before they got off the AerTrain. The balls on that one. Passed cops, hopped on the AerTrain, and just whaled on that man."

I nod. Of course I remember. That incident changed everything; now nobody knows what the Lineup Rep looks like until cops escort them off the AerTrain. I felt sorry for that Rep. Felt sorry for the boy who beat him. After cops stopped the attack, his family and friends watched cops string him to a tree in the middle of the wastelands—he was fourteen.

Boah elbows my arms. "Yuh hear about Curtis?"

"Flan? Kyra's brother."

Boah sarcastically waves the toke earned last night. "Yeah. Radius got him; rats ate the stubble clean off his knee bones. He didn't feel a thing, though. Still, it's just . . . bad."

I wonder if citizens in New Georgia find death talk respectable. Round here we don't think much of it. Just another part of conversation. Might sounds insensitive, but it's not. Here, death is a second skin. "When'd he die?"

"Last night. Was up late with Kyra talking about it."

"How's Peels holding up?" I wonder why Kyra's so mean when her mom, Peels, is so sweet.

Boah rubs the back of his neck, throws a pebble over the edge. "Like any mom would be, messed up."

"And you and Kyra?" I try to read his face, staring at his wide nostrils, round eyes, cleft chin—tracing his olive skin from his temple to the veins sticking out his neck.

He scoffs. "On and off. Off now . . . for the best, though." He sighs, looks at me. I gaze back. He knows what I'm thinking—always does. He continues, "I can't, Jo. Not this year; gotta be here for her."

Breath catches. "You both passed the exam, eligible for Lineup."

"I can't."

"Have you asked if she wants to?"

Boah nods. "She doesn't wanna leave Peels."

"Seriously? Peels would understand. I'm sure she rather her daughter be safe in New Georgia than another child dead. Radius doesn't exist there." I blow cool air through my lips, frustrated Kyra has a hold on Boah. I pinch my lips together, tight, tighter, then release them. "It's not like you're together."

Boah's cheeks expand with air; he huffs. "No, but we were. I owe her that much." He glances at me. "I'd do the same for you." And he did.

Two years ago, after Boah's mom died of Radius and my dreams of the jig resurfaced, Boah wouldn't leave my side. Night after night, we lay on my mattress in silence—his head on my stomach, his arms wrapped firmly around my waist. Then, every morning just before dawn, he'd kiss my forehead. Something foreign was growing amid our friendship—a closeness we'd never had.

I huff. "I'd never ask you to."

"You'd never have to." He sighs. "Radius breaks families. I can't leave her alone. Not now. Don't be so dramatic."

"I'm not dramatic. Just don't like being annoyed." Or changing plans . . . even if I'm used to life flip-flopping underfoot.

"That's interesting coming from somebody so annoying."

I inhale the world, exhale disappointment. "Alright—okay. I understand." And I do.

Boah leans into my shoulder. "But you should do it."

"Do what?" I blink the past away.

Boah laughs. "Lineup, silly. This Elenore 'whoever'"—Boah makes air quotes when he says the word *whoever*, then continues—"she'll want you. Yuh talented. Yuh could get over there, move into Transition House, take fancy art classes, and . . . and become this famous artist, make headlines. See what all the New Georgia fuss is about. Look, if they pick yuh, write tuh me—tell me how good life is over there and all that. Relay info on former Ashfolk livin' ova' there. I can see the front page of the *Expectation* now." Boah extends his hands, presses them together, making a triangle. He peeks through with one eye, says, "'Jo Monarch, from Rags to Acclaimed Artist!'"

Maybe Boah's right. I'm not a jig, don't have Radius. Scored good on exams, and sketch faces. But what if that's not good enough? John Ready says the selection process is based on whether or not the Hopeful makes a great rags-to-riches story. John's words echo like bullets in Moats Alley, make me think— "What if lining up is a mistake? What if they don't—?"

"Pick you?" he laughs. "Cut it out."

I nod, shrug—stare at charcoal dust smeared on the knee of my pants. I try to be positive, but even if I get picked in Lineup, many don't make past Gala night. Stories from Ashfolk who return the next morning after being rejected Gala night tell tales of only two or three Hopefuls making it to Transition House, where they'll live while dusting the Ashes off their feet to become full New Georgia citizens.

Boah bumps his shoulder into mine. "Seriously? Don't even think about it. You're lining up."

"No, I know. I'm going to, it's just—"

If Elenore likes me and I make it to New Georgia, it means I'll never see them again. Vye, Jessup, Neal, Boah—I mean, they'd be alive here, but I'd never see them smile again. I stare at light brown lines at the center of my palms like they'll change direction any second, disappear.

"You can't spend your whole life worrying about Neal. At some point, you have to let him pick up his own damn pieces."

Never told Boah this—never told anyone—but long ago, when Neal was heavy-busy robbing, beating, and stealing with guns, I asked the moon to take him away. But that's not all; sometimes, I hoped cops would trap Neal in the hole and never release him. It's not because I didn't love Neal. I do. Just didn't want him hurting innocent people. "Neal and Vye are the only pieces I have."

"Thanks a lot." He smirks.

I punch his shoulder. "You know what I mean."

"Ay," he chuckles, rubbing his shoulder. "Taught you too good. Yuh punch harder than me now."

"Yeah, well, maybe you did, so, watch it." I laugh. We laugh. We're silent. And it feels like two years ago on my mattress.

"You're my b—" Boah pauses, doesn't finish the sentence. He clenches his jaw, slightly nodding.

"Yeah. You're—" I don't finish either. He already knows. He's my best friend, too.

Boah places his palm over my hand. I want to gaze at our weaved fingers, but I don't. I want to look at his face, touch the scar above his lip. I won't. Still, I feel his eyes on me, tracing my lips with his stare. I don't have to look at Boah to see his face; I've sketched him so many times he's an imprint, a watermark; my optic nerve knows his name. I move my hand away slowly. Wipe red dirt off my pants, clear my throat, gaze at my watch: 6:55 a.m.

We lift our chins to the sky, chasing rising sun like we've done so many times over years. I hear my heart beating, feel my chest rising, up and down and down and up. And I feel like crying—I don't. I'm thankful for Boah. He's always been there—my reliable best friend.

Boah tugs his ear. "It's beautiful, right?"

I nod. "Yeah. It is." I wanna kiss him, but I'm scared. I close my eyes, part my lips. "Coming to Lineup?—to watch?"

"Wouldn't miss it."

"Yeah, everyone wants to see the circus." I laugh. Boah doesn't.

Boah scoffs, shakes his head, looks down. "No, Jo. That's not it. I don't wanna miss you."

3

COVE

And this is the way of it every morning. Me in bed watching sunrise over Saven, with New Georgia's state fair roller coaster in the distance, while my stepsister, Margo, buries her face in my chest. I stretch, scratch my hairless chin, yawn into violent summer sun, and sigh.

I turn away from the window, inhale Margo's sweet and sour breaths between soft snores, feel her skinny palm below my belly button, watch her hazel eyes shift under shut lids. I kiss her nose—she wiggles it—she hates it, but during sleep, she can't refuse butterfly kisses.

When Margo sleeps, her innocent parts rush forward like undying wind, blinding me to her manipulative woken state. She's cunning and has a way of making me see the perverted world as she interprets it when I'd rather cast optimistic judgment. But it's not just me; others feel her power. Larry, the first boy Margo broke, said he thought her insides were haunted by evil twins—said each soul craved different things—like one twin wanted sun while the other chased black sky.

From down the hallway, Stepmother calls, "Cove."

I lift Margo's chin, careful not to wake her. I slide white sheets away from my stomach, place my feet on cool bamboo floors, and ease out of bed. Through the oval pod window, the redheaded Fairmoth sisters, Edith and Victoria, are leaving our house after their daily gossip-fest with Stepmother. Aware of my nakedness, they gawk and blush. I smile. They smile. Then I grimace, giving them a look of disapproval. Even though they've done nothing wrong, next time I see those sisters, they'll do just about anything to make me happy. Stepmother's training hard at work.

With an exhausted gaze, I look past the Fairmoth twins, and I take in New Georgia. One could say it's beautiful here. Off to my right, Saven's neo-futuristic skyscrapers show off their distinct personalities, with tall and unusually decorative rectangular, circular, and triangular shapes. But these structures can't operate on beauty—they're controlled by iCom, the world's largest technology service, and powered by the sun.

Closer by, in my neighborhood, impossibly clean streets are eerily quiet at night, but in daylight, they burst with youth, couples holding hands at Hugo Park across the street. I sigh, lift my chin to the pastured mountains in the distance.

I wonder what life's like over the elevated green peak. Everyone here is well-mannered, put together like a clean machine—always on, never broken or messy. As a kid, when Stepmother and Margo weren't watching, I'd sneak outside after hard rain, plunge my hands into the fresh mud, and grin at earth matted to my palms.

Dirt beneath my fingers makes me smile. It doesn't take much to picture life in the Ashes: I'd walk around shirtless in broad daylight. Run in the middle of the street, across railroad tracks, screaming *I'm the king of the world!* like Jack did in the vintage film *Titanic*. I'd smell my dirty face. I'd feel my wild hair. And I'd know what freedom tastes like.

I'll get a whiff of it today, watching Elenore judge the Lineup.

I think back to when I was younger; the night Stepmother caught me playing in the rain. Without warning, she shoved me into a puddle, ripped the white shirt off my spine, and beat me until brown water turned red.

"Coventry?" Stepmother calls again. I close my eyes, roll them hard beneath tight lids, grimace.

I slide linen pants up my pale legs, pull a white tee over my head, walk barefoot through the corridor to Stepmother's large pod. As is custom, I wait patiently for her to speak. Her nose is buried in a circular compact, powdering her cheeks until the bony structures blush—oohing and aahing over her make-believe transformation from fifty to thirty. She's a southern aristocratic hermit fascinated with cosmetics, candles, and misery—and she worships maturity in young men.

Eight years ago, after my father died, Stepmother's sinister passion for education became increasingly known and left my ten-year-old bottom smoldering in red welts. To this day, she enjoys filling my mind with collegiate vocabulary via switches, extension cords, and leather flogs. Beating me until I sound like the man she lost, and the father I loved.

I'm convinced hate drives her to it—revenge for my face. When Stepmother sees me, she sees my father. And in seeing him, she punishes me for his young death and her aging loneliness. There's no warming her affections for me. I tried. Called her Mother once to bridge a connection; she didn't like it. Called her Stepmother soon after. For punishment, she struck my face with a wooden brush handle, insisted I call her by her first name.

"What's special about today?" Elenore puts down the makeup brush and picks up a bowl of rice, polishing off the last white grains. Rita, the maid, hovers next to her, waiting for the empty dish.

It's been a while, but when I was little, Rita and I'd talk late nights in the kitchen. Usually after the witch's punishments. We'd sit on stools in front of the kitchen island, share a big bowl of her handmade soft-churned vanilla bean ice cream. While eating, Rita'd tell stories of the Ashes. Confessed she left two sisters and one crazy brother behind. She was never teary-eyed about it, only big smiles—genuine grins—and gratefulness over being picked decades ago in the Lineup.

I once asked, in a life where you could be anything, learn any trade, why choose hospitality? Rita shook her head, ran her fingers through my unruly hair, kissed my skull, and said, "An ordinary life is a rich life."

Rita's house keys jingle on her pinky finger as she reaches into her apron and pulls out two envelopes with the words FIRST NOTICE written across them, PAYMENT DUE in large blue letters. Elenore smiles at the mail, stuffs it in her vanity drawer.

"Will that be all, my lady?" Rita takes the empty bowl from Elenore's hands. Elenore nods.

Rita wipes Elenore's hands with a towel. Her occupation is rare these days. Most citizens in this advanced age use nonbinary AI robots to cook and clean, but not the witch—she holds an unwavering interest in old-school human labor. As Rita leaves the room, I stare at the black rice bowl in her hands, and the leftover rice stuck on the side of it.

I watch Elenore chew, smack, and swallow the last of the rice, bits tossing around inside her mouth. I hate rice—white rice. Sightings of the tiny maggot-looking grains bring moods of agony, and the witch knows it. I lean forward to rub both knees, remember tiny white grains pressed into them.

"Don't slouch. You're not a baboon." Elenore scolds herself in the mirror. But I'm so startled, I lift my spine before the end of the word *baboon* leaves her cold tongue.

I fake unscathed and answer her question. "My birthday, ma'a—"

Elenore closes the compact, arches an eyebrow, pushes her favorite dangling diamond earrings into each ear.

"My birthday, Elenore."

"That's better." Elenore strains her eyes in the mirror. "Did you and Margo journal last night?"

I nod. "Yes, Elenore."

"Very well. I'll read them during lessons today." The witch flashes a quick malevolent grin. "Come here. I need your knees."

I walk over, take a seat before her vanity. Elenore sits on my leg, shaky thighs quivering from the draft in her emotionless room. Unbeknownst to her, I squint, peering into the wedged drawer above my knees. I can see it. The brown envelope guarding my future. I'm eighteen, legally three years from opening it. But Elenore says if I do what she wants, break one more heart, I'll be free, and she'll sign it over: two hundred acres of land called Plum Orchard—a fruit farm full of ripe lemons, pears, plums, mangoes, and meadows of mauve jaboticaba around thick bark. Plum Orchard keeps Margo and me hopeful during Elenore's beatings. Between lashes, we think about leaving this hellhole, and running around Plum Orchard barefoot, eating fruit all day.

Elenore's arms squeeze my waist. She smiles eerily, showing top and bottom teeth in the mirror, pushes her cheek against my forehead. I stare at her white hair, and I'm convinced she was born with it, as I've never known it to be any other color.

"Almost a man," Elenore says.

"Yes," I say, half grimacing, staring at an art piece depicting two sad, white face masks framed in flat glass. The crystal frame is built into the wall, next to Elenore's vanity. Margo says the painting depicts our faces. I think it's our souls; they're crying out, screaming, desperate for change.

"How'd the visit to the Fairmoths' go yesterday?"

My chest feels tight, repressed. "When she asked how she looked, I did what you said."

Elenore grins. "Expound," she says, eyes lowered, gazing over the taxidermy collection of exotic moths buried inside the surface of her vanity.

The witch wants micro details—she feeds off misery implemented during play sessions with Victoria and Edith. I've noticed Elenore's sinisterly more satisfied by stories about toying with Edith. To make her happy, I tell Elenore everything. About how yesterday, when Edith asked if she was pretty, I lied and said Victoria was the prettier twin. When Elenore asks how teatime with Edith went, I boast how I dropped a piece of bread on the floor and made Edith pick it up and eat it.

"You take instruction well, Cove. And did you see them? Did she do it?"

"Yes."

"What did you see?"

"Tears," I say.

"What'd you make her do?"

"Cry." You twisted witch.

"Did you like it?"

I lie. "Yes." Had I said no, she'd've beat Margo until her bottom bled red and blue—which the witch would enjoy too. Causing us pain in any form suits the darkness in her. I know why Elenore's this way because Margo can't hold water. She said before my father and I moved in, men passed through Elenore like voyagers twisting doorknobs. Random men left Elenore with tears laced with unrequited affections. This reveal didn't surprise me, as her experience with my father was similar. Elenore loved him, pleased him, tried to earn his love. And couldn't—my mother's ghost slept in their queen bed.

"Your heart is pure. Untouched. But never you worry. Remember my teachings, and no one'll make you cry. No one will hurt *you*." She places her palm over my heart, then wraps her arms around my waist, squeezes me tight, and kisses my cheek. "Now then, come, come, say the words."

I stare at the white tile beneath my feet. Elenore lifts my chin with her index finger. "Never fall in love," I say.

Elenore grabs my neck, squeezes it tight. "Why is that?" She smiles, pleased.

I swallow against her palm. "It steals parts we never knew existed and—"

"—And?" Elenore nudges.

One of her earrings falls out and onto the floor. Elenore leans over, picks it up, blows on it, cleans it with an alcohol pad. I've often wondered why things she loves fall away from her—it's as if her earrings are objects with feelings and want to run away from her as much as Margo and I do. Elenore continues, "Go on."

"—And when it finds the parts . . ." I say, sick to my stomach that she still has me this way—obedient, wanting to please the mother she'll never be.

Elenore flashes an evil grin. "What does it do with the parts?"

"Kills them."

Elenore releases my neck. "And never forget it. Especially today. I'll pick the girl you'll break. But just like every year, you'll need to control your . . ." Elenore glances at the seat of my pants, rubs her neck, tugging loose skin. ". . . extremities. There's beauty in the Ashes. A pretty face, no matter where it lives, destroys everything it sees." She pats my thigh, the touch that instructs me to move. Elenore stands. I leave her side, and she continues. "More hearts broken, plus knowing how love ticks equals controlled love. Voilà! Science behind love improves. Simple arithmetic. Don't you agree, Cove?"

"Yes, Elenore." I walk to her bedroom door.

"And why do you agree? Tell me." Through the mirror, Elenore stares at me.

I stare back, eyes fixed on her pale reflection. "Because science is only as good as its subjects."

"—And?" Elenore applies lipstick, purses her red lips. "What else does science behind breaking people do?"

"Helps us keep our hearts."

She nods in agreement, waves me off. "Wake Margo. Almost time for dance lessons. Turbo cab arrives in ten."

I leave Stepmother's room, eyes to the floor, sunken shoulders, heavy-hearted. Outside her door, I make a tight fist and bite my knuckles. I swear, sometimes being around Elenore feels like drowning, like quick gasps of air before submerging your nose deep in water. Other times it feels like I'm choking on sandcastles, like year by year, under Elenore's twisted tutelage, pieces of the boy my father loved slip away with the tide—transforming my heart into something unrecognizably numb.

In my pod, Margo sleeps. I wake her, tell her lessons will start soon. She rises, rushes over to hug me, then goes into the bathroom, prepares to wash.

"What's the witch's mood?" Margo jokes.

"Questionable."

Margo giggles. "Did she ask for the diaries?"

The witch makes us journal about the hearts we break. "Of course."

"Mine is under your pillow. Give it to her?"

Both our red journals are there. Sleeping toxically side by side. "Will do."

"A truth and a lie," Margo requests over running water.

I smirk. "I hate you. I like your mother."

Margo giggles with a snort. "Hey! That's two lies." She winks, closes the bathroom door, turns the shower on.

For four contemplative minutes, I stare at the crack along the bathroom door. I walk slowly toward it, steal glimpses of Margo's bare legs. The shower turns off. I could enter now, push the door wide open, disrobe, and Margo'd welcome the company. But I won't do it. Don't want it or her. I'm irritated with Elenore. I need to shake it off. I blink, remind myself that Margo and I are years past such play.

My saving grace is that Elenore's not my real mother. And I feel sorry Margo can't utter those words. She and Elenore share the same blood. But it doesn't matter; Elenore's claws hook us both, grooming her children into elusive creatures. I suppose my affection for Margo blooms from distress her mother causes. Elenore's darkness bonds Margo like unholy marriage to me. And because of this, I'll never let anything happen to her. I'd give my life for Margo, as she'd give hers for mine.

4

COVE

Turbo cab hums above the Savannah River.

For the most part, turbos are smooth, but not without imperfection. They'll never jerk over stones, but the solar energy used to glide over rivers and roads makes turbos lag sometimes. I blink, eyes skimming past the hologram floating above the cup holder in the front of the cab, displaying the turbo cab's plate number, traffic accident report, and car make and model.

We swish past Landmark Park—plantation land unchanged since Georgia became New Georgia. I stick my head out the window despite the drizzle, gaze up between tree branches dripping with rain and Spanish moss. It's a shame what Reps did to the river. They modernized it. Added glass cubes big enough to sit inches above the water. The Speres are fancy and stick out like a hangnail amid natural beauty.

Head back inside the turbo, I roll up the window—watch my facial expression through reflection. Five years ago, the day I turned thirteen, laughter and real smiles went away and transformed into snarky smirks, razor-thin grins, and scoffs. Upside-down frowns well-rehearsed in masquerading delight—lips pinched, poised. But this isn't the case with everyone. With Margo, smiles are real.

We pull up to Maple House, a sixteen-room brick mansion with large white pillars, located an hour away from home, nestled deep in the Historic District of New Georgia. Besides the annual Gala, few come here. It's not infiltrated by iCom tech, and therefore, not as cherished as modernized New Georgia. But its

36

traditional beauty chokes me. I hold Margo's hand walking up massive porch stairs, then release her grip to open its double doors for her and Elenore. Once inside, we enter the great dance hall. It's vacant now, won't be later.

Every year, the Rep in charge wakes early and heads to Maple House to oversee preparations for the Gala. It's not eight a.m. yet, and Maple House is busy. Waitstaff and servers are in relaxed clothing, setting both scene and mood for tonight's events.

This evening, this colossal ballroom will be full of Bambi-eyed teens from the Ashes chasing fairy-tale delusional ideologies of riches, connection, and love. Unbeknownst to other New Georgia Reps, Elenore uses the Gala to play her love games; even the years she isn't the Rep at the Lineup, she selects teen victims from the Hopefuls at the Gala—handpicking the vulnerable hearts Margo and I will manipulate and break. To "break" is simple. Pick girl. Woo girl. Make girl fall in love. Break girl's heart. Leave girl in tears. Breaking girls isn't exclusive to the Lineup or the Gala, but this year Elenore wants a heart from the Ashes.

Elenore starts up the music remotely, and Margo and I snap into a ballroom-dance embrace. Margo tugs my ear. I tilt my head, focus in on Margo's glistening red lip gloss layered over her pouty mouth. "A credit card for your thoughts, Covey?"

"It's 'a penny for your thoughts.'"

"Can you imagine living back when people actually counted printed money?—dashing around with change making all that noise in pockets and handbags?"

I humph, shake my head, begin to lead her in a waltz.

"You never answered my question. What are your thoughts?"

I pick up the pace, whisk Margo across the ballroom. With her feet barely touching wood floors, Margo giggles. Elenore watches from a shaded corner, nodding, okaying our form.

Distracting Margo with the change of pace is better than revealing my thoughts. Can't tell her I wish I'd never met the witch. Margo would take the comment, follow up, and ask: Does that mean I regret meeting her?

I can't tell Margo's perfectly bleached teeth I pity kids in the Ashes coming to the Gala. How it's shitty Reps plaster rags-to-riches stories on news outlets to bury ancestral guilt over normalizing injustice their ancestors bled to end. I slow down, even my pace, stare at the beauty mark shaped like a heart hidden under Margo's ear, thinking: Revolt 2030 could've ended differently. Had my ancestors lost their battle to end their poverty, everything'd be the other way around. Margo, the witch, and I'd live in the Ashes. We'd be Hopefuls.

Elenore claps her hands. "Chop. Chop. Chop." She walks over to one of the sixteen large windows, closes it, secures the latch to prevent rain from blowing in. Once back in the room's middle, she bangs her big white umbrella against the wood floor. "You're not a camel, Margo. Straighten your neck; lean your spine into his palm, gracefully. There. Beautiful, Margo. That's the way of it. We want to flow with the violin, not pop the strings."

Margo murmurs, "My strings were popped a long time ago, Mother." She comes up out of her dip and plays with a button on my shirt. "Weren't they?" Margo smirks, then glares at Elenore.

Like lightning, Elenore rushes over, and one of her diamond earrings falls to the floor. She doesn't notice the missing jewelry, she's lit, grabs the back of Margo's head, takes a fistful of her hair, and yanks her head back. Margo grins through the pain, while Elenore asks, "What's forbidden? What's the first rule?"

Margo scoffs. "No kissing."

"Expound." Elenore closes her fist tighter. Margo twinges.

"Kissing leads to broken hearts."

She'll never let her go without punishing her more. Elenore wants to see tears, but Margo, being Margo, will never give them to her. She's like her mother: spoiled, a solid tolerance for pain, and stubborn as hell. I have to stop this. Put an end to Margo's hair-pulled agony.

I rush over to the dropped earring, lift it from the floor, and present it to Elenore. "Dropped this."

Elenore loosens her tight lips, takes the earring, releases Margo's hair, and walks away. "That's the way of it."

Margo rubs the back of her head, smiles, and says, "You never answered me." I'll pretend with her that nothing happened. Our minds and bodies are trained to rebound quickly after Elenore's rough touch. Margo continues, "Weren't my strings popped long ago?"

"Yes, Jellyfish." I rub her head, gently twirl her around.

Margo buries her head beneath my chin. "I miss kissing you, Coveybear," she whispers.

I don't reciprocate.

Margo's the only girl I've kissed. When we started breaking hearts, kissing was the first thing Elenore instructed us not to do, to protect the most vital organ: the heart. Kissing is complex, equates with connecting. Connection is the origin of every broken heart and the square root of uncontrolled emotions. When one adds reckless sentiment to lip-locking, it turns into caring; the total sum of caring, multiplied by additional vulnerability, leads to love. And we can't have that.

Elenore pats her cane. "Beautiful. Beautiful form." A waiter brings Elenore a cup full of water encased in dissolvable pods. She pulls a transparent sphere out of the crystal glass and bites into it. With closed eyes, she swallows H_2O and licks her painted red lips. "Beautiful."

"If she says the word *beautiful* one more time," Margo says, "I'm going to fucking scream. Make her stop. Pretty please, Covey." She pouts. I humph.

The last note in the tune plays; I spin Margo around, place my hands under her arms, lean forward, and dip her. I look at Margo's snub nose, think of butterfly kisses I placed there this morning. We don't do much more than that—not anymore. Our flirtatious banter is delicate, overpowered by conversations related to who's broken the most hearts, and who the fragments belong to. Still, avoiding what we were is hard. Like now, every time I see the pearl bracelet she's wearing, I think of when I gave it to her.

We were fifteen. We were here. And it was summer—hot—New Georgia–devil hot, heat-waves-pinching-skin hot. Margo and I were splashing water in the middle of Havisham Lake. Margo'd just stripped off her tight white top and thrown it onto the lawn behind Maple House when I handed her the tiny steel box wrapped in pink ribbon. She clapped, anticipating untying the pink bow more than unearthing the present inside. But when I swam behind her, put the bracelet around her wrist, she turned around quick, weaving our hands together. That night, for the first time, we gifted ourselves to each other. 'Twas long ago, but I remember her minty tongue, and how her skin smelled like baby powder and tasted like fresh sea, and how I murmured "My jellyfish" in her ear.

"One more turn around the room. We need to leave soon. Will Pachelbel do?" Elenore says like it's a choice, though we know it's not—she ends every dance lesson with Canon in D Major.

The music starts. Margo rests her head on my shoulder. "And how are things in Fairmoth land?"

"They're desperately in love. Victoria's plucked. Edith's soon to follow," I say. "What about Larry?"

Margo grins devilishly. "Asked me to marry him, doesn't want me single at the Gala this year. He's just insecure . . . worried about the meat coming from the

Ashes tonight," she says. "I told him to give me a week to think about it; that was two weeks ago."

"You're cruel." I grin, but I don't want to.

"Yes, but it's so much fun—don't you agree?" She loops her middle finger in my hair.

I contemplate telling her, no, it's not fun. But there's no point to it. It's what we're good at. Pleasing Elenore is our life. When Elenore's joyful, our home stirs with her spoon of discontent, marinating in the misery she loves. Life is better when Elenore's happy, and in that vein, I suppose there's fun in that.

"How's James?" Margo says.

"Not interested."

"Come on, let me try him on. We used to share, remember?"

"Hard to forget."

"How hard?" Margo presses into me, nudging my chin with her forehead. "Can't we share your best friend? Let him stretch me like a starfish. Hmm?"

"He's dating someone."

"Oui, bien sûr! That's right, Edith Fairmoth. And what did you just say about little Edith? That she's next to pluck, right? Look at that pot, calling me kettle."

"Look alive, Margo," Elenore says, smacking a peppermint hard candy. I bet all the red stripes are gone. "Lift your chin, shoulders back."

"Yes, Mother." Margo lifts her head, arches her tailbone, presses her breasts into my chest, breathes in my ear.

After Pachelbel, Margo kisses my cheek. "Off to answer Larry."

I spin her around once more, watch her skinny fingers leave my palm as she exits the room.

Elenore takes a call. "Elenore here . . . Rose gold. Gala colors have always been dark gray and rose gold. Why are you asking me this, Aurice?"

41

I make my way outside, pace down the porch stairs. Below the bottom step, there's a mud puddle clear enough to see through. I gaze into brown water, reminisce about my father: his black hair, straight nose, fair skin, intense gray eyes, and thick eyebrows—those German features call my face home now. But I can't give Father all the credit; the height reflected is my mother's fault.

I take a knee, look over my shoulder at the door behind me and the window beside it. Elenore's still talking to her assistant, Aurice, on iCom. She's so excited to be this year's Rep, she'll spend ten to twenty minutes discussing how she hopes Lineup kids show up with clean clothes, fingers, and nails.

I twist my waist to face the water, brush fingertips across the surface. Dig fingers into moist earth like I did as a child. I wonder what five-year-old me would think. Would he be proud? Ashamed? Would he think me weak . . . strong? Or would he resent me—feel I didn't fight hard enough for him to keep his mind untainted? For a split second, I see a younger me inside the muddy water. His guiltless eyes resemble death, and tears stream down his chubby cheeks.

I rise, shake wet dirt and bronze water away, place my hands inside pockets. And ten minutes later, Elenore exits Maple House. "Our turbo is on the way. Don't want to keep Hopefuls waiting."

Margo comes outside, stands beside the witch, says, "The stains on their clothes have waited longer."

Elenore smirks, a subtle approval of her daughter's cruel joke.

We take a turbo cab to the AerTrain terminal, hop on an AerTrain headed for the Ashes. As the train silently swooshes over and through mountains, I stare into my right palm. The tips of my fingers are murky, unclean—smeared with brown stains mud left behind. I rub my thumb into my middle fingers, feeling residue crumble against tree rings in my skin. I'd forgotten how it felt to not be perfect. It tastes like shame and acute disobedience. It's glorious.

Out the window, I see the door through the mountains that'll lead the train to the Ashes' steel gates. I stare at the monstrously beautiful green mountain. Think of running through the Ashes like I'd dreamed as a hopeful kid—think of Ashes air blowing on my blushed cheeks, think of wrinkled clothes and wondrously dirty feet. And for a second, no matter how briefly the flash lives, for the first time in a long time, I think of showing teeth, of brightly smiling.

5

JOSEPHINE

Forty pairs of red shoes stand in line, nervous—soles of shoes tapping, kicking, and drawing lines in red dirt, waiting on New Georgia Reps. Well, one Rep—whoever this Elenore Wells is. All of us wait alike in thought and body—spines upright, hands to sides with a beehive of insecurities. We're all eager. Eager for acceptance. Eager to start a new life. We all want it, but I want it more. Want it so bad I taste it. I swallow hard.

I deserve good things, better things, rich chances, but somehow, I feel like this moment isn't real. Like the closer I get to what I want, the more I realize I'll never get it—like I'll never make it out of here. But it is real. I'm here. It's really happening. Fidgeting fingers twirling cotton dust in my pockets. I rock back and forth on the heels of red boots, sigh, stare at my watch. It's one p.m. Elenore'll be here soon.

With my hand inside my left pocket, I touch my Lineup card again. I can't read minds, but everyone standing in this line's thinking the same thing. If Elenore chooses us, we'll keep the triangular paper card after she scans the Gala crest onto it, a waning moon in rose gold. We'll use it to enter the Gala tonight. If she doesn't, she'll take it away.

Underneath my skin, impatient blood races. I'm excited about leaving, but sad for all I'll leave behind. It's no secret getting picked in the Lineup is the goal. I'd never be hungry again. For some, it'd be the end of dog legs for lunch and water for dinner. Downside to leaving is your family can't come wit'cha. Most Hopefuls

44

say it's worth it, but daunting, 'cause kids only get one chance to escape. One year. One exam. One Lineup. One Rep to impress. Zero failure. The end.

To my right, Neal shifts on his feet. I give myself a once-over. I'm as good as I'm gunna get. Vye convinced me to wear all black, said stains lose themselves in darkness. Other kids fidget with clothes too. Can't focus on them right now. Gotta make sure I'm straight. Clean black khakis. Check. Clean-ish black cotton V-neck tee. Check. Red boots a little scruffy on the sides, but the tops of both boots glisten in the sun. Check. Careful no one watches, I tuck my chin into my left armpit. No musk. Check. Behind the Lineup, the gathered crowd's full of fast tongues—they gossip over who'll be chosen and who'll be left behind. Among themselves, some Ashfolk accept and place bets with money they don't have. Other folks watch bewildered, wonder why we'd wanna line up in the first place, because for them, the Ashes is true north.

Kyra runs over, taking her place in line to my left, smiling ear to ear, and makes me think of Boah. Boah and I used to be the ones watching, dangling our scrawny legs over rooftops, or side-saddled in trees. We'd giggle, smirk, and laugh at the unchosen, but get sad when chosen kids boarded AerTrains.

I lean forward, scan roofs and trees—Boah's not here. If Kyra is lining up, why would Boah stay behind? Squinting past security is hopeless. Black combat gear, leather holsters, billy clubs, and black helmets are hard to see through. In my peripheral view, Kyra digs dirt out of her fingernails. Why'd she stand next to me? It's hard to think about it, but we used to be friends. As kids, after the jig incident, Kyra suggested a scavenger hunt, said we'd have to catch her. Holding sticks for weapons, we carried candles through blow pits, crack dens, and meth kitchens, searching relentlessly for the black woman with dreads. It was dangerous, terrifying as hell, but we had each other's backs.

Later, things got weird. Kyra started crushing on Boah and didn't want me around. Her mother, Peels, had sex with Bootleg Jules. Bootleg Jules gave Kyra expensive things. Fancy gifts changed Kyra's attitude—she got bougie. She lost interest in us, lost interest in me. Our friendship shriveled up and died like bad fruit. Kyra got mean. Her cruelty drove me away, and I stopped talkinnuh her. Soon, not being friends was okay; didn't hurt as much. Still, whenever I saw Kyra, I spoke—I didn't have to like her to keep the peace for Boah's sake. And besides, I felt sorry for her. There's nothing sadder than poor girls who make poorer girls feel like shit. But I'm not innocent. I've done bad things.

Back then, when Tessa heard about how Kyra treated me, we'd plan hangouts with Boah and other kids and didn't invite Kyra. Tessa said it'd give Kyra a taste of her own medicine. We'd drink and dance under the moon barefoot, roll over in bouts of laughter. Kyra out of sight wherever we'd go, but haunting my thoughts, making me feel bad. I don't know. Maybe Kyra deserved it. To know what it feels like in the cold. But it never felt right.

On Tessa's deathbed, the last phrase spoken before her tongue forgot words was, "Don't be afraid, Jo. Forgive her." When Tessa died, I did just that. Forgave. No matter how mean Kyra became, I held my temper. Death does that to folks— it opens them all the way, whispers inside souls, twists and confuses DNA, changes people.

A gust of wind makes me shiver. I glance at Kyra again. I won't be mean to her, but I don't wanna be fake. Don't wanna talk to her either. But she's the only one who knows where Boah might be. If she's here, maybe he got her to line up because he didn't wanna be in the Ashes without me. Maybe Boah was kidding this morning; he'll be here soon—he's gunna line up too.

I lean into Kyra's ear. "Where's Boah?"

"Not here." She rolls her eyes.

"Is he coming?—meeting you here?"

"How'um I supposed to know?" she says. Ugh!—why's talkinnuh her so hard? Kyra never makes it easy—there's always this maze you gotta hurtle through just'tuh get a straight answer.

Kyra's smart. She sucks at art, can't draw like I do, don't play instruments, but she'd make a good model. And in New Georgia beautiful things are worshipped. Beauty could be Kyra's talent. Why'd she come?—and more so, why'd she have to be right next to me? Elenore'll take one look at Kyra's doe eyes, blonde locks, long legs and pick her, and forget me. "He said you weren't lining up."

"Funny . . ." She sneers. "That's not what I told him last night." Kyra tosses platinum curls. "And why are you talking to me? We're in the same line, Jo. We're not fucking friends. And if Boah's not talkinnuh you, you might wanna reevaluate that friendship, too."

"Sorry about Curtis," I say. Maybe it's bad timing, but I mean it. Everyone loved Curtis. Even at his worst, folks spoke highly of him.

"Right. Thanks," Kyra snaps.

I make a tight fist, then quickly relax my fingers. I lean away from Kyra, insides red as an apple.

Neal elbows me. "You're friends with Kyra again now, huh?"

I scoff, tell Neal no, and keep my eyes forward.

"Well, stop talking to her, then. She's a bitch tuh ya, always has been." Neal bites and chews his nails. It's easy to believe he scored an 82 on the admit exams, but it's confusing why he'd participate in the Lineup, because he knows he won't get past Last Check—he smokes cigarettes. Maybe cousinly support? "You see Dulce?" he asks.

"Where?"

Neal points to the right. "At the end. The raven beauty, with the nice boot—"

I push Neal's shoulder. He laughs and continues, "Just saying, she's hot. And it ain't the sun."

I look to the right, scan the end of the line. And there she is, Dulce Palt. I don't know her much, but Neal's had a crush on her for a while. I think about what Neal said about Kyra, about her being mean to me. Well, I don't understand why he has a thing for Dulce, because she's mean to everyone. The bully. She won't make it. Half the battle of being accepted is being liked. No one except her family likes her in the Ashes. Can't imagine Elenore will like her either.

I smirk at Neal. "You're talking to her again? She's nice to you now?"

"Using my words against me, huh? Funny." Neal releases a sarcastic laugh. "Ha. Ha. Ha. Real clever, butthead."

"Well, stop talking tuh her, then."

Neal chuckles, elbows me, grabs my fingers, gives me a note. I open the tiny piece of paper. It's barely legible, but Neal wrote: *Smile butthead #1. Don't worry. You'll be badassery! Luv ur cousin, butthead #2.* I try to elbow 'em, but he dodges the contact. He smirks. He laughs. We laugh. And then we're quiet. Everyone is.

We hear the AerTrain's alerting horn in the distance. It's not here yet, but it will be in minutes. Officer Reed hobbles to the iron gate, the one circling the Ashes—live-wired to keep folks from hiking the mountains separating us from Saven.

Reed unlocks the fence. When he does, Jessup turns sirens on and rides down the red-clay road to open the ivy-covered door in the mountain. When Jessup returns, the train's not far behind. He parks the patrol car at the police station and, like the rest of us, watches the sleek AerTrain exit the mountain and glide through the massive iron gate.

I scrunch my nose. Air here smells like shitty diapers.

Officer Reed limps over to the engineer, shakes her hand—under her gray

48

worker's cap, her youthful smile's nostalgically familiar, but her mature features steal my memories, and I can't place her, can't remember where I know her from. Reed releases her hand, looks at his ankle, tugs pants, freeing fabric stuck along his brass ankle. Rumor has it Neal severed his leg with a machete and fed two three-legged dogs. Neal's never told me straight whether it's truth. Cops can't arrest him—they don't have proof. But it doesn't stop them from arresting him for everything else under the sun. I'm glad someone took Reed's leg. Maybe it'll slow him down—make it harder to hurt young girls.

Jessup slaps his dusty police cap against his pants, walks over to the mic, speaks. "Lineup will begin shortly." He gives the Lineup an awkward wave, smiles my direction, walks to his car, and leans on it.

Kids straighten spines and lift chins as the AerTrain's door whooshes open like hard wind. A black man in a navy suit, flap hat, and with a camera around his neck exits the train, laughing with an Asian man in a black suit and white lab coat, an old-fashioned stethoscope around his neck. Afterward, two white kids step off the train holding hands. Neither are Reps; they're too young.

I take the two kids in, eye them up and down. They look around my age, except their faces are stoic, their clothes clean. The boy's hair is dark, almost black, disheveled and cool without trying. Like he rolled out of bed, combed it back, then forward, with five fingers. The girl is thin with blonde hair. I wonder if they're dating, but a woman with white hair and skin, in a white pencil dress, emerges behind them. With slanted lips the woman scolds the girl—tells her to stand straight like her brother. So, siblings. The three of them's what I'd imagine folks over the mountain are like—elegant, off-limits, like furniture you can't sit on.

I think back to the *Expectation*, the article Boah read on the trestle. Elenore's favorite color is white. This woman wears white. It said she has two children.

49

That must be them. Which means the woman in white is Elenore Wells.

Reed offers his arm to Elenore, walks her to the white rug, where she, the other two men, and her children stand in silence. The Asian man adjusts his glasses, pushes round opticals high up a thin bridge. The black man removes his flap hat, places it in his back pocket, then takes pictures.

I turn my attention to the two teens, who stand pretentious in white dress suits. The teen boy gawks—gives us Hopefuls quick glances with tight lips. Most kids look down, avoiding the boy's gaze. But not me. When he looks at me, I stare back. Watch him, watching me. He gives me a look, like he's wondering what I'm thinking. Unlike Boah, his face is scarless, skin smooth like drawing paper. Ten seconds later, the skin between his eyes wrinkles; he blinks and looks away.

The microphone cries—screech's so loud, cops in helmets flinch. The woman in white gloves taps fingers against black foam covering the pill-shaped mic.

"Testing one, two, three—testing," the woman says, breathing heavy into the speaker. "Good afternoon. I'm Elenore Wells, New Georgia's Lineup Representative this year and head organizer of this year's Gala." The Rep to impress. "To my right, my assistant Aurice. And Dr. Gaitlin," she says, gesturing to the men beside her. "If selected, you'll meet Gaitlin in Last Check. And to my left are my children, Cove and Margo. Excellent examples of elite New Georgian youth." She pulls a glass bottle from her fancy white bag, sips water. "You all know how this works. I'm here to select the lucky youths who will be invited into New Georgian society. If, of course, you can impress us this evening at the Gala. I'll select those with promise; teen trinkets who show the most potential to contribute as citizens. Well then, let's begin."

Elenore steps off the white carpet, followed by Cove and Margo. They walk toward the line of Hopefuls. Never seen a Rep have help before, but Cove and Margo whisper in Elenore's ear, apparently comments or opinions. They examine us one by one for cleanliness and likability, then select or deny. I try predicting which kids'll be selected, but I shrug it off 'cause every year's a guessing game. Reps see potential however they want, something in our eyes or scuffed shoes. Suspicious whispers about who's chosen and why is endlessly questioned, talked around, but never answered.

I watch the line of forty Hopefuls become two lines. One line for chosen Gala participants. One for those rejected. Rejected kids fidget, waiting to run home runny-nosed. Just when I think it's my turn, Elenore skips past both Kyra and me and stands before Neal. I watch Neal spread his fingers so Elenore can see his clean nails. Elenore tells Neal he has a nice smile, and Neal chuckles and says, "I know."

Elenore smiles at Neal. "See you at the Gala."

Neal winks, waves wiggling fingers, and moves forward, takes his spot in the chosen line.

Elenore continues down the line, selecting and rejecting, until Kyra and I are the only ones left in the Lineup. Was skipping us good or bad? Chosen kids in the line before us smile, giving daps, excited they're going to the Gala. Elenore and her kids walk toward me. My palms are sweaty. My heart beats fast. I try to calm down and breathe. Vye raised me to be confident. But I'm unsure.

Elenore, Cove, and Margo's eyes are fixed on Kyra. I try reading their facial expressions, though it's a pointless task. Margo's eyes feel cold, as if nothing's lived inside her for years. Cove seems bored, like he'd rather be anywhere but here. And I feel hopeless, watching them ogle Kyra, until Elenore says, "Clean nails. Beautiful hair. Smile for me?" She shifts her attention, keeps her eyes on me while speaking to Kyra. "What is your name?"

"Kyra," Kyra says quietly, showing Elenore her Lineup card.

"Your name?" Elenore holds a hand to her ear, pushing her earlobe forward.

Kyra speaks louder. "Kyra."

Elenore nods. She lifts Kyra's hands eye level, inspects between her fingers. "Quite lovely. Soft skin. You'd clean up nicely enough for the cameras." Elenore caresses Kyra's cheek. "Yes, yes, this might work. Margo's a model in New Georgia." Elenore gestures at Margo to her side. "Thoughts, dear?"

With arched brows, Margo says lazily, "I'm 'the' model. And yes, Mother, she's quite beautiful."

Elenore instructs Cove to check "this one" for needle punctures. "This one" meaning: me. I glance at Kyra—she deserves good things too. But if she gets picked and I don't, I'll wonder if Reps would've picked me had Kyra just stayed home and not lined up like Boah'd said.

Cove moves before me—his eyes trace my face as if searching for answers. He makes me nervous. He feels cold and distant and untouchable, like nothing bothers him. I find myself wondering if he always seems miserable or if he ever smiles.

"Pay attention. Your fingers are dirty," Cove says, interrupting my thoughts. "Extend your arms, let me see your elbows." He's checking for needle marks, or Radius-induced red lesions and black spots.

I obey. I extend both arms, flip them over, show both sides, and expose my elbows, pointing them at him.

Cove narrows his eyes. "You're clean?"

"Yes." I shouldn't be irritated with him, but I am. It's perfectly normal for him to be surprised I don't do drugs. "Just say no, right?"

Cove ignores the joke without looking at me. "Show your hands. Spread your fingers."

I do. Cove moves closer to me. He's so close, I'm shaking, but tell myself to knock it off, *this is my chance.* I stare at him straight, never blinking, making sure he knows I know I belong in his world. I don't feel worthy, feel dirty standing before his clean white suit, but I'll never show it, he'll never know it—none of them will.

Cove holds out his hands for mine and I hover them above his palms. He investigates fingers without looking at me. Maybe my presence makes him sick. I turn my head, look away, focus on Elenore and Kyra's conversation, and flinch when his hands almost touch mine.

"You can have them back now," he says.

Eyes open, I meet his gaze again. He backs away. His eyes are warmer—no longer the icicles they were before.

Elenore tells Kyra she's made it to the Last Check, but that communication is very important, that if she wants to get anywhere in the world, she must speak up, be heard. Elenore's critique of Kyra's personality is wrong. In the Ashes, Kyra's known for running her mouth—she can't hold water. But I don't know—right now, the look on Kyra's face reads nervous, shy, and timid. Unlike her. Today, Kyra's not the richest poor kid. Today, she's scared and unsure like the rest of us.

Elenore continues, "That's it for this year. Let's go, children." Elenore and Margo walk away.

My heart stops and starts. No. Wait! What just happened? Is it real? They're done? I shouldn't've gotten my hopes up. John Ready's speech feels real now; his words echo in my mind, about Hopefuls needing to be charming enough. I didn't get a chance to charm, to speak with Elenore. She didn't even look my way. Elenore slowly saunters back toward the stage. The farther away she moves, the harder my heart pounds, louder and louder and louder. This can't be happening and yet it is. I didn't get picked.

Frantic, I think of tokes Vye spent on Gala gear that'll never touch my skin. And how it'll take Vye months to earn that kind of currency again. I think of food, people, experiences I'll never have. Not being selected means I'll end up like my parents, unhappy in love, wanting to take my life because I can't afford to live. Maybe the worst will happen. I'll end up a jig—live in Moats Alley, begging kids for Radius-infected food after heating silver spoons.

Cove doesn't move. His eyes meet mine, bewildered. "Wait—" He pauses, then continues. "What about this one?"

Elenore returns, stands in front of me. Her cold eyes travel up my red boots, charcoal-stained khakis, and stop at my forehead. I shouldn't've sketched this morning. My dirty fingers stained my pants. Charcoal's hard to get out nails. They're black pants; maybe Elenore won't notice.

"And your name, young lady?"

"Jo." I look beyond Elenore to the chosen line, where Neal makes weird faces and shoots birds.

"And Jo's short for?" Elenore arches an eyebrow.

"Josephine."

Elenore takes my fingers into her hands. "You're an artist."

I say yes, but Elenore says, "Wasn't a question, dear. A statement. Josephine's a strong name. You shouldn't shorten it. Be proud of it." Elenore reaches out, touches my braids. I don't flinch. She continues, "I've always wondered what these feel like." She sticks her neck forward, lifts her chin. "Well then," she says. "Now I do. You put them in yourself?"

"My aunt helps, but yes, ma'am, I do."

Elenore's smile disappears momentarily, she grimaces, then her smile reappears out of thin air. She leans close, into my ear; only I can hear. "Believe in true love, Josephine?"

Hesitant to do so, I turn my head to face her, looking into her black eyes. It's an odd question, but I answer. "Doesn't everyone?"

With a smile, Elenore glances at Cove and Margo, who stand like statues on either side of her skinny frame. "And what of those taught to fear love; do they believe?"

Who'd teach anyone to fear love? "Yes, maybe more than those taught to seek it."

Elenore chuckles. "And why is that?"

I shrug shoulders. "You gotta believe in stuff to fear it."

Elenore takes a step back. "Indeed."

Something about the way she says the word *indeed* feels condescending, like she doesn't believe my answer. So, I ask her if she does.

Elenore smiles eerily and says, "Congratulations, Josephine. Should you pass Last Check, you may attend the Gala."

I made it. I'm excited, but something about Elenore's smile feels odd. I try to read her, studying her silver hair, which's pulled tightly into a bun above her neck, and the deep creases in her snowy cheeks where big cherry smiles must've lived. Maybe she doesn't like me. I don't know. She's mysterious. Hard to read.

But does any of that matter when I've been selected for the Gala? I'm going. I've passed the next step on the road to New Georgia.

I know it does matter, though; my fate still lies in Elenore's hands. I gotta impress at the Gala, too.

Elenore faces the front line, walks toward the mic. Cove and Margo follow. Elenore says, "Congratulations thus far! Head to the police station for Last Check. Once done, go home, change. AerTrain departs in two hours. I'll see you at the Gala."

6

JOSEPHINE

At the police station, Reed leads us to a room with the words LAST CHECK in black letters on the door. The large white room has one door, zero windows, no mirrors, with cool air blowing from a vent in the floor. Reed glares at me, then leaves the room. Kyra nudges my elbow, giving me a *What's that about?* look. I ignore her suspicions and look forward.

Neal leans into my ear, smiling, rubbing his hands together. "Let the games begin."

Metal briefcase in hand, Dr. Gaitlin enters the room with Officer Hue. Hue closes the door behind them. Hue's Boah's cousin. Seeing her makes me think of him, wonder again where he is.

Gaitlin clears his throat. "This is Officer Rachel Hue. She's here to make the process go faster." Gaitlin's face is kind, nonthreatening. He continues, "Girls, please line up by the door in front of Officer Hue. Boys line up to the left with me. Enbies form a line in between."

Gaitlin hands out petri dishes. We're not dumb. Word of mouth in the Ashes is everything. After the test, if the petri turns yellow, detects the use nicotine or cocaine—banned substances in New Georgia—journey's over. Blue means drug free.

Gaitlin administers buccal swabs—sliding wood sticks with cotton tips, up and down our jaws—then dips them in the petris bearing our names. Liquid in some petris turn yellow; others fade blue. I gaze, amazed, fascinated by the science behind art, how different colors create new things. Reminds me of how much I enjoyed whenever Aunt Vye and I went over chemistry questions when preparing for the Lineup exam.

Science and art connect. I love how mixing acrylics and oils changes them in plain sight. It's cool how red and blue create purple, but no colors mixed re-create the color red. Red's a primary color, exists on its own. I look down, gaze at my red boots, think of the Ashes, its painful past. Red is constant, strong, like blood.

Gaitlin whispers to Hue. He faces us, speaks. "If your solution turned yellow, please follow Officer Hue; she'll see you out. Thank you." Gaitlin gestures to the door, right palm supine, directing them in Hue's direction. Three people, including grinning Neal, exit the room. Twenty remain.

———————

When I reach our warehouse, Vye's waiting, arms spread wide. She hugs me so tight I can barely breathe. "Come inside," she says. "I'll help yuh take the braids out and put 'em back in."

After Vye unravels my braids, nappy-headed and happy, I head to the kitchenette, where a hot straightening comb sits on the range; its iron tines marinate in orange embers, sizzling. Vye waits behind the chair adjacent to the stove. I take a seat in front of her. On the ceiling, a wolf spider spins a web; Vye grabs a broom, swipes it down, and crunches it under red flip-flops.

"A Gala Rep stopped by while you were at Last Check."

I glance over my shoulder. "Yeah? What'd they look like?"

"Dressed in white."

Elenore's the only Rep here today. I still ask, "White gloves?"

Vye nods.

"Were two kids my age with her?"

Vye shakes her head no. "But said she had some."

"What'd she want?"

Vye shakes her head with her bottom lip poked out and smiles. "The usual after Lineup. Meet the family . . . see what the Hopeful's like."

"Please say no embarrassing stories were told. Please say no embarrassing stories were told."

Vye laughs. "She liked your sketches."

"She went in our room?"

Vye laughs again, playfully swipes my shoulder.

I continue, "Was Neal's side clean?"

Vye pats my back, chuckles. "You know I cleaned that mess up."

"Which ones?"

"Oh, I cleaned every inch. Lifted his mattress and found a dead lizard. That poor thing probably died smelling Neal's feet."

"No, which sketches did Elenore like?"

"Ah, the ones on your wall." Vye protects my scalp by layering it with Blue Magic green hair grease.

There're three large drawings on my side of the room, taped horizontally on the wall—drawn on old white tees. On the fabric, I sketched my parents, mimicking the three photographs under my pillow.

Left to right, the first image is of my mom. She smiles with strands of silky black hair blowing over her right eye. On the second T-shirt, I sketched my father looking up, surprised, grinning, while tying his shoelaces. I sketched my father's hair like it's represented in the photo—coily like mine. The third drawing depicts my father winking, kissing my mother on her left cheek. Just like in the photo, you can tell her eyes smile behind closed lids. If Elenore liked my drawings enough to mention it to Vye, maybe I'm good enough to be a real artist in New Georgia. Good enough to have my art on a real canvas, on a wall next to real artists.

"You'll do good, JoJo . . . watch and see," Vye says, referring to the Gala.

"Yeah?" I gaze at her over my shoulder, questioning her certainty over how well I'll do. Just like the selection at the Lineup, the way through the Gala is a little blurry too. I know I need to connect with Elenore. I don't know how. What if attempting perfect isn't enough? What if I'm not enough?

Vye shushes me, pats my shoulder from behind. The universe is in her smile—you can hear it, feel it. "Yeah, you will. And you'll look good doing it, too," she says. She lifts the hot comb, blows it, and runs it through my hair, new growth to ends.

Vye tells me to hold my head down, stay still. And I do. I press my chin into my collarbone and freeze. I know what jerking can do when the comb's this close to the back of my ear. As a child, jerking during hair straightenings, scorched ears. And when that happened, Vye took butter out the icebox and rubbed it on the burn.

"Nervous?" Vye blows steam away from the hot comb.

I shrug. "Yeah."

"Only gotta impress one. That's it." Vye pauses, then says, "Heard Kyra was picked . . ." I nod. Vye runs the hot comb through my hair again. Vye swallows, says, "Don't be mean. Take care of each other. Yen gotta rob Peter duh pay Paul."

I smile at the Southern phrase Vye and most folks in the Ashes use when scolding kids about fighting, stealing, or being unkind. The meaning of the saying is simple: You don't have to be mean to get ahead.

When Vye speaks of childhood in the old Georgia, she spouts about how she and my mom would snatch unripe peaches from trees, bite into them, and count how many times their bitter nectar made 'em blink. And laughs recounting how their mother'd get on them for eating unripe fruit.

After bragging over how wild my mother and she were when they were young, Vye'd think of Yolt, frown, and go mute. They were childhood friends like Boah and I. Yolt and his family—mother, father, and twin little brothers— were murdered in Revolt 2030. She's thankful she found Officer Jessup. But the stars in every sky Vye sees are Yolt's eyes.

One day, I wanna feel the way Vye feels for Yolt. But I can't risk feeling that way living in the Ashes. Loving while broke is a waste of time. Waves of steam circle the room. The iron comb sizzles as nine heated tines meet greasy black hair. And the smell of burnt hair pushes me into the present.

Vye clears her throat. "Change is scary. Just be yourself . . . you'll do fine." Vye pauses, says, "They're the lucky ones. No matter what happens tonight, remember that."

Vye never talks about crimes she witnessed as a kid. Just says it wasn't right— it wasn't good. Just says even when the world was at its worst, good people of all races fought for those unable to resist.

Vye blows out the burner, places the iron comb on a cooling slab. "You'll be the only girl with braids, Jo. Other girls'll try tuh fit in, wear hair straight. Yuh sure?" she says.

I nod—think of telling her to leave my hair long, loose, and hanging—I don't.

Vye parts my hair with a brown plastic comb. I smell the chunk of hair grease siting on the top of Vye's hand, and the pine tar oiling her scalp. She checks my hair for kinks and wavy roots, plaits three long braids down to my tailbone. Once done, she knocks knuckles against the back of the chair three times, kisses the back of my head—says she wants to hear every detail via letter.

I turn to face her, smiling, feeling the strength of my long, freshly plaited braids. I sigh, feeling both scared and happy about my choice to attend the Gala as me. Scared, stressing over what being picked truly means. I'm still, body stiff in thought and reason.

I exhale. "If I get picked, that means . . ." *I'll never see you again.* According to Lineup rules, Hopefuls who make it through the Gala are permitted travel back to the Ashes under one circumstance: death of an immediate loved one. For me, that's Vye, and Neal. Officer Jessup and Boah don't count. I lower my head, watch a spider weave its web.

Vye leans over my shoulder, whispers, "We all got a time to go. And it's your time." She reaches into her apron pocket, pulls out a plastic bag full of the red clay only found here. "See? Now wherever you go, you'll have grains of home wit'yuh. Never forget who you are, Jo. That truth'll take yuh far," she says. She doesn't let tears forming leave the corners of her eyes. Instead, she knocks on the back of the chair again. "And I mean it—" She laughs. "Come morning, I wanna hear every freaking detail." She laughs some more. We laugh together.

7

JOSEPHINE

The Gala's an overnight event.

Entering my room, I trip over Vye's notebook, land in a push-up position. I rise, dust knees, and lift Vye's black notebook off the floor. It's an old-looking thing, full of short stories and poems she's written over the years. Some poems date back to when she was nine, a formerly rich girl transitioning to poor life in the Ashes. I place her notebook at the head of her mattress and walk to my side of the room.

I open the large cardboard box at the center of my mattress. I slip into the flowing skirt, pull the blouse over my head, glide both feet into heels, grab the little note Neal gave me during the Lineup, stuff it in my skirt's pocket for luck, and head out the door. There's no Boah on my walk back to the AerTrain. I'll leave without saying goodbye to him.

Twenty Hopefuls murmur inside the gate. We smile, lost in hope-filled giggles, anxiously waiting. AerTrain's doors whoosh open. Elenore exits the train, stands before us, silencing our chatter.

Elenore rocks back and forth on the heels of white stilettos. "Appearance is everything. How you're presented to New Georgian society matters. You see, the event is live. Broadcast across the country. It's imperative New Georgia has the most clean, talented, well-groomed group of Hopefuls in these New United States." Elenore rubs her slick hair, pulled back in a bun, and continues, "As you know, the Gala in the state receiving the most broadcasted views wins its state additional annual government funding. Let's bring those funds to our great state of New Georgia." Elenore smiles proud. "But it's not just about us. It's about you Hopefuls, of course. Your friends, families . . . Some of those funds go to the AerTrain trade . . . your monthly food, medicine, shoes, green sheets, clothes, keeping the Ash Mill operable. Et cetera, et cetera."

No one's ever mentioned the broadcast, the funding before. Do adults know? Other Hopefuls shift on their feet beside me like they don't know either. One by one Elenore studies us again. Some kids get a small black cloth bag full of tokes. Others, like me, Kyra, Rald, and seven other Hopefuls, get nothing.

Elenore claps. "Those who received tokes, step forward."

Elated, with wide smiles, ten kids in Gala-regulated colors step forward. Chin over shoulder, some smirk, jingling tokes in the palm of their hand. One kid counts his tokes aloud, showing off. When he gets to ten, he looks back at me, smug. It shouldn't bother me, but it does; he has enough tokes to feed his family for months. I look down at my garments, feeling selfish. I'm glad Vye bought the best Bootleg Jules had to offer, but suddenly I feel like she shouldn't've.

Elenore smiles before the front line holding tokes. "You won't be attending the Gala," she says blandly. "You can return home with the bag of tokes in hand, or with nothing."

Some boy I don't know raises his hand to speak. Elenore nods, giving permission.

"Yes?" Elenore says.

"What's wrong?"

"Beg your pardon?" Elenore says.

"Well, we were picked, and now . . ."

"And now you're not?"

"Why, ma'am?"

"Bless your heart. Look at the back line," Elenore says.

The front line turns, gazes over the back line, my line.

Elenore continues, leans into the boy's shaken face with a stern eye. "Do you understand why now? Can you see now?" she says without a blink.

The boy nods yes. And I agree. I see it, too.

Hopefuls in the front line have holes, stains, or tears in garments and shoes. Unacceptable for the Gala. That was one of the rules of appearance in the Gala edition of the *Expectation*. No imperfections in Gala-regulated gear.

Ten Hopefuls leave, tokes in hand, sad, wearing wet cheeks.

The air on the train is cold, canned. The ten of us, plus Elenore and her kids, don't even fill one car. I settle into a white recliner and gaze out dark windows reflecting stone walls. When the AerTrain exits the noisy underpass, tracks change color. They go from copper to silver as steep cliffs, jagged stones, and moss-covered boulders swallow the train. My own worry reflects back from the other Hopefuls, all thinking the same: What if they don't like us? What if we've done all this work to prepare, get over there, and they don't like us?

Seven seats ahead, Cove and Margo sit together. Margo giggles in Cove's ear. Cove doesn't laugh back; he looks serious, sad. He seems cold, distant, like he's hard to get to know. I envy them both—they're lucky to have lived their lives wanting for nothing. Cove turns his face, looks over his shoulder. Without a smile, he stares at me. I stare back. He blinks, then turns back around.

We glide up and over towering green peaks, coast above waterfalls splashing into ivy-cluttered ravines, and as we pass majestic hills, the flowers below mimic a quilt with lavender-and-blue fabric. I press the red button on the armrest, and the window against my right cheek rolls down. I stick my nose into the open space; inhale, exhale. The air is thin, digestible; not thick, rough, and polluted. So, I open my mouth, smile, taste the wind, and swallow it.

At the front of the train, a waiter offers Cove and Margo lemonade; they decline. When they get to me, I take it. Lemonade makes me think of Boah's aunt, Medicine Healer Marie. Marie gives what Ashfolk call prayer care—good words to lift us emotionally, spiritually, and physically. When Boah and I were little, Marie'd give us lemonade to distract us while she stitched and patched cuts and bruises we got climbing the roller coaster.

"Slice of pie, young lady?" the waiter says.

"Yes, thank you." I wanna try everything New Georgia has to offer. It's good pie, but not Vye's. And eating it makes me miss her. Vye's morning hugs are so snug and warm they'd melt snow. I remember watching *Charlie Brown* on VHS with Neal via battery-operated TVs, and grin reliving how he cracked up, dying laughing, whenever that raggedy ol' tree showed on screen.

I close my eyes, and Boah's golden smile appears. I think of this morning and the dozens of mornings before today with Boah. I see us climbing the old roller coaster, eating sunflower seeds, smacking—and relive every sunrise that brightened our hopeful faces. If selected at the Gala, I'll only ever see his face again if I sketch it.

I open my eyes, blink twice. In the window, Boah's side profile appears. I move my cheek closer and closer to Boah's image until it presses softly against the glass. This sucks. Once, Boah'd told me nothing could keep us from coming to New Georgia together. But here I am, gliding across the mountain without him. I turn toward Boah's image, watch it fade into blue mountains.

"Ain't it wonderful, Jo?" Kyra kneels in her seat, peering at blue mountains too. Buried in her voice is the sound of a friend I lost long ago. Her kindness won't last forever, but right now, we're those two little girls with skinny ashy legs, searching for the black jig with dreads. "I wish Boah could see all this," she says.

I nod. "Yeah. Me too."

8

JOSEPHINE

Skies are beautiful in Saven—they're ember and dark pink, mimicking Van Gogh's *The Starry Night*. They're better than any photo, cleaner than the mud-ridden potholes plaguing streets in the Ashes. Air doesn't smell like bad diapers. It's fresh, like our bedsheets in the Ashes when Vye washes them with milk soap and hangs them on clotheslines. And it's odd, but the moon is bigger this side of the mountain—radiant, luminously entangled with endless possibilities.

One by one, we exit the AerTrain, hop on the Swift Shuttle. Forty minutes later, we're divided into two turbo cabs heading to Maple House, where the Gala takes place. Five in each cab, we stick heads out of windows, taking mouthfuls of air, earfuls of winds, and eyefuls of stars.

Our turbo cabs pull up to Maple House. A massive hologram in the sky announces our arrival. Giddy, we watch our projected reflections display our eager eyes and smiling faces in the mauve sky.

Kyra leans into my ear. "Amazing, huh?"

I grin. Kyra's right. Outside Maple House, windows are bright, like sun sleeps behind white curtains. Inside, the house is full of art. And because Vye bought art magazines off Bootleg Jules every Sunday, I recognize lots of it. Some dates back to the early twenty-first century; I spot the bright primary colors of Kumi Yamashita, and an oversized canvas by my favorite artist, Yulia Brodskaya. I pause before it for a breath, wondering if when they were my age, they were like me—insecure over whether their art's good.

Kyra elbows my arm, gesturing toward a man and woman in black suits pacing toward us. When they reach us, their tags read: GALA GUIDE. We trade stamped Lineup cards for white envelopes with strict instructions not to open till morning. From previous tales of the Gala, I know the button is inside. The one that, come morning, reveals with just our thumbprint whether we've connected—made a good enough impression to New Georgia's Elite Society to start over here.

Guides lead us down a long foyer, into a large, lavish ballroom with dark floors. I see food I've had and others I've never even smelled before. Baked chicken, rosemary potatoes, collard greens, turkey, dressing, and macaroni and cheese; foods Vye raves about when reminiscing about soul food, in the good ol' days of the old South—foods headlined within the pages of the *Expectation*, but never in real life.

I don't wait. We don't wait. Most Hopefuls fill plates like nobody's business. Slapping slices of ham, chicken, and turkey on see-through glass plates; adding a spoonful of peach cobbler, yams, fried okra, barbecue ribs, and tacos. But Kyra and I are modest with food selections.

We're starving, ready to eat, but shouldn't stuff plates to stuff faces. Reps and Elites watch us. They've watched since we arrived. Precarious glances, gawking, tracing our faces and garments, up and down. Scanning for blemishes, observing imperfections. They don't know it, but I'm watching them, too.

Reps and New Georgia Elites keep to walls, watching us, judging, waiting for Hopefuls to make mistakes. Elites shake Hopefuls' hands. After the handshake, Elites sanitize their hands and dry damp palms with white napkins, erasing our touch from their skin.

On my way to a table with my full plate, cool fingertips touch my elbow. I turn; it's an Elite. Her hologram name tag reads: ELITE/VIMBERLY FAIRMOTH. When our eyes meet, Vimberly slyly wipes the index finger that tapped my elbow on the side of her long gown covered in rose-gold diamonds. "So, you're the one."

"Sorry, ma'am?"

Vimberly chuckles, puts rose-gold gloves on, then offers her hand. I take her hand, shake it. "Come now, don't be modest, Josephine. All Elenore can speak about is the artist in this round of Hopefuls!" She releases my hand. "Victoria! Edith!"

Two girls with wavy crimson hair approach. Vimberly continues, "This is Josephine. Mind your manners; greet this Hopeful."

Victoria and Edith roll their eyes and say, "Hello." I speak back, say hello, and then as quickly as the redheads arrived, they turn, leaving their mother at my side.

I lie, say, "They seem . . . nice," when neither seems nice at all. They seem like girls who only like you if you got something they want.

Vimberly crosses her palms across her heart, flattered. "Raised them myself."

I bet you did.

"They're twins, you know."

While both girls have long red hair, Edith and Victoria don't look alike. Edith looks like a model, sunken cheekbones, slender, tall. Victoria is short with a round face and fuller waist.

"They're pretty." This one is true. They are.

Vimberly says, "Well, aren't you just the nicest little thing. A pleasure, young lady." She removes her gloves, throws them into a waste bin. Without blinking, Vimberly takes a fresh pair of gloves out of her pocket, pulls them over her pale fingers, and walks away without saying goodbye.

Kinda'vuh a short interaction, but does short equal bad? She complimented me but seemed disgusted. I shake away from being negative; I guess if I were them, I'd think the same about touch. Folks in New Georgia have fears over catching Radius, since we know little about how rats contract the disease that passes to humans. Makes sense they'd worry. They're being careful. I could scream out loud you can't get it that way, but it wouldn't matter. Folks rarely believe what they hear these days, 'cause sometimes the line between true and false is blurry.

But nothing's blurry about how wasteful New Georgians are. They dump full plates of food into AI-operated bins that say "Waste contained, dissolved" after uneaten food slides into them. I sit down to eat. Steam levitates from my plate. I close my eyes, inhale savory chicken, sweet potatoes, garlicky spices. I chew with closed eyes. I swallow. Tastes so good, so rich. A sharp pain twists inside my belly. I open my eyes.

The pain in my stomach has nothing to do with the food. It's guilt. I look around the Gala, at my own plate of food. There's a lot of food here—food that'd feed entire families in the Ashes for weeks. I feel judgey. I don't wanna be, but I can't help it. Bet if these people didn't know where their next meal was coming from, they'd sneak those hot butter biscuits and golden sausage links into those fancy pants and push-up bras to eat cold later. It doesn't make sense. Why don't they just take what they need and leave the rest unwasted?

Repulsed, I look away from the Reps to watch other kids at the Gala. Boys from New Georgia wear dark gray suits; New Georgia girls prance around in expensive rose-gold fabric—their gowns make Ashes clothes resemble wrinkled loose-leaf paper.

Elenore stands on the stage in front of the room, blows into the mic. "I hope you're all enjoying the food. Very shortly, we'll start Conversations. Rules of the Gala are simple." She pauses for dramatic effect. "Be. Your. Self. You'll all sleep in Transition House, and come morning, check the envelopes we've given you for confirmation. That's it. It's that simple. At the end of the Gala,

I, with the help of the other Reps and Elites and even your peers, will select those who'll stay, and those who'll unfortunately return to Ashes. Pardon. I mean the Ashes."

Elenore said "return to ashes" as if Hopefuls are disposable nothings, devoid of the same blood running through her veins. I squeeze my fists. Maybe that's all in my head. Were Tessa here, she'd be pissed I was making lemons out of lemonade. I'm finally here, the place I've cursed the moon to reach, and I miss home. There are lights here. Real lights that switch on and off, and dim when you tell them to. There's more food than I've ever seen in my life. And yet, I can't help feeling like something's not right. I gaze over Elites and Reps speaking with Hopefuls with suspicious eyes, sporting forced smiles. Maybe that's it. I miss real smiles. Vye's smile. Jessup's smile. Miss Boah's smile. Well. I miss Boah's everything.

Elenore's voice rips through haunting nostalgia. Says she's prepared a welcome video. Tells attendees and Hopefuls to look ahead—the presentation will start shortly. Moments later, a young girl appears via a large hologram the size of a movie screen. The girl says, "The Transition Program changed my life."

When the girl says the word *life*, the word echoes like sounds in an empty cage. Then inspirational music starts—it plays over a video montage. One kid after another, I watch Hopefuls transition. Begins with past Hopefuls in the Ashes, standing in line, participating in Lineup. Were there cameras somewhere this morning I didn't see? It shows their happy faces arriving and attending the Gala, then studying their trade of choice at Transition House. Final images reveal the Fall Ball acceptance ceremony, where Hopefuls are inducted into New Georgian society. The video ends with kids in the presentation side by side. Holding hands, they smile in fancy clothes and say, "The Transition Program. It worked for us. Let it work for you."

When the presentation's over, Elenore rubs her throat, sips water, and says, "We welcome you to the fortieth annual New Georgia Gala. Now please, relax, have fun. Eat, drink, and be merry. And in the words of those who've succeeded before, the Transition Program works. Let it work for you." Applause fills the room and Elenore waves, smiles proud.

During Conversations, Reps introduce Hopefuls to New Georgia residents. It's the part where we connect with folks living over here. It's when impressing Elenore means the most. A waiter pours water nearby, the sounds so loud it fills my head. Thoughts of talking and connecting make me nervous, nauseous. Kyra whispers anxiously to the girl next to her; all three of us watch two older white men starting toward our table. What if I stumble over words and questions, unable to form complete sentences? Ugh. I hear water pouring, again. Can't hold my bladder, gotta pee. I excuse myself. Leave the ballroom and enter the hallway, searching for the girls' room.

A black boy with short hair paces at the end of the hall, in front of the entrance. When he finally looks up, he smiles, waves. I don't recognize 'em from the lineup—and he wasn't on the train ride over. Still, he walks toward me like he knows me, grins hard as he approaches. I spot the girls' bathroom, rush there. I wave at the boy, push the door open, and slip in fast.

After flushing, I leave the stall, walk to the sink. Elenore stands there lathering sudsy hands under steamy water. I keep a blank face, press the silver button on the clear washbowl. I watch hot water stream and grab pear-shaped soap from the glass bowl that separates us

Elenore clears her throat. "Enjoying yourself, Josephine?"

"Yes, ma'am. Everything's nice."

"Never call me that," she says sharply. She concentrates in the mirror, smiles hard, and checks her teeth for food. "No need to be formal, dear."

"Ma'am's how we address elders in the Ashes. Didn't mean any harm."

"I can't speak for anyone else, dear. With me, ma'am's unnecessary. Elenore'll do just fine."

I nod, ask Elenore if earlier, during the Lineup, she frowned because I called her ma'am. Tell her I thought I'd offended her.

"Whatever do you mean?" She brushes the question off with a short laugh.

"Maybe I imagined it," I say. I know I didn't.

"I have known stranger things to happen." Elenore nods, gazes at her reflection in the mirror. "Is life hard in the Ashes?"

"Yeah," I say, "but others are worse off. My aunt's woodstove baking makes it easier to earn tokes."

"Did you leave a boy . . . friend behind?"

"No."

"I overheard your conversation on AerTrain. Who is Boah?"

Inside, I'm whirling. Don't want Elenore to think I'm not here for the right reasons, that I don't want to leave the Ashes behind and transition here. Maybe I'll say Boah's no one special, but the smile on my face when she mentioned his name'll rat me out. And besides, lying to the one person I'm supposed to impress won't work in my favor.

"He's my best friend."

Elenore clears her throat, asks if my parents were proud of me being picked for the Gala.

I tell her they're dead.

Elenore's hand twitches. She hides trembling right fingers with a steady left palm. "How did they die?"

Again, I wanna lie, not bring it up, but I tell her the truth. Tell her my parents shot themselves. That Dad put a bullet in his head twenty minutes after my mom died, six hours after I'd been born. That my mother's sister Vye's proud of me, and that she raised me.

Elenore exhales. "Why'd they kill themselves?"

I tell her having kids is something Ashfolk try to avoid. That my parents couldn't afford to feed themselves, let alone me—and before they took their lives, they dropped me off at Aunt Vye's.

Elenore takes my hand in hers, says she relates to losing loved ones, says, "My only sister died young—tried to save her, but couldn't. I let her go." She stares at her reflection, traces her laughter lines mute as a turtle. Then says, "Death leaves a hole nothing beautiful can fill."

"Death brings sadness," I say.

"Yes, it's unfortunate. But we must never wallow in sorrow."

"Best to look on the bright side. Misery cures no one."

"If misery can't heal, what can?" Elenore takes a fingertip across her left brow, smoothing it.

"Love."

Elenore flashes an eerie smile. "Ever been in love, Josephine?"

"You mean with a person?"

"Yes, Josephine, a person."

Boah's profile pops into my head. "I don't know."

"Interesting."

I narrow eyes, forcing a smile, hoping Elenore can't read the confusion in my eyes. "What is?"

Slightly smirking, Elenore shakes her head. "Nothing, dear. Enjoy the Gala."

It's not nothing. It's something. What was it?

My chest is tight. And my forehead wrinkles over what Elenore's thinking. This might have been my one chance, one conversation with her. Did I say

73

something wrong? Something bad enough to send me home? Maybe being myself was bad advice. Maybe I should be who they want, to get what I want. And worry about my true self later. Elenore's the most important Rep to impress. I've been in New Georgia less than an hour and I can't help thinking I've failed.

Elenore places a hand on my shoulder before leaving. "When you're done here, come back to the ballroom. I'd like to introduce you."

"To who?"

"It's to whom," Elenore corrects me.

"To whom?"

"My children."

Elenore steps through the door. I plait an unraveling braid before following. I hear voices. Boys. I crack the door, listen. Through the opening, I see the black boy who waved earlier, talking to Cove. Cove calls the black boy Larry.

Larry points to the girls' room and smiles. He can't see me watching. Cove glances in my direction; he can't see me either, but I see him and I see it—his sadness. Sorrow sleeps in Cove's eyes, but his smirk makes me smile. Makes me wonder if he's into brown skin and giving black girls their first white kiss. As flirty thoughts dissipate, Cove's smirk shifts to a frown. Witnessing Cove's unhappiness makes me wanna fix him. Make whatever agony lives inside him disappear.

9

COVE

Maple House is alive. Jam-packed with well-dressed kids repping both sides of the mountain. Sitting at four round tables, on the other side of the dance floor, are Hopefuls from the Ashes. I count them. Organize them by gender. Four boys. Five girls. Hopefuls drink, eat, and chat merrily—smiles bursting with nervous delight. Ogling Hopefuls should conjure ways to torment their little hearts while plotting to break them. But fuck, I'm distracted. Can't get Jo off my mind.

No one makes me nervous, but Jo did when I touched her. I run my thumb across the tips of my fingers, think of the silk embedded in Jo's brown skin, feel the freedom in her smile. I scan the tables again for Jo's face, knowing she's not here. She must be in another room. But Jo's absence doesn't matter. I need only blink to see the way she looked at me at the Lineup and on the train. Her brown eyes are darts shooting through my dark places—made me feel naked fully clothed. I wonder what she thinks of me.

"A truth and a lie," Margo whispers. She grips the back of my chair, leans into my ear, nibbles on my earlobe. "What do we think of the new meat?" she says, breath tangy, crisp, pepperminty.

It's tough, but the older Margo gets, the harder it is not to see Elenore in her eyes. I shake my head. "Same ol' same ol'. No difference from last year. I'd rather be home." A server in a black pencil dress fills my glass, walks away.

"Ooh. Two truths. You're in a snarky mood." Margo sits next to me, fondles my collar. "But seriously, who will you pick? Who's the unlucky heart?"

I shrug and shake my head, sip Arnold Palmer. "And you? Which boy?"

Margo chuckles, biting her bottom lip. "A girl, maybe. It's a new year. New me."

I arch a brow. "Right."

I stare at boys from the Ashes. Sure, they're a little rough around the edges, but otherwise, they're like other boys I know, even myself sometimes. Seeking approval from girls through assholish behavior. Ignore girls we like, talk to ones we don't. We play it cool, but at home, when no one's watching, we're low-key afraid of hairy spiders and giant bugs just like some girls are. Meticulously, I'm contemplating who I'll ruin next. It's wasted thinking. The witch always chooses our prey.

Margo cups my knee. "I need cuddles. Want to after?"

I lift her hand and kiss it. "Depends on the toys," I say, eyes fixed across the room.

Margo looks too. She sniffs the ballroom and chuckles. "Smells like desperation. Delicious. Ugh, hope rats didn't ride the AerTrain with us. Last thing we need is a new Radius outbreak. Lassies get it worse. Heard they go bald first."

Lassies, as Margo calls her gender, receive affection differently. Most girls receive love via compliments, pretty things, and cute wooers who'll digest their angst without complaining. Elenore taught me that with girls the key is listening. And I do. I listen intently to every word spoken, to every phrase uttered. I listen only, never talk. Absorbing facts carefully, without interruption or judgment— offering no intimate details about my personal life. But it doesn't last long.

Soon, they're curious about me, too. When I don't provide answers, they'll verbally tackle anyone they see me talk to—try getting close to that person, to get closer to me, to know me, to find anything they can about me. Often it means

Margo, and we both know she'll never answer. I ignore them, mentally check out. Blame them for my disinterest—emotionally move further and further away from them, as they run faster and faster toward me, but it's too late. I'm so far away if they stood in front of me, I'd be invisible. Pretty soon, the chase exhausts them, leaving them with one card to play—their bodies. The horrible reoccurring events of my love interests—I am ultimately ashamed of it, but I must do as I am told.

We do as Elenore trained and emotionally feed on the misery we've caused. During emotional feedings, we keep in mind that their misery equates to love, the observation of misery is science, and science protects our hearts.

CHIRP! CHIRP!

The iCom alert near my ear makes me jerk. I slide my hand inside my coat, press the white button, answer the call. "Yeah?"

"Got a minute?" Larry sounds stuffy, like he just stopped crying.

I glance at Margo. And an evil grin splashes across her oval face. She lifts her right shoulder, shrugging palms up. "Larry," she murmurs, lifts her hand, wiggles her ring finger, and kisses it. "I said no."

I smirk, playfully scolding her. "Bad, bad Jellyfish." I uncross my legs, stand, pace past gawking girls, and exit the ballroom.

10

COVE

Larry's been Margo's plaything since Pull-Ups.

Elenore said she picked Larry for Margo because she wanted her daughter's first love game to be successful. I remember Elenore sitting Margo on her lap, telling her then-seven-year-old daughter that Larry was the perfect living cadaver, because there was weakness in his eyes—a rare tenderness that made him excellent prey.

Larry paces back and forth outside the girls' restroom, hands shaking in pockets. "You gotta talk to her, man."

"About what exactly?" But of course it's because Margo refused his proposal. It's beyond my comprehension why he'd wish for marriage at seventeen. I mean, Jesus fucking Christ, I just turned eighteen, and so far, I can't see myself tied to one girl the rest of my life. Some days, I don't want to be linked to myself that long.

Larry shows me the ring like I care. It's an enormous pink shiny stone. It's a good choice, actually, Margo's favorite color. But there's no diamond large enough in the entire world to make Margo disobey our mother.

Larry's drunk. Pathetically lovesick and sensitive to Margo's affection. I'd roll my eyes if I knew it wouldn't hurt his feelings. "Get back out there. Meet new people. Your life doesn't belong to Margo," I lie. His life abso-fucking-lutely belongs to my sister. And intrinsically, he knows it, too. But I swear, sometimes talking to Larry feels asinine; nonsensical, like going to the cinema to eat films and watch buttered popcorn.

"It doesn't?" he says, his face one empty question mark.

"No, Larry, it doesn't. It's yours. Take your life back," I say. "Go romance a dirty little easy girl from the Ashes. They're all the same. They'll dance with anything. Give them a little dance, tell them pretty things, pluck and toss them. They're not worth much else. Chin up, my friend. You're their dream—their meal ticket to the stars. You're rich, everything they aspire to be; they won't refuse you."

"What if they turn me down, like Margo?"

"There's only one Margo."

"Yeesh, thank God for that shit. You never have trouble with girls. They never ghost you or turn you down. They practically beg your ass to dance at these things." Larry shakes his face in his hands. "Ugh! Fuck-ah-ty. She kills me, man." Larry pauses, then starts again. "Remember when we were kids, what I told you about your sister?"

"The evil twin metaphor? I remember—"

"Yeah?"

I nod. "Yeah. What about it?"

"Well, it's like the identical fuckers grew up . . . they're godlike entities or something now. Like . . . every time I see Margo, I meet either God or the devil."

I grab his shoulders, shake him. "Then go inside. Choose an easy angel from the ashes, and all will be well, at least for tonight." And because there's beauty in Larry's torture, I lie to him. I tell him to try Margo tomorrow; maybe she'll change her mind after thinking about it. I say Margo's fickle, often changes her mind after a good night's sleep.

Larry smiles, eating the lie. "I'm a good catch, right? Yeah, why wouldn't she want to marry me?" He blows his nose into a wrinkled tissue pulled from his pants pocket.

"She'd be deranged not to," I say.

Larry flings his arms open, jonesing for a hug. I don't move an inch. I stand still, staring at his brown fingers, wrists, and forearms, with a *Don't hug me* look drawn across my face. Larry rushes into me anyway, wraps arms around my shoulders. I keep both arms glued to either side of my body. Larry sighs, releases his hold; I pat his back. We return to the ballroom.

At my table, Margo stares at Larry chatting with Hopeful girls across the room. "Is that your doing?" She looks at me.

I flash a one-sided grin, drink my Arnold Palmer.

Five minutes later, Elenore enters the ballroom with Jo. She's stunning—no, yummy—a Shakespearean sonnet in motion, scribed in chocolate letters. My chest feels warm and heavy. Like hair on my neck's lightning struck. Breathing is harder than usual; quick breaths become shorter as the witch and Jo move closer.

I'm never nervous, but I am now. With clammy palms, I stare Jo up and down, trace the hem of her muslin skirt. Her brown complexion's smooth, evenly painted over bones. I want to touch her full lips, grab her slender waist, gaze into her hooded eyes, and kiss her button nose.

Margo scoffs as Elenore and Jo walk across the room, heading toward our table. "Look at her shoes." Margo leans over my shoulder. "They're two sizes too big. Positively tragic." Margo insults when threatened. "Your chosen livestock."

When Elenore reaches our table, Margo and I stand. Elenore takes Jo's hand, cups it in hers.

"Trust you're behaving, Margo?" Elenore arches brows.

"Always, Mummy." Margo curtsies as most girls do for Reps at events. An old ritual acknowledging superiority—and also a bratty move. And Elenore knows it.

I bow, tilt my head sideways. "Elenore."

Elenore grins devilishly. I know that look—it's the one that says, *Are you ready to break another heart, Cove?*

"May I present Josephine Monarch." Elenore touches Jo's hair.

"Jo. Just Jo," Jo says.

I remain indifferent, glance at Margo; her face matches mine. No one corrects Elenore in private, let alone in public. "Nice to meet you, Just Jo." I smile. Jo doesn't smile back. She disregards me like people snub shadows on concrete. Jo looks to Margo, and her perfect smile appears. I humph and bite down on my bottom lip, grinning. Did Jo just ignore me?

Margo smiles, extends her hand to Jo. "I'm Margo; this is my brother, Cove."

"I'll leave you three to it," Elenore says, then walks away.

"Have a seat, Jo." Margo directs Jo to the seat next to hers—the one directly across from mine.

"Thank you," Jo says.

Margo lifts the empty cup in front of Jo. "This won't do," she pouts, waves a server over.

When waitstaff reaches the table, Margo asks Jo what she wants to drink. Jo says pineapple soda. The server returns with the yellow drink, asks if there's anything else we need. Margo waves the server off, dismissing him, the way Elenore discharged me as a child.

"Josephine's a cool name," Margo says. "Sounds old, in a good way. Where did it come from? Named after someone?"

Jo pulls her pretty lips off the crystal straw, swallows. "Not someone, something," Jo smiles. "A character from my mom's favorite book."

"Do tell." Margo wiggles in her seat, claps her hands like a giddy child. "What's the name of it—the novel? Maybe I've read it."

I'm annoyed, and I don't know why. What I do know is that since Jo sat down, she hasn't looked my way once. Overlooks me like I'm invisible, and won't talk to me.

"*Little Women*," Jo says.

"I know that book. Read it last year in high school. Jo, the rebellious writer. Are you a rebel, a writer, or both?" Margo asks, face soaked in mischief.

"I can draw," Jo laughs.

Margo laughs too. "Parfaite! An artist . . . how Victorian!" Margo claps, catching my eye. "Maybe you'll draw us someday . . . sketch my smile on my brother's face!" She reaches over, rubs my cheek.

I dodge her touch. Remain silent.

I stand, leave the table. Girls who smile pretty and read are like magicians. Jo's both; she's pure magic. At the refreshment bar, I grab a glass bottle of water. I unscrew the metal top and watch Margo and Jo laugh at the table.

Edith is suddenly beside me, places both arms around my neck—breath saturated in punchy liquor. "Would you like to dance with me?"

I lift her hands off my neck. "No."

Edith pouts, fills her glass with red wine, and walks away. Before reaching her table, she stumbles over her own feet but doesn't fall to the floor. Last year, there wasn't a boy in attendance uninterested in Edith; that was the Gala James first noticed her. And while I'll admit I didn't like everyone checking Edith out, this year, they can have her.

As Edith sits next to Victoria and their mother, Vimberly, a blonde girl from the Ashes walks over to the table where Jo and Margo still sit. Jo smiles, offers the girl the seat closest to mine, and the blonde girl accepts.

Elenore approaches; she stands beside me, holds my hand. "Jo's beautiful, yes?"

I nod. "She'll do."

Elenore pats my arm. "Larry is Margo's triumph. She's done a beautiful job with his misery, don't you think?"

Larry sits in a corner, eyes puffy, silver flask in hand. Every few seconds, he stares in Margo's direction, watching her every move from a distance.

Elenore continues, "Make her your masterpiece." Her eyes are fixed on Jo.

"Not a problem." I smile, faking control because Jo feels like a problem. She frowns when I'm near, laughs when I'm absent, and refuses to look my direction. "After her, I'm done breaking hearts. And the deed is mine?"

Elenore nods. "Promise is a promise. Ruin her, break her, and it's yours."

I nod and stare at Jo like she's forbidden fruit.

"So, what do you think of her?" Elenore asks.

"She's optimistically confident."

"Is that all?" Elenore nudges.

"She's stubborn as hell."

"Anything more?"

"No." I wonder why the witch is so fascinated with Jo. She never asked about the others.

Elenore tsks. "Feel it in my bones. There's destined to be love involved. You can't see it yet, but I do."

I scoff. "Agreed; she'll fall like the others. And I'll break her, like the rest."

"Jo has spirit . . . are you sure you're not biting off more than you can chew?" A conniving grin graces her face and raises her cheeks.

I humph. "Even the wildest of lions can be trained."

A satisfied look on her face, Elenore turns to the buffet of food beside us. Passes over shrimp cocktail, baked chicken, honey ham, and roasted vegetables to pile white rice on her plate. Disgusted at the sight, I down the bottled water and head back to the table.

As I sit, Margo says, "This is Kyra."

Kyra blushes, says hi. I nod, thinking that's better. Kyra's reaction to seeing me is more like the usual response I get from girls. It makes me feel better.

Margo giggles. "Kyra here was just telling us how Jo used to run around the Ashes as a kid, tugging at her kitchen, while reading a book."

"It's true," Kyra laughs. "It was glued to her tiny palms."

"She's right, I did," Jo admits.

I want to ask what a kitchen is, and how it's possible to tug it down the street while holding a book, but I don't. "Which book?" I say, staring at Jo, but she doesn't look back. She sips her pineapple soda.

"*Great Expectations*," Kyra replies, breaking the tension.

"That was a very long time ago," Jo says, her laughter singing its last note.

"Cove has a thing for crossword puzzles," Margo shares. "You two should talk words and stuff. Since you like reading," she says to Jo. Margo stands, narrows her eyes at Larry across the room. She continues, "Come, come, Kyra. We're going to be fast friends . . . let me introduce you to Larry."

"Is he cute?" Kyra's eyes gleam wonder.

"The cutest!" Margo chirps, then leaves the table with Kyra, their arms woven together like a porcelain basket.

Alone with Jo, I gaze at her. Hoping she'll look my way. I check her cheeks for redness—nothing. Black girls appear fearless. If they're not smiling, you never know if they're happy, sad, or pissed off. Girls, in general, are mysterious creatures with little to no knowledge of the power they possess. If they did, they'd climb inside male brains and crush senseless boys inside out.

I scramble for relevant conversation. She likes books; she's mentioned two so far. Louisa May Alcott's *Little Women*, and *Great Expectations* by Charles Dickens. Romantic novels crammed with optimism. Maybe books, not charm, are the key to capturing Jo's affections. "Why *Great Expectations?*" I ask, attempting to unearth why it's her favorite.

Jo twists in her seat. Facing away from me, she says, "Why does anyone read? It's a great book."

"When's the last time you read it?"

"I don't know—a while ago."

I run fingers through my hair, comb it back, away from my forehead. "What do you think about all this? The Gala?"

"It's everything I thought it'd be."

I want to tell Jo I like her voice, but don't. "See the table with roasted turkey?" Jo nods, and I continue, "When I was little, Margo and I hid under it during Galas."

Jo clears her throat. "Why?"

"It felt safer. Quieter." I shrug.

Jo nods.

The music starts—something slow I've never heard. The tune is perfect, catchy, woo inducing, love inspiring. Couples make their way to the dance floor. Margo's successfully matched Kyra with Larry. While holding Kyra, Larry watches Margo sway alone. Edith's slow dancing smothers her boyfriend, James, while her sister dances with two brown boys from the Ashes.

I stand up, position myself beside Jo's chair, offer her my hand. And it's odd. I don't dance with anyone at these things, let alone ask for dances. I don't question myself too much, but know it has something to do with a need to touch Jo. "Dance with me."

Jo looks from my hand to my wrist, forearm, neck . . . lips to eyes. "No."

"No?" My face is invidious. How could she say no? There's not a girl in this room I couldn't have right now; who is Jo to tell me no?

"No." Jo's nonchalant. "Ask the redhead to dance," she continues, referring to Edith. Jo was watching.

"I'm asking you." Inside I'm hot, like blood boils in my veins.

"My answer's no."

"Why?"

"You tell me." Jo stands. "Why do you ask? Do you ask because you want to dance? Or because I'm a romantic, dirty little easy girl from the Ashes? And I'd dance with anything?" Jo throws my own words back at me like a boomerang. Her nose is scrunched, eyes cold.

Confusion smears my face; how does she know what I said earlier to make pathetic-ass Larry feel good? Larry was the only one around. But he'd never tell a soul. We keep each other's secrets.

NEWS UPDATE! The tinny female voice of the alert system sounds off above our heads. Silence floods the Gala; everyone stands, heads tilted, eyes gazing up.

Jo lifts her chin toward the ceiling. I do, too. Together, we watch the words RIOT IN THE ASHES flash across the curved ceiling in light blue letters. I shake my head and scoff. It's degrading the news chose blue letters.

Jo doesn't know it, but every New Georgian citizen does. I glance at Margo, who's snickering. She knows it, too—knows the news displays emergency alerts in red, not blue. We consider blue holograms general news alerts, random, nonthreatening. News relating to the Ashes isn't displayed in red unless New Georgia citizens are involved, injured, or in danger.

Worry fills Jo's face as images of the Ashes display above us. They flash silently while text runs quickly below: fights between police and kids, kids lighting torches, and toddlers with mouths wide open mid-cry. Jo's mouth drops at the image of a boy around my age, with a scar above his top lip. When the boy appears to yell, Jo rises to her feet. She narrows her eyes as he fights off cops.

Jo doesn't turn to me. I watch her profile. She's barely audible, but she says, "I can't stay."

As Jo leaves the table and exits the ballroom, I think of the conversation with Larry in the hallway. Where was Jo when I went to talk to him? Was it when she wasn't at the tables? Could she really be leaving because she heard me? I scan the ballroom, heart pumping, drumming a mile a minute. I count the girls from the Ashes, include Jo this time. Six of them.

Jo heard the conversation in the hallway.

I ignore everything I've been taught and Elenore's ridiculous training, and I chase after Jo. In the hallway, I bump a decorative table and watch a crystal vase full of ghost orchids crash to the floor. I leave the chaos of glass shards behind, but I'm too late. By the time I reach the last porch step, Jo's in a white turbo, driving away. I watch the back of her head through the rear window. Out of breath, ignoring blood dripping from one of my hands, I just want to see it—the cab—as long as I can. I follow its path down the road bordered with enormous oak trees—watch its taillights with regretful eyes until it's unseen.

11

JOSEPHINE

AerTrain's terminal is crowded.

I race through human traffic, dodging passengers left and right. I'm lost inside the images flashed via hologram during the Gala—those clips won't leave my mind. And whenever an AerTrain passenger bumps my shoulder, thigh, or hand, a different image of the Ashes appears like swift blinks when eyes catch dust.

Bump!

A cop handcuffing a cursing girl.

Bump!

Kids chasing cops with billy clubs.

Bump!

Mothers and grandmothers holding wailing babies.

Bump! Bump!

The clip that pushed me out the door resurfaces. The camera zoomed in on the cut above his lip first. Before his whole face was shown, I knew it was Boah. Reed and two badge-less cops pushed and punched Boah in the stomach. Boah fell to his knees, fought them off. The clip ended with Reed's bloody, defiant grin.

"Please find the ticket booth for questions regarding your trip." The terminal's robotic voice jerks my mind away from hologram pictures and clips.

I follow white-and-red signs leading to the nearest ticket booth. What if Vye's hurt; what if Neal's in trouble? I try to think positive. Jessup'll take care of them.

I need to focus on getting out of here. Be anywhere but here. Try to think of something else. The Gala.

Aunt Vye was wrong. Elites look down on kids like me. I think of Cove's shocked face when I turned him down. My staying wouldn't change how he sees Hopefuls—how they all see us. Dirty little needy girl. We'll always be a headline away from less than nothing in their eyes.

I'm pissed with Vye. And I feel like shit for being pissed at Vye because at this very moment she could be in danger. I push those thoughts aside. Jessup wouldn't let anything happen to Vye. But thinking Vye's safe doesn't change why I'm upset with her. Stories Vye'd spout about kindness in Saven are lies. Or at least they're lies now. Or who knows?—maybe they're not lies and it's just Cove. And by chance, I met the only jerk who thinks girls from the Ashes are dipsticks, good for one thing. But all of Elenore's smiles were hiding something too.

The signs have brought me no closer to a ticket booth, or maybe I'm just distracted. I ask an old man with a cane for directions, finally find the booth in a wide domed hall.

"When's the last train?" I ask the brunette behind the counter.

"Headed where, dear?" she says, her smile reminiscent of Vye's comforting ones after jig nightmares.

Squinting, I check the time on the clock high on the wall. It's eight p.m. I turn, facing the clerk. "The Ashes," I say.

She nods and types on the holographic keypad, gazes at the information projected above it. "Can you run?"

"Fast."

"Good." She says a train leaves in nine and a half minutes. Loading's on the other side of the station. But if I hurry, take the stairs to the left, instead of waiting on the elevator or escalator to the right, I might make it before it pulls off.

I'm ashamed because—"I don't have money."

The clerk arches a brow, stares at my dress. "Mhm. You attended the Gala, yes?" I nod. "Transportation is free on Gala night for all attendees." She tilts her head slightly back, gesturing to the stairs behind her. "You'd better hurry."

I lift my muslin skirt off the floor. With fist full of rose-gold fabric, I turn and jog toward the stairs behind the ticket booth.

I glance down at feet descending—watch my too-big shoes take stair after stair, until I almost lose one. I stop, shove heel into shoe, and keep going.

AerTrain's intercom speaks. "The next train headed to the Ashes departs in five minutes. Riders, please board the train. Thank you."

I pick up the pace, mean-mugging down the narrow staircase. Rushing, I take two steps at a time, passing a little blonde girl hopscotching down the stairs. The little girl's resemblance to Kyra's uncanny. And suddenly, I'm back at the Gala, reliving what Kyra'd said opening the cab's door just outside Maple House as we arrived. "Amazing, huh?"

I reach inside my skirt pocket, feel for it. It's still there—the tiny envelope—the one with strict instructions not to open till morning. Come morning, I'm certain my thumbprint will detect that I haven't made a good enough impression tonight to transition into New Georgia.

The intercom interrupts my thoughts. "AerTrain to the Ashes departs in four minutes. Passengers, please board the train. Thank you."

I trip at the bottom of the stairs, grab the handrail quick. I'm exhausted, breathing heavily, heart racing against the digital clock in the sky, but I can't stop. My stomach kicks, growls, and grumbles. All that food at the Gala I wish I'd eaten. And I wish I could've gotten a little soul food to share with Vye.

Disappointment fills the spaces in my stomach devoid of food. I think of how wasteful they all were. And their food swallowed by speaking trash cans. I still see it, see them now, the Reps—their suspicious eyes on us. Those tight smiles, toting plates of food that'd never hit their bellies. I shouldn't judge them. But I can't help it. Can't stop it. Shouldn't bother me, but it does. Then again, maybe being born with everything means forgetting those born with nothing.

Through a wide doorway to the tracks and AerTrains swish above my head. I look up. Here, walls are mirrors and ceilings are see-through. I don't know which way to go. "AerTrain to the Ashes departs in two minutes. Last call for boarding to the Ashes. Thank you."

There're so many unnumbered and unnamed trains. Two trains to my left, a woman in white, wearing a white lace veil, lingers outside her train's door. Tired, I rush toward her, touch her elbow.

"Do you know which train's going to the Ashes?"

The woman doesn't look at me, keeps her head down, staring at the floor below her white heels. "This one," she says, stepping into the train before us.

I release a heavy sigh. "Thank you." I enter the train. Besides me and the lady with the veil, it's empty. It's not an odd revelation; no one hops on a train headed to the Ashes this late, especially on Gala night. Makes me wonder why the woman in white heels is headed there.

The woman nods her head without glancing my way. She walks to the back of the car, stares out the oval window to her right. Everything about her, besides her brown skin, feels rich, classy, and straight to the point, like Elenore.

Heart still pounding, I take a seat a couple rows behind her. As the AerTrain whooshes to life around us, she coughs into a white napkin. I wanna ask if she needs help, but she doesn't look sick—just seems lonely. She coughs again, harder.

I'll never end up like her; no white veils and heels in my future. The Gala was my chance to change my stars. And leaving before it's over, I know, pretty much ruined my one shot. Maybe this all has a purpose. Maybe I'm where I should be.

But maybe Vye should've never traded pies for these expensive clothes. And I never should've got in line.

AerTrain takes off, dashes out of the station in moments. I slump in my seat, gaze out the window, staring at tears rolling down both cheeks. I think of my parents I can't remember, and what they'd think about me giving up on the one chance to live a better life. All the hours Vye spent baking pies to buy this outfit were a waste. Tokes and time spent preparing for the night was for nothing. Now that I'm really on the train, it sinks in that I'm returning home empty-handed. Self-conscious over what folks'll think.

When I feel low, I try thinking of the Beautiful Things. They grew in the wasteland before the wasteland became a wasteland. For miles and miles, they sprouted from the earth. Was the prettiest flora in the Ashes, until acre by acre, cops chopped them down and burned anything left. The Beautiful Things had white petals that spiraled a black oval center. Growing up, no one knew what they were called, so we started calling them the Beautiful Things. I squeeze my eyes tight, tighter. Try imagining them, but I can't. So, I breathe deep, and take an eyeful of moon instead.

We pass between bright skyscrapers, until ten minutes later we leave the city behind. Soon, the AerTrain glides a little slower over smoky blue mountains, indigo meadow, and teal glen. I flatten my spine against the back of the seat, wiping beneath my nose. I wanna stop being mad but can't stop thinking about the Gala: Reps judging. Cove's mean words. Boah's troubled face flashing via live hologrammed news.

That's what's important now—getting back to Boah, and Vye, and Neal. Can't get the images out of my head, Boah being dragged away by cops with angry faces. I think of fire blazing in the footage, kids breaking laws. Not rioting—publicly protesting, raising silenced voices.

I think of Cove's frown when I left the Gala. I don't think he could tell, but I watched him watching me as the turbo cab pulled away. The look in his eyes was sad. Or it could've been regret. I don't know. Whatever it was punctured my skin and entered my veins like a vaccine. Made me think that maybe Cove didn't mean those hateful things. But if he did, it's good I left when I did. Had it not been for the emergency news alert, there's no telling what would've come out of my mouth. Leaving the Gala before morning's unheard of. But it doesn't matter. I'd rather be knee-deep in the Ashes than flying high in New Georgia. Right now, Boah's, Vye's, and Neal's safety's what matters. And if I ruined my chances leaving, so be it. It was worth it, just to see the smug look on Cove's face disappear when I told 'em I wouldn't dance with him.

AerTrain's bright rails swoosh across the track, pull me back to the present moment. As hurt as I am, Cove's smile made me smile. Cove's not Boah; I don't know him like my skin. And yet, his unhappiness pulled me in, made me wanna solve it. Solve him. Maybe feeling this is the start of love. Cove's rich. If we got together, we wouldn't fight about money, get suicidal, and kill ourselves from the depression.

The woman in the white veil stands up, nods at me, then turns and walks toward the front of the train where the conductor area is. In white numbers, the hologram on the seat in front of me reads: 11:00 p.m. Just fifteen minutes before we reach the Ashes. I don't have to be there to know what's going on. I hope Neal's not running the streets. Tonight's the last night he needs to get in trouble with how bad things looked on the news. Aunt Vye, is she okay?—tucked away safe from danger? Is Jessup with her? I wanna scream but I won't. So, I make a fist, press nails deep into palm skin.

The train stops outside the door built into the mountain—the door is large, rusty. It's made of old metal half-covered in moss. When the door slides open, it leads the train into the underpass, a bordering area inside the mountain with one bench. The lights inside the train flash on. Outside, it's so dark shadows don't exist.

AerTrain's automated voice announces, "Passengers, please stand by."

I narrow my eyes, puzzled. "Why'd the train stop here?" I murmur aloud to myself. I always see the AerTrain drive all the way through the door in the mountain until it reaches the high gates to the Ashes. Why would it stop at a desolate, dark, and unsupervised boarding zone first—an abandoned area AerTrain, and, well, no one really uses anymore.

A moment later, the automated voice again. "Due to tonight's riot, to maintain the safety of train, conductor, and our passengers, this is our final stop. We apologize for any distress this may cause. Thank you for choosing AerTrain. Doors opening soon."

AerTrain's double metal doors swish open. I step into the boarding area. The train closes its doors, heads in the other direction, toward New Georgia. I look down the other way, toward the Ashes.

Moonlight shines on the curved metallic stone walls, owls howl in the distance, and the spicy scent of Georgia pine fills my nose. Alone, surrounded by near darkness, the full moon's the only light, but that won't last long. In ten minutes, the entrance into this boarding area will close and I'll be in complete darkness. I gotta make it to the other door, the one on the other end of AerTrain's entrance.

I pick up the pace, start running like I do in dreams. I don't fall. But I run so fast a heel gets stuck in a grate, twisting my ankle. I slide my aching foot out of the shoe, pull the pump out, take the other heel off, and jog the rest of the way barefoot, shoes in hand. It's painful, but I don't stop. Thoughts of Vye, Neal, Jessup, and Boah keep me going—they're the moon in this darkness I run through.

The mountain door's ajar. I push the heavy steel forward with both hands. When it swings wide, I'm confused, worried by what I see. In the distance, behind the metal gate, frantic people protest, marching in every direction. Their voices thunder. Some cheer, hoot, and holler in front of the police station, which has flames lighting up windows. I scan the panic, then run toward the barbed-wire fence. I stick anxious fingers in diamond-shaped iron holes, shake the gate, yelling for someone to let me in.

"NO JUSTICE! NO PEACE!" they roar.

"Starve never! Fight forever!"

Bootleg Jules runs to the gate—he's been drinking, fiery breath baked in moonshine. He seems worried, eyes bloodshot, yellow, and dazed—clothes dingy and muddled. "Wait a minute." He searches his pants, anxiously looking over his shoulder at the riot behind him.

"Where's Neal?" I say.

Bootleg Jules mean-mugs me. "Don't ask me about that boy. Hope I never see 'em."

Unbeknownst to Ashfolk, Bootleg Jules and Neal don't get along; in passing, they don't so much as look at each other.

"What are you looking for?" I'm frustrated. "You don't have the key. Go get Jessup. He'll open the gate."

"What he gunna do? Cops ain't in control no mo. Not after what dey done done tuh dat girl." He pats down his wrinkled white shirt and red-dirt-stained brown sweatpants.

I squint at him. "Huh? What girl? What do you mean cops aren't in control?"

"Boah got duh keys. He in charge now. I—I—I'll go get 'em." Bootleg Jules backs away from the gate, runs dodging crowds, and disappears behind the torched police station.

"Wait! What you mean Boah's in charge?"

I shake the gate, again and again, stare at twisty razors at the top. I pull my skirt up, lift a knee, stuff my right foot into a hole in the fence. I climb up a little but freeze when Curtis Flan enters my head. I visualize him falling off the roller coaster—how he fell headfirst and lost his legs. I hear 'em screaming, blurting suicidal rants in the middle of the street. With a deep sigh, I glance down at my toes, shins, and ashy knees. I shake my head, sigh again, decide against hiking over the gate.

My body jerks back, startled, as the roof of the police station caves in. I watch orange and red and mustard embers push through crackling wreckage. I gaze, horrified, as thick smoke rises from blazing ruins, and ashes marinate on harsh winds.

Bootleg Jules resurfaces, Boah running next to him.

Boah spots me. He runs faster and faster, hurdling over blazing debris tuh get tuh me. When he reaches the gate, he grabs the lock on the fence. "Why'd you come back?!"

"The hologram, news . . . I saw you. Saw Reed, those cops, what they did. You okay?"

Boah checks his pants pockets. "It's nothing." He faces Bootleg Jules. "Go to the water hole—" Boah slides a key into the lock, jiggles it. "Tell the others I'm on the way. Go, now!"

Bootleg Jules nods, scurries off. I watch him disappear between the hundreds of protestors vigorously chanting, marching cracked streets, jumping fallen trees. Why'd Boah tell Jules to go to the water hole? Kids go to that isolated warehouse to make out, get drunk, or get high.

Boah pulls another key chain from his pocket, nervously stabbing the lock with different keys until one fits, clicks, and opens the gate.

I stare at him. "What others?"

Boah ignores me, pulls the gate forward to let me in.

"Boah? What'd'you mean by *tell the others*? What others?"

"Go home, Jo," Boah shouts.

"Don't tell me what to do. Talk to me." I grab his hand; he snatches it away. There's a seriousness in his stare I've seen before. It's not hate. But it's not love either. "What's going on! What's happening!"

"Just go home, Jo. I'll find yuh later. I promise."

"Like you said you'd come to Lineup because you didn't want to miss me? You'll find me like that, right? It's that kind of promise, right?" I'm so mad I could scream, and I feel hot. Like boiling water hugging tight skin hot.

Boah reaches for my hand. "Can't explain now. Won't be far behind yuh," he says. "Trust me, Jo. Alright? Just trust me."

I shake my head, pull away before his fingers reach mine. "Don't bother!" I walk away, and then I'm jogging—running faster and faster, so fast ashes fill my mouth, cover my arms, dirty my skirt. My heart's tight, like someone's squeezing it. I imagine someone's after me, like they'll come out of nowhere, grab me, shoot me, stab me, or beat me within an inch of my life. I cough. Smoke burns my eyes. But I keep going, dashing home—my arms, two bronze scissors swishing through wind, fog, and floating dust.

I gotta go through Moats Alley to reach home unseen. I enter Moats full force, thighs high, kneeing dusty wind. When I pass the green dumpster, chills dash up my spine. I see my nine-year-old self being held gunpoint next to it. Ever since, I've had trouble sleeping. So, I sleep with a rusty knife beneath a dingy pillow.

I fall, release a quiet "ouch" and rub my knee. It's scraped and stings. I ignore the pain, get up and keep running. I gotta get out of Moats Alley. Just before I reach the exit, I yelp as Boah jumps in front of me and covers my mouth with one hand.

"Scared the shit outta me!" I say, lips pressed inside his clammy palm. His hand smells like fire, smoke, and tree leaves.

Boah uncovers my mouth. "Quiet! Told yuh, I wasn't far behind." Chin over shoulder, he opens an alley door, shoves me inside, and closes the door behind us.

"What are you doing?"

Neal comes out a dark corner, grabs my arm, whispers, "Shhhhh, Jo. They'll hang us if they catch us." I don't like being shushed, but I'm glad to see Neal in one piece.

Gunshots fire on the other side of the door.

And then another *BANG! BANG!*

I'm shivering, sweaty, covered in ashes. We all are. We three stare breathlessly at the tattered wood door, mouths barely open with chapped lips, watching the door as someone on the other side twists its iron doorknob.

Boah locks the door from the inside. We listen hard as the person jiggles the knob, attempting to open the door. Boah grabs my hand and releases it once the doorknob stops turning.

Neal shakes his head. "Gotta get outta here."

12

COVE

Blood drips down my brown shoes, lands on the wood floor. The cut at the center of my palm stings, but every few seconds, thoughts of Jo, and how I offended her, numb the sharp pain in my hand, replacing discomfort with sharp guilt. But remorse doesn't visit long. Elenore's training bullies my thoughts of Jo, pushing them someplace so dark, light can't shine through. I squeeze my eyes tight, tighter. Elenore's words are disintegrating. I pop eyes open, watch red dots stain dark oak, and think of Father. He loved this room. The smoke tank, he called it. But it's not a tank. It's a cool office adjacent to the ballroom in Maple House, where wooden bookshelves climb dark green walls.

In the middle of the smoke tank, eight brown leather wingback chairs form a circle. I sit in my father's favorite chair, the wingback facing the large fireplace.

"Ouch!"

"Stop jerking. Stand still," Margo says, swiping my cut with three tiny alcohol pads.

"I'm not standing. I'm sitting." Skin between my eyes pinches, wrinkles—wincing.

Margo runs both hands up my thighs, feels up torso, neck, then traces my bottom lip with her index fingers. I move her hands away from my mouth, place them on my wounded hand.

"You're no fun." Margo narrows her hazel eyes, squeezes my injured hand.

I snatch my hand away. "Fuck!"

"I'm glad it hurts. What were you thinking? Running after her? Really, Cove? That witch'll beat us twice if she finds out." Margo side-bites her bottom lip, vigorously implementing skills learned last year during New Georgia's state-mandated CPR and first aid certification. "This cut is deep. Don't worry, Gaitlin's magic will do the trick."

It's not really magic. It's a healing scanner. Margo and others call it magic because the scanner decreases recovery time. It's extraordinary really. Depending on the injury, Gaitlin's scanner heals wounds, cuts, sprains, and broken bones in days, not months. Call me cray-cray, but I don't want it to heal fast. And I don't want to get rid of this scar. I got it chasing Jo. And its pain, no matter how long it lasts, reminds me of her. I deserve discomfort after treating her like that.

Alcohol enters my fresh wound. I flinch. It stings like hell.

"Stay still," Margo scolds.

Unbeknownst to her, I narrow my eyes. I'm twisted. Margo's helping, cleaning blood out of my wound, and I can't stop seeing her dead at the bottom of an ocean with her pearl bracelet floating up to the surface like round, glistening stars. It's odd, but at the strangest—and sometimes most normal—moments, my brain does this weird thing with her and Elenore, where it imagines how they'll die. I don't want them dead—I'd never wish that on Margo—but I can't control the thoughts.

Once I daydreamed Margo got hit by a car crossing the street, and an unkindness of ravens ate her entrails. Another day, in biochem, I imagined Elenore drowning in a pool of her own blood—I imagined she'd broken the wrong heart, and the guy she broke machete'd her heart into a million pieces, then fed her heartless body to the ocean. I'm never sad daydreaming Elenore's departure from earth. Instead, thoughts of her massive life insurance policy take over.

Last night, just before she took off her makeup, I watched her throw two envelopes with the words PAST DUE THIRD NOTICE stamped in red letters across the room, into the fireplace. Elenore looked like she wanted to cry, but didn't. I don't really want her to die, but her fat insurance policy—well—it'd cure financial troubles the witch covers with porcelain makeup.

I'd like to say I reserve dark inklings for Elenore and Margo, but I'd be lying. When I was thirteen, I tried to rewrite my mother's death. Instead of dying of starvation, she died with a hell of a lot of meat on her bones. I imagined her leaving this world lying sideways on my father's chest, a smile on her face, smothered cube steak in her full belly.

Margo wraps gauze around my hand. "Remember the chairs?"

It's a stupid question, but I nod. "I'll never forget." How could I? It happened ten minutes before the daydream of Elenore drowning in a pool of blood.

That day, Ian, a guy Elenore'd just broken, came to the house while she was out shopping for Margo's gown for Fall Ball. Trying to win the witch back, Ian took Margo and me for ice cream. When we returned, Elenore was furious, but an outsider would never know it. She's well versed in hiding anger with strangers. But when she walked over to Ian, kissed him on the cheek, told him to leave, and that she'd call him later, Margo and I knew we were fucked.

Once inside, Elenore slapped the ice cream out of our hands. She dragged us to the kitchen by the ears, stuffed our heads inside the open space on the back of the kitchen chairs, then whipped us bareback with thorn switches till blood trickled down our spines. It terrified Margo. Elenore terrified me. But that day, Margo and I swore Elenore'd never see us cry again. And from that day on, no matter how long or bad the beating, we kept our promise.

Chirp! Chirp! Chirp!

I glance at my watch. Margo stands, rushes to the wall, presses the button that opens the ceiling, revealing a skylight. She gazes up, staring at the white

101

hologram in the sky outside. It's iCom's emergency news flash—red letters.

Margo watches above; I stream it via my watch. A monotone male voice announces:

"Your attention is required. Important news coming soon."

Ten seconds later, iCom's number-one breaking-news reporter, Katie Childs, appears, her face as big as the moon. Her hair's the way it always is: red locks gathered in a bun atop her head, even bangs hiding her brown forehead.

Margo and I listen as Katie says there's a fire in the Ashes. I watch amazed as iCom drones show live footage of teens running mad, wearing black shirts marked #rr2070. It has to be a reference to Revolt 2030. She says police in the Ashes report the fire started after organizer John Ready publicized intentions to run for president of NUSA.

I look away, turn my attention to my hand, watch blood seep through white bandages while Katie Childs says, "Due to unknown dangers in the Ashes, New Georgia Reps have declared a state of emergency, implementing a statewide halt on tourist trips and transportation of goods to the Ashes until further notice. Stay vigilant. More information on this escalating story soon."

Margo shouts, "Good. I'm glad. Let them starve."

The hologram shrinks into my watch and disappears from the sky. Immediately I think of Jo, wonder if she's okay. I don't know her, or why she left. If it had nothing to do with the emergency news alert, and she left over stupid shit I said, and then Jo loses her life . . . I'll never forgive myself.

Fuck-kuh-dee-fuck. I don't believe in insta-love; it doesn't exist. But insta-energy does. Some people reel you in like a magnet the first time they smile, speak, or touch you. Maybe that's what this insane feeling is for Jo. Like somehow, her energy's calling out to mine—leashing my spirit to her first name like a moth to porch lights.

102

"Fake news." Margo laughs. She pushes the button on the wall again, closing the skylight. "Those people over there'd have to be pretty stupid to burn down an already dumpy place. I mean, it's like retorching trash. And, like, even if the story is true, the buildings over there are like shacks, right? Maybe fire makes them look better?"

I'm sick of hearing the term *fake news*. Nowadays, nine times out of ten, people use it to ignore shit they don't wanna face.

Margo kneels before me and kisses my bandaged palm. "Kiss my forehead . . . like you used to?"

I gaze down at my sister. On her knees she's angelic. Bambi eyes big and wide, staring at my lips. "Yes, Jellyfish." I take either side of her heart face and press my lips to her forehead.

Margo grins in delight. "We're still having the Gala after-party at the carnival?" She knows my mood is off, that I don't wanna go. "Come on, it's the last night, they'll take the rides down soon," she whines. "Say you'll come with, please, Coveybear?"

13

JOSEPHINE

Boah blocks the exit.

"Move outta my way, Boah!" Neal says, eyeing him like he wants to throw the first swing.

"We can't leave, Neal, not yet. Wanna get killed? Every block's flooded with badges." Boah points to the door. And for a brief moment, I imagine what this door used to look like when rich folks lived here, before jigs took over the street on the other side of this door, Moats Alley. It's bad timing, but I bet if someone cleaned this doorknob, it'd shine like a diamond. I imagine gleaming hardwoods replacing soiled, rotted wood floors. I see elegant furniture where bullet holes play connect the dots, creating a twisted pattern of their own.

Boah continues, "Cops gathering kids left and right."

Neal huffs, shakes his head. He backs away from the exit and sits at the bottom of a tattered staircase.

I grab Boah's arm. "What happened here? The riot, how'd it start?"

Boah places a finger over his mouth. "Shhh. Don't be loud. Moats Alley has ears."

Neal scoffs, "Jigs don't have ears; they're barely human. They're trash bags stuffed with needles and crack."

I ignore Neal's stupidity, get in Boah's face. I'm so close to him, I see peach fuzz on his jawline, fuzz I never saw before, or maybe it's been a while since I've been this close to him. "It was John's speech this morning, wasn't it? He got 'em riled up, protesting."

Boah sighs and pulls on his lower earlobe. Whatever he's gunna say, can't be good—he tugs his ear when delivering bad news. "After you left, cops beat a girl with billy clubs and bare hands. Folks tried to get to her, but cops had the area surrounded. Only thing anyone touched were her screams."

"They killed her? Why? What'd she do?" It's a stupid question. Living in the Ashes is enough reason for cops to hurt folks; probable cause is unneeded.

"She took a loaf of bread off the food bus. Officer Reed took her to the station. Cops beat her, took her to duh hole, left her duh die."

"They killed her over a loaf of bread?"

Neal shrugs, nods. "More fucked-up shit has happened. Heard she got a kid, a boy."

Boah nods too, agreeing. "Yeah. Bread was for him."

Can it be true?—he was killed for bread? I'm shaking. My skin feels hot.

"Neal, where's Vye?" I say, stumbling back onto a stack of John Ready's large READY FOR CHANGE campaign posters. No doubt cops snatched them from walls and stashed them in here.

Neal stands, walks over, and stands beside Boah. "At the house, I passed Jessup before seeing you. Said he's going over there to check on her, but one of us should go by—"

Bang! Bang! Bang!

Someone's banging on the door. Our six eyes are wide, our frames still as corpses.

We watch the handle on the door turn slowly, left to right, then right to left. Whoever's on the other side of the door's just as quiet and frightened as we are. I hear them breathing heavy.

The banging on the door stops. I reach for the doorknob.

105

Boah grabs the knob first and whispers, "No! No, Jo. You don't know who's on the other side of this door; they could still be there."

"And need our help," I say.

Boah's stare is firm. "You'll get us all killed and what good'll that do them? Huh?"

The door at the back of the home jiggles, someone trying to get in from the other way.

Boah moves away from the front entrance. "No one goes anywhere. Gotta lock this place down until it's safe to leave. Be right back."

Neal and I watch Boah run down the long hall, lock the door. Once the door's locked we watch Boah push old books, raggedy furniture, and anything with weight in front of the door to make sure no one can enter.

Neal grabs my hand and says, "In a few minutes, I'm gunna open this door. You and Boah go home to Vye. I'm not going. I'm gunna take care of Reed. With this riot going on, now's the perfect time. We'll take more than just one leg this time. Me and my boys should've finished him off last time." Neal wipes his face with his dirty shirt, then takes it off.

I grab Neal's shoulder. "Wait, you did that? Don't answer that. Don't do anything stupid."

"Not fighting is stupid. You weren't here when the riot started. Shoulda seen how Reed threw kids 'round, hitting 'em." Neal wipes sweat off his forehead, continues. "Besides, it's not about just you. Reed kills more kids than Radius. But listen, after I take care of him, I wanna be like you, both of you. I wanna be good like John Ready. Be good. Do great things. Just watch, I'm gunna make you proud."

Neal's always talking about going straight, but he never does. But something in his eyes tells me this time it's different. He really wants to change and be better.

"Hey, hey now," Neal says, trying to cheer me up. "Remember that day I brought all that food home?"

I squint, remembering, and laugh once I do. "All the fish slices?"

Neal laughs in his hand. "All the damn fish slices."

"There had to be at least—"

"Six tokes' worth of food," we say together.

Neal stops laughing. Says he sort of stole that food. Says he went to Bootleg Jules's Fresh Food Bus, and told Bootleg Jules the fish we'd bought from him the day before'd made Vye sick—that she could die from salmonella poisoning. And even if she didn't, she couldn't work sick, and therefore, couldn't earn tokes to feed family. Then Neal said he threatened Bootleg Jules. Told him if he didn't give him free food, he'd tell everyone the Fresh Food Bus sold rotten meat.

Neal opens the door, allowing faint alley light to fill this dark space. He sticks his head out the door, shifting his neck left to right. "It's clear."

Boah yells from down the hall, starts running, storming toward us. "Jo, don't! Neal, don't do this. It's not safe!"

But it's too late. Neal's right. I gotta check on Vye. I want to stop him from going after Reed, but I know my cousin. Once he sets his mind to something, there's nothing anyone can do or say to stop him. Neal takes my hand, leads me into the alley. We shut the door behind us, secure Boah inside, push a large black dumpster in front of the door.

My heart sinks into Moats Alley's wet cement. I feel bad for leaving Boah behind, but he'd've never let Neal and me leave. Besides, my whole life, Boah's protected me. Leaving him behind, safe from harm, is my way of trying to protect him.

Neal pushes against the dumpster, making sure it seals Boah in. I try to hug

Neal, but he pulls away. "Hug me later. You gotta run, go to the house, get my mom. Be safe."

When I reach the house, I push the door open, scream Vye's name until the back of my throat feels scratchy and sore—and then yell some more. The kitchenette's empty. The bathroom's blank. Inside the shared bedroom, Vye's mattress is devoid of her body. I put on untied red boots, grab my sketchbook off my mattress, head for the door.

On the porch across the street, two boys hold a gun inside a cop's mouth. The cop's face is covered in blood, but I recognize him. I'd know his face anywhere.

It's Jessup. His arms are tied behind his back; his left eye is punched shut. I recognize the two boys. It's Neal's buddy and Kyra's cousin, Hothead Frank, and his little brother, Lil Turk.

I dash across the street. "Don't do this, Frank," I plead, hands before me in freeze position. "He's a good cop," I beg, "one of the good ones." My hands quiver, and my head feels so tight it aches.

Frank scoffs. "A good cop is a dead cop." He cocks the gun inside Jessup's mouth, forces it deeper down his throat. Jessup gags, salivating over the black barrel. "Yeah, suck that steel, oink, oink," Frank snickers.

My throat feels warm, my chest heavy. Tears fill my eyes and stream unbroken down both cheeks. "No, please!" I beg. "You don't wanna do this. You don't have'tuh do this. Don't do this, Frank. Please don't do this," I say, praying hands over trembling lips.

Frank kicks Jessup in the ribs. "Whatcha gonna do for me if I don't?"

I nod my head fast. "Anything! Anything you want."

Frank takes the gun out of Jessup's mouth. Jessup coughs; blood exits his mouth profusely; he spits a tooth to the ground. Frank narrows his eyes. "Anything I want?"

I nod, wipe away tears. "Untie 'em first, and yes, anything you want. I promise."

"Alright, nosy JoJo." Frank tells Lil Turk to untie Jessup from the pole. And he does.

When the rope leaves Jessup's arms, his knees smash hard concrete—his bones make a cracking noise, and I flinch.

Frank walks over to me, pushes the gun between my breasts, smiles eerily. "You love pigs so much, kiss one, black girl."

"You want to me kiss a pig?" I'm confused.

Frank points the gun at Jessup, wiggles the Glock at 'em. "Kiss the pig," he demands.

Jessup uses all his strength to shake his head no, telling me not to do it. I walk over to Jessup, bend shaky knees before him. I lean forward, close to his cheek, and kiss him there.

Frank laughs. "Think I'm kiddin' around?" Frank leaps, swings his right leg forward, kicks Jessup in the stomach twice. "If you love a pig, kiss a pig, on the lips, Jo, or I swear to God, I'll put a bullet in 'em right now. Full-on tongue, you traitor slut. I ain't fucking wit'yuh, Jo. I'll fucking do it. I'll fucking kill 'em. Kiss the white pig in the mouth. Tongue 'em."

Frank and Lil Turk laugh, swing guns in the air, shooting bullets at the moon.

Jessup whimpers. "Don't do it, Jo. Let me die. Just let me die. It's okay," he coughs. "It's alright."

I whisper, "You saved me from Reed long ago. If you hadn't been there, you know what he would've done tuh me."

Jessup tears up, remembering. I do too.

Long ago, that night in Moats Alley, sirens from Jessup and Officer Reed's squad car scared the jig away. After Jessup and Officer Reed got out of their car, Reed wanted to bother me, but Jessup was my shield. Tonight, I'll shield him.

Lil Turk shoots into the sky twice. I blink the past away. I stare at Jessup's tall, thin frame soaked in blood and bruises, thinking—besides his potbelly, he hasn't changed much.

Hothead Frank kicks my stomach, bringing me back to present moment. "Whaduhyuh waiting for? Fucking do it . . . kiss 'em," Frank laughs.

"Don't." Jessup coughs blood. "Don't do it."

Belly stinging in pain, I cry without wiping tears. "I won't let you die. Vye needs you alive. We all do." I lift Jessup's bloody chin until our eyes meet, press my lips to his mouth, and kiss him.

I turn to Frank, stand up. "There, it's done. Let us go."

Frank and Lil Turk laugh; they scurry off grinning, saying, "I can't believe she kissed her aunt's boyfriend."

I help Jessup stand. Gotta get 'em to Healer Marie's house. If anyone 'round here can heal him, it's her.

Marie opens the door eyes wide. "Where's Boah?" she says with lines between her eyes.

I lie, shrug, tell Marie I don't know—that I haven't seen him. I wanna be truthful, tell her Neal and I locked Boah behind a door in Moats Alley to protect him, but delivering that news while our world burns to the ground doesn't feel right. Or maybe what I did was just wrong, and I'm a bad friend for leaving Boah in Moats Alley alone.

"Jessup?" Marie opens the screen door wider, staring bewildered.

Jessup nods, opens his mouth to speak, but no words come out.

I sling Jessup's arm around my neck, so he won't fall and me right along with him.

"Bring 'em on in," she instructs. "Take 'em tuh duh back. I'll get my herbs." Marie shuts the door behind us and walks to the kitchen.

With one arm around my neck, Jessup holds on tight. Once in the back room, I put him on the oak healing table where Marie patches and stitches wounded folks. "Have you seen Vye?"

Jessup nods. "Vye's okay. She and Peels are in the basement at my house. Safest place 'round here right now. It's an old doomsday shelter. Only way someone's gettin' tuh 'em is if they open the door from the inside. And we both know, Vye's not gunna let that happen." He coughs inside his shirt, then grabs my forearm. "Find Neal. He's in trouble. Reed's looking for him. Still thinks Neal's the one chopped his leg." I don't tell Jessup that Reed's right.

Jessup coughs again, and thick blood clots splatter onto his shirt.

I can't help thinking, if Reed's after Neal, Jessup might've caught the direction Reed was headed. "Where's Reed headed? Where would he take him if found?" Forehead full of wrinkles, I bite my thumbnail.

"They passed right before you found me, couldn't go after them. They're taking him to the hanging tree." Jessup hands me keys to his truck. "Find them before Reed does." Jessup says his car's parked in the lot outside the police station, says I need to hurry. I take the keys from his hand, turn around fast, bumping into Marie. She's carrying bandages, salve, alcohol, needles and thread, sweetgrass, sage, cedar, and tobacco plants in her Medicine bundle.

"Sorry," I say.

"It's alright, child." Marie moves past me, walks to the other side of the healing table.

Jessup grabs my wrist from behind. Chin over shoulder, I look at him. He mimes the words *thank you*. I nod with a worried smile, then leave Healer Marie's house.

Brown water fills every pothole in the Ashes like little coves of diarrhea. The world took a lot of shits today. It's a dirty place. I jet down boisterous roads, stomping in puddles, passing screaming crowds and barking three-legged dogs.

Before I reach the police station, I spot a cop in a corner alley, holding a pistol to a kid's head. I hide behind a dumpster unseen. I can't interfere this time; I have to find Neal. The cop calls the kid a white punk. The kid laughs—calls the cop a black pig with a lousy badge. I recognize the boy's laughter. I heard it moments ago with Jessup. It's Hothead Frank.

I lean around the corner of the dumpster, watch the scene unfold. On wet pavement, Lil Turk lies still with a bleeding bullet hole in his forehead. Frank lifts his arm, flicks the cop off, giving him the middle finger. The policeman nods with a grim smile and shoots Frank twice in the neck. Frank's skinny frame falls limply to gray cement. Blood gushes from his neckline—it flows like a river out his throat, makes a red puddle in the middle of the street. Just like that, Frank's gone. And the cop who shot him spits in his pool of blood.

I wanna weep for their lives, but I can't—won't. There's no time. I gotta reach Neal.

The police station's an unrecognizable fire when I reach Jessup's car. I could walk to the wasteland like I do every morning to meet Boah at the old roller coaster, but that'd take thirty minutes Neal might not have.

I put the key into the ignition, quiet music blasting through Jessup's speakers; make my way down the long-eroded road to the hanging tree. I pass burning buildings, looters, drunks, and teens holding up handmade signs that read REVOLT 2070 or #RR70.

A red light stops me. I keep my foot on the brake, wait for it to turn green; wonder why I'm following the law when the Ashes is in chaos.

Earlier this year, there were rumors of new Revolt Rebels. The talk came from

112

Boah's mouth late one night after every one of his Siksika cousins' shacks were burned to the ground. Boah filed a complaint, told cops how it all went down. But Reed said nothing could be done. "Buildings and grass get torched every day," he'd said. "Arson ain't illegal in the Ashes. Hold the devil dance party someplace else. Plenty'uh grass outside wastelands."

That night, we stepped outside the precinct, headed for Boah's favorite place—next to the water hole, the Halethrope: a pull-apart junkyard full of vintage CSX freight trains and stand-alone cabooses that can't move and haven't worked for decades. Boah's Siksika grandfather, Charlie Strikes With A Gun, used to ride trains in the old days. Halethrope made Boah think of him.

Boah grabbed my hand. "Change is coming," he'd said.

I asked him what he meant. He smiled, said, "What if there was a new revolution? New RR's. Imagine it, Jo. We could do it. Reverse history. Change it all, like Revolt 2030."

I squint. "That'll never happen."

Boah stopped me in the middle of the train graveyard, grabbed both of my arms, turned me to face him. "Yeah?—but what if it did, Jo? People are ready for change. They're tired of living and working for scraps. Never having enough food, hydrating via rainwater. Don't yuh ever get tired, too, Jo? Don't yuh want more? Wanna do more than just survive?"

Boom! Boom! Boom!

Startled, I bounce in the driver's seat. Three teens, including a Mexican girl who cried in her shirt at Lineup this morning, bang fists on the roof of Jessup's car, their pink tongues flicking between their index and pinky fingers. They wear vintage black Revolt Rebel T-shirts.

"Get out the car, Officer Jessup," they yell. A large red brick crashes through the truck's tinted back window and I flinch.

When they see it's me behind the wheel, not Jessup, they stop shouting, redirect their attention to the police car behind me. Laughing like wild hyenas, they jet to the other police car, force the black cop out of the vehicle, holding guns to her head.

The light turns green. I speed down the dirt road, nonstop thinking of Neal. I reach the wasteland in eight minutes flat. Outside the truck, police officers beat billy clubs against steel shields, cheering. I push through rows of cops before two security guards in the front row grab my arms, holding me in place.

"Let go! Let go of me!"

Reed walks toward me; his large pentagon shape blocks the view of the hanging tree. When he reaches me, he squeezes my jaw inside his hand, moves out of the way so I can see the tree.

Untied red sneakers dangling from the tree belong to Neal. His eyes widen when he sees me; he stops struggling against the rope squeezing his small neck. Neal tries smiling for me—an attempt to release the jokester inside. To hide the fear. Even now he's try'nuh be strong, so I won't cry.

I kick and scream, try freeing my arms from the cops to save him. I gotta try and help him get down—escape. I don't care if I die in the process, I gotta help him. But I can't break free—it's no use. Their arms are too big. Their grip's too taut. I'm not strong enough.

Crying blurs my vision, but I look up at Neal anyway. His nose is bleeding; there're purple bruises around his eye, cheeks, and hands. Cops beat him before stringing 'em up.

I shake my head, blinking, wailing, screaming inside. No! No! Then I say it aloud, "No! No! Neal! Neal!" My chin quivers. "Why?!" My nose runs, and my throat's so sore it feels on fire.

Reed whispers in my ear, "Not so high and mighty now, are ya, high yella?

114

Look at 'em. Watch that gangbanging black trash hang. Take a good look, girl"—Reed knocks his billy club against his artificial ankle—"that little black bastard's paying for my leg now, ain't he? Look at dem tears yuh got, girl. Did you cry for me when he chopped my leg off? Huh? Did yuh, high yella?"

I'm freaking out and numb—mouth wide open, watching Neal jerk. Feet like a swing beneath a tree. I squint, focus in on Neal's mouth. I can't believe it. Neal grins, raises an index finger to his lips, shushing.

Left to right, I look around; cops aren't paying attention. They laugh and cheer, backs turned away from Neal, while he digs inside his jeans pocket and pulls out his trusty pocketknife. I stare wide-eyed, watch the rope sever as Reed whispers pervy shit in my ear.

Neal drops to the ground, lands on both feet, and runs away with half a noose around his neck.

"Get back here! Duh boy done got loose!" says a cop in the crowd behind me.

The crowd of cops turn their attention to Neal. Some run after him; others pull guns, shooting, try'nuh take him down, but their bullets don't touch him.

"Run!" I yell to Neal, jumping up and down. "Run!"

Neal jets toward barren mountains in the distance where he and his friends collect bones. Cops chase after him, but they stop before catching him. I can't see Neal. He's gone. Cops'll never find him now. Neal knows those mountains so well, he might as well be their architect.

I sigh and smile, relieved Neal'll live to see another day. Feel air in my lungs again. Bad cops won't hurt him tonight.

"Think that's funny, high yella?" Reed grabs my arm, pushes past cheering cops, forces me into the back seat of his cop car, and drives. Ten minutes later, he pulls the key out of the ignition. He parks just outside Moats Alley, drags me out of the car. Reed spits on the ground, drives my face into the wall, presses it against the cold red brick, licks my face cheek to ear.

Reed spits in the puddle, then says, "Want you'duh look at me, high yella." He reaches for my Gala gown. I push his chubby fingers away, slap his face hard, shaking my head no.

Reed throws me to the ground, lifts my skirt, and unzips his black cargos. Something tells me now's the time. It's the moment to fight before this old man takes something I've never given. Fight 'em off, and fight hard, the voice tells me. And I do. I kick, and kick, clawing at Reed. Nails dig deep into his crater face, peeling his ugly pores like peach skin. Chunks of Reed's skin's buried in my fingernails. I tell myself I'm winning. I'm strong. I'm gunna get out of this. I gotta get out of this! I grab Reed's third eye, the mole at the center of his forehead, try tearing it off.

A hand reaches over Reed's shoulder and pulls him off me. Reed jerks back, mean-mugging me as he's dragged away from my body and pushed into a wall.

"Get off her!" Boah says—he jumps on Reed's back, puts him in a chokehold and tackles him to the ground, and kicks his gun. I watch the weapon glide and skid under the green dumpster.

Using elbows, I shamble away from them, wipe tears away as wet cement scrapes my legs. Reed pants on the ground, trying to catch his breath.

Boah runs toward me. "Get out of here, Jo!" Boah orders.

Reed's pistol goes *Click! Click! Click!*

Boah and I look toward the click.

Reed had a second gun—he flashes an evil grin, shaking his head. "Toou, toou," Reed says, clicking his tongue against his teeth. "Wouldn't do that, high yella. Ain't done playing."

116

BANG! Boah yelps in pain, drops to one knee, then looks at his leg. Reed shot him. *BANG!* Reed shoots Boah's other leg.

Boah spins on bloody knees and stands. With his head low, he rushes toward Reed, charges into his stomach, forcing his spine into a mountain of red bricks.

"Run, Jo!" Boah wheezes.

"I'm not leaving you!" I say.

Boah narrows his eyes. "Don't be dumb, Jo! Yuh need tuh go! Go!"

Despite mean words, Boah's looking out for me. I can't leave. I don't wanna die, but if I die tonight, my best friend won't die alone. We'll die fighting, together.

Reed's other gun peeks beneath the dumpster. If I can reach it, get it, I might hold Reed gunpoint long enough for me and Boah to make a run for it.

Boah forces Reed onto his back, towers over him, strangling him. I watch Reed pull a knife out of his pants; he stabs Boah in the stomach twice near his ribs. Boah falls to his knees and covers his stomach wound with a shaky palm.

I need to help Boah. Sprinting the small distance between us, the only thing on my mind is I gotta help him, save Boah—his blood's flooding the concrete. I gotta help him stop the bleeding. But before I reach him, Reed grabs my neck and shoves me to the ground.

When my spine hits concrete, Reed grabs an uneven rock. It resembles the giant stones I trip over in running dreams. He holds it above my eyes, bashes the side of my head with it. I can't see the wound, but it stings, aches, pounds like a heartbeat. I'm too out of it to reach up and touch it, but I feel it bleeding. My eyes are heavy. They open and close, and close and open. I'm drifting. I sense it, feel it— losing sight of the world.

I wanna fight back, I wanna scream, try to, but no noise comes out. Moonlight shines over Boah's blood. That's all I can see 'cause I can't focus. I'm outside myself, looking at myself, not really believing he's dying. Nothing matters anymore. Nothing but saving Boah.

I look over at him; his eyes are closed, his body still; he's barely breathing, starry-eyed and dying, and there's nothing I can do to help him. Boah gives me a forced smile before his eyes shut and head nods over to the side. There's no one here to save him. No one here to save me.

Reed licks my cheek again and chuckles; he fidgets with his belt, pulling tight pants down. I gaze over his broad shoulder—someone's behind him, standing over Reed with a gun inches from his bald head. My vision's too blurry to make out facial features, let alone tell who the person is. Boah's stagnant frame's a few inches away, so I know it's not him.

I'm fading in and out of Moats Alley light. The stranger has a halo of long hair. Not sure if her hair's dreaded or relaxed, but her skin's dark brown. And she smells like vanilla.

Vanilla.

Will vanilla be the last scent I smell before Reed hurts me and kills the woman standing over us? She needs to pull the trigger and release it fast. If she doesn't, if he sees, senses, or sniffs her behind him, Reed'll kill her, and finish me next. Please let her pull the trigger. Bullets don't have to kill 'em, just get 'em off'a me.

I'm drifting again; eyesight's blurrier now. The gun hammer goes *click-click, click. BANG, BANG!—BANG!* Reed's mouth drips red. He bleeds over my face and into my mouth—he falls on top of me, and the world fades to black.

14

COVE

Obsidian sky and thin white clouds claim both the night and my mood. Head sticking out of the cab window, images of the riot in the Ashes, one question haunts thoughts. *Is Jo okay?*

Margo tugs my arm. I take my head out of the window and she says, "Aren't you glad you gave in to me? Amusement park fun after the Gala always makes it better, Coveybear. You'll see. I'm always right."

I'll never tell her, but Margo has a point. The amusement park does make me happy. But after watching Jo leave, I didn't want to go anywhere. And yet, somehow, Margo convinced me. It's hard saying no to my sister. Her lips get pouty, her eyes get all Puss in Boots and I'm human putty. Margo gets her way when she's bratty, always has.

Four minutes later, we hop out the turbo and stroll the boardwalk alongside other kids we don't know. Margo holds Kyra's hand. Larry and James snicker behind Dulce, most likely betting over who'll pluck her first. And Rald, a chubby boy from the Ashes, walks ahead of all of us.

Fingers lost inside nostrils, Rald digs, picks buggers, flicking them to the ground. He wipes snot on his shirt, completely oblivious we're watching. I straggle at the back of the group, stopping to stare at a stray dog. It's a pathetic-looking creature—wet, shaking, probably starving. Margo runs toward me, holds me from behind, begging me to look at the Ferris wheel lights up ahead.

Aware she still doesn't have my attention, Margo releases my waist and holds a firm palm around my elbow, scowling at the shaggy, homeless canine who does. "What an ugly-looking thing. It's so effing dirty. Ugh. I smell it from here." Margo pinches her nose. "It's a kindness to put them down when they get like that." Margo laughs. Kyra follows suit, laughs too.

A large sign in front of the ticket booth reads LAST DAY. END OF SUMMER SALE: TWO FOR ONE. Soon, carnival crew impersonating clowns, fairies, medieval blacksmiths, and eighteenth-century whores will pack up unclaimed toys, box unwanted stuffed animals, and deflate cartoon balloon people. They'll disassemble roller coasters, the Ferris wheel, carousels, vomit-inducing revolving starships, and the gigantic pirate's boat; then get up and go—they'll travel one state over to New Tennessee, and two months later, they'll return—quickly assembling the rides they just took down, preparing for the Fall Fair on All Hallows' Eve.

On that night, precocious, greedy children will run around the carnival in face masks like horror-obsessed kids dressed in twentieth-century scary-man gear, like Freddy Krueger, Michael Myers, and Jason Voorhees. The little possums will hop ride to ride, yelling, "Trick or treat," jumping and cheering at the delight of chocolates and sour candies. Later that night, the Hopefuls who make it through the Transition Program'll be introduced into New Georgian Society at the Fall Ball. Elenore always makes us attend, so I have a closet of Victorian-age attire and decorative face masks from previous years.

Not all monsters wear masks; some have plain faces that look like Margo. On a red Ferris wheel seat rising, backward, to the top, Margo kisses Kyra's chin, and Kyra holds Margo's face, kisses her lips. Margo doesn't kiss her back, but she doesn't pull away either.

Larry and James rock back and forth in the blue cart above Margo. Larry leans over the safety bar of his seat, glaring down at Margo green-eyed, dyspeptic, drunk. Watching from across the wheel, I know what Margo's thinking. She enjoys Larry's torment, and is turned on by doe-eyed Kyra, who's sucking Margo's thin lips. Uncharacteristically, I feel sorry for them both. Within a week, Kyra will be Margo's little pet. And Larry . . . well, Larry will still be pathetic lovesick Larry.

But who am I to judge? Margo and I don't share blood, but our twisted parts are identical twins raised believing love isn't natural, it's a choice. How we treat that choice directly defines who we are. And in that regard, I'm no better than Margo. We're both monsters—monstrous creatures who treat love like shit because it shits on good people. Arguably, it's not the best ideology. And yet, I'd rather be true love's Grinch than Cupid soaring around with senseless arrows wearing soggy diapers.

After rides, we walk down to the beach. Larry bounces Margo against his spine, giving her numerous failed piggyback rides. Rald throws seashells into the ocean, eating cotton candy. Kyra follows me to the pier; sits beside me on the dock. She takes her shoes off, sets them beside her, and wiggles bare toes.

"Are yuh always this quiet?" Kyra combs her hair with skinny fingers.

I humph.

Kyra clears her throat, twirling hair around her index finger. "Margo seems cool."

I smirk, faking chill 'cause it's all I can muster. I keep seeing the news flash about the Ashes—worried for Jo. Wonder if she made it back. Wonder if she's amid the chaos right now. "What'd you think of the news flash? The story about the fire in the Ashes? Scared?"

Kyra says it's laughable.

I shift my gaze, facing her. "What's funny about it?"

Kyra's expression turns serious. "Looks beautiful from here, don't it? Those mountains." Kyra turns, looks at the roller coaster. Perplexed, she turns back, her blue eyes fixed to black ocean, and sighs.

I don't really care what she's thinking, but I give in and ask, "What's wrong?"

"When we were little, we used tuh climb a roller coaster, much like this one."

"There's a fair in the Ashes?"

"We call it the broke amusement park."

Jo facts. "When you say *we* climbed?"

Kyra giggles. She thinks it's cute; it's not. She continues, "Jo, Boah, and me. I stopped climbing years ago, but Jo and Boah climb it every day, just before sunrise."

I nod, staring at smoky blue peaks in the distance, wishing I could see Jo's roller coaster. I close my eyes, imagine her bravely climbing to its peak.

Kyra pivots, changes the subject. "Don't know if I'll get picked, but glad I'm here."

Hopefuls do this every year; they think kids they connect with have the power to secure their spot. But the Rep in charge of that year's Gala has all the power. The witch said she'd listen to others, but in reality, the Hopefuls' fates rest in her twisted whims.

Kyra repositions herself, moves closer to me, says, "Hey, yuh know, over there, saying someone got shot, killed, mugged, murdered is like saying the sky's blue." Kyra pauses, makes an exaggerated sigh, then says, "Sorry Jo left. There's not a hologram that'd show me anything important enough to go back there. Risk this chance? No way. Probably best Jo left, though . . . she's got a temper."

Temper or not, I'm a leech when it comes to Jo facts. Low-key, what I really wanna do is forget saving face. Drain Kyra of everything she knows of Jo's life. But I can't be direct. I play it safe, ask about Dulce instead of Jo. "Are you and Dulce friends?"

Behind us, Kyra watches Margo and Dulce kick beach water with bare toes. "Dulce isn't friends with anyone. No one likes her. And outside the buggers, Rald's okay."

I agree on Rald, but I couldn't care less. I can't wait any longer. I turn, face her. "And Jo?—how long have you been friends?"

Kyra tucks her hair behind her ear, smiling. "Ummm, since we were about four? Before the jig incident, that's for sure." Kyra sees my perplexed look at the word *jig*. "Y'all don't got 'em here, antidrug laws and all. Jig's a jazzed-up way a sayin' crackhead."

"What not just call them crackheads?"

Kyra shrugs. "Jig fits better. And 'cause modernized crack makes their wrists and hands jiggle. Beats me how they hold spoons to get high."

I clear my throat. "You mentioned an incident?"

"Oh, yeah. Jo was nine or ten." Kyra blushes and grins in the opposite direction.

"What happened?" I can tell Kyra's into me and thinks I'm into her. I'm not. She's an open window to all things Jo, and I want to know more, curious like prying people who get high off tabloids.

"A jig held her gunpoint. The junkie threaten'nuh kill Jo, shoot her in duh head if she didn't give'vuh the chicken. Chicken infected with Radius, no less."

"Did Jo give it to her?"

"Uh-uh, she told the jig no." Kyra wiggles her toes.

"Is that right?" The more Kyra speaks, the more intriguing Jo becomes.

"To save the jig's life . . . didn't want her'duh die of Radius." Kyra shakes her head in disbelief as if the story just happened. "Jo could'eh got shot! And didn't give a shit."

"I see. What would you have done?" I wipe sand off my hands.

Kyra shrugs. "Would'duh gave her the chicken. Most people back home would'duh. I mean, she was probably so strung out, right? Doped up. If rotten meat didn't kill 'uh, crack would'duh gotten her soon enough."

It's been a while, but for the first time in a long time, I wonder what life's really like in the Ashes. Because somehow, talking to Kyra, it doesn't seem like the place of freedom I built up in my head. It sounds like a snare of lost dreams, drugs, and violence.

I've been to the Ashes several times but don't really know what kids over there think. I know the watered-down version of themselves, the things they tell Reps, Elites, other New Georgia kids to impress them during Lineup and Gala. Makes me wonder. Is the Ashes full of teens who think like Kyra?—with no regard for human life? Or do most show the kindness Jo gave the woman holding a gun to her head? My mind ponders how I would've turned out had I lived there. Would I react like team Kyra or team Jo?

I ask Kyra about Jo's life and find myself pleased Kyra can't hold water. She tells me all she knows about Jo: About her mother's and father's suicides. Kyra laughs as she recalls Neal, Jo's crazy cousin, and beams chatting about Aunt Vye, Jo's hippie, pecan-pie-baking aunt. Kyra says the night Jo saved the jig, a cop named Jessup scared the junkie off, and days later, Jessup started dating Aunt Vye. Says everyone back home thinks it's weird a white cop'll date a dark-skinned black woman with braids.

I ask Kyra if Jo's seeing anyone. Kyra grimaces, says Jo has a thing for a boy named Boah. Says she and Jo fell out when Boah chose her over Jo. I ask her, "Jo likes Boah." I say it less like a question, more of a statement. Conversation being what it is, when it comes to Boah, I can't have Kyra thinking I'm . . .

Kyra shrugs. "Jealous. maybe. I don't know."

"Jealous of . . . ?" Kyra's attractive but can't hold lit wick to Jo.

She shakes her head, shrugs. "Me. Boah's connection tuh me. Not sure. But Jo got mean, so I cut her off . . . stopped talkin'nuh her. I don't do negative, you know? Positive vibes only." Kyra pauses, faces me. "I'm single now."

In synchronized voices, Margo and Dulce call Kyra down to the beach.

"They're calling you."

She shakes her head. "I'm fine here with you."

I wish Jo were here instead. Jo's stare makes me want to do better, be better. No matter how beautiful Kyra or any other girl is, Jo's the next chapter. I let myself forget that she has to be because of Elenore, and pretend it's only because I want her.

Kyra lays her head on my shoulder. "I like being here with you."

I don't want you here. "You should go."

Kyra frowns. "Oh. Okay. See yuh around, yeah?"

I shrug and shake my head no. "Sure."

Kyra blushes, joins the others on the beach.

I stare at the spot Kyra just sat on, imagining Jo beside me. While gazing into the black ocean, Jo's muslin skirt would be pulled just above her tan bony knees. I imagine trying to touch her pinky finger flat against the dock. If I did something like that, I bet Jo'd pull away—and say something like "Not yet. Be patient" or some other glorified phrase meaning no. I imagine how that no would make me want her more, hoping to reach the day she'd say, "Yes, Cove."

An hour later, I'm still sitting on the dock alone, staring at the dark sea, thinking of my father. He once said, "Nothing begins and ends without change, and the universal need to push against it." It's been eight years since Father's death, but his voice echoes like he's beside me.

Before he died, we'd sit on this pier, Ferris wheel in the background, splitting hot-boiled peanuts. After an hour or two, he'd reach into his brown admiral's coat, pull out photos of my disturbingly thin mother, baby me on her hip, pear-picking in Plum Orchard. Nostalgic, we'd gaze at the raven-haired woman, who dyed her hair black because she hated its natural color, red. And soon, like every time we'd sit here, I'd ask him the same questions: Why did Mother want to starve to death? And why did she stop eating when bones bulging under her skin screamed for food?

Father'd get teary-eyed, his answer invariable—it never changed. He'd say Mother couldn't help it—her polyphagia haunted her. And mirrors told her she'd never be small enough to exist in the world happy. So, she never ate and searched for happiness on an empty stomach. In my memories of the orchard, she never ate the pears anymore, no matter how ripe they were.

On his deathbed, my father made Elenore promise to sign Plum Orchard over to me on my twenty-first birthday. To this day, Elenore holds the deed over my head, ensuring I'll play her game.

Maybe it's too soon to think it, but I don't wanna play Elenore's game with Jo. I want Jo to make it back here from the Ashes even though Hopefuls aren't granted second chances. I wanna hold Jo's tears when they're heavy in her eyes; take her pain and put it inside me so she never suffers—shield her from bad things going on in the Ashes.

Everything in me screams to be near her, touch her, have her brown shoulder bump against my pale arm. It isn't scientifically logical I feel this way; I've yet to even touch her skin. She wouldn't shake my hand when Elenore introduced us, and refused to dance, and yet, something about who Jo is makes me feel as if maybe being Cupid wouldn't be so bad. I want to know her, not just things I can see, but facts unseen. I yearn to touch the parts of her she calls ugly. I want to greet her insecurities with tight hugs. Shit. I can't get her off my mind and don't want to. My brain montages Jo's glances, smiles, and frowns. And fuck, I want my nose in her hair to inhale her—breathe her pheromones in a Buddhist meditation.

A baby cries; the wail returns me to the present—back to the beach before me. I look over my shoulder to find a mother hushing her infant's cries. I face the ocean, curling my spine to roll gray slacks up calves—folding them just below pointy knees.

The fair will shut its gates soon; the Ferris wheel lights will dim. And the park will black out like deep space. I can't wait for that to happen because then I'll be alone. No babies crying, no people laughing, no couples making out—just peace and quiet and glistening ocean.

I ask iCom the time. It's 10:05 p.m. I ask iCom for updates on the Ashes, and its emergency alert earlier. I wait for iCom to respond, wonder if once it completes my research request, ghastly images of Jo will appear on a hologram.

"Request search complete. No new alerts," iCom says.

I inhale the world. It's saccharine, pleasant. Petrichor. I exhale, tilt my head back, extend both arms—fingers tiptoeing along the pier's edge, gripping the ledge with steady palms. Jo's perplexing, stubborn as hell. She ignored me the whole night, refused to dance, and ran off without giving me time to explain. It's baffling she's the same person who would risk her life to save a jig threatening to shoot her in the head. I'm intrigued, thoughts of her unshakable.

iCom chirps. It's Edith. I send her to iVoice.

Maybe getting under another girl'll get rid of thoughts of Jo. I'll admit it. Before her, life was colorless; shades of black and gray ruled it. Since meeting Jo, crimson, yellow orchid, cobalt, and burnt umber are taking over.

And fuck! Yes, I said mean things about Jo, and where she's from, but it never would've happened had I known she was eavesdropping. I only said it for pathetic love-drugged Larry. I run a hand over my face, sigh. It's not her fault. It's mine. But I've never felt so unimportant, unadmired, and ignored by a girl.

My stomach growls.

I leave the pier, buy a hot dog from a closing vender, and walk barefoot on the beach. My toes sink in velvet sand, heels press into seashells. I pull my shirt out of my pants, loosen the tie around my neck. I inhale, exhale, feel warm wind brush my nose.

"Incoming call," the female iCom automatic announcer says from the chip behind my ear. "Edith Fairmoth attempting to reach you."

"Accept call." Maybe talking to her will kick this Jo thing.

"Cove?" She giggles. "Come over? I want to see you . . ." she begs. "And please don't tell me tomorrow, you said that yesterday, and the day before that, and the day before that, the same thing. I won't keep you long. If this is about James, I'll ghost him. I just . . . I mean . . . I really miss you. Do you ever think of me?" she breathes.

"No," I say to her. Although it's the truth, I wonder why I'm saying no. I don't miss her, but Edith could be what I need. If I take her virginity, emotionally feed off Edith, maybe my heart'll stop pining for Jo.

"You don't miss me, or you don't think of me?" Edith pouts.

"Both." I zone out, trace the ocean to its black center, where the moon rests its eyes.

Edith huffs. "But you'll still come over, right? Are you still there?"

"Yeah, sorry?"

"That's the first time I've heard you say that."

"Say what?"

"The word *sorry*. You've never said that to me." Edith clears her throat. "It's nice to hear it."

Edith's right I never say sorry. And yet, I feel okay saying sorry to her. It's strange considering our dynamic, but Edith and I could be friends if I weren't irretrievably twisted by the witch's training.

Edith sighs. "Are you mad I mentioned the sorry stuff?"

"I'm not upset." And it's true. I'm not. I'm just confused as hell about this Jo shit.

"I like you."

I never tell girls *I like you*. "You're pleasant," I say.

"Just pleasant? I want you to be my first. I don't want anyone else. You know that, don't you?" she whines.

Inside my mind, the battle between good and evil erupts. *Toughen up!* I tell myself. *You've done this before.* I take a breath, steadily ignoring the queasy fluttering in my belly and the uncertainty running laps inside my brain. "Be right over."

I hear Edith part her lips to smile. I disconnect the call and walk down the damp road past that same pathetic dog—he's huddled in a dark corner, shaking in a puddle. I feed him the crumbs from my hot dog, then grab a turbo to Edith's house.

An hour later, I exit Edith's bedroom, pace across her front porch, and head back to the witch's house. On the walk home, I think *what?* and *why?* The "what" I did is clear. I still hear her moans, smell her sighs, feel her nails clutch my skin. And my *why?* is one word: "Jo." I had to get rid of it—those feelings for her, the way over them, was under Edith.

But already, Edith's face is fading, replaced by Jo's staring eyes. It didn't work. The walk from Edith's never takes long. I cut a few lawns, jog a few streets. And ten minutes later, I'm standing in the circled driveway in front of my house. Dress jacket and tie clenched in my fist, I squint, suspiciously staring at—"Aurice?"

The back of Aurice's head faces me; his suit's covered in soot. In his arms, light brown slender legs and mud-soaked toes drape over his left forearm—a round head and three long, bloody braids dangle over his right arm.

Aurice turns around, facing me. His russet skin is tainted by gray debris. The girl's skin is smooth, covered in ashes. Barely moving, her head shifts toward me.

It's Jo.

She's bedraggled, bloodied—eyes closed, inaudibly weeping.

Aurice hefts her in his arms. "I brought her back."

I stand frozen, eyes fixed on blood gushing between Jo's black braids. With parted lips, my tongue won't move. It's stuck in some section of my brain where words go to die. I'm worthless. Jo's bleeding like a hit deer, and I'm standing on stale limbs.

"Cove!" Aurice says.

I blink out of my frozen state. "What happened?"

With watery eyes, Aurice lifts his chin, his gesture for *turn around*, and I do.

Across the mountain, the night sky's on fire—clouds stained dark orange, mustard yellow, and deep red. There's a fire in the Ashes.

"Get Gaitlin," Aurice says.

Without words, I sprint to the back of our house, past the tiny pond, through Elenore's field of lavender, race up the stairs of the tiny white cabin—the one Elenore reserves for Gaitlin to keep him close for the nights Margo blacks out, drinking, popping pills.

Bang, bang, bang!—the side of my fist punches the cool steel door.

"Just a moment," Gaitlin says on the other side of the door. He sounds tired. He was sleeping.

Bang, bang, bang!

"Two seconds," he says.

Jo might not have two seconds, let alone one. I lift my fist, ready to bang hard again. The door opens.

Gaitlin adjusts his glasses. Sleep in both eyes, he says, "What's wrong?"

"Come quick," I say. "It's Jo."

Part II
FEAST

". . . and we aspire to be a nation of welcoming hearts, equality, and fruitful wealth."

—New United States of America Preamble

15

COVE

Jo's eyes are bloodshot red—her breaths are faint, quick, softly marinating inside whispery wheezes, gagging coughs, and inaudible words.

Gaitlin treats Jo while Aurice and I watch, fearful and amazed, from the foot of the bed in one of our guest rooms. I've never seen Gaitlin move so fast. Vigorously, he cleans dry and running blood away from Jo's head injury, elevates her swollen ankle, and adjusts the transparent oxygen mask covering Jo's mouth and nose.

Some sort of frenzy hits me like a brick when her breathing stutters. Wrinkles pinch my forehead. My heart races. Why is my heart racing? I take a hand to my chest, make a claw, drag short nails diagonally across my heart. This shouldn't faze me, but it does. Shouldn't give two fucks. And yet, I do. But why?

All this emotional angst can't be romantic. It's pity. I feel sorry for her. Yes, that's it. That's all this odd sense of care is. Pity. After all, she's a poor kid from the Ashes. A Hopeful with dreams of being one of us. And what happens to her? She comes all the way across the mountain for a better life, only to be treated the way I treated her. Had I not said those mean words to Larry, had she not heard them, Jo never would've left the Gala. Never would have gotten so wounded back home. She wouldn't be in the witch's house, two doors down the hall from my bedroom.

Gaitlin administers eye drops to Jo. She blinks twice. Gaitlin wipes the leaking drops away with a napkin and she closes her eyes for a few moments, then opens them again. I shouldn't be thinking about this. But Jesus fucking Christ. At her worst, Jo's brown eyes could melt an icy summit.

An hour later, Jo settles, breathes normally while sleeping. Eyes closed, she's an angel. Skin glows dark amber as if the moon and stars claim her cheeks as home.

Without thinking, or knowing why, and without wanting to, I open my mouth. "What can I do?" I feel the creases in my forehead deepen. "I'll do anything."

Gaitlin adjusts the white cloth bandage circling Jo's perfectly round head. He looks away from Jo, turns to me. "You got me here. You did your part. And I've done mine, for now." Gaitlin taps the medical bag on the night table beside Jo's bed. "I'll teach you to change bandages. Clean the wound." He arches a reassuring smile. "Sound good?"

I swallow, nod. "Anything." Anything? Who the hell am I? Anything? Why would I say anything, when what I want to convey is nothing. Without consent, my tongue speaks, puppet of the barely unconscious pretty brown girl—a girl who, when conscious, doesn't like me. "How long will she be in and out?" There it goes again.

"One, maybe two days. She's suffered massive smoke inhalation. It'll take time. She'll come around. Be good as new."

Gaitlin packs up his things. Asks if I mind staying a while, watching Jo. Make sure she's okay. And I do. It's all I do.

———◆———

Jo's in and out of sleep for two days. Come morning her eyes are awake, but dead. She's mute when I speak, ignores me much like she did at the Gala. Only speaks to Gaitlin, Elenore. Margo hasn't spoken to Jo—she doesn't like her. I suppose that's my fault; ever since Jo arrived, mornings don't find Margo's head buried in my chest.

Mostly, it's because I'm not worried about Margo. Much like me, years with the witch have tamed basic emotions. Yes, Margo . . . she'll be alright. Even if she's a little bothered by my absence, she's spent all the extra time at Transition House cuddling Kyra and Larry. Says she'd rather be with them because she can't stand to be home. Home isn't bearable because of the witch, but more so, Jo's screams the first day drove Margo away. Says there's no way she could sleep with her here. I'll admit it. Jo's screams are viscerally unbearable for sleeping.

But her screaming is sensical—she's grieving a massive loss. Death is a bastard impossible to adjust to. Elenore's training aids in romantic heartbreak prevention. But what about the other forms of heartbreak? Death of neighbors, friends . . . parents. Sometimes, the first people to break our hearts are parents. Losing my father broke mine.

The night Aurice brought Jo to the witch's house, he told Gaitlin and I what happened. Said he found Jo in a pool of blood that wasn't her own, with a half-naked dead cop bleeding out on top of her. Said Jo's last audible words were, "You can't save him. Boah's dead." Whenever I think of Jo, I think of this. That Boah was her best friend. And maybe her heart feels as mine felt when Father died. Broken—a little empty.

Jo's settled a little, sleeps a little less during the day. As for most of the past two days, I sit in an uncomfortable wooden chair to the side of her wide white bed, watching every uneasy breath. I've been here since the sun sank and the room darkened. I see more than hear her murmur Boah's name, again. I want to save her from the misery of traumatic thoughts. I need—no, crave—to help her, but how?

This morning, Gaitlin stopped by to fill Margo's prescription and change Jo's head bandage. Before he left, I asked if there was anything I could do to make Jo less sad.

As he opened the front door to leave, he said when his late husband was in a coma, he sat next to him night and day. He nodded, thinking, and said, "I read to him all night, all morning. It was only a few moments, but . . . reading woke him . . . to say goodbye."

I wonder if reading to Jo will help her resurface—escape the mind that traps her, forcing sleep. This afternoon, I checked Elenore's massive library for *Great Expectations*, but it wasn't there. A drone order, however, came within the hour.

Now that the house is quiet, I move to the edge of Jo's bed and read the title of the thick novel aloud. "*Great Expectations.*"

I think of touching Jo's forehead, but don't. I think of caressing her cheek, but won't. I want to shake her awake, but I'm too scared. Who's to say me reading to her at night won't freak her out? Make her think I'm crazy. Well, crazier than I am.

At the foot of Jo's mattress, I continue reading. This book starts sad, but I see parallels in Jo's life and the character Pip's. And immediately I want to protect Jo from the Ashes like Pip's uncle protected him. I want to bottle Jo's trauma via mason jars, then drown them in the ocean. Then Pip meets Estella and Miss Havisham, and I quickly realize how Estella's life mimics mine.

I devour chapter after chapter aloud, half impressed with Pip's insatiable drive for nobility and the other half in awe of Charles Dickens's writing—to create work this tragically beautiful, Dickens must've had a tough life. I close the book and leave Jo's side. I stop for one last look from Jo's doorway, get captivated following the back-and-forth motion behind her closed brown lids.

A hand touches my back. "What are you doing here?" Margo says. "Careful, brother. If I didn't know better, I'd say someone has a lit-tle crush." She sings the last part.

"And I'd say someone's a little high."

Margo moves in front of me. "I'm not a lightweight. It was one pill. Stop dodging. You like this one, don't you?"

Yes, I do. "Careful, Jellyfish. Like's a strong word." Besides Jo, Margo's the only girl I've "liked." "I wouldn't wish Jo on anyone." I chuckle, because a little laugh always shakes away shit I don't want to talk about.

Margo giggles. "You're right. She's pathetic." Not what I meant, but I don't tell Margo she's wrong. She continues, "No need to feel sorry for her. Big deal. She got attacked. It's how it is over there, you know? Guns, violence, blah, blah."

I tune out Margo. I'm incandescently thrilled by Jo. I've never fallen in love. But what if this is it? And what if it's not? Instead, it's some other twisted form of lust. Jo's attractive and special. But she's not the kind of special that's magical, is she? And besides, with Margo monitoring my actions, any other emotion besides annoyance with Jo is intolerable. I shake my head, dust Jo off my mind. "What're you dressed up for? It's past midnight."

"Larry wants a three-way with Kyra."

"You can handle it, Jellyfish," I tease.

Margo stretches her arms around my waist. I look up and out the window, trying to catch a glimpse of the stars. "I've never asked," she says, "why you call me that. Don't care all that much, but indulge me . . . what made you call me Jellyfish?"

"They're beautiful . . . touch them and they . . ."

"Sting," Margo finishes.

I nod.

Margo sighs into my shirt. "Ever miss us . . . the way we were?"

iCom chirps. Margo's.

"Larry?"

Margo shakes her head, no smile or smirk. "It's my Kyra. Staying at Transition House tonight. Have my back with the witch?"

I nod.

"Invite her to Bonfire Night." I know she means Jo, though she doesn't say her

139

name. "Should be . . . interesting. That is, if she stays awake long enough for you to ask her."

Margo's voice, I recognize it. It's—"Jealous, Jellyfish?" I smile.

On tippy toes, Margo kisses my chin. "Should I be?"

I watch her white hair leave my dark gray shirt; listen to her red-bottomed heels echo down the hall.

Bing! Bing! Bing!

Someone's at the door. In white numbers, the digital clock on the wall says 1:00 a.m. The bell rings again. God forbid it wakes Elenore; her pet peeve's interrupted sleep.

When I reach the front door, Elenore's standing in the doorway sideways, braless, open white silk robe, hair tied in a knot just above her neck. She holds a brown envelope in her right hand addressed to Josephine. In front of her feathery white slippers, a silver briefcase stands upright with the letter *R* in black imprinted in the center.

———◆———

Before the turbo cab fully stops, a thin red head pulls open Elenore's door. "Hello, dearie." Vimberly Fairmoth drags out the first *e*.

I withhold a sigh. Vimberly's a Mock, a New Georgian citizen who believes Ashfolk shouldn't be allowed NG citizenship, that they should go back to where they came from. Somehow this doesn't stop her from attending the Gala. Shamefully, I've overheard Vimberly say people in the borderlands in all fifty states should be injected with Radius, eliminated.

Elenore presses her index finger into the window, and with her lips, mimes *one moment* to Vimberly.

Elenore speaks into the phone, says, "Hello, Greer, dear!" It's Greer Landing Sr., her accountant.

I listen as the two discuss how Greer Sr. is sending his son, Greer Jr., to handle her concerns today, because Greer Sr.'s under the weather. And how Greer Jr. will assist her in creating an account in Jo's name, using the funds discovered in the black leather suitcase left on the front porch last night. Elenore turns away from Vimberly's curious eyes and tells Greer Sr. that it's strange for a girl from the Ashes to be gifted a black metal money card. "Paper money or plastic red cards aren't that unusual," she says. "A black metal card is something else entirely."

Hate to admit it, but Elenore's right. Anonymous New Georgians often gift transitioning Hopefuls red money cards to assist with living expenses while attending vigorous training at Transition House. Benefactors support their chosen Hopeful until they can present their protégé at Fall Ball. The accepted Hopefuls—new New Georgians—select a career path that coordinates with skills developed or fostered while living in Transition House. Red cards have an expiration date, with limited funds. A black card signifies millions.

I exit the turbo slowly once Elenore hangs up, linger behind the two women as they gossip outside the bank.

Vimberly grabs my right bicep and tugs it, forcing me to join them. "Well, don't you get manlier every time I clap eyes on you? Working out?"

Vimberly's a little fresh. Suppose it runs in the family. Maybe it's cosmic destiny to give in to Vimberly's advances—now that I've plucked and chucked both her daughters. I should do it, really should, but I'm intellectually allergic to plucking venomous humans.

Elenore slaps Vimberly's hand clutching my arm. "Don't be desperate, dear."

"I was just, umm," Vimberly starts.

"I know what you were just umm. He's promised," Elenore says.

"Of course he is." Vimberly glances at me. "Are you happy with your choice?"

Besides me and Margo, Vimberly's the only one who knows how twisted Elenore is.

I nod. "She's interesting."

Vimberly laughs. "Interesting's better than boring, is it not?"

I humph. "Indeed."

Vimberly tucks loose hair into her tight banana-shaped bun. She faces Elenore. "Did you hear about New Florida?"

Elenore arches a brow. "No. What about it?"

Vimberly's ecstatic she has news unknown to Elenore. "Rumor has it a little white girl, only thirteen, crossed the bordering river, and stood at the top of the stairs at the Justice Department. They say she was holding signs up that read *Starve Never*, or maybe it was *Fight Forever*? Doesn't matter much what it said. Border people know full well protesting's illegal."

"Indeed." Elenore digs into her purse, pretending she's not bothered she didn't hear the information about New Florida first.

Vimberly continues, scratching the top of her wrinkled hand as she speaks. "It's that John Ready. And all his Ready for Change posters. I hear he's been going state to state, rallying. Riling up third citizens, brown gangbangers, making them hope."

"Hope's a crime now?" I make a fist, tight, tighter. So tight, I feel nails imprinting crescent moons inside my palm. Elenore grabs my elbow, squeezes it a little, then a little more.

Vimberly giggles as if I've just made a joke. "Why on earth do they need hope, dear? They have Trade Trains. We give them food. Our taxes pay their medical bills, and for the Transition Program. Oh my, I declare, Elenore. What more can we do? Will it ever be enough? I heard you've ended up with a brown girl staying with you. I do hope she is a positive influence and won't interfere with our plans? What's her name? Josephine?"

"It's Jo." I pull my elbow away from Elenore's grip.

"Attached al-rea-dy?" Vimberly clears her throat. "Yes, yes, I know her name. Met her at the Gala; she is lovely." She glances at Elenore with a raised brow.

Elenore catches sight of Greer Jr. heading into the bank. "Everything is as planned. Let's tea next week."

"Sounds like a plan." Vimberly narrows her eyes, then flashes a smile at Elenore. "We'll spill tea over how our Gala was a national success. And who'd have thunk it after that night's nonsense? That riot made our Gala the most watched ball in the history of NUSA. Ratings haven't been that high since Revolt 2030."

Before entering the bank, I look over my shoulder. Vimberly watches me. Glad to leave her shark smile behind.

Banks are snobbish places, filled with suits, heels, silver walls, holograms, and New Georgia citizens seeking loans. Today's no different.

Greer Jr. grins when Elenore and I catch up to him. "If you get any taller, you'll pet the building." He towers above me, but then again, Greer towers above most people. Some folks joke about how tall he is. Say his mother, Priscilla, cheated on his father with an unknown giant, because she's five-two and Greer Sr.'s five-five.

I nod.

"You and Margo attend UNG, right?"

I nod again.

"It's your . . . what? Second semester at University of New Georgia?"

"First semester," I say.

Greer Jr. rubs the back of his neck as we enter the elevator together. He's tired. "Go, Bulldogs!" he says, cracking a smile. "Picked a major yet?"

"Agriculture."

Greer Jr.'s office is on the ninety-first floor. Inside there's no space for art; large windows take up the walls. Greer sits behind his massive steel desk, in a high-backed brown leather chair. He extends his hand, directs Elenore and I to metal chairs opposite his desk. Our chairs are cold, and Elenore looks uncomfortable.

When I was little, I asked Greer Jr. why he smiled so much. He said he smiles because he doesn't want to disappoint God. With the turmoil Elenore'd put Margo and I through as a kid, I found Greer's answer strange. Back then, I didn't know if I believed in God. For what supreme being would allow innocent kids to be raised by monsters, demons, and witches?

Elenore slides the black briefcase onto Greer Jr.'s desk. "Can you trace it? Where it came from?"

"I'll run it through the system." Greer Jr. opens the briefcase, removes the metallic money card, swipes it across his desk. "All donations are private, which'll make finding the donor difficult."

Elenore grins. "But not impossible?"

"Give me a few days. I'll see what I can do."

"How old are those adorable children? Well, they must be as tall as you now!" Elenore laughs, scratching the bag beneath her left eye.

Greer presses one of three silver buttons on his desk, and a photo of three boys and a little girl appears. "James is seventeen, Chris's seven, Matt's five, and Zozo's three."

"Oh, those terrible threes," Elenore gushes.

"Don't we know it," he laughs.

"How's the wife?" Elenore says. "You two have your hands full."

Greer smiles. "And we wouldn't have it any other way." He clears his throat. "Now, my father said you wanted to create an account for Josephine Monarch. It's odd she's left and come back, but now that she's got a black card, I can't imagine she'd be turned away?"

Elenore, tight-lipped, says, "Turned away? By whom, I wonder? I'm Gala Rep this year. Doesn't matter that she left, where she's been. I select. I decide. I picked her. She stays."

Greer nods meekly, then clears his throat. "All funds deposited into one Josephine Monarch's account?"

Elenore nods. "Yes."

"And the other matter?" Greer and Elenore stare at each other, speaking without words.

"Would you mind, dear?" Elenore gives me a look that says *leave*. I stand, leave the room, shut the door behind me.

Outside Greer's office, I listen. He tells Elenore taxes on my mother's land are due, and they haven't been paid in four years. Greer coughs, then tells her the property will revert to the bank at the end of the year. My parents' land, my land, will be auctioned off and sold to the highest bidder.

16

JOSEPHINE

Yellow sun stretches over both eyes, warming cheeks. My forehead throbs, pulses, hurts. I don't want to wake. Wanna keep both eyes shut, fight the inevitable—the being fully awake thing. Gaitlin'll be here soon. Yesterday he said he had a gift for me, said it's something I'd need in New Georgia. It's crazy, but I still don't know how I got here. Crazy enough, I don't really care. It only matters who's not here.

Boah . . . he's dead.

I feel numb about it all. And I don't know. I wanna cry, but tears won't come. I still can't believe it. Boah being dead is a waking nightmare. He's gone and I don't want him to be. I want him breathing, eating, sleeping, climbing roller coasters even if I can't see him do it—I want him alive, kidding around about stupid stuff. It doesn't feel real. I wanna play make-believe. Pretend it never happened. But that's impossible. It did happen. Boah's not coming back. He's gone, gone.

Fuming lawn mowers, pungent grass, and irritatingly loud chirping birds force closed eyes open. And then I feel it again. Inside out. I feel it. Pain. Excruciating pain's all I feel. My mind's angry—pissed—still throbs along with my racing heartbeat. The monitor near my bed matches it too, in quick beeps.

My stomach growls. I grab it, rub it, think of food I'd like inside it. Food only New Georgia has. Bacon, eggs, cheese grits, oh, and pineapple soda. I shouldn't be so happy about stupid soda when Boah's gone. Fragments of happiness feel like a betrayal of the life Boah lost saving mine. From here on out, happiness is forever attached to death. Like I can't be too happy, because if I am, when I am, bad things are close behind.

Gaitlin enters the room, interrupting dark thoughts. "Aha, you're awake. Good." He closes the door behind him and walks over to my bed. He waves a small flashlight into my eyes—its sharp white light shifts from one eye to the next, attacks dilated pupils like blinding sun. "How do you feel?"

I'm not really sad. Not really angry. Just not good. Maybe numb. "It hurts," I say.

"And it will for a while." Gaitlin turns the flashlight off, stares with a worried look on his face. "Besides the headache, how do you feel?"

"My foot hurts."

"It's your ankle. Sprained it bad. It'll heal. Just takes time."

I twisted it when my heel got stuck in the bordering area under the mountain, and I bet running during the riot made it worse. Couldn't've made it better.

Gaitlin moves fingers in front of my eyes. "How many do you see?" he asks.

I blink. "Two." Gaitlin nods.

Sun shines brightly into the room. I cover my eyes with my hand.

"I'll close them." Gaitlin walks to the window, shuts the curtains.

I untie the wrap around my head, wondering if the rock Reed bashed into it left a scar. I slide my two fingers under the white bandage. The scar isn't as big as I thought. It feels like a raised thin, straight line the length of half my pinky finger.

Gaitlin rushes to my side. "Easy. Easy now." He moves my hand away from the bandage, helps me rest against the headboard. He rewraps the dressing. "It's the scanner makes it heal quicker. There's no instant fix. Mental healing, well, that takes time. Try to relax. There's no rush."

147

But there is a rush. I've been in New Georgia three days now. I want to get the hell out of bed. Jump on the next train to the Ashes. I'm worried about Vye and Jessup—I'm concerned about Neal's safety. Gotta know they're okay.

Gaitlin hands me a glass. "Drink up."

"Drink what?" I squint at the clear round balls in the tall glass. "Are these . . . drugs?" Addictive drugs are illegal in New Georgia. But still, don't wanna get hooked on painkillers, get kicked out of the Transition Program, and return to the Ashes a jig after all.

Gaitlin narrows his eyes, as if thinking, *You're kidding, right?* "Water."

I feel the skin between my eyes touch. "No, it's not."

Gaitlin laughs, shaking his head. "They make the round pod with transparent seaweed." He takes a pod out of the glass, pops it into his mouth. "See? Bite the pod, release its water, drink. You can swallow the pod, too. It's edible."

"Do you have regular water?—the kind you pour?"

Gaitlin chuckles, nodding. "I'll get water from the fountain in the bathroom. Be right back."

Gaitlin enters the bathroom in my room. Water runs. Now's the time. My chance to break free, get out of here, and head back to the Ashes. I need to know Vye's okay, that Neal made it home after escaping the hanging tree, find out if Healer Marie was able to save Jessup.

Like a wild animal, I snatch the IV out of my right hand, covering the puncture with a middle finger. After a few seconds, it coagulates—no more blood.

I feel savage, out of control, like protestors in the Ashes. What I'm doing is dangerous, but I can't stop. Flustered, I rip thin square pads with blue and red wires off my forehead.

Water stops running in the bathroom.

I swing legs off the bed. And when my feet touch the floor, the bathroom door opens.

Gaitlin rushes over—he grabs my arms; it triggers me. I think of Reed grabbing, pinning me to the ground while watching Boah take his last breath.

Gaitlin pushes me back toward the bed. "I'm not gonna hurt you. Trust me. Breathe. Come on, now. Breathe, kiddo."

And I do. I take a deep breath that leads to ten more deep breaths. Gaitlin's face is kind; I remember thinking so during Last Check after Lineup. I listen to Gaitlin's steady voice. I don't know him that well, but feel I can trust him.

I close my eyes, calm myself, and breathe. My heart rate decreases. It pumps slower and slower and slower until it reaches normal pace. I count the beats. One. Two. Three. One. Two. Three. I sigh. Breathe deeper and deeper. And open my eyes.

"There we go."

"How'd I get here?"

"Aurice brought you. Carried you," Gaitlin says. "Aurice was at the police station. Protesters entered the building, torched the place. He hid inside the floor vent in the Last Check room. The vent led him to the sewer, where he escaped, and later, found you knocked out in Moats Alley, barely breathing."

"What was Aurice doing there?"

"He never left. Stayed after the Lineup. He makes secret trips to the Ashes. Sort of a vacation to him."

I shrug, holding my hand flat against my throbbing forehead. "Why'd anyone wanna visit there, when they have all this here?"

"Suppose he feels connected to it. He dresses flashy, but many years ago, he was just like you. A smart kid from the Ashes, lining up for Reps. Selected photography in Transition House. He excelled, became the first black artist in

Transition House history. Elenore made him famous." Gaitlin smiles. "Anyway, after the riot, he brought you here. Elenore's house. And, oh, you already know it, or should because you're here; this belongs to you." Gaitlin reaches into his pocket. He said he had a gift for me; maybe this is it. When Gaitlin removes his hand from his pocket, it isn't what I expected. It's the envelope from the Gala.

Trouble-minded, I open the envelope, take the translucent button out, gently place it on sheets covering my legs. I hesitate for a moment, close my eyes, press my thumb into the button.

Gaitlin speaks. "Open your eyes, Jo."

I open my left eye, slowly look down at the button. It glows blue. They accepted me before the riot. Elenore picked me. She likes me. I don't know why. I'm still trying to figure out if I like her.

Gaitlin sighs. "Well, young lady, a lot happened while you were sleeping."

"Like what?" Worry for Vye fills my stomach alongside the hunger. Maybe Vye wasn't as safe as Jessup said. Maybe kids broke into his house, went down to his basement, found Vye, and killed her.

Gaitlin rubs the back of his neck. "Four Hopefuls made it through the Gala, but there's only three of you left. One's already been kicked out of Transition House for mistreatment of staff."

Gaitlin reveals the four who made it. Kyra, Rald, Dulce, and me. Says four's a large number. Then Gaitlin says, "Transition House isn't full of kids. Usually only one maybe, two Hopefuls make it past the Gala each year, and move to Transition House." He reveals Dulce was the Hopeful dismissed for telling a teacher she needed to lose weight. I was surprised Dulce made it through Lineup, so I'm not shocked she didn't last long. Elenore didn't see past the mask Dulce wore during the Lineup, but I knew someone would. And besides, New Georgia's an anti-bully state. She would've been found out one way or the other.

I'm exhausted by Gaitlin's news. "Anything else?"

Gaitlin shakes his head, adjusts glasses, and says all communication from the Ashes to New Georgia stopped immediately after the Gala. Says Reps stopped mail and food train trips to the Ashes after the riot. The only trips allowed to the Ashes are one-way AerTrains transporting goods from New Georgia, ensuring the Ashes has basic supplies to survive—things like canned Spam, pork and beans.

"Can I go back?" I try lifting my tailbone, but it hurts my brain to move, so I sit still.

Gaitlin touches my head. "You're no prisoner, Jo. Free to go whenever you want."

"When's the next train?"

"After Fall Ball," he says gently. "Elenore says she hasn't witnessed raw talent like yours since Aurice's Lineup year. She has high hopes. Wants you to succeed, to transition to life here."

"What if I don't succeed?"

Gaitlin narrows eyes at me. "Do you want to?"

I think about Gaitlin's question. Transitioning's what I wished on the moon for. But I left, made my decision. And now, Boah's death changes everything.

Gaitlin coughs hard, clears his throat again.

"That sounds bad," I say.

He coughs into a handkerchief. "We're testing a cure for Radius. Inhaled the lab fumes too long."

Wide-eyed, I sit up straight. "We?" A Radius cure would mean everything to Ashfolk.

Gaitlin opens his mouth to sneeze—nothing comes out. "Colleagues at iCom Technologies Research Center."

151

I lean down and rub my ankle. The pain's sharp—it pulses under the bandage like a heartbeat.

Gaitlin says, "Radius is complicated. But who knows, if you chose science as your program of study, maybe you'd like to help?"

I smile. But I don't give Gaitlin an answer because I'm confused. In the Ashes, I always thought I'd pursue art in New Georgia. But now that I'm here, I'm fascinated with thoughts of all the other great many things I could be.

Gaitlin takes a rectangular scanner out of his black bag. He removes the bandage from my ankle. He places the white scanner over my ankle, waves it back and forth over bruised tendons and muscles. After a few seconds, Gaitlin tells me to—"Stand up."

"But it's not healed. It still—" *Hurts*, I start to say, but it doesn't anymore. Doesn't even sting. I gaze, amazed, then look up at Gaitlin. He beams.

"Stand up," he repeats.

I obey. Stand. "How is this possible?"

"It's in the beta phase of testing. We don't know all the side effects. But it works. It heals. Glad you feel better, Jo."

I nod. "Why didn't you do that earlier?"

He chuckles. "You had to be awake so I could tell if it worked." He pats the front pocket of his white lab coat. "Your gift. Almost forgot." Gaitlin hands me a tiny round transparent triangle and says to place it behind my ear, tap it once to turn on. And I do. I ask what it is; he says it's iCom's communication service. Says once I tap it, the interactive AI will answer any questions, send messages, and make calls when requested. Said it sends spoken messages to friends in New Georgia. I think of that word: *friends*. And then I think of him: Boah. I shake my head away from the bloody images of the last time I saw him. Friends here in New Georgia. I don't have friends here. At least not yet. Kyra and I were friends;

we're not now. She was nice on the train after Lineup, even nicer at the Gala. Maybe things will be different since we're here.

Gaitlin watches me turn iCom on and off and on and off. "Before I go . . . need anything?"

"Anything?"

Gaitlin nods, smiles.

"Sketchbook and charcoal."

I wake to music, cheery music playing outside my bedroom's door. Hours and days have run together. And I can't help thinking . . . there's something terribly wrong with me. Staring into the moon's face, I try squashing bad feelings by wishing them far away—but I cough, vomit a little in my mouth, and ta-da-hocus-pocus, I'm back sulking. In bed rewinding and fast-forwarding time in slow motion, feeling like blah-blah, alone with wicked spirits and ugly vibes. And cheerful music outside this bedroom brings no joy.

The music part's sad, the ugly vibes can kick rocks, and it all just sucks. I don't wanna go anywhere, do anything, see anything. I'm not interested. Just wanna stay in bed and melt recklessly, berate the night sky—yell at it for letting me down because life's so fucked up, you can't trust stars, and the jacked-up moon isn't taking damn wishes.

Will this feeling ever pass? The nothingness? Possibly. But that doesn't change that now, I don't feel like me—the me before Gala night, before Boah's murder. My brain's broke—stuck on pause like those old vintage VHSs.

I blink out the trance, feel my cheeks; they're wet. I stare at my ankle. It's a little red, but doesn't hurt—my head hurts, my heart hurts more. No one wants to see depression, not even me. I wanna skip past it and get to the next part, the good part, the sunny place, but I can't. I'm lower than I've ever been now. And

I don't wanna be here. Just wanna scream, shout, pull my hair out—and I do, moaning into the dark.

And that sucks too, because I was doing better, hadn't screamed in twenty-four hours. But here I am. Back in bed, I'm this human sound machine yelling profusely at the top of my lungs. My sobs deteriorate into coughs, gaudy, nasty coughs that make my head pound.

Doors to my bedroom swish open. I've been gagging so much, I've awakened Elenore, Margo, and Cove. I feel nauseous.

Elenore places a cool rag that smells faintly of lavender over my forehead. Margo grimaces in the doorway. And Cove enters the room holding a silver wastebasket. Shouldn't feel this way. There are more important things to worry about: like missing Vye, Jessup, wanting to hug Neal . . . grieving Boah. And yet, seeing Cove is irritating.

I hurl again and again in the trash can, holding my belly, wailing from pain I can't touch. Every time my eyes squeeze shut, I relive Neal's attempted murder, Reed unzipping his disgusting cargos, and the mysterious woman planting a bullet in his head. And then I smell it again—sweet, sweet vanilla.

I wake hours later. It's still dark out. I touch my forehead, reach for the cut, the scar, but I can barely feel it. It's nearly gone. Gaitlin's healing scanner works fast. I squint. Something's in the corner opposite my bed. I lift my head, blink hard. Someone's here, but who? They rise, walk out of the dark corner toward the foot of my bed.

I sit up right. "Who are you?"

"Rita." The woman's face comes into view. "I work here, live here." Rita's heavyset, dimples for days, warm brown eyes, with russet skin like Aunt Vye's. She stops at the foot of my bed. "You hungry?"

17

JOSEPHINE

Rita's smile is warm. She paces around my bed. I take her in. She wears a black dress—hair pulled back in a bun. Her black eyes narrow when she smiles. Moonlight makes the tip of her bulbous nose shiny.

"Nice to see you awake. It's late; the house is sleeping." Rita tilts her head to the right, says, "You didn't eat earlier. You want something?"

I'm so hungry. I nod. "I could eat."

Rita smiles her warm smile, pats my shoulder. "Right this way, Miss Jo."

Watching bamboo floors, I move slowly, follow Rita to the kitchen, peeking into open doors and entryways we pass to get there. Bedrooms are like tiny houses with bathrooms of their own. Bathrooms aren't holes in the walls— they're wide-open spaces with tubs big enough for three people and massive uncracked mirrors.

Rita enters the kitchen first, and bright lights flick on. Chin over shoulder, she winks, says, "Body temperature operated. An adjustment, yeah?"

Amazed, I say, "Yeah." I think of Boah and other workers at the Mill manually processing the *Expectation* the old-fashioned way via the vintage printing press.

But Boah's not at the Mill . . . he'll never work again. Never wake to sunrise.

Rita moves purposefully, places a plate of food before me. Bacon, fried eggs, pancakes, fresh orange juice. Foods I've never had. Unlike at the Gala, I don't waste time worrying over what Rita'll think if I eat too fast or too much. I wanna taste every flavor. Bite after bite, I dig in. Hardly breathing between bites.

"Good, Miss Jo?"

Mouth full of food, I nod. "So good." I'm full but I won't be like them, waste full plates of food, when folks in the Ashes are starving.

While I stuff sadness and breakfast down my throat, Rita reminisces. She tells me she was like me once—a Hopeful living in the Ashes. That she lined up, got picked, and moved into Transition House. Says that, just like me, the year she was Hopeful, out of the eleven picked in the Lineup, only four were selected to transition into full New Georgian citizens. Then Rita clears her throat and says, "Well, three for now. One was sent home."

She's talking about Dulce.

"You made the front cover," she continues.

I lift the glass of orange juice off the island, bring it to my lips, and sip. "Who?"

"I'll show you." Rita taps her watch, and a hologrammed news article appears.

Hopefuls chosen made the front cover of the *New Georgia Times*. I didn't notice pictures being taken at the Gala. There's close-ups of all three of us, Kyra, Rald, and me. The article below is long. Depicts Kyra as an undiscovered beauty, Rald as the next great chef, and me as the futuristic artist with immense potential.

I wish Rald didn't eat buggers in public, but he's not just the boy who picks his nose. He's desperately kind and deserves to be here. Despite our past, with everything Kyra's family is going through with the death of her brother, she deserves a chance too. Elenore made good choices.

I shake my head, think of Tessa. Were she alive, she'd be Hopeful number four. I'm sure of it. It's unrealistic, but right now, I can't help thinking the same of Boah. Had he not changed the plan, if we'd've lined up together—he wouldn't be dead. He'd be alive. Alive, chest pumping, breathing, here . . . with me.

Rita lifts my empty plate off the island, brings me back to now. She takes my dishes to the sink. While washing, Rita says New Georgia changed her life. Says if it weren't for the Rep who picked her, she'd be stuck in the Ashes eating the legs of her family's sixth dog. Then Rita changes the subject, says there's a library; I should have a look. To use the elevator, get on it, press the number 2, and when the doors open, you'll be in the middle of the library.

The thought of being in a room full of books, new books, makes my belly flutter. "Thanks."

Rita's smile reassures me. "What you went through—couldn't've been easy, Miss Jo. If you need rest, that's okay. You don't need to visit the library tonight. The books won't disappear."

Rita's right. Books don't disappear. People do.

Rita smiles warmly. "He's been sitting in your room, constantly, every night."

The skin between my eyes wrinkles. "Who?" She can't mean Co—

"—Cove."

"Ah." I look away from her, pause, turn to face her, and ask, "Doing what?"

"Reading as you slept."

"Oh."

"It's an impressive library, Miss Jo."

Although I'm tired, I follow Rita's directions. Take the house elevator to the second floor, and when the doors open, I'm surrounded by books.

The first thing I see in Elenore's library is a small café. I've only read about them in books. I walk over to that corner, stand in the little doorway. Air is sweet. It only takes a few moments to understand why. On a long back counter sits an assortment of sprinkled doughnuts. I'm not that hungry, but I can't resist. I close my eyes and savor every bite.

After snacking, I return to the main library. It's massive. I walk over to the bookshelves. I've never seen so many books. It'd take years just to count them.

The spines are in good shape, pages glued hard inside frames. Pages aren't worn, torn, dog-eared or moldy, like books in the Ashes. Books don't smell like red dirt here. They smell fresh, like clothes drying on wired lines. I wonder if New Georgia kids know how lucky they are to have nice things, unlimited food supply, piss-free mattresses, and new books free of musk.

Excitedly, I search for the classics, books read while studying for the exam. Books like *Little Women*, the one with characters my mom loved so much she gave me one of their names. The book I love, *Great Expectations*. I've read them many times in the Ashes, but I want to see how they look new and unused. I find *Little Women*, flip to the first chapter, and read.

"What are you doing in here?" a voice behind me asks.

I gasp. Drop the book. Something about being startled, and the book falling to my feet, reminds me of Moats Alley. I think of the jig, and my sketchbook falling into the puddle at my feet, mud splashing on my face.

"Are you gonna turn around?" he says. I think of picking the book up, but don't.

I turn, face him. "Cove."

Cove chuckles, looks down at the book. He lifts his chin, stares at me. "Jo."

18

COVE

"Are you going to say anything?" I ask, but Jo looks past me, unresponsive. Her coldness is hauntingly beautiful—like transparent ghosts in white sheets lingering in tattered mansions. But Jo's no ghost. And that's no sheet. She wears a nightgown that is nearly see-through, thin enough to make out her silhouette beneath pearly fabric.

The silence between us reeks of bitter death. I don't want to say anything but want to do something. Must do anything. I stare at the dropped book touching Jo's pretty brown toes. Walk over, slowly kneel before her. I pick the book up, then look up at Jo. "Here." She doesn't take it—doesn't take my gaze either.

I stand, glare at the rejected book, held by the rejected boy. Close my eyes and sigh. When I open my eyes, I find Jo staring back. Our eyes meet until I blink. Fuck. I can't hold Jo's stare. Her eyes are too deep. Or her soul's too heavy, filled with galaxies beyond my comprehension. This feels odd, peculiar. I don't like it, but I seem to crave it, the way she makes me feel. Jo has a way with me—she's human catnip and I'm the silly obsessed pale pussycat.

She walks past me.

I catch her hand and her eyes snap down to our woven fingers. It is a bold move; she could hit me, yell at me, reject me once more. I place the book in her hand. I don't know how she feels, but inside my chest I'm a fluttery mess. I watch Jo's chest rise and fall. Skin around her eyes is tense, and then it's not.

Book in hand, Jo moves her fingers away from my hand. She continues to

159

walk away from me. I want to, it hurts not to, but I don't turn around to watch her leave. I don't turn around until she says, "You're like a sweet-and-sour candy—but opposite."

"Pardon?"

"You know, the candy that tricks you into thinking it's sweet, but the longer it's in your mouth the sourer it gets."

I want your mouth. Those lips. I look down at Jo's hand. I want her skin close. To touch you without you pulling away. "Like sour gummies?"

"Yeah, like that. Only you're sour first, and sweet later."

I've never heard that before. I like the metaphor, but—"Is there a compliment in there somewhere? Because if there is, I'm not catching on."

"Which are you? Are you the boy in the hallway at the Gala? Or the boy who picks up my dropped books?"

I'm tongue-tied, as if under some sort of binding spell preventing coherent sentence structure. I want to say I'm sweet, not sour. But that'd be false. Truth is I've been both. The boy who picked up the book is the five-year-old inside me, fighting Elenore's twisted training. The boy at the Gala is sour, bitter, treading oceans without a life jacket.

I open my mouth, speak. "Both."

Her eyes tighten, jaw clenches. "Be honest."

"I'll never lie to you."

"Alright. Did you mean those things you said? In the hallway. At the Gala."

"Honestly?"

"Said you'd never lie to me, right?"

I nod, answer her question. "I'm sure you hear stories about us here as much as we hear stories about you. Doesn't make them true. Or false. Just stories. The reasons behind the words don't matter. But if you need to hear it . . . no, I don't think those things." I refuse to say I'm sorry. It'll never happen. I like her, but not that much, right? Besides, I never tell girls I'm—"Sorry . . . I'm sorry, Jo. Forgive me?"

Jo turns. With her back facing me, she walks toward the library's exit. Then stops. Chin over shoulder, she says, "A little."

Isn't the answer I want. But given my harsh words, it's fair.

I walk toward her, grab her hand. She looks at my hand gripping her fingers, and she doesn't pull away.

19

JOSEPHINE

In *Little Women*, there's a part where Jo March cuts her hair and sells it for money. Vye said that part is why my mom named me after her, because that part made her brave, like she knew I'd be, or at least hoped I'd be.

I stop reading, think of Elenore's massive library, its shelves of books, Cove's ivory hand holding my brown fingers, and how it felt being that close to him, that connected after how mean he treated me—how after leaving the Gala I thought he was an asshole. I reflect on how I once treated Kyra. How mean I was to her. In Cove's defense, if anyone knew how mean I'd been to Kyra after our friendship ended, they might call me an asshole, too.

I tuck *Little Women* under my pillow, bury my face in the silky fabric, breathe hard into it. I can't make sense of it—barely know him, but when I see Cove, the inside my belly feels like feathers landing on cushy white pillows.

Someone knocks on the bedroom door. I sit up in bed. "Come in," I say.

Elenore enters. I summon a pleasant expression to my face, knowing I should be grateful that Elenore is kind enough to let me stay in her home when the other Hopefuls are at Transition House. The elephant in the room wonders if the next words to leave Elenore's tongue will question why I tried to leave. But the elephant must exist only in my head. Elenore doesn't mention it. She sits delicately in the chair by my bed. Says my benefactor left something for me. Says they donated a large sum of funds toward my New Georgia transition effort. Before I can ask, she says the benefactor didn't leave their name. Says it is unprecedented;

benefactors like being thanked by the Hopeful they're supporting. In the history of the Transition Program, no benefactor has ever given a Hopeful this much money. "Did you or your family connect with anyone from New Georgia before the Lineup? If you did, that wouldn't be fair to other Hopefuls."

I shake my head. "I didn't," I say vehemently.

Elenore nods, says, "Good." She seems to believe me. Says banks restrict Hopefuls from opening new accounts. Only New Georgia citizens are allowed to do so. Says she already opened an account for me, that I'll have access to the funds in forty-eight hours.

"How much is it?"

Elenore hands me a black chip, says to tap it. And I do.

A hologram displays my bank account balance.

My lips part. Semi-speechless, the only words that come out are: "The zeroes."

"Yes, dear . . . millions." Elenore walks over to the window, opens the blinds. "Gaitlin left a gift for you. It's on the balcony. Beautiful day out. I'm sure you'll put it to good use."

My charcoal. "Where's Gaitlin?"

"He's teaching at Transition House. Gaitlin spearheads the science career track. I'll set up a tour this week. Once you're better, feel up to it. No rush necessary. You can stay here as long as you want, dear." Before Elenore leaves, she says she's taking Margo out of town for the day. That she'll be back later tonight.

To rest my head, I lean against the cushy headboard. Grinning ear to ear. I think about how rich I am. What kind of house I'll buy once I become a permanent resident of Saven, New Georgia. And how it wasn't so long ago, I was standing before the cracked mirror in the Ashes, pretending to be one of the rich folks. Now here I am. I'm finally here. I'm one of the rich ones.

I wonder what Transition House is like. Supposed to already be living there if

I wasn't recovering at Elenore's. Wonder if Ashfolk like living, teaching, transitioning to New Georgia there. Some Hopefuls stay, I've heard, long after their Fall Ball. Wonder how their lives are. Are they joyful, filled with happiness, with poverty behind them? I wanna talk to 'em and figure it out. Maybe they'll make being out of the Ashes worth it. I don't know.

Curled bare toes to cool bamboo floors, I rise from the bed, stand tall, walk toward large double doors leading to the balcony outside my room. On the balcony, the clouds in the sky are puffy like they wanna cry. I spot a rectangular box sitting on a white leather chaise longue. It's wrapped in brown paper with a red ribbon tied around it. I pick up the box, sit on the lounger with box on my lap. The ribbon is thin and silky and smells minty.

Inside is everything I asked Gaitlin for, but a little altered. Instead of buying one sketchbook, Gaitlin bought four, all different sizes. I flip through their lineless pages, run my fingers across the paper. It's soft, like fabric. I caress my cheek with the pages, close my eyes. Turn my nose into the sketchbook and inhale. There's nothing like the clean smell of drawing paper. I wonder if all artists feel this way, attached to blank paper they'll mark up soon. Wonder if my parents felt this way when they discovered their love of sketching.

Beneath the sketchbooks is a large flat wooden box. I loosen the latch on the box, then flip it open and smile. Charcoal sticks. And they're not all black. There's charcoal in every color. One by one my fingers dab smooth pastel sticks. Wide eyes gleam over shades of yellow, pink, blue, red, black, and gray. I lift the box of charcoal out of the rectangular box, and two brown envelopes fall to the balcony's wooden floor.

I pick the letters up. They must be from Gaitlin. I flip them over, discover Aunt Vye's handwriting in sender and receiver spaces on both letters. Gaitlin'd said they canceled all communication to the Ashes until fall. If that's true, how'd

Vye deliver these? One envelope reads *Open now*. The other reads *Open after Fall Ball*, even though there's no guarantee I'll make it through transition to receive an invitation to Fall Ball. I obey Vye's orders, open the first envelope.

JoJo . . .

    I didn't get a chance to tell you that the lady in white who stopped by after Lineup, you know, the one who liked your sketches; she came back to visit with Aurice two days after the riot. I asked her for a favor. Asked if you made it into the Transition Program, if they'd get you this. If you're reading this, it means you connected at the Gala and, oh, Jo . . . I'm so proud, so very proud. Neal says congrats butthead. Seriously, he's right here, right next tuh me, making sure I write his words how he wants. He just said he loves you. Well, we both do. But you know that.

    I won't write too long. It's like my mother, your grandma, used to say, if a letter's longer than a few paragraphs somebody's lying. Truth doesn't take pages, it takes sentences.

    Don't forget to write. Don't forget to have a blast. Don't forget who you are. And remember you're enough. And they're the lucky ones.

Always,
Aunt Vye

20

COVE

There's a knock at the front door. I know who it is. I'm uneasy, queasy, as if seasick under the witch's roof. I regret it. Never should've happened. Never should've plucked with my head in the clouds over Jo. Since the night of the Gala when it happened, Edith's been blowing up my iCom—calls nonstop. I ignore her, which results in unexpected house visits. And here we are. Edith on the other side of the peephole. And me, on this side of the door, realizing the deed to Mother's land isn't my only entrapment.

I gaze through the hole, eyeing her up and down. She wears a white blouse, yellow skinny pants, black flats, flowing auburn hair, and pretentiously bratty smirk.

Fuck! This is karma; karma for not facing feelings for Jo, and sliding into Edith's bed instead.

Edith knocks, again and again, finger fucks the doorbell so the ringing never stops. I back away from the door. Stare at the video of Edith on the other side of this door. I know what she wants. It's not Elenore; Margo's not here. They flew to New New York City this morning in search of Fall Ball gowns, leaving Jo and I here, alone. I clear my throat, look at my bare feet.

Doorknob in palm, I twist it, then let it go. If I open the door, she'll want me to pluck her again. I'm not in the mood. Walk away from the door as she knocks harder and harder, then head to Jo's room.

Outside Jo's bedroom, I watch her sleep. I sit in the chair across from Jo's bed, pluck *Little Women* from her nightstand. I've been switching between it and *Great Expectations*. I watch Jo sleep, listen to her breathe, stick my nose in the book, and read, murmuring aloud.

There are so many things about the character Jo that puzzle me. Sometimes Jo March is this beautiful, kind, and generous girl, wise beyond her years. Like when she cuts her hair and sells it so her mother can visit her injured father. And then other times, Josephine March is selfish. Her relationship with Laurie is a perfect example. Laurie had to be big mad, pissed. Throughout his childhood, Laurie gives Jo his heart, only to have her stomp on it when she falls in love with Bhaer, the older professor.

I wonder, if I open my heart to Jo, the one outside Louisa May Alcott's world, the one sleeping in the bed across the room, would she do that to me? Break my heart? Maybe Jo's like Josephine March. If she is, that makes me Professor Bhaer in the story, and Boah is Laurie. This Jo's Laurie is gone, dead.

I close the book and walk over to Jo's bed. I stare out the window behind her bed, watch airplanes transport passengers in the sky. I wonder when Margo and Elenore landed.

Earlier, Elenore and Margo said they'd make a trip of it and spend the night in the five-star Hilton Hotel in New New York City. Before they left, I heard Elenore call Greer. She begged his bank for more time to pay.

I look over at Jo—her mysterious donor left her a lot of money; money she can't use sleeping. It'd take one click to transfer Jo's money into my account and pay Elenore's debt. I know how much her benefactor gave; she wouldn't even notice what I took.

Fuck. I can't do that. I try to shake sinister thoughts away. Maybe I don't have to steal it. Maybe I can make Jo love me. Love will woo her into giving me the money to save Plum Orchard herself. But who am I kidding? Forget love; Jo'll never like me enough to be that generous.

With a curved spine, I lean over, watching Jo's face, and carefully open the third drawer in her nightstand. I stare at the metallic money card with JOSEPHINE MONARCH written horizontally in shiny silver letters. I run my hand down my face, take a deep breath, and exhale. Has it come to this? I'm a heartbreaker turned thief contemplating stealing from the girl I'm into.

I lift the card from its square placeholder inside the drawer. I blow air through my lips. Electric shock waves speed through me. I'm ashamed. Stare at Jo's chin. I'm evil. I stare at Jo's nose. It's the only way. Her eyeballs race left to right under her eyelids. There's got to be another way. I can't do this. I slide the card into my pocket. I close the nightstand's drawer, step away, and leave Jo's room, closing her door quietly behind me.

Back in my room, I sit on the bed, staring at the card like it's mystical black magic, ta-da-ing troubles away. I hit myself in the head one, two, three, four, five, six times. There's good in me. There's more to me than this—robbing a girl I like while she sleeps. There must be another way to keep the orchard. I've got to figure it out. And if I can't, well . . . I'd rather lose my mother's land than risk what little soul I have left.

I'm not stealing from Jo. I need to put her card back. I dash out of my room and into the dark, dim hallway. Bright lights flick on.

Margo stands at the end of the hall, wearing a green pencil dress, with her fingers on the light switch. "We're back!" She does a happy dance, slides out of her green pumps, and carries her heels in the hand not clutching a green shoulder bag.

"What happened?" My hand rubs over Jo's card burning my pocket.

A pained expression replaces Margo's smile. "Why the long face?"

"Edith. She was coming over." I fake-message Edith, hoping to God Margo can't smell bullshit.

Margo perks up. "Purr. Purr. The intrigue. Plucking James's girlfriend. Doesn't it just taste . . . delicious?" She licks her lips and then stuffs her bottom lip into her mouth, biting it playfully.

Hate to admit it, but even though James has another love interest, I feel bad about plucking Edith. "Why the early return?" I glance past Margo's shoulder toward Jo's door. It's ajar. It shouldn't be open. I closed it. "No dress?"

"There was an issue on the AerTrain there." Margo walks to her room. I follow her, looking over my shoulder at Jo's cracked door, before I enter behind her.

Margo turns her purse upside down. Lip balm, lipstick, and more flavored lip balm spill out and onto her bed. She counts the lip balm with a spoiled grin.

"What issue?"

"Nothing, really." She peers at herself in her vanity mirror, smears a new shade on her lips. "Bottom citizens. You know how they are . . . causing trouble."

It's been a while since I've been to NNYC, but I remember coasting over the Bottom via AerTrain, thinking it's what the Ashes are to New Georgia. Every state in the New United States has one—waterless borderlands full of brown grass, Radius-ridden rats, disorderly cops, and poor people. "Anyone hurt?"

Margo shakes her head no. "Not really. Just the girl."

"What girl?"

"The nobody from the Bottom who hijacked our AerTrain during a trade stop. A reporter on iCom news said that bum has Radius. The girl kept screaming, going on and on about spreading it around to rich people. It's like we can't even deliver them food. Government should feed them like animals, sprinkle their food via plane and make them catch it." She giggles at her own suggestion.

"What happened to the girl?" I scan Margo's face for an ounce of concern, but I can't find a smidge.

Margo looks up from her makeup. "I don't know." She huffs, puffs, parts lips. "Pray she didn't cough on anyone."

I scoff. "You pray now?"

Margo rolls her eyes.

I continue, "Radius doesn't spread through human contact."

Margo pouts. "Ugh, Coveyyyyy, you're being weird. Since when are you worried about border slums?"

"When did you become a snob?"

"Around the same time you became an ass." Margo throws lemongrass lip balm into my chest.

I turn the balm's metal top, threatening to break its seal. I pretend to smell it through its wrapper.

Margo glares. "Don't you dare."

I toss the balm on her bed and leave.

In the hallway, I watch Elenore leave Jo's room. She says, "Did Margo tell you about the girl from the Bottom?"

I nod.

Elenore passes me, enters her cold room. "There's no controlling those animals." Her door snaps shut.

Jo's softly snoring while sun falls on her forehead. I open the third drawer in her nightstand, reach inside my pocket, and pull out the black money card. The metallic money card clicks into its holder inside the drawer. I close the nightstand. Can't believe I almost did that. I know I'll feel the weight of this almost betrayal forever.

21

JOSEPHINE

Sparks of fire circle midair above blackened lumber. Turbo cab's windows are up, yet burnt wood and evergreens fill the inside of the taxi. It's dark outside the window. But darkness can't hide the immaculate view of Transition House in the distance; nor can it conceal the tiny bright stars twinkling like fireflies in the night sky.

Cove touches my arm. "Night doesn't bite." He opens the door next to him, slides out the turbo, walks around to my side of the car, taps on the window with his knuckles. "Coming?"

I nod, press my index finger against the window. I touch my forehead. I feel dizzy, close my eyes, inhale, caress the thin raised scar—think how it'd be nice if Boah were tapping, not Cove.

The door slides open, and outside, wind rustles leaves and branches. I take the world in, inhale deep. Burning lumber fills my nose. Kyra waves in my direction, signaling I should join her—she leans against a tree, surrounded by bugger-picking Rald, Margo, the redheaded Fairmoth sisters, and other kids I don't know.

Cove reaches for my hand, but I pull away.

Margo jumps on Cove's back. "Almost dragged you guys out of the car."

When we reach the group under the tree, Margo asks Kyra to get her another drink.

Kyra narrows her eyes. "That was your third one."

Margo flashes an evil grin and plays with Kyra's hair. "Cute. I didn't know you could count. Don't Ashfolk count like one, three, ten, two, four, and dot dot dot?"

Water fills Kyra's eyes before she walks off. I'm not a twenty-four-hour fan of Kyra, but she didn't deserve that. I mean-mug Margo, then run after Kyra.

When I reach her, I find her sniffing, sitting on a massive fallen tree with bark covered in moss.

"Some party, huh?"

"Just say it."

"Say what?"

"That it's karma. I had it coming."

Don't say that. "You didn't deserve that."

"Don't I, though?"

I shake my head no.

Kyra continues, "How I treated you back home, ruined our friendship. Thought I was such a big shot in the Ashes, Mom started fucking Bootleg Jules and then suddenly I was the rich poor kid. That was the only thing that kept me from falling apart, and then Curtis..." Kyra's eyes turn pinkish red, cheeks marinating in tears. "I just had to get out of there, yuh know, had duh leave to survive. Surrounded by all that sadness, depression. You know how it can be sometimes. Just got so bad, yuh know, JoJo, I couldn't, I couldn't breathe anymore in that shack, suffocating and all. All my mom did was cry. She wouldn't talk about it. Just cried and cried. So, you see . . . I had to line up even though I didn't want to. Then I get over here. And I'm reminded I'm a nobody. I swear, Jo, right about now, all I'm saying is, if you ever wanna leave this place, go home, and I'd go with you."

I feel exactly how Kyra feels. I don't wanna go back right now, but I know what it feels like to want to. Sometimes I feel like I'll never fit in, too. I wonder if all Hopefuls feel this way. Or if after the Transition Program, they magically feel like their lives matter here.

Kyra pauses, stutters, "I . . . I . . . I don't know . . . what if coming here was a mistake?"

I feel Kyra's words. It shouldn't be a surprise, but it is; I never imagined crossing the mountain would rekindle our friendship. "You're not a nobody. Come here." I take Kyra into my arms, hold my long-ago dear friend.

Kyra pulls her head away from my shoulder, blows her nose, sniffs. "Sorry I was that way with yuh. I know that now, knew then, but couldn't stop. Do you think—" Kyra pauses, takes a deep breath, exhales, and opens her mouth again. "Will yuh be my friend, Jo? Think yuh'll forgive me?"

We might not get back what we had, but maybe over here, we'll have each other's backs like we did back in the day. Instead of searching for the jig who held me gunpoint in Moats Alley, get used to New Georgia together. I nod. "I'd like that."

Kyra smiles, sniffs again. "Me too." She laughs. "Can't believe he's dead."

I don't say anything. Don't know how she found out, but thank the moon I don't have to tell her. Kyra continues, "Yuh know, if Boah could see us now . . . he'd like it, too. He wouldn't believe it, but he'd like it."

I fight tears. "Yeah, he would."

We stand; Kyra grabs my hand.

I watch our arms swing back and forth in the space between us. "Let's head back."

In the distance, I watch Margo slide down Cove's back. She grabs Larry's arm, then heads in our direction.

I drop Kyra's hand with a smile and sit next to Cove by the bonfire. The red-haired girl—Edith, I remember—cuddles close against him.

"Gonna introduce us?" she asks Cove coyly, as though her mother didn't already at the Gala.

Rald staggers in our direction with three beers—two bottles in one hand while drinking the third.

Cove looks at me, looks at the redhead, then back to me. "Edith, Jo. Jo, Edith."

Rald laughs as he collapses beside us. "Edith and Cove are—"

"Good friends," Edith says.

"Nice to see you," I say carefully, and stretch across Cove's body to offer my hand to Edith. She doesn't take it immediately. For seconds that feel like hours, she stares at the palm of my hand like it's covered in feces.

Cove narrows his eyes at her. "Don't be rude."

Edith takes my hand, shakes it—her fingers feel like feathers. I wonder what she smells like. When she releases her grip, I fake scratch the hood of my nose to see if I can tell. I smell like milk soap. Edith smells better than me, like sweet lemonade.

Edith's better suited for Cove—what I imagine his type would be. Model tall. Thick arched red brows. She's not without imperfection—her nose slightly crooked. But attached to Edith's face, it isn't a bad thing; her curved, pinched nostrils add to her beauty.

In the distance, James arrives via turbo cab. Edith rolls her eyes at me, runs over to James. When she reaches him, she jumps into his arms and gives him kisses all over his face.

Rald yells behind us. When we turn around, we see him and other kids head in the opposite direction, climbing a small hill that leads to Transition House.

Rald opens his mouth, releases a long, loud, lingering burp. "Skinny-dipping in the pool, bruh!"

174

Kyra waves me over. Cove gazes at me. Our eyes meet briefly before I hop to my feet to catch Kyra.

It's dark inside Transition House—so dark, I can't make out the color of the walls. Even still, it is big, echoey, smells like pine needles, and is internally more futuristically designed than its modish exterior suggests. We pass pod chairs, hologram teaching boards, drones on glowing wheels, and passcode-protected entrances to every room.

I glance in the classrooms as we move down the hallway; each one is the size of my entire home in the Ashes. Doors are labeled according to concentration. And Transition House has everything: visual arts, fencing, dance, architecture, and all the usual courses, such as math, composition, science, and history.

I stop in front of the visual arts room. I don't need the code. It's open. As kids sprint the halls, headed to the indoor pool, I step inside. Student art hangs on walls. Every medium is represented carefully labeled below the works: oil on canvas, watercolor, digital art, and other forms of art I've never heard of like anamorphosis, reverse graffiti . . . A painting of white and red and blue flowers is labeled FLUID ART. I don't know what fluid art is, but I recognize one of the two flowers.

One is the Beautiful Thing, the flower that looks like white sunflowers, that grew until cops cut 'em down and burned the fields. The other is blue, with tiny round petals.

"A kid—" a voice from behind says. I jump, turn in its direction. It's Cove. "Didn't mean to scare you."

"If you were any closer I'd've hit you."

"Apologies. They headed to the pool—saw you here."

I turn back around to face the canvas painted in red ink, again.

Cove walks over. "A kid accidentally cut his ankle on broken glass last year . . . he put the blood from his injury in a jar and painted the red flower."

I shake my head, narrow eyes gazing at the blue flowers. "Blood's not blue. How'd he paint the blue flowers?"

"He dyed his saliva with blue ink."

"Ah. Fluid art."

"Yes."

"Makes sense now."

"Good."

The odd medium makes me curious about the science behind art, and the materials combined to create beautiful images. "This white flower, I recognize it. It grew in fields in the Ashes when I was little. Haven't seen them in years."

Chills rush over the back of my neck as Cove touches my hair. I jerk, startled, but I don't move. Usually when someone touches my hair, it bothers me. But right now I like Cove this close. His hand leaves my hair and I close my eyes, listen to my heartbeat, thump, suck my bottom lip into my mouth. I swallow hard, lick my lips. I shouldn't feel this immediate wanting, craving. It's so intense it feels unnatural, unreal, and yet, I want to curl into his arms like a scared millipede. I open my eyes, turn around.

When I do, Cove's so close I smell his tangy, spicy cologne. I wonder what chemicals or plants mixed to form the way his skin smells. With my forehead beneath his cleft chin, I place a hand over his shirt and watch his chest move up and down, and down and up. I count, taking this moment in. I don't want it to end. One, five, ten, fifteen, seventeen seconds. And suddenly it feels like I felt with Boah on my mattress.

Twenty seconds.

"Jo," Kyra says from the door. "Yuh coming to duh pool?"

I back away from Cove, lift my chin to meet his gaze—he doesn't stop staring.

Cove and I follow Kyra to the large, dark indoor pool. No one turns the lights on and nearly everyone besides Cove and me skinny-dips. We roll our pants up and get our feet wet, before jumping in fully clothed. Screeches echo off glass walls. After, we head back into the woods, covered in wet clothes and stolen white towels.

We sit around the bonfire, attention on me, Kyra, and Rald telling Ashes stories to ogling New Georgia teens amazed life's so bad there.

I let Kyra and Rald blabber; don't wanna share everything. I slap the back of my neck hard, look at the palm of my hand. I killed a mosquito. Skin throbs around the bite site. Mosquito carcass and the blood it stole stain my palm. I take the towel off my head, wipe dead mosquito on the towel.

"They'll eat you alive if you let them." Cove nods.

"You're right." I wipe my hand on the damp towel next to me.

"Follow me?" he murmurs.

"To where?"

He stands from his log, extends his hand. "You'll see."

I think back to the Gala, and how everything inside me rejected taking his hand when Cove asked to dance. But this time it's different. I kinda wanna hold his hand. I take it.

We hike a steep hill of stacked, massive moss-covered rocks until reaching the top—a flat rock surface with amazing views of New Georgia in the moonlight. In the distance, I see the mountain that leads to the Ashes. Think of Neal, Vye, Boah. Jessup, even drunk Bootleg Jules.

Cove sits down beside me, legs swinging over the rock hill. I think of Boah and me on the roller coaster chasing rising sun. Cove places his palm over my hand, and my chest feels heavy, warm, cool, like a solar eclipse is happening behind my rib cage.

The world is silent, like we're the only ones in the universe sitting beneath stars. Inside, I'm smiling so hard toes curl. In the Ashes, worry is default. I spent so much time keeping Neal out of trouble and convincing Boah to line up for a better life. But Cove's different—he doesn't need me.

"You look nice." Cove rubs the back of his neck.

"Yeah, right. I'm barely dry."

"Even still." Cove's uneasy.

"You okay?" I try to read Cove's facial expression, but his face's as it always is: stoic, measured, controlled. His actions and facial expressions don't match. Makes him hard to read. So hard, sometimes I wanna magically split his brain open and use the moon as light to read his thoughts.

Cove forces a smile. "What? I don't look nice too?"

"You're ugly."

Cove laughs. And I realize it's the first I've heard him truly laugh. "More than you know. Do you trust me?"

I tell Cove, "A little." I don't know him enough to give the response he wants.

Cove nods. "That's fair. Trust me enough to walk a little more." Cove extends his hand.

I take it.

Cove leads me back down the hill, into the dim woods on a narrow path. Five minutes later, we turn left, and he says, "Look down."

Inches from Cove's brown boots is the blue flower with tiny petals. It looks just like the painted one in the visual arts room. Its blue petals remind me of tiny quills.

I reach down to touch it, but before I do, Cove says: "Don't do that."

"Why?"

"They're endangered. It's against the law to pick them."

I lean down, sniff them; they still smell like . . .

"How does it smell?" he says.

I smile into the flower. "Like honey?" I scratch the mosquito bite burning my neck.

Cove nods, bends down, picks a green leaf. "Let me show you something."

He reaches for my hand, pulls me up. I stand tall. Cove stands behind me, rubs the leaf across the mosquito bite.

"Feels cool, doesn't itch much. What is it?"

"Peppermint leaf. It heals bites."

"How d'you learn it?—about peppermint leaves, that they heal?"

"Family of farmers. Mostly fruits, but my mom owned a farm. It was passed to my father. And when my father died, it was temporarily deeded to my guardian, Elenore."

"Your mother taught you this?"

"Yes, when I was little. I asked my mom why mosquitoes bit me more. She said my blood's pure sugar."

I laugh. We laugh. And then we're quiet. Cove places the leaf in my hand. "Better?"

I nod. "Yeah . . . better."

And it is better. I barely feel the bite, but another question stirs. I want an answer. "Are you and Edith—"

He looks into my eyes. "—Yeah?"

"—together?"

"Why do you ask?"

"At the Gala. She was all over you. And then tonight. She was—"

179

"—We're not together. She dates my best friend, James."

I stare at his bottom lip. "I didn't mean to pr—"

"—Pry?" He smiles. "It's alright." He frowns as if his mind's no longer here. "I'm private."

"Oh."

Cove takes my hand into both of his. "But I don't want to be that way with you. I like how you see me. I'm just broken."

"Broken how?"

"Scattered like glass on the ground, and if someone picked up every piece to put back together, there'd still be missing pieces."

I don't know Cove well, but time speeds up with him. It hasn't been long, but I feel close to him in a way I don't understand, and yet, it's a way I like, a way I kinda sort of wanna melt into. I want to tell Cove his pieces are beautiful even though they're broken. That if he'd just give up what he believes he is, and believe in what he could be, he'd see himself the way I'm starting to, as a beautiful, fragmented human. But I don't. I exhale, change the subject. "Sorry about your parents."

Cove releases my hand and clenches jaw muscles. "Me too."

We stand at eye level, lips almost parallel. I dig my feet into the earth, attempt to ground myself. I feel so light, as if I'm levitating.

Cove leans into me—his breath's minty. I close my eyes just as he closes his. I feel clammy and jittery as Cove's lips move closer and closer to mine. We lean in. Warmth fills my chest and tiny bumps rise over my arms.

"Cove!" Margo calls in the distance.

I open my eyes.

Cove opens his. "I'd better go."

22

COVE

Margo didn't want to leave early, so I left her at the bonfire. And I can't stop thinking about it. Had Margo not interrupted tonight, I would've kissed Jo.

I'll no doubt think about this all night. I stretch over my bed, think of taking the edge off. But I don't want to cheapen Jo by putting thoughts of her in a sock. Elenore'd call this thinking weak, pathetic. It doesn't matter. Being vulnerable with Jo tonight felt like strength—made me feel useful for something more than breaking hearts.

I move my hand away from my navel, place both hands behind my head and stare into the skylight.

I lean over, reach under my bed, retrieve the leather flog. No matter how beautiful the sky will be soon, it's Saturday night. And no matter what, she'll come. She hasn't missed a lesson since I was ten.

I place the flog at the end of the bed, then lie on my back again, eyes closed, until I hear the front door. Margo's home. But she's not alone. Voices accompany her giggles down the hallway.

Margo opens my door. She stands in the doorway, trash drunk, with Larry's and Kyra's arms around her waist.

Margo places her index finger to her red lips. "Shhhhh, everybody shhhh." She laughs, hiccups, then laughs more. "Cove's studying."

With narrow eyes I say, "You know what tonight is."

Margo holds up a bottle of clear alcohol. "That's what this is for." She kisses Larry and Kyra on the cheeks. "What they're for."

I give Margo the look. The one that says: *This is serious.*

She rolls her eyes. "Ughhh! Like usual she won't be back till later; she's with Vimberly. By then I'll be so trashed I can't feel it. Don't worry, Coveybear. I'll make them leave before lessons." I'd be shocked she said this in mixed company if my sister wasn't known for speaking gibberish while drunk. Margo turns around, then says to Kyra and Larry, "Now, let's go have some fun."

I hear Margo's door shut, and soon after, her loud house music.

Tonight's sky is stunning. I lift my arm, point to heaven-tracing constellations. I connect the dots as Aquila, Cygnus, Hercules, Lyra, Ophiuchus, Sagittarius, and Orion light up the indigo sky.

Before he died, Father said my mother called me Orion—her little hunter. Said there wasn't anything I'd seek and not find. That being a hunter was my superpower.

I wonder why my father couldn't be a hunter and seek someone good before he died—why he fell in love with the stepwitch after loving an angel like my mother. I realize fear of love isn't all Elenore's fault—it started with my father.

My father was senseless in love—love made him fucking stupid—made me hate him. Hate he allowed Elenore to take his money and treat him like shit. I know that makes me afraid to be vulnerable. Vulnerable on my father looked pathetic. I don't want to be my father. And as much as I like Jo, I don't want to look stupid.

Fireworks crackle high in the sky. I marvel at wild colors bursting like rainbow popcorn under thin clouds.

My bedroom door opens. Without checking, I know it's Margo. "Done already?"

"No." It's Elenore. I lift my spine off the bed. She continues, "I'll apply her lessons tomorrow."

"Don't do that."

"No?"

"Give me hers too."

Elenore extends her arm and stares at the flog. I stand from the bed, hand it to her. I bend over, press my fists into the bed, spine facing the skylight. As leather marks my back, I numb out, vision focused on the window, watching the red, blue, yellow, orange, pink, and green shadows fire in the sky.

Minus the fireworks, this is Saturday night. Curled over my bed, fist denting the mattress, while Elenore smiles and marks my skin. I bring my lips into my mouth, bite my bottom lip with top teeth.

Whip by whip, I'm soundless, can't feel the sting, used to it. Elenore can hit as hard as she wants. I won't give her tears. I won't make sounds. Unequivocal silence is all she gets.

I wish I could same the same for Elenore, but I can't. She enjoys conversing during lessons.

She clears her throat. "I need you available tomorrow."

"For?"

"Josephine. She will paint your portrait."

"What time?"

"First light." Elenore strikes my back fast five times in a row.

After adding fifteen lashes for Margo's disobedience, Elenore leaves my room out of breath, and closes the door.

23

JOSEPHINE

Fireworks explode in the glistening navy sky. I can't compare the light show to anything I've experienced in the Ashes, but it feels like art. Like the sky is this big canvas above my head and the elaborately designed firecrackers are the paint being sprinkled and splashed onto it. I sigh, think of what it would've been like to watch the explosion in the sky with Cove at the bonfire.

I think of almost kissing Cove, and I wanna melt into the cement beneath me. I slouch on Elenore's roof, legs swinging over the edge, barefoot. Stars shining behind loud firecrackers remind me of Boah and the night he gave me the moon.

On the midnight I turned thirteen, Boah gave me a straw hat filled with tiny pieces of cardboard paper. When I asked what it was, he said it was a puzzle—asked if I'd help put it together. When each piece was in place, it created an image of the moon surrounded by hundreds of stars. After, Boah picked the puzzle up, towered above me, and sprinkled puzzle pieces over my head. He laughed.

I laughed. "What the hell are yuh doing?"

Boah placed a finger over his lips. "Shhhh. Shooting stars. My Siksika ancestors called them Kakatosiks. Close your eyes, Jo." I obeyed. And Boah continued, "Make a wish."

I wished for New Georgia. I wished for us both. I sigh, kick the air, adjust myself on the roof, scooch closer to the edge. I need a sign, or just someone to say it's okay to be happy. Because it's crazy to live in the place of my dreams, feeling half-empty.

Back in my bedroom, I kick off my shoes, slide them under the bed, and relax between cool sheets. I think of home. In a few months, it'll be cold outside, and when that happens Ashfolks'll either survive the freeze or die shivering in it.

I stare at the hologram heat and air system in my room. Yesterday, Gaitlin showed me how to use it. He said talk to the room, tell the room you're hot or cold, and in five seconds I'd be comfortable. "Make it more . . . cooler, colder?" Seconds later I need a blanket over chilled legs. "Make it a little warmer." I remove the blanket. Now it's not too cold, it's not too hot, it's just right. Back home weather control isn't easy.

Come winter, Ashfolks'll warm shacks, warehouse homes, and hands with lava rocks and fire bins in daylight. At night they'll store heated lava rocks under covers at the foot of their bed. Night or morning, it takes hours to warm frozen bones in the Ashes. Just a little of New Georgia technology would do wonders in the Ashes. It'd save lives and limbs lost to winter, too. I fall asleep imagining Vye huddled under thin sheets.

———————

In the morning, eyes wide, spine against the white wall, I sit in bed, sketching Cove's profile, while sun shines on my sketchbook. I flip the page to draw Boah, but voices outside my bedroom make me panic. I close the sketchbook, put the charcoal sticks away, and get out of bed to press an ear to the door.

I listen to conversation, staring at sunlight seeping through white curtains.

Gaitlin speaks. "Good to see you, Margo."

"I need more pills. Ran out yesterday," Margo says in reply.

Gaitlin coughs. "The diazepam? So soon? Taking only the prescribed daily amount, yes?"

"What are you insinuating? Of course I do. I kind of accidentally left my bottle in a turbo cab yesterday."

Gaitlin hums. "Experiencing side effects?"

"It's fine, thanks again. For writing the prescription, I mean." Then something rattles like a bottle of pills.

"Glad to hear it," Gaitlin says.

"Umm, before you go." Margo's voice is filled with worry. "Is it supposed to make me feel, I don't know, off? Sometimes it feels like I'm walking in slow motion?"

"It's a low-dosage benzodiazepine. Drowsiness is normal. Just don't take it with anything else. We wouldn't want another situation like last time."

"I understand," Margo says. Margo's need of pills is like aloof jigs leaning over silver spoons. Beige crust isn't coming out the corners of her eyes; she doesn't shake uncontrollably whenever I see her. And yet, I can't help thinking Margo feels like one. Suddenly I can't wait to move to Transition House. Even though I'm sad about Boah, I came to New Georgia for a future devoid of fear of dying from suicide, starvation, or unwarranted bullets.

"You're a smart girl, Margo. Make smart choices. I still have Dr. Bland's iCom contact information. It can't hurt to talk to someone about what's going on."

Margo sniffs. "Just . . . say nothing . . . to her."

Gaitlin clears his throat. "Do I ever? Call if you experience side effects."

Silence.

Gaitlin continues. "And Margo? Remember what I said. I won't approve another refill until you agree to see a psychiatrist."

Footsteps stop right outside my room. It's either Gaitlin or Margo; whichever it is, I can't let them know I heard anything, so I jump into bed, hide my face to play sleep and save face.

My bedroom door opens. And then . . . more silence.

It's so silent it's like I'm alone until the person sits on the side of my bed. Sniffs and sits on the edge of my bed. She's so close, I almost taste the peppermint she sucks on.

A soft *hmm* vibrates Margo's lips. "Jo . . . are you sleeping?"

I don't say a word.

Margo kisses my ear, then sighs inside it, "He's mine."

He's mine? Who's hers?

I open my mouth to speak, but Margo is already out the door.

She must leave it open, because I hear Elenore clearly. "It's good to be nice to her. She needs to feel loved. Welcomed. I'll want you on your sweetest behavior. I insist."

Margo snickers, "The sweetest. Got it. Veins full of lollipops."

Then more steps, and Gaitlin's voice again. "Headed to the lab. Jo is doing much better. I expect to see her at Transition House soon."

Elenore bristles. "I'll supervise her training here. And Cove and Margo can assist with her transitional studies. Besides, after such a terrible ordeal, she should stay here. With you by her side, she'll have the best around-the-clock medical care."

"Studies show after traumatic experiences, victims heal faster in places where they feel safe, alongside familiar faces. With her fellow Hopefuls there, former Ashfolk she might know, I recommend Transition House. Best place for Jo to heal."

Elenore clears her throat. "And you're sure she wouldn't be better suited here? Margo and Cove are excellent examples of well-mannered youth."

Gaitlin doesn't agree or disagree. He coughs twice, says, "You take care of Margo."

"Oh, Margo's good as ever," Elenore says lightly. "She and I just went with Edith Fairmoth on a dress-hunting trip."

"Ah, I see," Gaitlin says. "Won't be long now. Edith excited about the big day?"

"Beyond thrilled. The only issue is who'll do the ceremony. Vimberly's persistent as usual. Insisting on using Edith's childhood priest," she sighs. "But what the bride wants, the bride gets. It's her day." Elenore chuckles.

Edith and James are getting married? I'm surprised, given how much she seems into Cove.

It's silent again. I pull the covers away from my body. I wanna go outside. But I can't let on I've heard anything, so I gotta be careful.

After a few minutes, the coast sounds clear. Then more faint steps transition to louder steps, which pause in my doorway. I even out my breathing again.

A shadow towers over my bed.

It's not Gaitlin; he smells like the hospital and alcohol pads. It's Elenore—she's a mixture of peppermint and lavender, like her daughter. She thinks I'm sleeping.

Elenore sits on the bed beside me. She tells me a story about Cove. He was four, begging his dad for a dog. Cove's father drove him to the local animal rescue to feed stray puppies. Cove wanted a dirty dog. And on his fifth birthday, his father got him one and named the puppy Henley. Three days later, Margo left the back door open. And Henley went missing for days. A week later, Cove found Henley unresponsive and ice cold in an alley four blocks from the ocean.

It's strange. I can't see Elenore's face. But much like I can hear Vye smile, I hear Elenore grin when she says the bit about Cove's dog dying. I think of pretending to wake up, but what if I do, and Elenore accuses me of faking, pretending to sleep—which I am, but I don't want her to know that.

Elenore touches my shoulder. "Josephine," she whispers.

I extend my arms, fake stretch, slide white covers down my face, rub fake sleep out of my eyes, and sit up.

Elenore is flipping through my sketchbook. "You're talented," she says, eyes fixed on a sketch of Boah's face.

"Thanks."

She stands up. "Come with me."

"Where?"

"To draw a portrait."

———————

In the middle of the library, an easel carries a large white canvas. Beside the canvas, on a small three-legged oval-top table rests an array of black and white charcoal drawing sticks. I sit on the stool in front of the canvas, staring at the expensive pieces of charcoal—they're in a wooden box with a glass top. Elenore clears her throat to talk.

"My mother added this library to the house on my twelfth birthday," she says. "Never gave it much use, but my sister did. Absolutely loved this room, the smell of drafty old books. Every time I open a book I see her, cross-legged in the middle of the children's aisle over there." Elenore lifts her chin, gesturing to the massive shelves of books behind me. She continues, "Whenever she read a passage she loved, she'd get this Bambi-eyed gaze in her eyes. I could never replicate that gaze, its innocence. Suppose some people have it naturally."

I glance up, taking my eyes away from the charcoal. "Naturally?"

"Yes. Purity. Kindness. Love. We're born with them. As we get older, people snatch them away."

"People can't steal those things."

"No . . . but hate does. Once it's in you, it works alone—doesn't need permission." Elenore's fingers run over book spines; her gaze is far away. "People think the devil is the root of all evil. They're wrong. Hate's the culprit. Responsible for everything: self-hate, racism, fear. Hate's a monster."

I think of the Ashes, my attack, Jessup's attack, Boah's murder, my parents' suicide—everyone who left me without permission. For years hate marinated in my bones—told me how to talk, walk, eat, sleep, dream. Had it not been for Boah and me climbing the coaster before dawn, wishing on the moon, hate would've won. I didn't let it. No matter how many people hate kills, I won't let it win.

Elenore takes a seat on the white lounger, adjusts the white fluffy pillow behind her. "Am I under enough light?"

I nod, yes, then pick up black chalk, sketch Elenore's long face. Is she this block of ice with tight lips, wrinkled white skin, thin bones, and skinny fingers? Or does warmth live inside her, invisible 'cause it's hiding from the hate that stalks it?

"Aurice told me about your friend . . . Boah."

The sound of Boah's name closes my eyes, shakes my fingers, and sends goose bumps up both arms.

Elenore continues, "Sir Thomas More."

"I'm sorry?" She brought up Boah. "Who's Thomas More? What does he have to do with Boah?"

"He wrote it."

"Boah?" My comment is nonsensical. Boah hasn't written a book. But I can't connect the dots Elenore is sketching.

"More."

"Huh?" She's hard to read.

Elenore stands from her pose, saunters past one massive bookcase to the next, gently touching book spines. "More wrote *Utopia*." She opens a hidden drawer built into the bookshelf.

I press, "What does this have to do with Boah?"

"Patience, Josephine."

"Just Jo."

"Indeed."

I clench teeth and my jaw tenses. Why'd Elenore bring Boah up when he's dead? Then not even talk about him. She's smart; she must know it'd be hurtful to think about. But maybe pushing thoughts of Boah away is not the best way to go. And maybe Elenore knows this, and she's trying to heal the hurt.

When her hand leaves the hidden drawer, she's holding a leather-bound journal with brown straps tied around it. She walks toward the easel, skinny fingers gripping the journal. "More wrote, 'What else is to be concluded from this, but that you first make thieves and then punish them.' You see, Just Jo, Boah's death is a product of his upbringing. An unfortunate series of events, yes, but these things were bound to happen. By no means saying it's just. Simply saying it couldn't be avoided."

I unpack Elenore's words. If she feels the way we're treated and excluded in the Ashes is unjust, why won't she do something about it? If Hopefuls bring fame and more wealth to New Georgia, why can't NG transfer wealth to the Ashes?

Elenore continues, "It's tough in the Ashes, sure, but it's better than it was for my ancestors."

"Better doesn't equate to good."

Elenore stands, towers over me, staring at the sketch. "Interesting."

I lift my chin, gazing up. Elenore's eyes are narrow—her lips hide in her mouth. "I've barely started," I say.

"Well then, that settles it—" Elenore makes a *tic-tic* sound with her tongue. "You've a great talent, Josephine."

"Thank you," I say, but her drawing isn't done. Can't get her eyes right.

"I've known many a great artist in my time. And you've got something,

Josephine. Almost as if you inherited it." Elenore tilts her head left to right, inspecting the sketch of herself. "Were your parents skilled in the arts?"

"Both of them. Painters."

"Knew it!" Elenore claps in excitement. "I'm always right about these things, you see. Art is your passion then, yes?"

I wanna tell Elenore I'm good at art but that as I get older, I realize I do it to be closer to parents I never saw in motion, parents I never knew outside stories Aunt Vye told me. But I don't. "Yes, it is."

Rita enters the room, carrying a silver tray with small black cups and a black teapot. She walks over to Elenore. Elenore smiles, whispering in her ear. I try reading her lips, see if I can make anything out. It's hopeless; I can't.

Rita nods, straight-faced at Elenore's inaudible words. Once Elenore pulls away from her, she sets the tea tray on the table next to the lounger in the middle of the room and exits, closing the door behind her.

Elenore ambles back to the lounger, takes a seat. "Gaitlin says you're well enough to go to Transition House, strong enough to make the move. But you're welcome to stay here. Your choice really."

"I appreciate all you've done. Your home is beautiful. But, if it's alright, I'd like to go to Transition, be where I'm supposed to be, with the other Hopefuls."

"Of course, dear." Her words are smooth; only a tightness in her eyes betrays the argument she made to Gaitlin earlier. "Transition House is an essential education before acceptance into New Georgian society. Hopefuls must learn our ways. How to dance, choose a creative outlet, sport, or instrument to play, learn how to eat at a table, et cetera, et cetera." She waves her hand under her chin, fanning. "You're ahead of others; you were born talented. Your art. It's special, Josephine."

I can't stand when she calls me Josephine. But she won't stop. No use calling her out on it. Besides, Elenore's been nothing but kind; she didn't have to let me stay here, heal here, but she did. What harm can come from allowing Elenore to call me Josephine? It's the least I can give in return for her kindness. "Should I pack now?"

Elenore presses into the pearl ring on her wedding finger and a hologram of Rita's location in the house appears. "Rita, please pack Josephine's things."

Rita nods, "Yes, Elenore. Right away." The hologram fades.

Elenore turns her attention to me. "It's settled. This week, you'll move to Transition House, like hundreds of Hopefuls before you. But today, I'm going to give you a head start on your training."

I'm confused. "How do you mean?"

Knock! Knock! Knock!

"Come in," Elenore says, rising, still gripping the brown journal.

The door opens; it's Cove.

"Where do you want me?" Cove walks over to Elenore.

"Here is fine, dear." Elenore smirks.

"Fine for what?" I say, staring at Cove's bare feet and closed white bathrobe.

"The human form is best captured live, Josephine. Your art, though good . . . could be better. Would be excellent with practice."

I want to say something, defend my talent, but how can I? Elenore has a first-rate education from New Georgia. All I have is the Ashes. I know I'm smart, but I don't know everything. Elenore knows famous artists. If she sees potential in my work, maybe she can help me get better. Be better. "Should I draw you again?"

Elenore laughs. "No, dear. I was the warm-up. Cove will sit for you."

Cove disrobes, wearing black boxer briefs over hairless skin. With a smug look on his face, Cove stands in front of the lounger, legs shoulder width apart, arms held straight down on either side of his body. I trace his frame, foot to cocky grin.

"It wouldn't hurt, you know," he says.

"What?" I ask, keeping my eyes on the sketch.

He chuckles, briefly looks between his legs. "It might a little."

"Ugh," I say with an exhausted breath. I look away, shake my head, annoyed. We connected almost kissing, but then he says arrogant things like this to put up a wall. And yet, I sorta kinda wanna know Cove past what those lips may do. "Stay still."

Minutes pass, until Cove says, "Look, I'm sorry. I suck at this."

"At what?"

"The being-open thing."

I nod.

"Doesn't come easy."

He's scared, trying, so I meet him halfway. "That's what she said."

He laughs, the real one. Our eyes meet. We stop laughing. Cove looks away. I look away. Silence fills the space between us. I sketch his hairline.

Cove covers himself with his robe. "What are you thinking?"

"That I'm glad you put the robe on."

He humphs with a genuine half grin.

I clear my throat. "What are you thinking?"

Cove opens, then closes his mouth as if he's trying to suffocate the words that wanna come out.

"What it is? What are you thinking?"

"Tell anyone, I'll deny it."

I stop sketching, shift my gaze to focus on him. "I'm a vault. Tell me."

Cove releases a heavy-hearted sigh. "You scare me."

I gently set the charcoal on the easel, meet Cove's worried eyes. "I scare you?"

Cove's chest rises and falls; he nods. "Yes . . . shitless."

24

JOSEPHINE

iCom's morning weather alerts says a storm's coming. I narrow eyes; the sun is bright out, and storm clouds aren't suffocating light blue skies.

A tap on my bedroom door startles me. My heart beats fast. Maybe it's Cove. It didn't seem like it when it happened, but maybe my seeing him almost naked made him feel some way, like awkward—the same awkwardness I'd felt sketching his body.

Before speaking, I watch shoe shadows pace beneath space separating bamboo floor from steel door. I swing my legs off the bed. Bare feet to cool wood, I walk swiftly toward the shadow moving left to right.

"Who is it?" I don't wait for a response. I open the door. It's Aurice in plaid straight pants, white sweater, brown penny loafers.

Aurice asks if I mind taking a walk with him. I tell him yes, but I gotta get dressed.

"Five minutes?" I ask. Before he responds, I ask him where we're going.

Aurice grins, pulls a camera over his head, and holds it in his right hand. "The Market Center. Then we'll come back this way across the street. Hugo Park. Take your time. Wear pants. Gotta ride bikes where we're going."

"Why? And what's the Market Center?"

"You'll see," he says, smile mischievous.

Turns out Market Center is located a twenty-minute walk from Elenore's, outside in an enormous field. People walk down well-beaten paths. On either side of us are booths housing fresh meat, fish, fruits, and vegetables. I watch a kid take an apple from a farmer without paying for it and run away. I wait for something bad to happen. Think about Hope, the girl in the Ashes killed over a loaf of bread. But moments pass by, and nothing happens. The farmer doesn't chase the kid, and cops don't shoot him. The farmer acts as if nothing happened and serves the next customer. The kindness warms my heart.

Grocery bags in hand, we leave Market Center, headed for Hugo Park. When we reach the park, Aurice rents two bikes. I hop on the yellow one; he rides the red one, bags piled into a wicker basket. After ten minutes of riding a narrow, rocky path through dense woods, I understand why we needed bikes. The section we just entered has a NO PEDESTRIANS PAST THIS POINT sign. Beneath that, the sign reads: MOUNTAIN BIKE TRAIL. I didn't realize Hugo Park stretched so far from Elenore's.

Five miles down the trail, we reach the other side, where the green stops and elegant cobblestone roads begin. We turn down an alley, come to a green door with *105* nailed above an oval peephole. The door's not modern. It's old, pre-revolt. Walls on either side of the door are brick—clean brick, devoid of staggering human bodies. Thoughts of Moats Alley and the black woman with dreads make my forehead wrinkle and stomach ache.

I steady my bike, kick the kickstand, and look at the sky, clean streets, sniff the air.

Chin touching his shoulder, Aurice grins back at me. "Yeah, I know, takes getting used to."

"Used to what?"

"For starters, there's internet here. I know it's still the same in the Ashes—wanna look up who to contact if you get hurt, you gotta walk to the nearest healer, knock on their door. Wanna see a friend, hear their voice?—gotta walk miles to hug them. Attacked in Moats Alley?—911 doesn't exist in the Ashes. And if they did, the last person you'd wanna reach in case of an emergency is the wrong cop. The changes, Jo, take getting used to. Reprogramming the way we see the world and people in it."

I nod. Aurice gets it.

His camera hits concrete, breaking my thoughts. He leans to pick it up, worried, but sighs. "It's not broken."

I look back whence we came, notice a thin person in black standing behind a far tree, watching me, watching us. I can't make out their face—a black mask covers it. I turn my neck to Aurice. Maybe he sees them too. But he's too busy getting off his bike to notice.

I turn back around, and as my eyes meet the stranger's across the long distance, thunder erupts, and lighting bolts touch ground behind them.

"Can't find my keys. Maybe I dropped them? Dear, dear," Aurice says.

I volunteer to trace our steps on foot. I rest my bike on the side of the building.

Before I walk off, Aurice releases an exasperated sigh and says, "It's got to be in this bag somewhere."

I pace forward, farther and farther away from the safety of Aurice's view. Closer and closer to the person in black. Part of me thinks if I get closer, the stranger will back away, turn, and run. They're not running. Stepping over uneven cobblestones, I move quicker. Walk faster and faster down the road toward the park, until I'm a little sweaty, light jogging, then fast jogging, nearer and nearer to the shaded oak tree concealing the stranger's identity.

The balls of my feet hurt—they did not build this path for runners—but I can't stop. I can't see the stranger's eyes, but I feel them staring.

"Jo!" Aurice calls from behind.

I stop jogging dead in my tracks, almost tumble over my shoes. I face Aurice's voice—he waves me down, flailing a single key high above his head, with a relieved smile.

"Got them," he says.

Hands on hips, catching a breath, I wave back. "Coming!"

I turn around to face the stranger in black again. They're gone.

We leave mountain bikes outside the green door. Aurice enters a password into the keypad next to the handle, uses a skeleton key to open the bolt, and the door creaks open—its modest imperfection makes me smile. Every piece of furniture, art, photographs, and oddly shaped human statues is eclectic. None of the pieces in this place should fit together, but artistically they do.

"What is this place?"

Aurice looks around the front room, smiling. "Home."

Wall to wall, Aurice's studio is covered with photos of Ashfolk. The only thing in color is our red shoes. But he's interested in more than people—an entire corner's dedicated to the broke amusement park. Capturing the roller coaster Boah and I climbed every dawn, with the trash heap in the distance. He took a photo of the wastelands, capturing little pieces of onion grass, and dandelions sprouting out of dry concrete and dry soil. And the next wall over are frames, trophies and medals and news articles awarding his talent.

"Be right back." Aurice leaves the room, turns a dark corner in the house.

I explore Aurice's home, snooping and lifting framed photos of him when he was my age or a little younger. In a couple, Aurice is shirtless in beat-up jeans and torn sneakers. I inspect the photos. I recognize the building in the background. It's the old police building I watched burn in the riot. These photos weren't shot here—they were taken in the Ashes.

I think back to what Gaitlin said about Aurice. That he was just like me, grew up in the Ashes, took part in the Lineup and gained citizenship in here. I wanna be like him—another poor kid from the Ashes capturing the world through art. Aurice and I'd be side by side in magazines—him next to his photos, me next to a canvas full of charcoal strokes. I wonder how often he sneaks back to the Ashes. Whether I could too.

I want to see everything here—fascinated more every second. Each picture reveals milestones in his life. A picture of him at the Gala and another of him dressed in all white at his citizenship ceremony, and another where he smiles ear to ear, hugging Elenore. I lean over, lift a small frame away from the side table; in the shot, Aurice kisses a man wearing a BIG BOYS KISS BIG BOYS T-shirt. I smile, leave the living space, and enter the kitchen.

Aurice's kitchen is no hole-in-the-wall. Two bamboo triangular light fixtures dangle from the ceiling. Shiny pots and pans and plates and glasses line walls. And fruit from the market joins a large fridge full of fresh vegetables. I touch the shining gas stove, thinking of all the tokes Vye could make cooking pies in an oven this big.

"Hey, Jo!" Aurice calls from somewhere in the back of his house.

"Yeah?"

"Down the hall, take a left. I wanna show you something."

"Coming!" I leave the kitchen, follow Aurice's vocal map to his location in the house.

After taking the left, I enter a dark room, find Aurice's face covered in amber-colored light.

"What's that smell?" It's pungent, metallic, smells like someone poured a gallon of vinegar on the floor.

Aurice chuckles. "Best smell in herstory."

I narrow my eyes.

He laughs, confirming he saw the sarcastic glare in low red light. "Be with you in a sec."

I nod, quietly scan the room. Some corners are so dark, squinting doesn't help; it's impenetrable. A swift rush of cool breeze brings goose bumps.

"Check behind the door, put it on, it'll help." A shadow of amber light shows little of his gentle smile.

"Sure you don't mind?"

Aurice shakes his head, says, "Girl, if you don't put that cardigan on? And when you're done, come see, Jo."

"Okay, okay." I obey, take careful steps around the large table, where Aurice leans over a large square white pan.

"This is where the magic happens. Look."

I lean in. Aurice counts down. "In five, four, three, two, one. Real-life magic."

Eyes fixed on the clear liquid in the pan, I watch a blank piece of white paper transform into a photo of an old woman sitting in a tattered rocking chair. A white bandage covers her left eye. Doesn't take long to notice the location. The picture wasn't taken here. "It was taken in the Ashes."

Aurice nods yes. "The night of the riot."

It's a beautiful black-and-white photo, but it makes me pause. Make me think unpleasant things.

That night. What almost happened to me . . . what happened to Boah.

Aurice hangs photos across two-wire lines, using old clothespins.

"You know I grew up in the Ashes."

I nod. "Gaitlin told me."

"It never leaves you. The Ashes. It's always with you. It's why I chose photography as my creative outlet, during training. I told myself that one day I'd go back, give back."

There's dust in my left eye. I rub it. "I wanna say, thank you."

"For?"

"For . . . saving my life."

Aurice smiles. "Allow yourself to live, Jo. There's no shame in wanting a better life, wanting to start over. No one'll fault you for being happy." He places a hand on my shoulder. "Did you get your money?"

I take the card out of my pocket. "Yeah. But . . ." I feel ungrateful; I should just take the money without caring who sent it, but I can't help wondering . . . "Do you know who the donor could be?"

"Nope. Elenore said they're unidentified."

"Could it be Elenore?"

Aurice shakes his head no. "Possible, but highly doubtful. Truth is, no one knows. What we know is they donated it to you. The largest donation gifted to date."

"Why me, and not others?"

"Why not you? Listen, it's free and cleared the bank. Enjoy it. Don't worry who it's from." Aurice sighs. Shaking his head, he taps my money card. "You've grieved enough. Try living a little, yeah?"

John Ready's words the day of the Lineup are getting to me—I hear them now. His words make me feel guilty for wanting a better life. Was he right when he said everything I needed was in the Ashes, that I can't find it here? Or maybe Aurice is right—that there's no blame in wanting a better life, wanting a fresh start. Aurice started over, without forgetting who he is or where he came from. He's found a way to go back. I can do the same.

Aurice catches my smile and beams. "Heard you're moving? Transition House tomorrow? Loved my time there. The art career program is college level, but worth it. Learned a lot there. But had it not been for Elenore, I'd not be this fabulous. She has an eye for talent."

"So I've heard." I force a half smile.

He nods. "Yes!" He claps playfully, continues his pep talk with an Ashes accent. "And soon, after yuh all moved in, we gunna have fun."

25

COVE

Jo and Rita left the witch's house twenty minutes ago for Transition House. I don't like it, but maybe Jo leaving is a good thing—she should've moved into Transition House days ago but didn't. The witch will say Jo didn't move in right away due to her injuries. But I know the twisted truth—the witch dragged the move out. Elenore wanted Jo to live here longer to watch me break her heart.

To be fair, I don't want Jo to move out either, but my reasons aren't distorted; they're pure—well, half-pure. I like Jo close. She wasn't close enough sleeping two doors down, and now she's farther away. Distance from Jo makes my muscles ache. I rub my chest, think of something more pleasant. Jo sketching me. Her eyes on every inch of my skin.

I should care less, but I don't. I want her to like me, because I like her. "What are you thinking about?" James asks, watching me splayed across his bed. He's sitting at his writing desk, next to the only oval window in his pod room.

I shrug. "Nothing," I say, staring at the porcelain ceiling. James's mansion is the biggest in New Georgia. His mom, Emily, runs the deli everyone prefers, and his father's Greer Jr. And his grandfather Greer Landing Sr. runs the bank, and owns the New Georgia transportation system that controls AerTrains.

"Liar." He balls up a piece of paper, throws it at me, and misses.

I chuckle. "It's the new one."

James flashes a glare that says *really?* "Jo?"

I nod yes with closed eyes. It's a shock to me too.

James chuckles. "You got it bad, bro."

"Don't laugh." I open my eyes, glance at him. "Yeah, so do you."

James grimaces. "I don't wanna talk about it."

"Yeah, me either."

"Talked to Edith?" he says, with a suspicious glare. He knows she's after me, has been since we were kids.

"She's your girlfriend; you talk to her."

"You know what I mean. She's into—" James stops himself from saying what he wants to say, and what every kid in New Georgia knows.

Edith's into me. "I know," I say, turning to look at him. "Haven't seen her in a few weeks."

"She got mad I didn't go to the Gala. One Gala is pretty much like all the rest. Anyways, bro, she stopped taking my calls. Larry said he saw her over your house the other day."

"Yes. Planning with Elenore."

"She seems excited?" Worry lines fill his forehead.

I shrug. "Doesn't matter." I stand from the bed, walk over to the window.

"How's Larry? Still pining for Margo?" He releases a half-hearted laugh.

I humph and ha. "She asked about you the other day."

"About?"

"Plucking you."

James laughs; he's seen glimpses of the other side of Margo, the one she hides, and only truly shows me. "What'd you tell her?"

"That you're off the market."

"Not so sure anymore. Edith's not talking to me. Haven't had a real conversation with her since before the Gala. Look, do me a favor. Ask Margo if Edith's seeing anyone? Got a feeling, you know? Like there's someone else."

"It's not me," I lie. It fucking is me.

"Despite the twisted game your stepwitch makes you play with her . . . I know you'd never cross that line."

Back toward him, I say, "I'd never do that."

"Cut it out, bruh, I know that. But I need to know. She's saving herself for me. I don't want some clown swiping her before I pluck."

I wanna tell James the truth. That the clown is me. That I plucked Edith. That's what friendship is, right? It's honest, transparent. Friends don't keep secrets, but I do. How can I tell my best friend that in a moment of sheer confusion and weakness, I swiped his girlfriend's V-card? "I'll ask around. If there's a clown, I'll find him." I walk over to the mirror nailed to the back of his bedroom door. I mouth the words. *I'm the clown.*

"Heading to Transition House?"

"Yeah. Margo messaged me earlier; she's high, can't drive home. You wanna come?"

"See Jo? Heard she moved in today. But you knew, huh, bro?" James laughs hard and places his left hand over his heart. "All your talk about how I'm a sucker for Edith and you're puppy-dogging over Jo."

I shake my head, a failed attempt to hide red cheeks.

James laughs. "Hate I know you so well, huh, bro?"

I walk toward his bedroom door. "Shut up, man. Let's go."

James claps his hands, laughs harder as we leave.

26

JOSEPHINE

Reddish-orange monarchs soar above Transition House. Pointing in their direction, I try counting 'em. A hopeless mission, but it's magical. A large one with big brown wings lands on Rita's forehead. Startled, Rita jumps and waves it away.

Vye says our last name, Monarch, hails from ancestors from Kentucky back in the 1800s. But that doesn't matter to me. I enjoy thinking I'm named after butterflies. When I was little, in the Ashes, I'd daydream of butterflies—wish I was one of 'em. Fluttering free, with wings big and strong enough to fly to New Georgia. Now that I'm here, doesn't seem like I thought it'd be. Then again, maybe Aurice is right. I need to let go of the Ashes, give this place a chance.

I smile up at the curved metal staircase leading to Transition House's entrance. Never believed in heaven or hell, but New Georgia built heaven: tall white walls, elegant, elongated steeples, and too many big oval windows to count.

"Ready, Jo?" Rita carries my black suitcase. I take it from her. We follow a little egg-shaped, four-axis drone on white luminescent wheels.

The drone speaks. "Please follow me."

And we do. Rita and I pace slowly behind the drone as it hops up the metal stairs, through Transition House's massive double-door entrance, onto the see-through elevator. We coast up to the third floor. On the ride up, the drone says there are three floors in Transition House, each one with a purpose. First floor is careers and talent hall—the classrooms I peeked through on bonfire night. When the elevator passes the second floor, the drone says it's reserved for Hopefuls on the Science Program Career Path. Says because of dangerous chemicals, no one's allowed on the second floor without supervision. And Transition House has a strict curfew, ten p.m. Hopefuls in violation of the curfew can't reenter the building until seven the next morning.

Soundless, the elevator doors open on the third floor. Air rushes into the elevator.

"What's that smell?" I breathe it in. It smells spicy, salty, roasted.

"Calculating a list of smells." The drone glides out the elevator first. "Popcorn," they conclude.

"Never had popcorn."

"We'll fix that, Jo Monarch."

"Jo?" a voice from behind says.

I turn to face the voice. It's Kyra. She's hand in hand with Margo. "You're finally moving here?"

I shrug and smile. Happy to see Kyra's familiar face. "Yeah."

Margo doesn't speak.

Kyra's smile is wide, welcoming. "We're headed to my room. 211. Come find me. We're all hanging out tonight. Catch yuh later, yeah?"

I nod. "Yeah." I watch Margo and Kyra saunter down the hall, all smiles and giggles, until they disappear around the corner.

The drone rolls to the wall opposite the elevator and says, "Floor three is residential hall. Hopefuls, new citizens, and hall monitors habituate here. I'll show you to your room. But first . . ." They point toward a hologram that reads RESIDENTIAL POLICY on the wall opposite the elevator. "Please read all New Georgia Resident documents, and holosign."

"Holosign?" I say.

206

"iCom, show holosign instructions," the drone instructs.

Within seconds, the Hologram shows what holosigning is. In the video a young boy signs the document by writing his name midair on the hologrammed line that reads SIGNATURE.

I stare at the hologram, thinking it'll magically turn the first page. When it doesn't, I face Rita. "How do I . . . ?"

"Turn the page?" Rita completes my thought.

"Swipe your hand to the left to move forward, and to the right to access the previous page," Rita says.

The drone speaks. "Once all documents have been signed, you'll receive your assigned room. Good luck and goodbye."

I swipe left to: New United States of America Preamble. I've read it before. It's required knowledge on the Lineup exam. I don't have to read it, but since I don't know who, or what's, watching, I skim through it.

New United States of America Preamble

We, the Representatives of the New United States of America, in order to formulate a more balanced social system, will create a durable working class, train sustainable lower classes, provide health care regardless of social station, gender, race, or sexual orientation, and extend a kindness to bordering citizens ungiven to our ancestors pre-Revolt 2030. We pledge that those born into Ashes shall have opportunity to rise from dust. We ordain, establish, and shall enforce this Official mandate for the New United States of America.

I swipe left to the NUSA Constitutional Peace Doctrine, which I know and

skim, then find the Transition House Mission, Career, and Residential Policy. I
read this one more closely.

Transition House Mission and Career Policy

The Mission and overall purpose of Transition House isn't to
learn a select career path in its entirety, but rather to instill
foundational educational knowledge, the basics of a selected
talent or field. Our training prepares Hopefuls for optimal
transference into New Georgia's Elite Society. Failure in
successful career path selection decreases positive economic
outcome and could result in denied or revoked NUSA citizenship.
Should any Hopeful select one career path and later decide it's
not for them, they must immediately return to Transition House
to select a different path. Successful completion of selected
career path training is at the discretion of the career path
instructor.

I write my name midair in cursive, watch my name appear in blue.

"Required documentation complete," the increasingly familiar iCom voice
says. "Click done for room assignment."

Rita reads the number over my shoulder and silently leads me down a hall.
She opens the door. I sniff, inhale. Smells good. Popcorn in a bowl sits on my
fancy metal desk. I rush to it, chew, smack, and devour buttery popcorn. It's salty,
crunches soft onto back teeth; it's delicious.

There's one bed in here. I don't have a roommate. It's my room—my white
walls, white sheets, and covers—

"Does everyone have a room alone?"

"No," Rita says. "When I was here, and every year since, it's been two Hopefuls a room."

"Then why me?"

Rita wraps her arm around me and smiles. "You're blessed. And your donor is generous. Affords certain privileges."

I should be happy, grateful. And I am, but I can't help feeling privileged and unworthy too—like somehow, it's not okay to accept nicer things, things other Hopefuls aren't afforded. But it feels good having beautiful things. I sink onto the white couch, smooth linen against my legs and fingers, and look out my window over the hill we ran up on bonfire night.

Rita hugs me, says Elenore's set up art lessons with Aurice at her house, that Elenore or Aurice'll be in touch. When she leaves, she says she doesn't know me well, but'll miss me being around, says my presence made Elenore's house warmer.

I unpack my small bag in just a minute, set my charcoals and sketchbooks neatly on the desk. I'll be glad to keep practicing at Elenore's . . . but part of me doesn't wanna pick art because everyone here and back home expects me to. I can't find a way to lock my door, but maybe that's just how Transition House is. I'm curious about the science floor and take the elevator to the second floor even though I'm not allowed.

Elevator doors open with an AI automated greeting. "Welcome to the science hall."

I step out of the elevator. Pace down the wide hall of endless transparent aquariums. Wall to wall. I'm amazed. Picturesque rocks and stone rest glistening at the base. Seaweed and algae float, dance freely at the bottom of tanks. Holographic words pop up as I watch, identifying mandarin fish, butterfly fish, and angelfish breathing gracefully through gills, flapping fins, weaving among starfish. And translucent jellyfish wiggle tentacles bouncing up and down, their soft bodies glow like lightning.

Next, I observe scaly and spiky bodies behind thick glass. Holograms by the tanks offer detailed information regarding each species: Lizards can detach their tails while escaping predators. Porcupines have very poor vision, and their babies are porcupettes. Alligators' medulla oblongata, the part of the brain that controls aggressive behavior, makes 'em mean. Pythons take sunbaths to increase the temperature of their cold-blooded bodies.

Farther down the hall, separated from jellyfish, fish, and reptiles are bigger fish. Hammerhead sharks swim around and above my head. Amazed by the futuristic infrastructure, I gaze up, eyes watching their every move, as they swim fast in tanks, left to right. Round and round. Transition House is like the TARDIS, bigger on the inside.

"Jo?"

"Gaitlin." I jerk back away from the shark tank. I'm not supposed to be here.

"Enjoying Transition so far?" Gaitlin holds a lab coat and face mask, and face shield.

"For me?"

Gaitlin chuckles. "Yes. Put them on. You'll need them. Can't enter where we're headed without them."

We take side stairs that lead to the entrance marked RESTRICTED AREA— VISITORS UNPERMITTED WITHOUT SUPERVISION.

I follow Gaitlin into one of the science labs. Once inside, my eyes toggle over fancy telescopes, rows of petri dishes, pipettes, and beakers, a fake skeletal body with labeled internal organs.

At a large steel sink, Gaitlin and I wash and sanitize our hands. Then he hands me a set of lime-colored rubber gloves.

"Considering a career in the sciences?"

I shrug. "I'm an artist."

"Yes, an excellent one. You're also much more. We all are." Gaitlin pauses, then continues. "Let me show you something."

Gaitlin leads me into a small room off the main lab with sterile silver walls and a large steel table at its center. Rubbery petri dishes filled with vibrant colors make an intricate design across the tabletop.

I wanna say many things, ask many questions, like how'd he get paint to look like hard Jell-O? What are the wild colors and what has he discovered in them? But the only word that comes out is, "Wow."

Gaitlin's pleased with my response. He seems positively proud, chest puffed, chin up, high cheeks.

"It looks like art, but it's science?"

Gaitlin chuckles. "It's both. Science and art. I told you I've been researching Radius, trying to find a cure. I realized how beautiful the bacterial cultures are, brought some here to try preserving them. These are epoxy cast molds."

"They're what cast molds?" I question.

"Epoxy." Gaitlin pulls out bottles, explains a chemical reaction between two components to harden a resin over the bacteria and agar. Says one component inside the petri is paint.

"I wanna make one."

Gaitlin smiles. "I don't have any real cultures we can use, but I'll show you the principle. I'll teach one. You'll do one. Sound good?"

My cheeks hurt; I can't stop smiling. "Yes."

Gaitlin stirs clear liquid in a plastic cup for three minutes, says timing is important. Then he fills a clear, empty petri dish with liquid resin halfway, careful not to spill it. With a pipette, he drips different colors of paint at different corners of the dish. In another petri filled with resin, he adds dried flowers and leaves. From the cabinet along the wall, Gaitlin grabs a small torch gun and traces the object with its heat, then pours another layer of resin over the paint and flowers.

It's my turn now.

Step by step, I do what Gaitlin did to make his mold. Instead of putting paint and flowers in separate petri dishes, I create a mold using a kaleidoscope of acrylic paint and dried tiny blue flower petals. "How long before it dries?"

"In the old days, curing took twenty-four to seventy-two hours, but now . . ." Gaitlin carries our petri dishes to a small contraption near the door, places them inside like an oven. Sets the timer for sixty seconds.

When we pull them out, the resin is hard and translucent, stained glass singing of art and science.

My heart feels light. I can love art and science. I don't have to choose one—I can do both, be both, like Gaitlin. An artist and maybe someday a scientist. I tell Gaitlin he'll need to teach me the culturing half of his experiment too. Being here feels right, and though it's not the Ashes, it feels something like home.

27

COVE

Margo sits between Larry and Kyra. James cuddles Edith. Edith's predatory gaze hasn't left me since I arrived at Transition House. And I sit at Kyra's study desk, elbows on knees, head down, curious which room on the residential hall belongs to Jo. I stare at Margo and Kyra, wonder if they know. I should ask them, but it'd be a dead-ass tell. Margo'd know I am seeking Jo's face; she'd never shut it.

Kyra's gaze meets mine. "Yuh always this quiet?"

Margo lifts Kyra's hand, kisses it. "Only when he's thinking."

I scoff, close eyes, shake my head, and look away from them.

"Are you blushing, dude?" Larry chuckles. "Didn't know you did that over girls."

Margo releases Kyra's hand, narrows her eyes in my direction. "He doesn't."

Think of something to say, Cove. If you don't, Margo will automatically assume it is about Jo. And that's worse than thinking about Jo because I don't want to hurt Margo. The witch bruised her enough; she doesn't need more scar tissue. "Biochem. Test tomorrow."

"You'll ace it like all the others, bro."

"Not all of them." I made a B-plus the exam after the Gala. The accelerated Honors program at University of New Georgia is brutal. But they transform a four-year bachelor's degree into two. Saves time. I wanna hurry up, graduate, and live on Plum Orchard.

"Covey hates Bs. Allergic to them. Got a B-plus last exam."

"Perfectionist, Cove?" Kyra smiles.

"We both are." Margo grabs Kyra's chin, kisses it.

I stand. Can't see all this happiness—this affection. What I feel for Jo's intense, like I can't breathe without thoughts of her, unless she's occupying the same space. And even then, I'd use our shared space to do nothing but stare at her, try to smell her—take her fragrance in like a monk's meditation. "Be right back."

I pace down third-floor hallway, climb the last level of spiral stairs that leads to the roof. When I reach the top, I open the tiny window, step outside it, sit inside the window on the windowpane. Sometimes, the best way to think is climbing the highest peak alone without smooch chatter.

I stare into the horizon. Clouds are heavy, thick. They crowd skies: birds and bees and full sun take up the rest of its faded yellow space. I wish it were night; maybe I'd get answers to calm the mania of wanting to see Jo's face right now. Because when stars glisten in the night sky, the universe is thinking.

Not sure the sky thinks, if it's true. But my mother said so before she died. The night of her passing, we lay in bed, quiet, my head on her slow-beating heart. We gazed at those sparkling bubbles of hopeless gas, and Mother said, "Coventry, when you miss me, look at the sky. Every time a star sparkles, it means the universe is thinking for me, to carry a message to you. A message from me."

Five-year-old me held on to her frail fingers. "What message, Momma?"

"This one . . . always remember, Coventry, love doesn't understand absence or time. No matter how far I am, no matter how many days, months, or years pass without the sound of my voice . . . I'm always here." She placed her hand over my heart. "And here, too." She placed her hand over my head.

"In my hair, Momma?"

Wind rushes over my face. In the present I remember her response like she's standing next to me. She kissed my forehead and said, "Yes, my little love, in every strand."

"Covey?" Margo says from behind, kicking the reminiscence away. "What are you doing up here? It's chilly."

I scooch over silently, let her sit beside me on the sill, bodies touching side to side.

"Feel like we're losing us." For once my sister seems sober. We both keep eyes to horizon.

"I'm here."

"Are you, though? Since Jo arrived, you've been different. Stopped sharing stuff."

I don't trust my thoughts with you. You grow more like the witch every day. "I tell you things. Ask what you want to know. I'll tell you."

Margo shrugs. "Used to leave your door open at night. We'd fall asleep together, wake up the next morning, you holding me."

Curious and patient, I wait for the tough kicker. The question. Margo's real question. But she doesn't ask it. It doesn't matter; I hear it unsaid. She wants to know *why* my door's locked at night, why we don't sleep together. The answer to her question would piss her off. Hurt her. Make her feel unwanted. How is it Elenore spent so much time teaching us to fear love, but never discouraged our closeness—a closeness she's well aware of?

Margo sighs. "I miss them. I act unbothered, but I do."

I know what she misses, but how can I tell her I do not, that the thought of my lips pressed into anyone's except Jo's is inconceivable, cardiovascularly impossible? I've zero knowledge of what Jo's mouth tastes like. Never kissed her tongue. And fuck, I don't know what it's like to hold Jo while she's sleeping, but she got me. Owns my heart like white on rice. It's not the most glamorous or even the most romantic of metaphors, but I don't want a perfect entanglement with Jo. I crave Jo messy, disheveled like wild morning hair the night after a party.

"I miss them a lot." Margo turns, wraps her arms around me, rests her ear on my chest.

Alright, I'll give. "Miss what, Jellyfish?"

"Love it when you call me that." Margo blushes, buries her nose in my armpit. She never blushes. "Butterfly kisses come morning. I played sleep. I liked them, like them. I miss them, miss us. I miss you."

I don't respond. I wind an arm around her. I stare at the sky, eyes narrow, breathe in fading day. *Stars or not, I know you're thinking, sky. I'm thinking, too.*

I want Jo.

28

JOSEPHINE

Transition House is devoid of bodies. With just a handful of residents, it's full of objects instead, unmovable beautiful things like untouched beds covered in silk white sheets and fluffy pillows. Lavish uncracked mirrors held by unblemished shiny wood. Eggshell walls covered in art nobody sees. Pristine white bookshelves hosting books that haven't been dog-eared. These halls reflect the numbers of Hopefuls accepted as new citizens. And I can't help thinking that this building alone is going to waste. How many Ashfolks these walls, beds, and covers could shelter from rain, sleet, snow, or those long, hot summer days when folks literally die of thirst. I swallow, run to the nearest vending machine, and press the button for water. When the water drops out of the machine, I unscrew the glass bottle's top fast—dry tongue and guilty conscious screaming for H_2O. Hoping water'll drown the shame I feel having access to unused things that could literally save lives in the Ashes.

"Josephine Monarch," the egg-shaped drone says. The hallway echoes its words. "You have a visitor on the first floor. Waiting room. Visitor's name: Aurice."

The drone and I take the elevator down to the first floor. Aurice beams when he sees me.

"Done with science?"

My cheeks hurt from smiling. Aurice promised fun things. I can't help wondering—"Where are we going?"

Aurice claps his hands, rubs them together; face full of mischief, he says, "You'll see."

———•••———

Aurice only says he has something he wants to share—something he usually does alone, but he wants to take me with him. We turbo cab across New Georgia, take Aurice's personal jet, and an hour later we're high in the sky, hovering over a small town.

Aurice presses the button used to communicate with his pilot. "This is the place."

I look at Aurice. "Place for what?" We're high in the air, surrounded by fluffy clouds. I gaze out the window and glare at the mossy mountains below.

Aurice reaches under his seat, grabs a black vest. He slides his arms through its straps, fastens the latch across his chest, and tugs it as if making sure he's locked and secure. "Yours is there, put it on," he says, smiling, pointing at the matching vest under my seat. "We're gonna jump."

"Huh?" I think of Kyra's brother, Curtis—how he lost his legs when he fell off the roller coaster, how losing his legs made him want to kill himself. I think of all the things that could go wrong. I touch my legs. I grab my neck.

That's how I feel about the ground. That life feels too good right now, and soon, it'll all come crashing down. Like somehow, this'll all go wrong, something'll snatch me down and watch me smash into hard concrete.

Aurice removes specs, replaces them with thick goggles, and stands. He helps with my vest, fastens it, makes sure it's secure, and instructs the pilot to open the door. When the door swooshes open, a rush of cold wind fills the jet and goose bumps race over my entire body.

Aurice stands in front of the open door, spine facing bulky clouds. "Your vest will take care of everything. You just have to trust. Life starts with a leap. But to truly enjoy life . . . we must jump." Aurice dives out of the jet and vanishes.

"No!" I rush to the open space, as if by some miracle I could grab his wrist and stop him. I gaze down into open sky, searching for Aurice as he shouts in laughter.

"Jump, Jo!" Aurice's voice is faint. I'd have to jump to reach his words.

"I can't," I say, but I know he can't hear me. Just like Jessup couldn't hear me yelling from the top of the roller coaster.

Hard wind makes my cheeks dance, pushes them back to meet my ears, and then up to kiss my eyes. I can do it. I can jump. I take a deep breath. Think of all the things I've let hold me back in life. Think of good and bad times—times that ruined my life or made it better.

I put my goggles on. Close my eyes tight and tighter, gripping either side of the jet's open door. The jig who held me gunpoint, the riot. Reed's attack. I reminisce over the noose cops forced around Neal's neck, the hanging tree. I evoke the sweet aroma of Vye's pies and warm hugs, Jessup's smile. I smile as an image of Boah's profile appears, then disappears, replaced with Cove's face. I see the veins in Cove's neck, the care in his stare, the fear and sadness that make me wanna fix him, make him the kind of happy he pretends to be.

Hesitant, I release my grip on the open doors. I squeeze my eyes tighter, shutting them more than I thought possible, and jump. With open arms I hug fast wind. I'm flying. I open my eyes to beautiful pink and light blue skies. Misty blue mountains come into view; smoke oozes from every peak. A myriad of colors fills my eyes. Blues, greens, orange, reds, and yellows brighter than the huge sun on my left. I smile big, inhale, take in fresh air, open my mouth in laughter and scream.

iCom starts a countdown to parachute release in my ear. I hold tight, take a deep breath, feel the jolt of a black parachute expanding behind me. Watch the patchwork of fields come into sharp focus.

When my feet touch ground, I roll, laughing, tangled in the chute. Aurice runs over to help me remove it. "Let's do it again!" I say.

Aurice bursts out in laughter. "Ready for what's next?"

Nodding my head fast, I take both lips into my mouth in pure excitement. I jump up and down like a kid waiting for drones to deliver toys. "Yes!"

29

JOSEPHINE

I arrive on Elenore's doorstep with arms and hands full of shopping bags and sweet treats, trying not to drop them. With much difficulty, I reach for the call button, and press it. Two minutes pass before Rita opens the door.

She smiles, takes a few bags. "Good to see you, Miss Jo. Aurice said you'd be spending the night. Your room is ready. All settled in Transition House, yes?"

"Yes, thank you."

I love my room at Transition House. But on the ride back from parachuting, Aurice asked if I'd mind staying over at Elenore's. We're having art lessons earlier than usual since he'll be out of town a while. His work's being shown in Paris. Sounds like a dream. I've wondered what the world outside of NUSA is like. Is it much like NUSA: Poor folks in borderlands, while rich folks live it up in mainlands? Or is it different?—everyone lives where they want, how they want, doing whatever career path they want with everything they need?

Rita leaves my bag by my bedroom door. I spread my new things over my bed, watching them like they'll disappear any second, as if all these pretty things and sweet treats aren't mine. I jump back first onto the mattress, my body splayed over presents Aurice bought and things I gifted to myself.

After skydiving, we went to Genius, the gown shop where Aurice says most girls shop for Fall Ball gowns, or get 'em custom made. In the clean parking lot, I noticed how happy everyone was. They wore big smiles, glowed with laughter, left their car doors open with keys in the ignition while chatting. People in New

Georgia are trusting. In the Ashes, that'd never happen. There, Ashfolk would wear locks on their shoelaces, and swallow the key if they had to, to keep shoes from being stolen.

In the little boutique, I took a hand full of dresses from the racks. Aurice selected a few too. When my arms couldn't hold any more gowns, I entered a dressing room, Aurice outside the door in the viewing area.

One by one, I tried on silky and velvety and satiny dresses, running my hands up and down the fabric until Aurice would call for me to come model. He oohed or aahed or nayed each one for hours, until we narrowed it down to three. A black one, a pink one, and a red one. I chose the red for two reasons. One, it's elegant like something tattered history books in the Ashes show Marie Antoinette wearing, and two: It has hidden pockets.

To celebrate our success, Aurice and I shared the biggest ice cream cone I've ever seen. We don't often have ice cream in the Ashes, and when we do, by the time AerTrain delivers it, it's melted and tastes like creamy milk soup. With milk soup, I never experience head freeze. I ate the massive ice cream cone so fast it made my head hurt so bad I stopped eating it, but it was worth it for the cold, rich flavor.

Aurice's iCom chip sounded off with a call. Elenore called him with an errand, and he had to go. I overheard Elenore say there was trouble in New Massachusetts. Said three kids, two boys and a girl, wearing black hoodies, crossed their border walls, robbed a gas station but only took food. New Massachusetts's local cops apprehended the bandits—sent them back to the Dumps, where dirty cops dragged 'em through mud and hung 'em.

I think of those kids. Being poor isn't fun. I know how hungry they must've been to risk crossing their border. And how scared they must've been—just like Neal—when cops strung 'em up. I can't explain it, but the world's changing, shifting.

I grab my sketchbook, quickly sketch those three kids crossing the border. Once done, I carry my sketchbook to the large oval window next to the bed and push it open.

On the balcony, I sit on a steel stool. Gazing out, I see Cove in the garden. He sits at an iron table with one, two, three, four books spread over it. His eyes are narrow, index finger over his top lip, thumb hiding beneath his square chin.

The doorbell rings.

After a few minutes, I hear Edith's voice, and Elenore's laugh.

Edith is often part of the group, whether here or at Transition House. Sometimes she and Margo have their heads together, ordering stuff via drone— shopping for hours until they crash. Sometimes Edith goes off to speak with Elenore. They never speak to me. But it's alright; I've been getting used to the New Georgia kids. Despite Margo cuddling Kyra, I see the look in her eyes. Larry's, Edith's too. Like Kyra, Rald, and I'll never be more than immigrants— poor kids living among them as illegals. Guess it's almost true till Fall Ball, but New Georgia invited us. It's not our fault we haven't made it to Fall Ball yet.

To prepare for the Fall Ball, Elenore wanted to go over dinner etiquette and afterward teach me to waltz. One night after dinner etiquette, Elenore instructed Cove into the library. At room's center, Cove and I met.

"I don't know what to do," I whispered.

"I got you," Cove said. And he did.

Classical music filled the room as Cove directed my feet. Before I knew it, I was waltzing. I moved gracefully, stepping forward then backward, feet miming the shape of square boxes over bamboo floors.

Below on the grass, Cove gathers up his books, and I duck back into my room before he looks up and sees me.

30

COVE

Some mornings Jo comes to the witch's house for art lessons with Aurice. Lost in pastels, acrylic, and charcoal sticks, the two spend hours on the balcony in the room that still seems to belong to her—they sketch and draw or partake in sporadic lessons of photography. And sometimes, like now, she comes to the house anyway to sketch by herself.

When she's up there, every so often Jo gazes down briefly, finds me sitting outside in the garden, legs crossed in a lounger, nose deep inside my philosophy, biochem, statistics, or anatomy hologram textbook.

Chin to sky, I sigh. It's dreary today, feels like someone or something pissed the universe off and it decided to make sun leave the sky earlier than usual. Swiping right, pixelated page after page, highlighting need-to-know passages. I color diagrams of skin, muscles, and bones, while outlining medical terminology for the week's exam and ignoring Edith's phone calls.

As always, when I tire of studying, I look up at Jo. Watch her sketch a world she's optimistic about, inside a house so cold Lucifer avoids it.

Aristotle comes to mind—theories involving relationships of shared virtue, those of pleasure, and those of utility. The "pleasure" kind of relationship from Aristotle's theory is all bump and grind, minus the mind. It's a quickie. Relationships of utility are superficial connections, using each other to gain richer friends or obtain a higher social status. People who can build relationships of shared virtue don't lie—they talk about everything under the sun, revealing their darkest secrets, letting someone else live inside the twisted workings of their mucky little brains. I think of Elenore—she's utilitarian: a money-sucking leech, milking her reputation off false wealth, living vicariously through the children she fucked up, drinking us dry.

Is Jo the stuff of virtue, pleasure, or utility? She seems the stuff of virtue; I can't know for sure, but there's a quiet confidence in Jo other girls didn't have.

Which am I? Pleasure? Virtue? Utility? I'd prefer somewhere in between. I want to connect with a girl, but without losing my identity in the process. Without being weak like how Larry and Kyra are pathetically crazed for Margo. Maybe I don't fit into Aristotle's relationship theories. Maybe almost stealing from Jo brands me incapable of affection without a twisted angle attached to it. Maybe I'm evil—unclean—dirtier than mud.

Maybe I'm just an asshole.

31

JOSEPHINE

Soft pastels in shades of pink, blue, yellow, and white stain my fingers. Today's morning art lesson at Elenore's went well. I practiced shading images with color. Class with Aurice ended forty minutes ago. And I'm still at it, sketching, layering tone after tone, shading—re-creating my parents' images on a large white canvas.

I'm tired.

I leave the balcony, wash hands, and walk out Elenore's front door.

Outside, I cross the brick street, enter Hugo Park. Children chase each other. They fumble into green grass laughing. Some couples hold hands. Most talk and walk, while others sit on benches cuddled into each other. I wanna be close to Cove in that way, but I'm afraid he doesn't feel the same.

I stroll around Hugo's cobbled paths, until I reach a human-free spot beneath a large cherry tree. I sit on the ground, take two fistfuls of onion grass, and stare at the mountains in the distance. Eyes closed, I inhale. I think I'm close to happy. In the Ashes, unless you're sitting out front of a house of people you know, it isn't safe to be alone. Solitude is risky. Yuh might not make it home in one piece. Yuh not might not make it home at all.

A hundred feet away, a tall cop walks in my direction. I tense up, habit from life of knowing law enforcement in the Ashes. Nothing good comes from cops you don't know getting close. My heart races as I watch the white man adjust his holster as he gets nearer. I feel like crying, but I don't. I breathe deep, think of what Vye's mother'd taught her—she told her, "Black girls don't cry, they fight."

When Vye tells this story, she ends it saying her grandmother was wrong. That crying's a superpower not many have. So, I gotta have thick skin, but I cry a lot. Brown girls have tears. We're like everybody else.

The cop is getting closer. He looks nice enough, but you never know. I feel tears slip down my cheeks. I tell myself I'm exercising a superpower for doing so. And I believe it, somewhat. But is there a reason for me to be crying right now? I haven't done anything wrong. Maybe it's true what Aunt Vye said about the law in New Georgia a long time ago. That cops are pleasant, considered friends to locals.

I shield my eyes from the sun; the cop's almost here. He seems hard and stern like Ashes cops—broad shoulders, handlebar mustache, beard, and all. But there's something different about his demeanor. I see dimples, a smile—his eyes look happy. I wipe my tears away.

"It's a pretty day today," he says. His mouth is full of shiny, straight white teeth. "But don't let the sun fool you. It gets dark pretty fast around here."

I nod, inhale, swat a mosquito on my arm, scratch the bite.

The cop extends his hand. After hesitating for two seconds, I shake it. The cop chuckles. I breathe out the nerves, take a lungful of ease, and smile. His badge reads OGGERS.

"Don't worry about formalities," Oggers says. "Just call me Ogg." He lifts his forehead to the sun and continues, "Just making my rounds. Didn't mean to startle you. You're new. Didn't catch your name, though."

"Josephine. Jo, sir."

"Prefer Jo?" Ogg says.

I nod. "Jo's good."

"Well then, that's what I'll call you. Nice to meet you, Jo. Now you enjoy your day. Let me know if you need anything." Ogg whistles across the park, shaking hands with people who pass. He stops to pet leg-humping dogs along the way.

I take a deep breath, pick at green grass and dandelions.

32

COVE

"Have you seen Margo?" Elenore's lean face invades my bedroom doorway. "She didn't come home last night."

I shrug, shake my head no.

She doesn't look like she believes me. "When you see her, tell her I'd like to speak to her."

I nod.

Elenore clears her throat. "A word, dear?"

I follow her skeletal frame to her cold room. I close the door behind us, and she sits behind her writer's desk. I take a seat at her vanity on the opposite side of the room. Every so often she looks up from whatever she's writing to watch me watch her through the mirror's reflection.

I study the lavishly clean room filled with late-afternoon light behind me. White bed. Ivory quilt draped perfectly over a round mattress. Sheer curtains. A white rug that looks like poodle hair is splayed across her floor. Elenore's desk sits in the corner near a large oval window—it's tidy. Pencils and papers just so. Files and envelopes stacked high. I envision pushing all her items to the floor. Adding surface-level chaos to her miserable old life.

Elenore stops whatever she's writing and throws the paper into a small glass trash can near her desk. A devilish smirk graces her face as she pulls an envelope from her drawer. She stands, walks to her vanity. She pats the back of the chair I sit in, hands me the envelope. I open it. My gaze lands on my mother's calligraphy—it's the deed to Plum Orchard.

I raise it to eye level. "Blackmail is unnecessary." I'm livid, but I don't show it, can't show it. Misery fuels this twisted-ass woman, and I'm not about to fill her tank. "I told you, Jo won't be a problem. I know what I'm doing." I glare at the painting with two sad white faces, ruefully contemplating the state of my soul.

Elenore runs her fingers through my hair like a mother might do. "Of course you do, dear. It's not blackmail. Think of it more as a gentle reminder. I know you'll not disappoint me. But I saw you."

"Elaborate."

"It hasn't happened in a while, but I heard you." Elenore straightens her sinister spine.

And just like that, I know what she's referring to. The reading.

"Night after night after night . . . the reading . . . the constant, sickening reading like a foolish lovesick puppy." She pauses, pats my shoulder, the touch that lets me know she wants to be the one sitting before her vanity, so she can put her face on. I don't move. She grinds her teeth. "Glad all that reading is over. But tell me . . ."

"Tell you what?" I can't fix my face. I know Elenore can see my distaste for this conversation. And I don't care. I'll gladly take the beating for it.

Elenore reaches over me, grabs her makeup bag. She returns to her writing desk. She grabs a tiny mirror from her drawer and props it on her desk. Looking into it, she pulls her hair away from her face and into a tight bun that sits just above her sagging neck. "Tell me, how did reading to Jo contribute to the science of breaking her?"

I wanna tell Elenore the truth. At first, reading to Jo was step one in breaking her. I figured if I read to her every night, that one night, she'd wake up, hear me reading, and fall in love. Then I'd sleep with her, dump her, and throw her away like the others. She'd return to the Ashes destroyed. I'd win. Game over. Period.

That was the plan. It was a good strategy. But I can't play games with Jo; she has a slice of my heart.

"She's no different from the others," I lie.

Elenore grins eerily. "When did it happen?"

"When did what happen?"

"Your desire to tell lies," she says.

"She's no different." I slide my hands into pants pockets while a migraine burgeons, pressing against my temples.

"Then I guess you somehow lost your senses. Since you insist on playing ignorant, I'll tell you what you already know. Jo's not like the others. I knew it when I saw her in the Lineup. It's in her eyes. She's strong. She's not shallow or easy to pluck. She's beyond her years and loves smart men. She'll never give you her heart without you exposing yours first." Elenore contours, angling and highlighting sections of her oval face.

What Elenore says is true. Jo's strength radiates even while sleeping. And my addiction to her is stronger when she's awake. "I can handle it."

Elenore chuckles. "I see you, Cove. You haven't kissed her, and you're still falling for her. I wonder what she'd think if she really knew you, if she knew the games we play?" She applies rosy blush over cheekbones that've long forgotten to sit high. "Oh, no, no. I'd never tell her that of course. I won't have to. Will I, little Cove?"

I stand, stare at her reflection in the mirror with all kinds of smug written on my denying face.

Elenore leaves her writing desk, walks to me. "She's too much for you. She'll shatter your heart into a thousand shards of glass, and the rest of your life you'll walk barefoot on the pieces. And when it happens, you'll look back on this moment and remember: I tried to save you." She snatches at the deed in my hand.

I lift my arm, removing it from her reach. "It's under control. Jo won't be a problem." More lies.

Elenore pulls the deed from my fingers. "We shall see." She sits in the chair before her vanity, applies red lipstick.

I turn toward her bedroom door.

"And Cove?"

"Elenore?"

"When giving pieces of your heart away, which parts do we avoid?"

Elenore's chair shrieks against the floor. Without turning to face her, I know she's looking in my direction.

I remember that moment years ago. My thirteen-year-old self invades my eighteen-year-old frame, and I want to respond to Elenore the way I did back then, by finishing the sentences she welted into my skin as a child.

"Which pieces of the heart are best left untainted?" She repeats the question differently but seeks the same answer.

I want to say *the parts you've stolen, the parts you've robbed from me and Margo.* But I don't. Like the trained, abused science project I am, I say, "Heartskin."

"And what's Heartskin?" she probes.

I shake my head and run my tongue over my teeth. "Memories and emotions closest to us."

"Give an example and tell me why."

"Stories about parents we've lost, people we love. Any person, place, or thing that evokes real emotion. When people don't know who you are, you're never vulnerable. And the heart is safe."

"Now," Elenore says, rising from her seat. "Say it." She walks toward me.

"Never fall in love."

"Why is that?"

"It steals parts we never knew existed."

"And?" Elenore reaches for my chin, covers the cleft with her thumb. "Go on."

"And when it finds the parts . . ."

Elenore grins. "What does it do with the parts?"

"Kills them."

———•••———

Outside Elenore's bedroom, Margo bumps into my chest. "You've been drinking," I say.

"It's five o'clock somewhere? Doesn't matter. Don't be lame."

"I'll take you to your room. You don't want her to see you this way."

"I don't care if she sees me. Or hears me!" Margo leaps into my arms. I catch her, then put her back down on her feet. She points to Elenore's bedroom door. "That witch, she's the living embodiment of misery. How come we're the only kids in New Georgia without an aunt or uncle's house to run to when shit's tough? I wanna run away but I can't. You can't either." Margo sings the word *either* and continues. "It's a good thing her sister died young. But maybe—" This word is sung too. "Maybe her sister didn't drown in Havisham Lake like she told us. Maybe the witch misery'd her to death. I should go in there right now, tell her she's fucked up lives, my life."

"You're not doing that." I block her from entering Elenore's room.

"She screwed you up too. You can't even admit you like the dirty girl from the Ashes because of that witch! Slit my carotid artery, why don't you? I'll bleed out faster. Take back the brain she stole!"

Jo's not dirty. "Shh. Seriously?" I say, trying to hush her.

"Just got off in the cab, too. Pity masturbation. I'm pissed and sorta sad. No lassie or boy'll ever want me." Margo huffs. The liquor on her breath's so strong, it makes me blink. "Larry sees Kyra behind my back. I caught them last week."

233

Her voice goes singsongy again. "And they don't know that I saw them fucking without me." She burps. "Told Kyra I loved her. And she says she's into Larry. And then Larry iComs me, right? Fucking iComs me! Says he wants that poor blonde bitch, Kyra, more than me. Me!" She hiccups, blows air through lips. "But she was into me, right? Both were. Now they're not!"

"Shh," I say again, but it's no use. I gotta get her to her bedroom without her causing more of a scene.

She belches. "Then I start crying and crying, and I threw up something orange and green and something else like a yellow noodle. Then Larry said he didn't want to be with me anymore because I was pathetic, and that he doesn't like emotionally needy girls. Then he says that the only reason he liked me was because he thought he couldn't have me. He said I wasn't fun anymore. I'm the queen of fucking fun, Covey."

Margo's hazel-green eyes roll upward. She passes out. I grab her waist to keep her tiny frame from slamming into the floor. I glance down the hall as Jo's door opens. She stayed after her morning art lesson. I lift Margo's feet from the floor, holding her in my arms—Jo stares at me. I look at Margo, then back at Jo.

I carry Margo to her room. Her hair dangles over my shoulder, and her green stilettos bob against her heels.

I put her to bed and sit on the mattress beside her. I push her blonde hair away from her face; pull covers over her body, up to her neck. In her drunken state, I see the girl I cuddled as a child. I wonder what her five-year-old self would think of the drunken mess she is now.

I stand; Margo grabs my wrist. "You read to her."

"You're drunk. Sleep."

"I know that."

I grin wide. "You need a toothbrush." I fan the air below my nose.

"Stop it, Covey." She stops my fanning. "I saw you. Every night, reading to her. You never read to me. Checking on her, doting on her. The bonfire, almost kissing her. I kiss people all the time; you've only kissed me. How do you think that makes me feel? I was so mad at you. Told Elenore too. That was satisfying. The witch got so mad." She laughs. "She started spying on you. Betcha didn't know that, huh?"

That's how the witch knew I read to Jo. Margo snitched. Can't be mad at Margo. Madder at myself for breaking Elenore's rules.

Margo's voice cracks, her chin trembles, water fills her eyes. "You like her more than me, don't you?"

And Margo passes out again before I answer. I close the blinds, turn her bedroom lights off, and shut the door behind me.

I knock on Jo's bedroom door.

"Who is it?" she asks, like she was standing by the door.

"Cove." She opens the door. "Want to show you something."

"What?" she asks, eyes piercing.

"Can't tell you. I wanna show you. Ready?"

"Now?" She looks down at her blue jeans and white button-down top. "I gotta change first."

"You'll be perfect where we're going," I say. She's always perfect. "As long as a bathing suit's underneath."

"And where's that?"

I just smile, leave, wait for her to put on a bathing suit. When she opens the door again, she's changed into brown flats, fitted dark blue jeans, and a blue-and-white polka-dot silk chemise. I can just see a bikini through her top.

"How's this? Are you sure I look okay?" she asks.

I want to tell Jo she'd never ask that question if she knew how she melts me.

Her brown eyes remind me of undiscovered hazel-shaded planets. If the world were crashing, I'd live in a deserted galaxy without food and water just to be near her.

I think of Margo, and Larry. And how drastically Larry changed after Margo confessed how she felt. Margo gave Larry control by showing him her heart. But maybe that's what love is; it's giving another human being permission to see your heart, and copyrights to break it. Right now, it feels like Jo's slicing my chest wide open. I'm the voodoo doll, Jo's the pin. Every word, every phrase, every sound Jo makes pricks my thin skin, pokes my heart.

"Cove?" Jo says.

"Yeah?" I blink away the thoughts, and stare at Jo's nose, think of kissing it.

"Well? Are you sure I look okay for where we're going?" She fidgets with her fingers, tucks her hands into her pockets.

"No complaints," I say.

Jo grins. "Gunna say where we're going?"

I offer my hand, and she takes it. "Nope."

33

JOSEPHINE

Spanish moss dangles over thick tree branches outside Bonaventure Graveyard. Cove said we gotta trail through this cemetery to get where we're going. Side by side, we walk down curved dirt paths circling the cemetery like mazes. It's tragically beautiful, loved ones buried beneath lush greenery and brown understory, aged marble headstones, porcelain mausoleums.

Five minutes into our walk, Cove says, "Look at that."

"What?"

He points. "That bird. It doesn't like me." It's a crow, sitting on a tree branch, seemingly uninterested in us.

"You can't see that?" Cove flinches; I laugh.

"It's not thinking about you."

"Yeah, but it's looking." Cove stops moving. Glares at the bird.

I stop too. The bird doesn't move, doesn't blink. It stares in our direction. "Maybe you're right."

Slowly, Cove and I move forward, watching the bird watch us. At Transition House the other day, at the bird exhibit on the science floor, I read a bird fact that said: Birds can attack when humans approach their nesting area. Maybe the bird has babies nearby, worried we'll take 'em. Cove speeds past the bird; when he does, it flies toward him, shits on his jacket, and soars away.

I laugh.

Cove scoffs at feces on his jacket, disgusted. "JFC." Cove removes his jacket, rolls it up, carries it.

"JFC?"

"Jesus fucking Christ."

I push my iCom communication chip. "iCom, what does it mean when birds shit on clothes?"

Cove laughs. "You're a little annoying."

I scrunch my face, wiggle my nose. "I know."

"Can't believe you're asking . . ."

"Ah, come on, that never happens. I've known no one, and I mean positively no one, who got shit on by birds. Has to mean something."

"Answer retrieved," iCom says.

"This should be good." Cove shakes his head.

"There are three probable meanings of birds defecating on humans. Possibility one: Birds are message carriers, and travel crossing borders. A bird's feces could mean you're wanting to go on vacation."

"Wanna leave New Georgia?"

Cove doesn't respond. His lips part as if preparing to speak, then close. I don't force his answer.

iCom continues, "Possibility two: Birds symbolize spirituality, and were once worshipped as gods. Possibility three: Economically, birds defecating on humans signal good fortune, luck, or an increased income soon."

We pace down the path. "Do you believe in God?" I ask.

"Birds' shit turns into a conversation about belief, huh? Alright, I'll give. Umm, God. I don't know. Maybe."

"What do you mean?"

"Religion"—he clears his throat—"When it comes to that stuff . . . I eat the meat, spit out the bones." Cove's answer isn't straight, but I accept it. Don't wanna make him tell stuff he's not ready to share. He searches the sky for more birds and speaks. "What about you? Do you believe in God?"

"Yeah, but it's genderless, without body or name."

Cove walks a little ahead. His arms are bare, veins visible tracing down to his hands. I wanna hold his hand, but I don't. I wanna jump on his back, but I don't. I want too many things with Cove. And I haven't felt this way about a boy since Boah. But I knew Boah like freckles on skin. I don't know Cove like that, but when Cove's close, it feels like that's where he's supposed to be.

Cove humphs. "I wish . . ."

I try meeting Cove's eyes, but he won't look back. "What do you wish?"

"Nothing."

"Why do you do that? Close up like that."

"Like what?"

"Like you just did. It's like you're suffocating in thoughts."

"I don't know what you want." Cove reaches for my hand.

I back away, put both palms up, then drop them. "I'm gonna take a walk." I shouldn't walk away. But Cove's walls are so high, doesn't seem like his heart and mind are reachable.

He scoffs, "We are walking."

"Alone." I leave Cove's side, irritated. I feel him watching me leave, but I won't turn to meet his eyes.

In the distance, I spot a mausoleum. It's dingy, eerie, exquisite. I find its entrance slightly open. Inside, I sit on the stone bench that circles the space, and shortly after, I stretch my body along the cold stone. There is a peace in this darkness, peace inside my head, no noise, sounds to drown out what's on my mind.

I want Cove to open up, but he won't. I wanna cram Cove like he studies biochem. But he won't let me in, and I don't know why. He's afraid of something. I know it isn't me, and I'm irritated. I'm in the dark, playing Guess Cove's Mind. Cove's like Boah was in this way—I suppose he's a lot like most boys his age, and some girls, too. Why is it this way? It's like the more folks know about you, the less they try to keep you.

I reach down to retie my shoes. The mausoleum's door closes. I stand. Trying peering through darkness. Shoes scrape against the cement, but they're not my shoes. Someone's here. In here with me. On the other side of the dark room, echoes of their breaths fill the surrounding space. If there were light in here, it'd reveal my large pupils, reflect arched, frantic brows and wrinkles between my eyes.

And there it is again, the scraping; it's closer. It's so close it feels touchable, reachable. I move forward, toward the scraping. And the scraping stops. My heart drums, my pulse races, head tenses; I feel blood flowing up and down my veins.

I stick my neck out. I sense them. Hear their light breathing. They're in front of me. Inches away. It's too dark to see; I extend my arm, reach for them, but the scraping starts again. Slow, barely audible.

"Jo!" Cove calls from outside. I back away from the person here, toward the wall behind me. The tips of my fingers brush over icy walls as I walk toward the door.

The doors crack open. I search for the handle behind me. Jerk the door ajar, but it's hard to get it wide enough to squeeze through.

"Jo?"

I turn, press my face into the cracked door, speak through the slit. "In here." The sun warms my nose and blinks on my chin.

Cove dashes to the door; we open it together, allow outside light to fill this dark space. When the door is wide enough, Cove helps me out; he breathes heavily, eyes wild with worry. "You hurt? Okay?"

I don't respond. I turn, scan the mausoleum. It's empty.

34

COVE

It was a mistake bringing Jo here. So far, she's watched me chicken out over birds, been stuck in a mausoleum, and got pissed when I shut down her questions. Being vulnerable feels naked—like being nude before a stadium of strangers—naked and dangerous. Being here with Jo feels dangerous. I'm going to like Jo more before the night's through, and the stepwitch won't approve.

Paranoia sets in. I skim the riverbanks as we glide down the Savannah River in a canoe. Were Elenore spying, she'd hire a drone to follow me—have it hide, taking shots to show later. I push radical thoughts of Elenore's rage aside, concentrate on controlling the paddles. Oars whoosh as whitecaps meet metallic-blue waters. I inhale the scents of wet dirt, onion grass, pine, and river water. Swans float on the outskirts of the river, basking in hot sun.

At the end of the canoe Jo sits with her arms spread wide, the tips of her fingers reaching toward huge trees and mountains cradling both sides of the mighty river. She grins like a kid at the sight of diving beavers, dragonflies whirling just above her nose, and herons wailing in the blue sky.

When the canoe dives over small rocks, Jo clasps her life jacket, eyes closed waiting for the fall. A bumblebee lands on my nose. I try to play it cool, but I'm afraid of yellow jackets, wasps, and anything that stings, so I flinch, swiping at the buzzing insect with a scrunched face.

Jo catches my fear and laughs. "Scared of insects, too? Not just birds, then?" she teases. At least she's talking to me, not mad anymore. I hope.

I lower my eyes, knowing my face is red. "Maybe."

She smirks. "Mhm."

"And you . . . scared of anything?"

Jo shrugs, smiling. "I've been skydiving. So, I'm fearless."

I smile, almost laugh, shaking my head. Our chins to the sky, we watch a murder of crows spread their wings and pass overhead.

"Why *Great Expectations*?" I ask. "At the Gala, Kyra said you carried it around nonstop."

"It gave me hope. I'd open *Great Expectations* and the crazy world disappeared. Charles Dickens made the gunshots go away. In my mind, I became Pip—a blacksmith optimistic about the future, who gets a mysterious benefactor who changes his stars. I was always waiting for the Lineup."

I nod. "At the end, what happened to Magwitch was sad."

It's too far to be a threat, but in the distance, walking on grass, Jo spots an alligator and smiles. With her arm extended in front of her, Jo claps her hands together to mimic an alligator's mouth. She's silly. I like that about her. But I can't let her make me laugh. Laughing's worse than kissing sometimes. It's my firm belief only geniuses create laughter in others. If she's smart enough to make me laugh, she's crafty enough to make me feel, make me open.

"What are those?" Jo points at the globes gliding inches above the river.

"They're called Speres."

"What are they used for?"

"Non-platonic activities."

Jo chuckles. "Gotcha." She glances over her shoulder, gazes away from me. "Back home we have the water hole."

"Like a water fountain?"

242

She laughs, shaking her head no. "It's an old warehouse everyone used to make out in."

"Who did you go there with?"

Jo grins, but she doesn't answer the question.

The canoe stops, floats in a little pond area. Surrounding us, birds rattle in and out of whistling trees. Chattering squirrels tackle one another, racing, chasing tails, spiraling up and down massive pines. In the near distance, a thunderous cascade flows over moss-covered stones, spraying as it crashes into thrashing waters.

This is the other thing I want to show to Jo. This waterfall—it's picturesque and charming like her. It's my safe place. I visit it to escape Elenore's voice and Margo's pill problem.

Jo buries a surprised smile behind her hands. Eyes wide, she faces me, then turns back to look at the waterfall. She grips both sides of the canoe and twists at the waist. In sheer joy, she pulls her bottom lip into her mouth, smiling. At the sight of this, I'm like butter in a hot pan, sliding from one space to the next, melting slowly at the center.

Elenore's in my head, so I heed her advice, try not to get too personal, too attached. But I'm a fucked-up chameleon, and my brain's a bag of wacko Skittles. But my mind's not so fucked up it can't see that Elenore's teachings about love don't apply to everyone. And I'm scratching my head because Jo's not like girls Elenore warns about—girls who toy with love like airheads twisting gum around index fingers. Jo wouldn't break a heart for the hell of it. Jo's good. She's not like me, Margo, and the stepwitch.

Jo braids her three long braids together, and her hair blows in the wind. She lifts her shirt, pulls it over her head, and reveals a black bikini top. Then wiggles out of her jeans, revealing smooth brown legs. She folds her clothes and sets them in the center of the canoe. She grins, then dives headfirst into the river.

It's been sixty seconds, and Jo hasn't surfaced. There are no rivers, oceans, brooks, and streams in the Ashes. All their drinking water comes from New Georgia. Since the Ashes is barren and waterless, there's no way she'd know how to—Fuck. Jo can't swim.

It's been two minutes. Still no sight of her. "Jo?" I call out. "Jo!"

I set the oars in the middle of the canoe and jump into the river fully clothed.

I search for her, neck circling, shifting direction every few seconds. Scanning above, below, and beyond the river.

"Cove!" Her voice comes from above the water. I break to the surface, relieved to hear her voice. "Over here," she says. With a smile, her slender arms extend above her head. She's waving me over.

Jo sits on a high moss-ridden hill left of the waterfall. I exhale, releasing air I'd been holding.

I've never swum in this river. For years I've paddled these waters, never feeling its warmth or allowing the current to touch me.

Jo lays her back against the mossy stone. I climb toward her. Climbing is new, too. The rough texture pressing into my palms, the brittle grass rubbing my toes, the earthy smells of moss filling my nose. This is the life. I feel wild, free. It's as if I've been living in a coma of my own making. Now I'm awake. Alive.

When I reach the top, Jo's upright, her arms hugging her knees, her eyes full of wonder.

"What took you so long, slowpoke?" Jo smirks, wrings water out of her long coily tresses. I stare at the water dripping from her black hair. I like it flowing, but I prefer it braided.

"How'd you learn to swim?"

Jo's face is a sea of mischief. "The Brown River," she says, adjusting her legs so she's sitting cross-legged.

"Where's that?" I twist water from my clothes. I reach to take my shirt off, then stop. I can't take the risk. How do you tell the girl you're crushing on that you're a eighteen-year-old boy who allows his stepmother to beat and manipulate him? Easy answer: You don't. You keep up the facade or push her away. Not being near Jo isn't an option. I'm selfish with her. She's my secret treasure chest. I wanna hold on to her, protect her. So, the mask stays on, and the facade continues.

"Sure you wanna know?" she teases.

I nod. "Wait. Brown River? That's not what I think it is, is it? A river full of sh—"

Jo narrows her eyes at me, pauses, then playfully hits my arm. "Ewww. No, nasty." She laughs. "In the summer and sometimes near the end of spring, we'd get these horrible, beyond terrible, dangerous tropical storms in the Ashes. There're no rivers. No oceans like here. So we'd pray for storms. 'Cause when it rains hard, streets flood, and waters flow into our homes. And so OldTimers—"

"OldTimers?"

"People who live in the Ashes now, but before Revolt 2030, they lived here, in New Georgia," Jo explains.

I've always felt the revolt was a great cause to end discrimination, but the aftermath of the revolution sounds a lot like the travesties that started the uprising in 2030 in the first place. It's as if RR's back then were fighting for revenge, not justice. Or maybe they fought, protested for both, and sometime after they formed the New States in 2030, they lost sight of the real purpose.

But maybe in a way, the Lineup and the Gala, the Transition Program, and all of it, makes up for all the bloodshed and freedoms lost. The generations of kids affected by the class switch get a chance to change their stars, get rich, and be successful over here and all that. That didn't exist for my ancestors pre-revolt.

Jo continues, "When rain hits dirt it turns brown; brown water filled the streets. It was our pool. So we called it Brown River. OldTimers taught us to swim in it."

"Glad it wasn't the other thing."

Jo smirks. "Mhm." She bumps her small shoulder into my right arm.

I stare at her spread fingers behind her back—she brings them to her lap. I take her hand in mine, place it on my lap. Jo doesn't look at me, but I see her. She's smiling. Me too.

I lean back on elbows, stare at the moon-phase tattoos running down her spine. Jo's stunning as fuck. And Jesus, I want to know what her skin feels like, smells like.

None of the girls in New Georgia have tattoos, and I've never seen one this close up before. Just in pictures Aurice showed us from his excursions over the mountains.

There's magic in our differences. Jo's unique in a way that's not cheesy. She's a fountain of secrets, a perfect mystery. Freedom lives in Jo's smile—there's so much life in her teeth, I want to be a part of that freedom. I ask if she'll tell me more about her old life. She tells me about violence in the Ashes. Explains turmoil in a fashion sympathetic to the bully and bullied. "If folks are taught and raised in violence, doesn't make sense getting mad when they respond to problems that way." Jo lifts her chin to the fading sun.

Jo's rare, special. It's mind-boggling she can do that—inspire sympathy for individuals who treat good people like shit. I feel good with her. Like nothing Jo touches'll ever turn evil. She sees the good in everything. I think of telling her about my past. I don't, but if she asked, I wonder what I'd tell? I feel like she's the kind of girl who'll consume all the shitty shit of my life. Like I can throw all my darkness in a cauldron, and somehow, Jo'd magically turn it into chicken noodle soup.

I smile at her. "It's getting dark. Let's head back."

Night hasn't arrived, but it will soon.

The river's nothing like the riot it was earlier. It's steady, calm like whispers. The moon glistens on still waters and borders sharp, uneven gray rocks. I stroke forward, continue farther downstream. It's narrow and murky here, but soon we'll reach a space so wide open night sky will glisten over ripples in the water.

I paddle slowly, not really using the oars, just allowing the current to steer our path.

"You're hard to read," I say.

"Ask your questions."

"What are you thinking?"

"Are you always so serious?" Jo says.

"What makes you think I'm serious?"

Jo watches the oars dip in and out of water. "You never laugh."

She's right, but I'm not about to admit it. I shrug, tilting my head. "And what? You laugh all the time? You're always happy?"

She hums. "Is that it, then?—you're unhappy?"

I shake my head, humph. "Has anyone ever told you, you ask a lot of questions?"

"Yes."

"Oh yeah?—who?"

"The same person who said you avoid them," she says.

Coyotes howl, frogs croak, and crickets sing. Dry wind blows Jo's coily hair forward. I think she's beautiful. I push the unspoken compliment away; replace it with Elenore's warning label for Jo. She'd said Jo's the kind of girl who won't open up unless you come clean first.

There's gotta be a way to work this to my advantage. So that Jo can't win.

Maybe I'll ask questions implementing Elenore's training, surface topics I don't mind answering. Controlling the narrative's the only way. If I can do that, if I succeed, we'll stay clear of the "are you happy?" query, the "boy loses parents as a kid, now an orphan" storyline, and the "evil stepmother beats stepson" logline. That should work. It's possible.

The canoe's steady, rocking, floating like a baby's cradle. And the scenery's cool, crazy-chill, like an old black man playing guitar, puffing a vintage pipe.

Jo stares at me. I focus on paddling, contemplating safe questions. I shake off cowardliness, mentally drink a little courage. I part my lips to speak.

Jo stretches her legs across the canoe, rests the back of her head against the boat. "I could stay out here forever," she says.

"Could you?"

"Couldn't you?"

"Seen one river, you've seen them all, right?"

"Wouldn't know." Jo points her nose to velvet sky, like she's taking the whole wide world in. "Is Margo okay?" Jo draws the letter S on top of the river. "Earlier I saw you—"

"—carry her, yeah. She, uh, had a little too much drink last night," I say. "And a little too much this morning too."

"You drink?"

"Not if I can help it."

"Why is that?" Jo says.

"It killed my father." I look away, into the ripples in the water, biting my lip, confused I've shared this with a girl. I realize this is the moment, the moment Elenore says to avoid. Heartskin. It's too late, I can't take it back, but maybe I can slow it down. Control how much information I hand out for the rest of the night.

Jo lifts her head off the canoe, stares at me. "Mine too," she says.

"Father, too?"

Jo nods. I can tell she wants to know more—more about me, who I am. I'm shit-fuck afraid to give her more. And yet. I open my mouth. "More questions?"

Jo parts her lips to speak, pauses, and continues, "What's your biggest regret?"

More Heartskin questions. I want to seal my lips, but I can't close my mouth. "The night before my father died, he wanted to take me out to eat. I refused, told him no. I wasn't tired, sleepy, wasn't even not hungry. Hadn't eaten at all that day. I didn't go because I was ashamed."

Jo touches my knee briefly. "Of what?"

"Him. His bones. A year before his death, my father became like my mother— stopped eating. He was thin, skeletal. I regret not spending that moment with him. I could've gotten one more hug—" I pause, my voice cracks; I clear my throat and speak. "I miss her smile and how she'd drive for miles for my favorite ice cream. I think of all the times shame kept me from going out in public with her. It embarrassed me how the world would see her—how it would see me."

Jo's face is angelic and nonjudgmental. "How old were you when it happened?"

"Young. Ten. You get one more serious question."

"One, huh? I better make it good." Jo rubs her palms together with a sly look on her face. "Do you believe in love?"

I nod. "It's complicated."

"How do you mean?" she says.

"Let's just say Elenore has a unique perspective on love."

Jo stretches her arms above her head. "Which is?" Her arms fall into her lap.

"That it's unnatural, dangerous." I wanna tell her we're creatures of habit, made of lessons taught by parents. I say nothing. Watch a brown leaf blow into

Jo's hair. I remove it and paddle on. Make deep strokes into the river. "I used to dream of life over the mountains, what it'd be like."

"Oh yeah? What'd your dreams show you?" she asks.

"It's silly."

Jo frowns. "Don't do that. Tell me."

"In my dreams I'm dirty. Mud all over my clothes kinda dirty. Crazy, I know. But, everything's so put together here. Abnormally clean. I had to be the only boy who'd rather run topless in the middle of the street barefoot than spend money. I guess I thought if I wasn't here, and lived there, I'd—" I gaze at blue mountain peaks in the distance. It feels safe with Jo, like there's almost nothing I could reveal to her that she wouldn't accept, and possibly one day, love.

"You'd what?"

"Be free. Dirt face and all, I'd be free. Free without—"

"Without what?—people thinking you're crazy?"

"Yeah, something like that."

Jo fans gnats away, swats a mosquito eating her thigh. "We're all crazy, playing normal."

I glance at Jo's toes. I like them. They're eight light-brown tiny fingers, beside two chubby pinky toes.

Jo curves over her knees. With an extended forearm, she slides her fingers inside jean pockets, searching for something. When her hand resurfaces, she's holding a tiny bag full of red dirt.

"Where'd that come from? No red dirt like that here," I say.

"Vye gave it to me before the Gala."

I think back to the conversation Kyra and I had at the pier. "She talks to Jessup, right?"

Jo gives me a curious look. "How'd you—" she says.

"Kyra," I say.

"Should've known—chatty, that one. She can't hold water." She smirks. "What else she tell you?"

"The jig story," I say. "And Boah."

Jo rolls her eyes. "Don't give me that look."

"What look?"

Jo reaches into the river. "That look." She splashes water on me, and I duck. She continues. "The condescending one that says Boah's not just a friend."

"I gave that look?"

"Mhm, you did."

Jo never addresses the Boah issue. It doesn't matter; he's dead. Still, I want her to open up to me about it. But it's cool. And besides, we're all allowed little secrets. I have more than a few myself.

"You think you're slick." She laughs, then reaches out and playfully pushes my leg.

I laugh. "Nah, not me."

Jo beams. "Cove has teeth! Who knew?" She giggles, reaches out to tickle me; I grab her fingers before they reach my belly.

I look down at her fingers in my hand; trace her skin with the tip of my thumb.

Jo nervously takes her hand away. She wiggles the sack of red dirt in front of her nose; she kneels in the center of the canoe, knees pressed in folded jeans. "Come over?" she says.

"Why?—what are you up to?"

With an index finger, Jo points down to her jeans, grinning. She has a dimple on her left cheek.

I bend down, thighs parallel to hers, knees meshing into denim.

Jo loses her balance. The canoe rocks a little. I grab Jo's elbows, balancing her and the narrow boat. She looks down at the space between us, clenching the bag of red dirt. She pours a little in her palm, grabs water from the river, and turns red dirt into red mud. "Stay still," she says. And I do.

She lathers her hands with mud, reaches for my face. I flinch, pulling away from her. The canoe wobbles. "Trust me," she says. I lean into her. "Close your eyes." I want to question her, ask her why. I don't.

Jo draws lines up and down my face with red mud. It's squishy, a little gritty, cold. Yet weightless. I feel wild, free; adventurous—the eleven-year-old in me smiles, cheeks cheesing hard ear to ear. I open my eyes.

"My turn." Jo closes her eyes. "Do me."

I take the mud from Jo's hand and put it in mine. Mark her face with red mud, like she marked mine. With ease, I paint three horizontal lines below her cheekbones, two zigzags across her forehead, and one line straight down the center of her face, forehead to nose to chin.

Jo takes my hands in hers. "See, you don't have to wish for it anymore."

"Wish for what?" I say.

"The dirt. You're part of the Ashes now." She looks over my shoulder. "Look," she says.

In her eyes, I see them before I turn to look.

Fireflies, thousands of them, surround us; they're brightly burning, floating like lassoed stars. I could not have planned a better romantic scene to make Jo fall for me. But I realize now, it's not a game with Jo. I don't wanna be a fuckboy and whisper pretty little lies in her pretty little ears. I want to hold her—cuddle her—treasure her like a leprechaun hoarding gold coins.

If Margo could hear me now, she'd call me a pussy for wanting that. Right about now, she could call me whatever she wants. I don't care. Feelings for Jo are real. Purer than anything I've ever felt for a girl. And not having Jo is more terrifying than fear.

I never tell girls *I like you close.* "I like you this close." I pull her into me; our bellies touch.

Jo shakes her head no. "I don't like it," she says.

"What's that?" I say with mild panic. "What don't you like?" My eyes shift left to right, searching for answers in Jo's eyes.

"I don't like that I like being this close to you." She looks away from me, avoiding eye contact. "I heard you."

I find her eyes. "You heard what?" She's going to bring up the asshole night again. The Gala. I swear, in the history of bad moves, I'll never live that night down.

She hums, with a light chuckle, wipes her tears away. "The reading. I heard it."

Oh. "I didn't know you could hear me. I thought you were sleeping."

"I know you did. And I was. But . . . somehow, I was awake, too." Jo pauses for a second, then adds, "Is this the cool thing . . .? What you wanted'deh show me?—the fireflies?"

"Part of it." I stare at her bottom lip, then her top lip, then her eyes, then back down to her bottom lip. Jo's heart moves fast under her skin. I watch her chest rise and fall and fall and rise. I lean into her, press my lips to her shoulder, and smile there. I'm a ball of nerves.

Jo takes my face into her hands. I weave our fingers together and move close, closer. Kiss her forehead soft. I rub my nose left to right across her nose; I feel butterflies. And I'm counting in my head . . . 150 . . . 181 . . . 205, 206 seconds.

Time moves, even when we're standing still. I reach 240; we've been staring at each other for four minutes. I wonder if Jo's chest feels as warm and heavy as mine does. Warm like sun, heavy like bricks.

"I like you," I say.

Jo releases a heavy sigh. "I like you, too, Cove." She presses into my torso, shaking, a little sweaty. I'm sweaty too.

My heart's beating so fast I can't track my pulse. Now I'm panting, nearly breathless.

I place my hands on either side of Jo's waist, press my lips into her mouth, sigh there, kiss there.

Kissing Jo is like drinking terror and excitement. Scared shitless feeling these things. And yet, every vein in my body desires more doses of Jo. Feeling this way makes me understand why Elenore's against kissing. I'll never tell Jo, but her mouth makes me feel tender, soft, gentle like my skin's made of water. Like if right now, someone gave me the nicest of compliments, it'd make me wanna cry.

35

JOSEPHINE

Cove thinks he's faster than me. I'll let him think it for a little while, but he's wrong. I'm faster. While running, scents of wood fill my nose; warm sun kisses my bare shoulders. And every now and then, leftover raindrops on tree leaves drop, watering my forehead.

"Hurry up, slowpoke."

"Slow, huh?" I sprint past him.

"Oh, no you don't—" Cove grabs me from behind, scoops me up, and swings me onto his back. He gives me a piggyback ride through hundreds of massive white birch trees until we're standing before a vast meadow quilted with unusually tall red sunflowers.

The stunning flora surrounding us reminds me of one-on-one science classes with Gaitlin at Transition House. Gaitlin enjoys dissecting flowers more than pig's brains. Together we plucked living petals from stems, tore them into pieces, and viewed them under high-tech microscopes, then processed the parts from the outside in, examining the stamen, pistil, and ovaries of daffodils, tiger lilies, orchids, and sunflowers. Afterward, Gaitlin'd instruct manual examination of flowers via hand lens, observational art sketches. Lately, Cove comes to get me right after.

Cove picks up the pace; arms holding my legs around him, he stops again. His breathing is calm. Arms around his neck, I place my hand on the part of his shirt covering his heart; it races.

"You cheated," I accuse.

Cove runs to the center of the lush field and pats my thigh gently. "Ready to climb down, slowpoke?"

I kiss the back of his head, slide down his tailbone, and snatch a sunflower, inhale its sweet scent. If Valentine's Day had a dedicated flower, this would be it. I tug it from the root, pluck petals and count as I blow 'em away.

I lie down with my neck on a bed of clover, letting sun warm my nose. Cove lies next to me on his back, and our shoulders touch. He places both hands behind his head. I roll onto my side, staring at him. I want my tongue in his mouth. Wanna kiss him again.

Cove faces me. "A toke for your thoughts."

I wanna tell him that he's strong, intelligent, and confident, but sometimes, when he's talking with Elenore, I fear he doesn't think he's good enough. And last thing I want to do is make that fear worse. "I don't know, you tell me what's on your mind."

He smirks, says, "Hmm, *Little Women*? Charles Dickens?"

I throw a petal at him, grinning. "What made you read tuh me?"

Cove clears his throat. "Let's play a truth and a lie."

"What's that?" I climb on top of him, rest my head on his chest.

He kisses the top of my head. "Just this game my sister and I played growing up. I ask you a question, and you respond with one truth and one lie."

"How will you know truth from fiction?"

"That's why it's a game." He kisses my head and rubs the small of my back. "And if you can't figure out which is which, just ask."

"Okay." I nudge Cove's chest with my chin. "A truth and a lie."

"Alright, ask me something," he says.

"Like what?" I say.

"Anything you wanna know."

"You go first." I bury my nose in his chest.

"Sure?" he says.

I nod, then he says, "You know what? Let's just talk. No lies." He wraps his arms around me.

My cheeks rise, chin upright against his sandalwood-scented shirt.

"Your cheeks are moving," he says. "Why?"

I hear 'em smiling. "The no lies part."

He lifts his head, stares down at me, eyebrows raised.

"I like that."

"Ready for your question?" he says.

"Sure." I brace myself for Cove's question. He can ask me anything really, but deep down, I hope he doesn't ask about Boah. Boah's a topic that's hard to think about.

"Play any instruments?" Cove asks.

I relax a little. "I played viola," I say. "Wanted to play the cello, but it was too expensive to rent."

"Enjoyed playing it?—viola?"

"I did. I enjoyed it, but like all things growing up in the Ashes, I knew we didn't have enough money to sustain my interest, so I quit before money was an issue."

Cove nods.

I pluck more petals. "What about you? Play anything besides girls?"

"What makes you think I—"

"Edith. What's the herstory there?"

He shrugs. "What's the story with you and Boah?"

I shake my head. "Instruments?"

"What?" He narrows his eyes, confused.

"You play any?"

"Nice transition." He chuckles.

"I thought so."

Cove stares at a bumblebee feeding on the flowers. It flies toward his face, sits on the tip of his nose, and then flies away. "Uh, yeah. Piano."

"Did you like playing it?"

"Lessons didn't end till fingers were bloody." Cove laughs, but his eyes are frowns.

Cove gets a call from Margo in the meantime. He answers it, says he'll see her when he gets home. After the call, he asks, "What's a kitchen?"

"Ummm, where you cook things?"

Cove laughs. "Now you're the one with the jokes." His lips part like he's itching to say something he doesn't want to. "That night at the Gala, Kyra said you were tugging at your kitchen while reading *Great Expectations*."

I reach behind my back, remove Cove's hand, and place his fingers on the back of my neck.

"What's wrong?" he says.

"Feel the little curly hairs—the nappy ones?" I say. "That's my kitchen."

"Ah, I see, but why's it called that?" He's serious, genuinely wants to know.

I grin at his ignorance, but I wanna tell him so he knows. "Vye says it's called a kitchen 'cause when America had slaves, cooking areas were in the back of the house, near chimneys and backyards, 'cause cooks and field slaves weren't seen or heard—they were hidden. That's where the term kitchen comes from—curly parts of hair hidden in the back, just above the neck."

"It doesn't feel nappy," he says. "Curly, maybe."

"Trust me, if I took a comb to it, I'd yelp," I laugh. And then Cove laughs, and then it's my turn to ask him a question.

Cove arches his lower spine, stretching.

I lift my cheek from his torso, plant my chin there, watching his nostrils flare—then I roll off his stomach, lie chest up, rear end comfy-cozy against warm ground.

Cove lies on his side, props up on one elbow. "What's your question?" he says, smiling until my question comes out.

"I like you a little."

Cove laughs. "That's not a question."

"Why don't you tell me more."

"Tell you what?"

"That you like me."

Cove shrugs, stares at my head, removes three red petals from my hair. "I'm an asshole sometimes."

"Plan on being an asshole anytime soon?"

"Not to you." Cove fans a petal off my thigh. "What about you?"

"What about me, what?"

He scoffs. "Plan on being an asshole? I have it on good authority, girls are assholes too."

"Yeah, but—"

"Yeah, but what?" he says.

"You don't strike me as the kind of boy who has to worry about that . . . seems it's the other way around with you," I say.

Cove humphs, releases a soft chuckle, and places the palm of his hand over my belly button.

"What's on your mind right now? Don't think about the questions this time, just blurt it out," I say. Cove gets this look on his face—a somber gaze. Makes him more attractive, something I'd not thought possible.

He moves his hand away to scratch his neck. "Sometimes, you zone out; it's like you're somewhere else. And wherever that place is, I can't reach you. Where do you go inside your head?" He plays with a curl of my hair. "I can't figure you out."

I know exactly what he means, and there's too much to say. I settle for "I didn't leave home in a good place. Every now and then, my mind drifts there."

"What do you miss most?"

I face him. "Vye and—"

"—Boah?"

"Yeah . . . Boah. I never got to say goodbye. He died, and, well . . . I woke up in New Georgia. It's not like I can chat or message them with iCom. There're no landlines or cell towers in the Ashes."

"How do you communicate . . . reach people?"

I sway my feet left to right, stare at four shoes. My red kicks. His white sneakers. "Ike and Mike, bikes, or if we're lucky, by car. Life's better that way, like real human connection, you know?"

Cove nods. "Oh, I get it. I just can't imagine life without iCom."

"Vye always says, it's amazing whatcha don't miss when you don't use it. She was born here, pre–Revolt 2030."

Cove just watches me, until I turn on my side toward him. He says, "I want you closer."

"I'd like that."

Cove pulls me into his chest. "What else do you miss about the Ashes?" he presses.

I feel the rise and fall of his chest, his arms warm around me. "There's an old roller coaster near this place called the wasteland in the Ashes. Has the best view of the sky. Morning time, the sun was huge up there. I miss it. Climbing it—"

With Boah, I wanna say, but don't. Don't mention Vye. Jessup, Neal.

I push bad thoughts to the back of my head. I flatten my scrunched forehead, force a smile between my nose and chin.

I reach a hand around Cove's body. "Tell me something nobody knows." I rub Cove's back; he jerks away with what sounds like a faint ouch, then pulls away from me, sits up. Why would a light touch hurt him?

"We should go. Promised Margo I'd help her study," he says, agitated.

I figure I've done something or said something wrong, but I don't know what that something is. Cove doesn't seem up to talking about it. He's sitting right here beside me, and he feels miles and miles away.

I wanna ask 'em why he jerked when I tried to touch him, but I don't. "What subject does Margo need help with?"

Cove won't look me in the eye. He wipes dirt away from his shirt and shorts. "Anatomy, I think."

I nod like I believe him, but I don't.

He's lying. You don't have to think about the truth—it's quick—tight like a second skin. I watch dirt fly every which way off his clothes. And then I see Cove's pale fingers, strong pale palm, smooth tan hand, reaching out for me to take it.

And I do.

36

COVE

Margo bursts through my bedroom door. "Jo's nails are in your back so deep, you'd think *she* put the scars there."

Staring at her pink stilettos, I finish my last set of push-ups, and stand bare chested before her.

After checking me out, Margo narrows both eyes and throws my white towel into my chest. "I used to look up to you. Thought it magical how effortlessly you broke hearts without an air of conscience. But you're pathetic now. You know? Useless." Margo's words slur. I remind myself interrupting drunk Margo is fruitless. I bite my sarcastic tongue. She continues, "And to think . . . I wanted to be you, so my mother—*my* mother!—would love me, like she seems to love you. She's my mother! Not yours. Yours couldn't hold food and died." Margo snickers, but when all I give her is an impassive stare, she frowns and shrugs away from the doorjamb.

Moments later, her bedroom door shuts, followed by loud sappy tunes. Margo's words don't sting. I'm used to my sister's drunken rambling. But there's truth in Margo's rage. She wasn't lying about Jo.

Caring for Jo is peeling me, breaking me down. It feels like a crane hit me— divided me into fractions. I'm two halves—a sagittal plane—dorsally Elenore's, ventrally Jo's. And fuck, I'm tired of lies. This secret's devouring me. Denying Jo's touch in the forest consumes me, swallows me whole like pythons consuming rats.

But what other choice did I have? Truth didn't feel like an option; running did. So, I pushed her away. Had Jo touched my back, she'd've felt the scars. No one's ever been that close to me. Besides Margo. I care about Jo—I do—but . . . I don't know. Something hiding inside's not ready for her to see the scars. Guilt pinches, berates, and claws me—makes my insides roll into a tiny ball like a terrestrial crustacean. I gotta call her, make her understand it's not her, it's me, and do all this without telling her the truth.

I instruct iCom to reach Jo. The call goes through, but Jo's not picking up. Thoughts of her ignoring my calls because she's mad at me drive me insane. I've fucked up, and I can't think straight. I've never been afraid of losing anything, especially a girl. And here I am tripping over one. I call her again. No answer. With sweaty palms, my mind paces, wondering if Jo'll reach out, call or message. I wanna tell her I'm sorry without saying *sorry*. And then I do just wanna say *sorry* and be so fucking wide open my heart erupts. Were Jo here I'd kneel before her, and the hell with it, I'd show her my scars and be done with damn secrets.

But Jo's not answering, and not knowing why, or if we're even okay after today, feels like a new desperation, bordering on nervous breakdown. I'm weak and ashamed. Anxiety wells in my chest. And it feels tight there, just above the rib cage. It's convoluted with self-doubt, unworthiness, and insecurity I've never felt before.

Maybe all boys feel this way. Maybe that's why they're assholes sometimes in the first place, and never wanna say "I like you" or "I love you" first in relationships because the person who says the mushy phrase first is the loser and the other the victor. Maybe it shouldn't be this game of freeze-tag-you're-it in things like this. Perhaps honesty is the way. But being open is scary. It's like convincing myself to bungee-jump without a harness.

iCom chirps. I stop pacing the floors in my bedroom, flash a brief smile, frown, and huff. It's not Jo. It's Margo from down the hall. I tell iCom not to pick up.

It's nine p.m.

iCom says I have a call from Margo, again. I think of answering this time, but I don't. Why doesn't she come back down the hall? I wonder where Jo is.

Outside in the backyard, I climb the ladder on the side of our house that leads to the roof. Up here, I sit on the edge, elbows on knees, gazing at happy couples entering Hugo Park across the street.

I want to do that with Jo, walk with her, have that with her. But that kind of happiness doesn't come with lies.

I look over my knees, think of stories Jo told about climbing the old roller coaster in the Ashes.

I back away from the edge of the roof, stand, make my way down the narrow white ladder and back into the house.

Something CRASHES.

It's something that sounds like glass . . .

And that something's in my bedroom.

In front of my bedroom door, I twist the knob, suspiciously turning it until it clicks and the door pushes open.

"You son of a fucking bitch!" James swings, gunning for my left eye. I duck, swing, jab him in the stomach. James falls back, holding his belly. And I shut the door behind me. "You plucked her?" He swings again, gets me this time, straight in the chest.

I stumble back, lunge forward, punch him again in the stomach. Give him a left hook, uppercut, right jab. James falls to the ground, rises like the dead, scrambles to his feet, shoves me into my dresser, where my crystal high-school rowing championship trophy crashes to the floor, shards of the glass rushing under my bed.

I grab him—he holds me back, tries to steady himself with my weight. "Are you done now? You wanna talk?" I gasp.

"Not even close, fuckboy," he says. James wraps a firm palm around my elbow; he swings me around, slams my spine against the wall on the other side of the room. "You could have anyone. You can have anyone you want, and you just had to swipe her?"

James breathes heavy; his hands reach for my throat, but I'm stronger than him and grab his neck first. I spin him around, pin his back to the wall. While I grip his pulsing trachea, James's fingers stretch toward my eyes, trying to push 'em out of the sockets.

In a swift move, I press my forearm into his neck; he grabs my arms with both hands, struggling against the hold. With my free hand, I position myself behind him, put him in a chokehold.

"Listen, James, let's not do this."

"Why'd you fuck her, bruh?" James says, elbowing my ribs.

"I don't wanna fight you," I say. "I'm not letting you go until you calm down."

"Don't tell me to be fucking calm. You calm down, bruh," he says, panting. I loosen my grip so he can breathe better, but I don't release him. He continues, "How could you do it, Cove? How could you?"

"How could I do what?" I hate myself for pretending I don't know.

James chuckles sarcastically. "Don't play fucking dumb. You plucked Edith."

"How'd you find out?" It's something I don't have to ask. He should know. Edith's his girlfriend. I'm a shitty best friend. I release the chokehold.

James turns around, socks my right eye. "What the fuck does that matter? She's mine . . . been mine three years. How do you think I know? She told me, you bastard." He swings for my face again.

I duck, dodge the hit, put up my dukes. "Help me out, James, 'cause I'm racking my brain, trying to figure something out here."

"Oh yeah?—what's that?" James raises both fists, moves his feet fast, dancing around like Creed in classic Rocky films.

"You've known since we were kids. Who she belongs to. She was never going to be yours."

James's voice is like thunder. "Motherfucker, I know that." I've never seen James this angry. I'm not scared of him, but I'm more than a little uncomfortable not knowing what he'll do next. And I'm worried about the mean things we'll say or do to each other, things that once said will ruin our friendship, because we can't take them back. He continues, "Her future isn't now. She's mine now." He thrusts toward me. I step back, avoiding another punch. "That should count for something."

"We both know it doesn't. But that's not the point I'm trying to make here."

"I'm about two seconds from pounding your face. Make your point," he says, breathing heavy.

"Why do you care?"

"What do you mean, why do I care?" He lunges, tries to uppercut me. I sway, and he misses, slams his fist into the wall, and yelps. "She's my girlfriend, that's why," he says.

I shrug. "So, again, I ask. Why do you care?"

"We've been together three years," he repeats.

"Yeah, so what? I know you, James. And I'm asking you, when you know that I know who you really are, why the fuck do you care?" I drop my dukes, release my fists, hands flat against either side of my frame.

James socks me in the jaw.

I stumble back, landing on one knee. "Feel better now?"

James releases an exasperated sigh, falls heavily onto my bed, nose facing the ceiling. "No."

I check my throbbing eye in the mirror; it's red, a little sore, nothing ice won't cure—might not even bruise.

On the bed next to James, I stare with him through the wide skylight.

"You could've picked someone else," he says.

"You know I didn't have a choice! I didn't pick her. Shit was arranged after my father died. You know this. Knew dating Edith was temporary. But she called me, alright? Should've kept it in my pants. It's too late now. Right timing for me kinda thing. It was forever ago. Gala night. It's not an excuse. Wasn't thinking that night." I elbow James's left side. "Come on, now. You, more than anyone else, know I dodge her. And Edith is—"

"Persistent," we say in unison. I laugh. James laughs until it fades.

He clears his throat. "Talked to Larry tonight."

"Did you? And?"

"He's in love with Kyra. Leaving Margo for her. Wants nothing to do with me anymore." His voice cracks, shatters like the shards of trophy under my bed. "I knew about Edith's V-card being swiped the night you took it. Wanna hear something crazy?"

I shrug, shaking my head.

"When Edith told me, it relieved me."

"Why?" I say, but I already know. And besides Larry, I'm the only who does.

James exhales. And the heavy sigh makes his lips poke out. "Took the pressure off. My dick doesn't work around her—it has a strict XY prerequisite."

I laugh, run two fingers over the cut on my lip. It stings a little and tastes like old pennies.

James sighs. "Sorry about socking you. I just flipped. I don't want Edith like that, haven't for a while, but she's one more person I'll never have. This is all so fucked up. Why'd I fall in love with someone who won't love me back?"

"Larry loves you."

"Yeah, not the way I love him. I was this experience, his entry card to boy sex.

His guide to figuring out who the hell he was. And the funny thing is, he hit on me first, bruh. Didn't think about it before. Didn't want this life. This acute case of gayness. But he loved me, touched me, and since then . . . all I could think about was him . . . and the next him, and the next him, and the next him. Larry should come with a warning label that reads: Do not enter my ass unless you wanna be fucked outside it too." James laughs, reaches over to me, places an arm around my waist. "Love sucks."

I flash a one-sided smile. "It's not all that bad."

James arches an eyebrow. "Jo really did a number on you," he chuckles. "Hey?"

"Yeah?"

Moonlight shines on James's face. He releases a heavy sigh and shakes his head. "Why couldn't you be gay?" he teases.

"'Cause then you'd really have a problem."

"Oh yeah?" He stares at my lips. "How's that?"

"I'd fuck all your boyfriends, too."

"You're such a dick." James chuckles, moves his arm away from my chest.

I take a hand to my face, massage both eyes using my thumb and middle finger. "Yeah, I know, but seriously." I turn away from him, gaze at the stars. "People are born gay. I was born to love her. I don't know, man. Maybe love comes and goes like seasons. It's natural. Nothing causes it, nothing can stop it. It just exists, floats around like electrons on an orbit waiting for covalent bonds."

James has no answer. Scrolls through photos of him and Larry projected from his watch.

My iCom chirps.

It's Margo, again. When she stalker-calls me, she's realized she was wrong about something and wants to apologize. But I'm so exhausted, there's no energy to answer the call. I drift to sleep.

An hour later, I wake to five missed calls from Margo. I don't call her back. I call Jo. But still she doesn't answer. I leave James in my room, head down the hall to check on Margo. Four knuckles to her door, I knock three times. No response. I tap three more times, still no answer.

"Call Margo," I say to iCom.

"Calling Margo," iCom confirms.

On the other side of the door, Margo's iCom rings, but she doesn't answer. I realize the crash that sent me running to my bedroom last night might have originated in Margo's room; I'd gotten so distracted by James that I forgot. Margo keeps her room locked when she's home, so I enter 06 10 58 into the white keypad on the wall beside the knob. The lock click-clacks, and the door opens.

"Margo?" I call out. Dead silence without an echo. "Margo?" I check her large dressing room before entering her bathroom.

Margo's half-dressed, eyes half-open, lying in her claw-foot tub full of alcohol and her favorite red ribbons: the strings of blood exiting her tiny porcelain wrists.

Frantic, I lift her from the tub, carry her to the bed. I pat her cheeks, calling her name.

"What's going on?" James says in the doorway.

"iCom Gaitlin."

"Fuck, man. She passed out, barely breathing?"

"James! Fucking call Gaitlin. Please!" I wanna tear up but can't. Margo needs me to be stronger than that. I feel for her featherlight breathing while James iComs the doctor.

I'm afraid—a piece of shit because Margo's been calling all night trying to reach me. And I've been so consumed with James and with Jo, I'd forgotten how troubled my sister is, how much she needs me, who we are . . . what we mean to each other.

"Gaitlin's on the way?"

James nods.

I nod. "Good. Good." The only thing that matters is saving my sister, the girl I loved before Jo. "What were you thinking? Trying to kill yourself?"

Margo coughs and slurs. "No. I just drank too much. But she's evil, Covey."

I don't care what she says—only that she can speak. "Gaitlin's on the way. Stay with me," I say, looking at her nose. Margo's cute button nose, and tiny nostrils; I think of butterfly kisses I planted on the tip early mornings in bed. I hold her tight.

Margo pants sharply, inhaling, shaking, and exhaling softly. It's like when we were kids and she'd freak out when it stormed, and I'd hold her close to my chest until she slept. All I want to do right now is make her happy, make her smile— take her away from this house.

Margo shudders like the room is cold, but it's not. It's warm. "The witch's journal . . ." she murmurs. "Brown leather straps." Margo coughs, chokes on saliva. "Let me die. I'm not strong like you. I feel so . . . so . . ." She nods in and out, drooling.

I panic, afraid I'm losing her. "A truth and a lie." Nervousness fuels my speech. "Remember?—don't close your eyes. Open them. A truth and a lie. One more game. Come on, Margo, stay with me. Gaitlin's on the way."

Margo flashes a quick smile before frowning. "She killed them both—" Her words slur together, barely audible. "Just like she's killing us." Margo coughs, again, and again; her eyes roll to the back of her head. Her fragile frame lurches. Vertebrae by vertebrae, she jerks, convulsing.

Part III
Ashes

". . . despite our past, shall we never forget that life leaves Ashes,
and Ashes birth new life. As citizens, our past is not the end, and we
humans are more than the future ever reveals."

—New United States of America Catechism of Moral Code & Law

37

JOSEPHINE

I hurt myself. I push the pain aside and dust the gravel off my black jeans. I've never considered myself particularly clumsy. But on the way to Gaitlin's research lab, I fell. After the AerTrain ride, I wasn't looking, tripped on the platform, skinned my elbow on rough concrete, and bruised my knee. It happened fast, and it's my fault.

Outside the Grand New Georgia Station Port Authority, three turbo cabs pass me before I'm finally able to wave one down. The black driver with tan skin gets out the turbo cab and opens the back door.

The seat is plush and soft. Through the rearview mirror, the driver asks, "Where to, miss?"

"iCom Technologies." The words come out of my mouth like a question mark.

Gaitlin has been promising me a tour of his iCom research labs for a while, to show me more of his work for my science lessons. Late this afternoon, he said he had news about the Ashes, and I should come as soon as I could. Good or bad, I don't know.

I lift my nose to dark skies. Just below the clouds, AerTrain tracks shine bright white, transporting folks left and right above the city. I slide into the back seat, and watch the turbo pass tech-savvy people, whiz past extravagant monuments, and swoosh beneath metallic skyscrapers and past mosaic parks resembling outdoor museums.

The cab driver brakes in front of iCom Technologies Research Center. He opens my door. And the air that enters the cab smells like fresh buttered popcorn.

I lift my chin, stretching back to look at the top of the building—it's a hammered-silver dome.

Nervousness wrinkles skin between my eyes as I enter the massive research building. A wheeled drone greets me inside the large doors. "Welcome to iCom, Josephine Monarch. Dr. Gaitlin Chan is expecting you. Please have a seat. He'll call shortly."

I hold shaky hands together, inhale, say, "Thank you." I walk to the center of the lobby. I stand amazed, staring into the glass ceiling revealing clear skies, the domed top of the building visible high above. The sleek, bright room is filled with chairs that look like white glossy globes made of cotton fabric that rotate on steel swivel bases.

Three people sit in the waiting room: A black woman in shades sits legs crossed with a nose stuck inside a fashion magazine with *Plastic Surgery* written on the cover. A short white man adjusts his toupee, while scratching an ashy ankle. Most folks don't think white folks get ashy, but they do. And a brown girl drinks milk from a carton.

I take a seat like the iCom greeter suggests. The drone offers entertainment—any book or film I'd like—but I am too nervous, wondering what Gaitlin has to tell me. Instead, I bounce my knee anxiously until the drone announces, "Dr. Gaitlin will see you now, Josephine. Please follow signs to the elevator. Dr. Gaitlin Chan's office is located on the ninth floor."

I obey, do as told. Take the elevator to the ninth floor. Dr. Gaitlin's name is listed by one of the metal doors, and inside there's a larger version of the lab at Transition House. There are pieces of equipment Gaitlin has been teaching me to use, and wall-to-wall centrifuges, telescopes, and glass testing tubes.

He motions me to a back corner, and he holds his arms out, fingers spread wide for examination, rotating his hands supine to prone. "What do you see?" He slouches with a lowered neck. With a smile on his face, he watches my eyes, waiting for a response.

I shrug. "Tan skin?"

He laughs. "Tan skin is right. Clear skin's a better answer." He sticks out his tongue. "No black spots."

"Huh?"

"Five days ago, I had full-blown Radius. Today I don't."

"What? How is that possible?"

"Thanks to this little fella—" He pauses, walks to a large glass cage with breathable holes at the top, where a chittering baby rat's feeding on black worms.

During my time here, this is my first time seeing a rat. But it's not just rodents. I haven't seen a cockroach, stink bug, or any other eight-legged or long-winged creepy-crawlies.

The rat stretches its short neck and hisses. "I injected a pure strain of Radius into my bloodstream." Gaitlin pulls his sleeve back. He runs his hand over his arm. "No black, oozing lesions. No fever blisters. Radius-free." He almost leaps.

I run my hand over Gaitlin's lean arm. "But that's impossible." I knew he was working on a Radius cure, but my brain is slow to catch up.

"Not anymore."

A smile creeps wide on my face. I gulped before entering Gaitlin's research lab, under the impression the news would be bad information about the Ashes— something like murder, madness, and mayhem. I'm glad I was wrong.

I stare at the fuzzy rat. "How'd it get here?"

With glowing eyes, he talks to the animal. "After two rats were captured years ago in the Ashes, the rest were bred and raised, right here in this lab." Gaitlin knocks on the cage with a knuckle, then faces me. "This little guy is my favorite. Morones's a fighter." Gaitlin laughs.

"You named the rat?" I frown at it. It's filthy, round, and hisses, flashing crooked teeth. Its presence angers me. I think of all the lives its ancestors must've taken. Countless mothers, fathers, sisters, brothers, cousins, and friends died from their nasty bites. "Why name it?"

"Why not? It's a life. There's much to learn from disease, even the deadliest. No matter the infection, if we study it, we learn the flaws of nature. Inconsistencies we'd not know were they not present. They teach us where society falls short, help us make the world better."

"So why the name Morones?" I tap the rat's glass house, mean-mugging it.

"It means a small hill. Look at his round belly. Turn him upside down, he's a giggling little hill." Gaitlin chuckles. "Tickles me pink."

"Did you give it the cure?" I stare at Morones's death-seeking, beady-black eyes.

"Yes. Four times now."

I rest my elbows against the lab table, place my hands on either side of my face. "I don't understand."

"Morones had Radius four times. And was cured four times."

Gaitlin reads the confusion on my face.

He reaches for a tiny corked bottle on a top shelf. Inside the bottle, a translucent white substance whirls. Gaitlin holds the bottle eye level. He stares off into space.

I study his face, try reading him. But can't make him out. "Are you okay?"

He smirks with a half smile. "I trust whatever's shared stays here? You won't tell anyone."

I nod. "I'd never do that."

"For the past twelve years, Dr. Laclos and I've worked toward this. You may've met him. Laclos ran the medical clinic in the Ashes for years."

I nod, yes.

I knew Laclos; anyone who ever lost a family member, friend, or neighbor to Radius knew Laclos. I think back to how I know him. He's the doctor who gave Boah three tokes to get home from the hospital the night his mom died of Radius.

Gaitlin stares into the serum like what he's about to say next is painful. "Before my husband—" He pauses, looks at his feet, shaking his head. He looks up, looks at me, then gives a short-lived smile. "—before Laclos died, he dedicated his life to people in the Ashes. He ran the medical center over there with hopes to eliminate Radius. He's the one who brought Morones's ancestors across the mountain. He wanted Radius destroyed. So much so, we joked he was more married to this lab than he was to me." He stuffs the tiny bottle of serum in the pocket of his lab coat, then continues. "He'd stay up hours and hours, late into the night, testing serums against every strain of Radius he could find. One night he called so excited, said he'd figured out a way to prolong life after infection. Said it'd add two weeks to the infected life. Was close to a cure, he'd said. Said a single flower was both the cause of and cure for Radius."

"Wait, it's not the rats? Radius doesn't come from them?"

"Well, yes and no." Gaitlin pauses, then says, "Radius originated from flowers."

"But there aren't any flowers in the Ashes."

"Or there aren't anymore." Gaitlin gazes into Morones's cage. "Rats and mice were eating the plant, passing sickness to offspring, generation after generation." He glances at me. "Let me show you something."

I follow Gaitlin to the back of the lab. We stand before massive medical shelves stacked with bottled herbs, powders, syringes, medical pads, bandages, pills large and small. "What happened to Dr. Laclos?"

"Though I loved him, my husband was ambitiously stubborn, a rule breaker. Wanted to skip past lab animals, use himself instead. He infected himself with Radius. He was sure he had the cure, wanted to test it on a human immediately. But his first try was his only. The serum extended his life with Radius but didn't save it. He didn't know it'd take ten years to perfect the serum. Or that he'd not be the one to perfect it."

It makes little sense. Everything I know or have heard about Laclos says he was this brilliant MD. It's strange. He didn't seem like an irrational man—or someone who'd inject a life-threatening disease into their veins without an antidote. "Why inject himself before knowing if the cure worked?"

Gaitlin reaches into his pocket, hands me a pair of clear gloves. "Science is only as good as its subjects. Without them, without sacrifices of brave regular people and scientists, dead and alive, we'd lose the world, cease to exist. And medicine, well, it wouldn't be what it is today. Those methods aren't for everyone. Science is a lot like fate; sometimes, it needs to be pushed for progress." Gaitlin releases a heavy-hearted sigh.

I think about Dr. Laclos's trips to the Ashes. I wonder how Laclos could've been Gaitlin's husband. Most women in the ashes gushed every time they saw Laclos; back then, he looked too old to be Gaitlin's husband. But maybe I'm wrong. Maybe Gaitlin's older than forty—some folks age better.

Gaitlin types 03 24 20 12 into the keypad next to the door. He presses the enter key, and the vast medical shelf splits in two, revealing a shiny gray door without a handle. Gaitlin presses his bare palm to the door's center, and it swishes like a bottle of soda, releasing a silky-cold vapor when it opens.

We walk through the thick fog until we reach a steel wall. I lift my chin, follow the shiny wall to the steel ceiling.

Gaitlin draws a perfect circle on the silver wall. It reminds me of mirror writing—like when someone breathes on a mirror and writes inside their breath.

Whoosh. Swoosh. The wall slides open to the left, revealing another steel wall that slides open to the right.

We walk through the open space. When the fog of cold air disappears, the Beautiful Things appear. The large indoor greenhouse is full of the white feathery flower.

Gaitlin walks over to one flower, inhales.

I walk over to him, sniff the Beautiful Thing next to the one he's inhaling. It smells just like I remember. "Baby powder," I murmur.

Gaitlin nods and takes his nostrils away from the center of the flower. "In the seeded center, the flower produces a liquid that smells like baby powder and looks and tastes like milk. From this flower comes both the cause of and cure for Radius. Smells wonderful, I know. Rats think so too. It's catnip to them."

I want to tell Gaitlin that I've seen this flower before, but I don't wanna come off stupid because I don't know what they're called. I could call them Beautiful Things because, well, they are. They're prettier than the red sunflowers. How do I ask a question without sounding stupid? Then I remember something Vye always says. And her words give me courage. Vye says the only dumb question is the question never asked.

"What are they called?"

"Plumes."

"Plumes." The word leaves my tongue like the flowers' silky white petals. The flowers that brought so much joy to kids in the Ashes had a name—a real name. Plumes.

Gaitlin pulls a small, corked bottle with a butterfly needle from his pocket. He drives the butterfly needle into the center of the Beautiful Thing. I watch the white serum flow down the needle's tube, disappear in the brown cork, and drip into the tiny glass bottle.

"We call it *les blancs plume fleur de la génie*—translates to 'the white feather flower from the genius.' Both beautiful and deadly. So much so, Laclos ordered officers to cut every plume down, burn the fields they grew in, and bring them here for research. For years Laclos focused on the flower's white petals, until I discovered it was the liquid inside I could transform into magic." Gaitlin pulls the needle out of the plume. He covers the butterfly needle with a see-through sheath.

Now I know why cops cut the Beautiful Things down—the flower infected rats feeding on it; those rats bit people and gave them Radius. Dr. Laclos gave the order to burn the fields they grew in—the wasteland by the hanging tree—to save lives. Cutting the plumes down wasn't this malicious act carried out by cops to make our lives more miserable like I'd initially thought. I was wrong about those cops. I don't know. Maybe I'm wrong about a lot of things.

Gaitlin fills another corked bottle with plume essence. "I'm taking the cure to the Ashes. iCom barely supports my research. They don't care about Radius, Jo. It's been a slow process because it lacks funding. They won't pay for human trials . . . If they did, I'd worry about them infecting *more* Ashfolk with Radius to do their tests. The risk is as low as I can get it, so I want to bring it to Ashfolk who are already dying of Radius, give them a chance."

I nod, think of all the people I've known who would have tried anything. Who are gone.

Gaitlin continues, "The winter Trade Train leaves early morning after the Fall Ball in two weeks, four a.m. sharp. I'll be on the train—we'll ride back together."

We'll ride back together. Gaitlin's words run through me, pierce me like a needle. The word *home* feels a lot like where I am now, and less and less like it's over the mountain.

I'm conflicted, like ripples in a river flowing different directions. If it were scientifically possible, I'd clone myself. That way, I'd be in two spaces. Couldn't let anyone down that way. Everyone'd be happy. Strange enough, I got what I came here for—love. And it's crazy. I wish I could clone that, too—take it everywhere I go. Am I selfish for wanting to stay?

A knot grows in my throat. It feels uneven, unfair like the world. I try swallowing it, punching it down, but it's not having it. It rises higher and higher. It travels up my esophagus—makes my throat burn—water's in my eye.

"Those are the best tears—tears of joy." Gaitlin hands me a bottle of serum, closes my fingers around it. "I'm an outsider. And with everything going on in the Ashes, tensions are high post-riot. They won't readily trust me. That's where you come in." With gentle eyes, Gaitlin places his hands on my shoulders and continues. "You'll help them trust me; you'll help me. And together, we'll save lives."

I flash a nervous smile.

Cheerful, he grabs another corked bottle with a butterfly needle sticking out of it; exsanguinates another plume. "We did it, Laclos. And it's just the beginning."

iCom chirps.

I reach up, touch my ear. It's not my chip sounding off, but Gaitlin's.

Gaitlin holds his index finger up. "Dr. Gaitlin here." He pauses, sighs. "Wait a minute. Slow down, James," he says, monobrow wrinkled. "Breathe, James. Good . . . good. Yes, I can hear you now. Tell me what happened?"

38

COVE

I open the front door to the witch's house, walk down the dark hallway. It's amazing how different our house is when the witch's not here. When she is, Elenore's house feels alive and hisses like rattlesnakes.

I stand in the hallway by Margo's bedroom door. Her words are in my head—a brown journal with leather straps. I hear the crackling of her frail voice as she uttered, "She killed them both. Just like she's killing us."

Which both? And killed whom? The "she" part, I already know, is Elenore. But who was she saying Elenore killed?

An hour ago, before I left the hospital, Elenore was sitting beside Margo. Just before I walked out of the room, Elenore grabbed my wrist. She told me to break it off with Jo. That it was time, that nothing good would come of disobeying her. Then she said:

"You're in love with her . . . Jo. Doesn't matter. If you don't break her heart, you won't get the deed."

After Elenore's sinister comment, Gaitlin entered Margo's hospital room. He apologized for arriving late, said he rushed over as soon as he could from the lab. He asked Margo if she wanted to go home, where he'd keep watch over her, or if she'd rather stay at the hospital. Margo didn't want to go home, said she wanted to stay in the hospital the maximum days allowed and agreed to psychiatric evaluation.

Gaitlin exhaled. "How long has she been drinking, and does anyone know the cause?"

I didn't answer aloud, but inside the words flowed. Margo bought the bottle, but Elenore's twisted game is what Margo's trying to drown. My sister's good at hiding pain behind cheerful smiles. I know her better than anyone. But I didn't know Margo'd reached her breaking point.

I waited for Elenore to answer Gaitlin's question. Hoped she'd admit the harm her game caused. Or at least say sorry—some half-hearted version of the truth holding her responsible for Margo's overdose on alcohol.

Elenore removed tight white gloves from her hands. "She had a fight with a boyfriend. Broken hearts are dangerous."

Gaitlin adjusted his glasses. "I'll take care of her."

Elenore touched Gaitlin's forearm. "And you're a good friend."

"She'll be out for the night. It's a good time to go home and get some sleep. I'll keep an eye out for her," Gaitlin said.

Elenore shook her head no. "I'd never forgive myself for leaving her here alone."

Some parents are like that. They fake being good—only nice when watched.

Rain pounds the skylight. I lift my chin to the hallway ceiling, stare at the dark sky. Swift wind blows outside and falling leaves block stars from view. I pace down the long corridor to Elenore's large pod room. I've made this walk many times before, but this time's different. Elenore's usually sitting behind her vanity, picking blemishes and wrinkles with the tips of her fingers. She's not here tonight.

Elenore's room's always been unusually cold, but tonight, it's warm, like the cold is only here when she is.

I rifle inside her desk drawer carefully. Elenore's meticulous in how, when, and where she positions objects. This makes searching tedious, but it's doable. Lifting papers is the hardest. Before lifting them, I scan the corners of the edges, precisely calculating each sheet's alignment before shifting the stack and touching another pile. I don't see a journal.

After searching drawers in Elenore's room, I want to give up. Maybe Margo didn't mean to say Elenore killed someone. Maybe she was too out of it to remember the color of the journal, or perhaps she was just talking nonsense and there's no journal—her intoxicated self hallucinated.

Or maybe I'm the one who's hallucinating. The two sad white faces by her vanity aren't frowning anymore, but smiling.

I remember when we were young, Margo said the faces were ours. I'd always thought they were our souls trying to escape this wretched house.

Taking steps toward the faces, fear makes my palms itch and bones shake. Yells not to go near it. But I don't step back. I keep walking. Inching closer and closer—extending fingers, reaching toward it, touching it—caressing the glass like delicate skin.

"Hello, soul." I half expect the painting to answer back.

I pull the art away from the wall. In an empty, square space behind it, I see it: a large brown journal bound with leather straps—just as Margo described. I grab it, take it out of the wall. It's heavy, filled with thick off-white paper. I push the art back into the wall, making sure it looks untouched.

I open the journal to the first page. The table of contents is in Elenore's handwriting. There are eight chapters.

1. Beginning.

2. Margo.

3. Ethan.

4. Abigail.

5. Holt.

284

6. *Cove.*

7. *Rashad.*

8. *End.*

Ethan's my father's name. Abigail's my mother. Holt is Margo's father. I don't know who Rashad is.

I flip to chapter three.

Cove's a sensitive boy. Optimistic eyes. Big thumping little heart.
And it all disturbs me. So, I'll cut him down, crush the seed before it
matures. Train Cove to fear that which ruins me. Make him lovable and
unable to love. Treat him like secondhand goods . . . the way his father
continually reminds me I am. And the photos . . . all the blasted . . .
skeletal . . . horrifically tragic photographs of that pathetic excuse for a
dead wife, Abigail.
 I'll never be anything but second place to Ethan. Not good enough . . .
never will be good enough, or fairer than his precious starving Abby.
Soon I'll—

I stop reading, slam the journal shut. It's too painful.

I carry the journal back to my room and stop in my doorway. Jo's here. Her skin glows olive in the moonlight. She seems confused, staring out the window like she's searching for something beyond it. I close the door behind me. Startled, Jo gasps, turns around like she's seen a ghost.

"What is it?"

"Yuh scared me."

"What are you doing here?"

Jo sighs. "I heard about Margo." She stares at me. And when she does, it feels like she can see through my darkness—through the lies.

Nodding, I sit on my bed; elbows on knees, hands clasped together, head hanging low, eyes to bamboo floors.

Jo studies the brown journal beside me.

I flip through the journal like it's insignificant, and not the malicious work of evil it is. "Just an old book."

She nods.

I slide the journal under my bed. Push it farther back with the heel of my shoe. Jo won't be here all night. I expect Elenore to feel like she has to stay with Margo for another day or so. I'll have plenty of time to read it and put it back in its place unscathed.

Jo walks over, slides hands around my neck, presses her belly into my forehead. "How's Margo?"

I place my hands on either side of her waist, shake my head against her torso. I don't want to think about Margo, or picture her lying in a hospital bed, both wrists wrapped in bandages—monitoring wires glued to her arms and temples. "How was your day?" I lift her shirt—stick the tip of my nose inside her belly button.

Jo giggles and twists away. "Alrightish." She leans over. She curves her back, rests her cheek on my messy hair, and holds my head in her arms. "How's Margo?" she says, repeating her question.

"I don't wanna talk about it." I rub the back of my neck, stand up, walk to my bedroom door and open it. "You should leave."

Jo faces me, stares into the dark hallway. "Why?"

"Reasons. Many." I can't look at her. I gaze at the floor—I belong there, right next to the dirt shoes dragged in.

"That's not good enough."

"No. This?—whatever this is we're doing, isn't good enough—end of discussion. Period."

She narrows her eyes. "What happened to you? Why're you doing this?"

I don't deserve you. "Why are you still here?" What's it gonna take for Jo to see I'm not worth the trouble or effort? I'm not worth her time, or anyone else's. I'm damaged goods—broken. Too scared, and too trained in the art of anti-love to be loved, accept love. And I'm too fucked up to deserve it. Elenore knew I wasn't worthy of love when I was a child. Why can't Jo see it now? "You need to go. Now."

She walks toward me. And I swear to God Jo's walk could dim stars. "Don't do this." On tippy toes, she kisses my forehead. And I let her. It's soundless to the world, but inside my chest, my heart is on fire—out of control—drumming louder and louder and louder—its cadence robs my throbbing ears and fills the space between us.

I glance down at Jo's nose. She lifts her chin, and our eyes meet. I can't feel my knees, but I fake feeling them, and stand tall; maintaining cold eyes and distant stare. "There's a lot you don't know about me. Things you don't wanna—I'm not who you think I am," I say.

Jo holds my face in her hands, brings my eyes to meet hers. "Show me who you are."

I'm indexing my brain's monolingual dictionary for ominous phrases to say to Jo. Something that'll push her away, really piss her off, so she'll stay far away. I'm toxic, an infection worse than Radius.

And all this inner conflict is insane because deep down inside, I know I'm not trying to hurt Jo so she'll walk away. I'm doing it to see if she'll stay.

Jo kisses my chin. "Open up to me."

"It's just . . ." I inhale, exhale, quivering inside. Some calm rushes over me, because Jo just stands here with her big heart thumping, all beautiful and shit. And it's pissing me off because being near her is tough and smelling her skin is a fairy tale. I don't want her to go, but I can't stop being an asshole. And, *fuck*, I'd rather touch her than breathe.

She takes my hands into her hands. "I wanna see you. The real you. Don't hide from me." Jo's voice could woo Hades.

"Words are so . . ." I humph. "I'll show you." I release her hands.

Jo steps back. "Show me what?"

I pull my V-neck tee over my head. I'm bare chested.

Jo stares, making a face that's the very definition of a question mark. It's as if she's thinking *why did you take your shirt off?* Eyes to bamboo floors, I turn, showing Jo the scars on my back. I hear a gasp, then silence. Like behind me Jo's hands are covering her mouth. I imagine her doe-eyed in a way that's not adorable, but shockingly stunned. She's unnervingly silent. What's she thinking, gazing over the deeply layered scars that crisscross down my back like a jacked-up jigsaw puzzle?

The deep quiet lingers. Waiting for Jo's soothing affirmation is emotional torture. It is absurd. I'm supposed to be this cold, controlled human machine without emotions. And the uncertainty over if Jo'll still want me, after seeing my scars, makes me feel like a mad person—revealing how insecure I am with her.

With other girls I felt like a king ruling weak subjects. I think we're different with different people, because Jo's my equal—we're similar scribble pages. She slaps me off my high horse. Shows me we're both grown from the same tree, just raised on different branches.

Clenching my jaw, I end the silence. "My father wasn't in the ground six days before the beatings started. Rods and flogs came soon after . . . She believes in the whole . . . spare-the-rod spoil-the-child thing." I scoff. "Cried myself to sleep too many times to count. Margo and I made a promise to never let her see us cry again." I lean forward, roll pants up my legs. "Misery's her kink. When we wouldn't cry, it pissed her off. One night, Elenore dragged us out of bed. Said she'd give us something to cry about. She spread uncooked rice on the floor, made us kneel on it. To this day rice repulses me."

Jo takes a few steps forward. She stands directly behind me, breathing on my shoulder blade. She doesn't speak for a while; presses her ear just below my neck. "The welts are fresh. When's the last time she . . ."

"—Yesterday. Happens once a week. Not as often as it used to. She's older. Doesn't have energy for both of us."

"Us?"

"Margo, too." Guilt burns my chest. Margo's story is hers to tell, not mine. But there's no me without my sister. And I'm done with half-truths.

I close my eyes, just feeling Jo. Listening to my heartbeat. Watching the red veil behind my eyelids. I flip lids open and sigh. "I've done things. Things I'm ashamed to admit."

"No one's immune to imperfection," she says. And I swear, I love her twice for saying it. She continues, "In the Ashes, after the Gala, a cop attacked me."

I turn around, but Jo stops me.

Jo places both palms to my back, preventing me from facing her. "Not yet, don't turn around." She pauses, and then continues, "He pinned me to the ground. Bashed me in the head with a rock. Blurred my vision. Boah died trying to help. A woman saved me. I couldn't make out her face. She pointed a gun at him. Shot him three times in the head—killed him. I'd never wish death on anyone. But that night I wished him dead." Jo sighs. "We're some version of messed up."

And I'm angered, pissed someone'd do that to her, or anyone else. I'm not for murder either, but low-key glad whoever did it is dead. I feel bad for thinking this way, but then Jo touches me and guilt subsides.

Jo traces my scars with the tips of her fingers, drawing up, down, and across raised skin like tic-tac-toe. While she touches my back, I imagine there's a crossword puzzle there. One down spells out *baculine*. The *n* in *baculine* creates two across and spells *retribution*. In *retribution*, the first *i* joins three down, *malignant*. Four across grabs the *u* in *baculine* to generate *supposititious*.

I reach around my back for Jo's hand. I turn, lift her chin, and kiss her nose. She slides out of her shoes.

Jo unzips her jacket. Her fingers shake. There're goose bumps on her skin. She walks to the bed and sits on it. I sit beside her, take her hands into my palms and kiss them. Her eyes are innocent, free of the guilt I feel for wanting to make Elenore happy by taking Jo's virginity.

Jo stares at my chest, blushing while biting her lip. She removes her top. I stare at her bra—melting at the rise and fall of her cleavage.

I take my pants off. Jo peeks between my legs with eyes wide. I look down too, grin, and then glance up at her. Our eyes meet. I lean into her to kiss her, and we both fall back onto the bed.

"Sure you wanna do this?"

Jo nods yes with tear-filled eyes.

I wipe them away.

I gaze into Jo's eyes as the tip of her nails graze up and down my spine, calling me to enter her, take her.

It's that time. The time with any other girl, I'd grab a rubber out of the nightstand, slip the rubber on, and ease in. Afterward, I'd leave the bed, get dressed while she's naked, then break her heart. Ask her to go. But I can't with Jo.

Why can't I do this? I've done this more than once. Why the FUCK can't I with Jo? I'm procrastinating. Chickenshit's my name. I lie above this gorgeous black girl, second-guessing myself. With each passing moment I'm making a choice—the decision to not have sex with her tonight. I gaze into Jo's trusting dark eyes, frozen, fearing her.

Caressing Jo is terrifying; embracing her creates little earthquakes under my skin. I can't enter Jo, break Jo, or feed off her misery. Her heart's too big—its light'll consume me—swallow my darkness whole.

I lift my body away from hers.

Jo sits up on elbows. "What's wrong?" She swipes at her eyes.

You're a virgin, I wanna say, but I don't. "Nothing."

Elenore'd be so proud if I took Jo's innocence, but I can't do this. Caring for Jo kills me. And taking her virginity right now'd be for Elenore's benefit, not mine. The witch's influence tugs my brain, but I can't do it. Can't rob Jo of something she can only give once and hand Elenore something I thought the witch already stole—my soul.

I tuck a wild strand of hair behind her right ear. "Lie back." And she does.

I give Jo the side of the bed by the window. I slide under the covers beside her and kiss the back of her cool brown neck. And this is the way of it for hours . . .

Jo presses her back into my chest. Her ear buried inside the fluffy white pillow beneath it. I take her in. Her tongue tastes like cinnamon. There's a hint of coconut in her hair. And I'm happy. Unapologetically into her.

I trace her long eyelashes, sloped nose, and sharp cheekbones. Locking my arm around her waist, I pull her into me, close. And as she sleeps, I butterfly-kiss the back of her neck. I'm at peace next to Jo. Mind at ease, heart light as feathers. As I drift, nose buried in her coconut hair, I think, this must be like love.

39

JOSEPHINE

Moonlight washes over my face. I open sleepy eyes, wondering why boys I like don't want me. I'd have given myself to Cove, but he refused—just like Boah when he chose Kyra. Maybe Cove's more like Boah than I realized; maybe all boys are—full of kind words that don't really mean anything.

I blink twice, turn to Cove's slumbering face. His snores are faint whispers. I run a soft thumb over his closed eyes, across his thick eyebrows, and down his straight nose. Wending fingers through his hair, I crave that peace—the kind born inside quiet minds while sleeping.

A quiet mind. Sleeping.

I'd give just about anything for a quiet mind and easy sleep. But it's hard to sleep when you think you're followed.

I've noticed the follower three times. First riding bikes with Aurice. Second time was at the cemetery. Third time was tonight, while staring out of Cove's window just before he came home. The person stood next to the magnolia tree in Elenore's yard. They're gone now. I couldn't see their face. But they wore all black and a long trench coat.

Anxiety makes my lip twitch; nerves writhe in the pit of my stomach. I take a deep breath and exhale. I scooch to the end of Cove's bed, place feet on cold floors, and search for shoes.

On all fours, one arm extended, I pat around the bamboo for red sneakers. Under Cove's bed I feel a pencil, a marble, a folded pair of socks, and a big brown book.

I drag the book forward, stare at it. Push it back under the bed. A shard of glass pierces my palm. I shriek, but it's not loud enough to wake Cove.

I fall back, sitting on my heels. And pinch my skin, plucking the thin glass, until it's out of my hand. I suck the wound. In the dark, I scan the open space for my red shoes. They're next to Cove's closet door.

I bandage the cut, slide shoes on, go to the room that still feels like mine. I grab my sketchbook and a charcoal stick, and head outside, moving quickly in case the watcher is still close by.

There's a ladder on the side of Elenore's house leading to the roof—climbing its rungs reminds me of the broke-down roller coaster in the Ashes. The moon burns bright up here. It feels palpable, like a lassoed coconut husk rope could hug it.

In the distance, to the north, where the city is, AerTrains swoosh and swish, arriving and departing the train station. Glowing night trains glide left to right in every direction except the Ashes. I think of home, Gaitlin's serum for Radius, and the good I'd accomplish for my people if I returned with Gaitlin.

In my sketchbook, I draw Vye's strong face—her sharp cheekbones beneath dark brown eyes. I flip the page, draw Neal's portrait. Sketching his golden smile makes me smile, makes me wanna hug tight and never let go. On the next page, I draw Boah's profile looking up at the moon.

I close the sketchbook and place the charcoal stick on my thigh.

It's been close to two months since the riot. And for the past three days, I can't get her out of my head. The person who saved me from Reed. I know it was a woman's figure with long hair. I can't see her face. But she smelled like vanilla. And that's all I have, those three things, three facts: Woman. Long Hair. Vanilla.

I shake the sugary smell away.

Cove's scars. I can't get them out of my head either. Or the woman who put them there. How could Elenore do that to him?—to Margo? How could anyone hurt someone they love? Margo and Cove are good at hiding pain.

Dysfunctional effects of their childhood made them strong like Teflon. So strong it's as if the glass that cut my hand a few minutes ago wouldn't scratch their skin. Skin . . .

I think of the jig, her skin. Dry, chapped, bruised, bloody lips, and her eyes. I open my sketchbook. I don't know why but for some reason tonight feels like the night I'll get them right. Once I get them right, I can let her go. Get her out of my mind, like the spirit of her in my head is waiting to escape through my sketch. I draw uncontrollably. I can't stop. Twenty minutes later, I stare down at my work. It gives me chills. Her lips, perfect. Her nose is shaded correctly. Her chin is well done. And her eyes . . . her eyes are . . .

"Jo!" Kyra yells from the ground.

Index finger over my lips, I shush her, but she can't hear that. I press my iCom chip, call Kyra from Elenore's roof. When she accepts the call, I tell her, "It's the middle of the night. Quiet, you'll wake the house." I lean over the edge, look down past untied shoelaces. Kyra's holding a little flashlight. When the bright light lands on my nose, I shield eyes with both hands. The sketchbook slides down my legs; I grab it quick. Manage to grab hold of one page, which rips from the spine: the jig sketch I just finished. The rest of my sketchbook hits the ground in front of Kyra's feet.

Kyra jumps back, her infectious laughter boisterous in my ear. She lifts my sketchbook off the ground. "Got it!" Then continues, "What'duh ya doing up there? Come down." She waves. "I want you'duh meet Larry." Sober Kyra knows I've already met Larry, but she's drunk, memory questionable, pale arms flailing through night fog. I wave back, tell her I'll be right over, and end the call. Then Larry chases Kyra off Elenore's lawn, and into the park across the street.

I don't wanna go, but err on the side of friendly, even though Kyra lied to Cove about me being jealous of her and Boah, and that it was me, not her, who ended our friendship because Boah chose her. Ugh. I tire of being the bigger person all the time. But if I don't, if I'm not the bigger person with Kyra, we'd spend every interaction bickering over small nothings.

I scooch away from the edge of the roof, rise, fold the sketch of the jig, slide it into my jacket's pocket. I bend over, tie shoelaces, and wonder why they keep coming loose. They're so expensive I should never have problems.

Few days ago at Nine-Points, while Cove and his best friend, James, picked tuxes for the Fall Ball, Margo and I went shopping for heels, and by default, these hella-expensive red sneakers to remember Neal.

Before we entered the shoe store, Margo said she noticed the heels I wore to the Gala were two sizes too big.

"You have money now. We'll get you the best heels for the Fall Ball and a few others you don't need." Margo laughed, weaved her arm inside mine as we walked in the store and picked out dresses and shoes that fit.

Shopping with money is every bit of fun I'd imagined it'd be—knowing cost doesn't matter. There's freedom in saying, yeah, I want that, robot lady, put it in a bag for me. After it was all rung up, guilt hit. No one person should have so much, while hundreds of thousands of people in the Ashes starve.

The park has paths made of brick and layered with fallen crimson maple leaves illuminated by tall globe lights. Beyond the bare branches of the cherry trees, massive oaks border a vast, lush meadow. Couples squeeze each other tight, hold hands under trees, smooching on benches, or thin blankets spread over fresh-cut green grass. I lift my chin to the sky. Branches block stars and the moon from view, embracing like clasped fingers.

"Over here, Jo!" Kyra calls. I turn toward her voice. Larry stands behind her, hands on her back, pushing her on a tire swing.

When I get close to them, Kyra jumps out of the swing. Larry chases her, and they run into a dark tubular tunnel paved in stone; a dim light flickers halfway down.

At the start of the tunnel, I look over my shoulder to the well-lit park behind me. Kyra laughs. Larry laughs. They're too far down the shaft to see. So, I place one foot inside the tunnel, walk slow, following laugh echoes.

Dry leaves crunch under my shoes, mush between crevices in the stone pathway. There's a pebble in my shoe. I stop, place my left palm on the clammy cement wall, pull my shoe off, take out the pebble, and then fling it to the other side of the dark tunnel.

I wait for the pebble to hit ground, but it doesn't. Seconds later, it rolls back to the heel of my shoe.

Something's breathing.

I freeze, pause everything, even breathing. I cover my mouth to make sure it's not me—that I'm not hearing my own breathing. It's not. Someone's here with me, and it's too dark to see who.

"Jo! Are you coming?" Kyra yells. The person here's not her. Kyra's voice is too far down the shaft for it to be her.

I walk away slowly at first, but pick up the pace when footsteps clickety-clack behind me. I'm speed walking, faster and faster and faster until walking becomes a light jog. And then I jog and jog and jog until jogging becomes a light sprint and run and run and run . . . Until fuck! I extend my arms, and my fingers stretch wide, bracing for a fall. After my palms slap down hard against the wet stone, I feel my earlobe. The iCom chip isn't there—it's gone. And there's no use searching for it. Wouldn't find it now anyway, especially without proper light.

Footsteps several feet in front of me echo against the stone streets. One, two . . . three, four . . . five, six, *clack . . . clack—clack*. And then silence. No more footsteps. I dust the dirt off my jeans as I stand. A kid screams in the park outside the tunnel. I turn, facing the shriek; the sound ricochets, bounces like a trampoline; in and out of my ears like a game of Ping-Pong.

I turn in the other direction. Forget Kyra. I have to get out of here. Feeling like at any second Reed'll come back to life, pin me to these curved walls.

Footsteps again. I hear them, clacking—they're close.

Heart's beating like hard rain on a tin roof. And yet, faster, quicker I run. Coughing on the wind, arms slicing through the air like my running dreams. The footsteps are thunderous; they're running too, behind. And they're close. I don't stop. I see the light at the end of the tunnel. I see the green meadow.

Sprinting, I reach the weak light of the outdoors. Footsteps stop. And I quit. I don't know why, but I stop. I'm out of breath, too. I'm dizzy; feel woozy, off-balance, like a Slinky.

Breathing heavily, I turn around. Dry-mouthed, swallowing oxygen. Catching more rapid breaths. I peer into the darkness with narrow eyes. I reach down, pull my pant leg up, and frown at bloody abrasions. The cuts aren't terrible, but they sting, tingle, and itch.

A long arm in a black leather coat hooks around my neck—a leather glove covers my mouth. I scream behind the black glove, heels scraping concrete, as I'm dragged farther and farther into the dark tunnel.

40

COVE

I extend my arm, reaching across the bed for Jo. I grab fistfuls of white sheet, inhale the space she slept in; it smells of her coconut oil, but she's not here.

Thunder opens my eyes, and roars like lions in the sky. I wonder where Jo went. Whether she's mad I didn't sleep with her. I wanted to. But when I realized it had nothing to do with Elenore's demands, and was more about craving to be that close to her . . . it scared me.

Emotional sex is alien to me. Like if I have sex with Jo, it'll be the last of me.

I pinch the bridge of my nose and clean the sleep out of my eyes.

She must've left in the middle of the night. Returned to her room. God . . . I miss her already.

I shift to the left, lean over the mattress, and drag Elenore's journal from under the bed. Open and study it. Elenore's an eccedentesiast—well skilled in hiding pain behind the porcelain smile she wears. Chapter after chapter, I discover that every relationship she's had, including the one with her mother, is perverse.

In chapter one, Beginning, I learn Elenore's mother had three children. Triplets. Three girls with platinum hair. Two perished in childbirth, leaving one: Elenore. Elenore's mother married a black man two years later, who had a daughter from a previous marriage, Rashad. The man died of a massive heart attack six months later. And Elenore's mother raised his daughter as her own.

During childhood, Elenore's mother played her daughters against each other, making high marks, accomplishments, and scholarly awards a competition, driving the two sisters apart. When Elenore's mother was upset, she shunned one or both girls, comparing one against the other, creating hostility and jealousy between the two siblings.

In Margo's chapter, chapter two, Elenore raves over the first day her silver-haired offspring made Larry cry—underlining the scene in crimson ink. I relive the day.

Margo and Larry were seven. Margo told him that if he really loved her, he'd stand on her tall dresser, wearing a red cape, and fly. He tied a red sheet around his neck, plunged from the dresser, and burst his chin wide open. Margo giggled.

Larry cried. "It's bleeding. Hurts terrible. Why are you laughing?"

Margo smirked. "Why not?"

Ethan Harding's chapter reads like a hate letter to unrequited love. In it, Elenore complains my father didn't love her; he was still in love with my mother, Abigail. Says he treated her like shit. In all caps she wrote: *Abigail had his heart on our wedding day. He spent our honeymoon calling her name before climaxing.*

She goes on to say how once he fell in love with her, she made him suffer. That he didn't deserve love, because he didn't know to take care of it. She wrote:

> *Ethan died of a broken heart, because God made it so. Jesus felt my need to escape marriage to a man who loved me only when his cock ceased to stand for others. Strange enough, I'm both sad and happy he's gone. It's disturbingly unusual, but I could've loved Ethan outside his wallet, had he not spent so much of our marriage in love with someone else.*

Chapter five dictates how Elenore's first husband, Holt, didn't want a girl. While pregnant, Elenore hid Margo's gender. After she gave birth, the nurse asked Holt if he wanted to hold his baby girl.

Holt took our daughter into his arms. With narrow eyes, he gazed into Margo's pinched face. "You were stupid enough to get pregnant. Didn't know you were dumb enough to have a girl."

Before tonight, I've never understood Elenore's fear of love. Men broke her. Love broke her. Maybe teaching Margo and me to fear love was her twisted way of showing she loves us—or carries enough affection for us to not let love break us. I skim chapter six, my chapter. Flip to chapter seven. Rashad.

On the first line, Elenore wrote and circled: *Rashad's the fairest. Loved more. Destroyed more.*

"Reading anything I'd enjoy?" Elenore stands in the doorway.

I jump, slam Elenore's journal shut, stand. I hold the leather-bound book next to my thigh. "You're home. Early. Margo okay?"

"She's fine, dear." Elenore tilts her head eerily from left to right. She walks to the window beside my bed, gazes at the rain crying down the glass. "Gaitlin says she'll recover with faint scars."

"Not surprised. She's a fighter."

"Surprises are nice, aren't they?" Elenore leaves the window. She walks toward me, glaring at the journal in my right hand.

When she reaches me, she takes it away. "I met Abigail in grade school. She entered the classroom and poof, magic happened. Like moths to porch lights, we connected." She walks to the window again, flipping through the journal. "You have her eyes. Mmm . . . she was a word so superior to beauty it's undiscovered. It cut deep when she married your father. Broke me when I discovered she'd have a child . . . you. Because having you killed her."

"More lies." Not eating killed my mother, not me.

Elenore sneers. "Truth is hard. Truths are . . . surprising."

Truth doesn't exist in her words. I just read her past. Page by page. I know

300

how twisted her mother was, and as a result, she is. I skimmed the roots of her teenage angst. Discovered the why in her twisted need for sibling rivalry. Elenore can't love—fears love—because as a child, love was a dark platter; a plate full of hate, envy, and manipulation.

"You know nothing of my mother," I say.

"Hmm."

"But I know about you. Your mother. The sister—Rashad—we've yet to meet. The men you loved who never loved you."

"No," she snickers.

"No?"

"No, this isn't that moment."

"What moment?"

"A mother-and-son one. We'll never have that. I'll pass along something better. Gift what your father's weakness could not. Truth. Ethan gave you rainbows, without rain. Started with that damn dog, Henley. The fleabag had cancer. So I killed him. Injected liquid rat poison into his veins, then dumped him at the pier."

I don't answer. I listen, face turned in the opposite direction.

Elenore's eyes are cold. "Margo's cat suffered the same fate." It makes sense now. Margo's words. When she mumbled "she killed them both." She'd meant Henley and Iggie, our childhood pets. Elenore says, "Your father lied about the dog like he lied about your mother. He said Abigail died of starvation. And well, that's one version of a complicated story."

"It's not a story. I've seen photos—her frail body."

"I've no reason to lie. I'd say ask your father, but he's dead, isn't he?" I've never hit a woman before. But I want to slap her for saying that. I ball both fists, tight. "There isn't a woman alive who doesn't fear food. Margo is bent over the toilet, toothbrush down her throat every morning after breakfast. Do I have photos of her gagging? Does it make it any less true? It's true Abigail didn't eat. But starvation wasn't the cause of death. Your father was. He's not the hero you think he was. Your mother died attempting to live up to his expectations. His high standards. Your mother killed herself. Would you like to know how?"

Speechless, I turn away from her, holding angry tears.

Elenore's heels clack, move closer to me. "Abigail was troubled. While it's true her struggles with food made her unhappy and eerily thin, it didn't kill her, her prescription did. Abigail overdosed on purpose. I watched her do it."

I turn to face the witch—heart aching—my tears wetting both cheeks.

Elenore continues. "Afterward, you came running out of your bedroom. Still see your little face now. I blocked you from entering the room. So you wouldn't have to see. And while your mother took her last breath, on the other side of her door, I held your hand."

I shake my head. I remember that night. I couldn't sleep, had a nightmare. I left my room, ran to my parents' room, only to be stopped by Elenore snooping outside their door. I didn't know why she was there, but I told Elenore I'd had bad dreams. Elenore took my hand, offered to tuck me in. My mother and I both fell asleep that night, only one of us didn't wake.

Elenore licks her fingers, flipping through the journal. "Finish your chapter."

I can't look her in the eye. "I've read it."

"Who's the liar now? Had you read it to completion, you'd know I speak the truth." She thrusts the journal in my direction.

I read and read and read until the words Elenore spoke appear on the written page. It's true. Shaking my head, I close the journal.

There's a positive to all this. I have leverage. Elenore can't make me break hearts anymore. Or blackmail me into letting her punish me. Not with what I have on her. She loves her reputation too much. "Sign the deed over. I'm done with your games, the lessons. All of it. I'm done. So is Margo. You'll never hurt her again. Your twisted shit's the reason she slit her wrists. I know about your money problems. Plum Orchard? How you tried stealing from my trust to pay back taxes. Parading around like you walk on money. Spending what you don't have. Trying to steal from me."

Elenore fakes surprise, then smiles. "Pot. Kettle. Shhhh." She rushes up to me, places her index finger over my lips. "I know your secret. You stole Jo's money card."

"No, I didn't."

"It wasn't in the drawer when Margo and I returned from New New York. It was missing. Rita's worked for my family since Margo was in diapers; she'd never steal from me. You were the only one alone with Jo."

"I put it back. I'd never steal from her."

"Thinking the sin is committing it. How'd you feel overhearing the conversation with Greer Jr.? Did you say, 'I forgive Elenore for trying to steal from me'? Or did you get mad and cast me as the monster in your fairy tale?" The smell of peppermint in Elenore's mouth makes my stomach turn. She sucks on the candy and continues, "How do you think Jo will see you when I tell her what you've done? That you stole her card to pay the taxes on your mother's land."

"Tell her. I'll take my chances."

"Let's say Jo's forgiving. Will she accept the other secrets? The incestuous past with Margo? Edith? And the hearts broken to prove my theory? Does Jo know the sole purpose of your courtship is to break her heart?"

Elenore's right.

Jo'd never speak to me again if she knew the truth—the heinous acts I committed just so Elenore'd release the deed to Plum Orchard.

Jo's good. Her heart's wide open, thriving, and honest. I'm damaged goods. And my heart's that little dent along the rim of a tin can.

303

I've slept with so many girls. Broken too many hearts. Margo and I swiped each other's V-cards. I built my and Jo's relationship on stacks of lies and a sick love game. And to top it off, I stole the money card while she was not just sleeping, but in a near coma of grief. I'm a monster.

And it's hopeless because no one loves a monster—no matter how beautiful it is—everyone hates it, doesn't wanna understand it. And'll do anything humanly possible to rid themselves of it. But I don't know. Maybe we're all the insidious monster beneath our bed. The torturous creature grabbing our own ankles—the demon laughing as we dig our own nails into hardwood floors—the fantastical evil dragging us under the mattress.

All this mental seesawing makes my head spin. I'm weak. Confused as fuck about what to do about Jo. She can't find out the truth. I wasn't born this way; monsters are made. It sucks to think this way, but it feels like the world is full of ugly monsters walking around faking normal, hoping like hell no one'll figure us out. Doesn't matter, though. If love is honest like Jo says, then I'll never have her, because Jo can never know my dark past.

"You win," I say quietly.

"I what, dear?"

"I'll never reveal what I've learned in the journal. And we can just stop all this. I'm tired of it."

Elenore grins. "But we're not done. A heart is on the table—Josephine's. Make Jo your masterpiece, I said. To which you said, 'Not a problem.' I told you she was different. And you replied . . . ? What was that beautiful quote, dear? Ah yes, that's it. 'Even the wildest of lions can be trained.' But maybe you failed . . . the experiment backfired?" Elenore pauses. She covers her mouth with her hands, smiling behind them. "Do you love her?"

A knot inside my throat chokes on the word. Love. And I hate it. The aching, this wanting to do anything and everything for one person just to be seen by them, liked by them, and fuck, dare I say it, just to be loved by them. When people don't know who you are, you're never vulnerable. And the heart's safe.

Elenore narrows her eyes with a sharp grin. "Lie. Tell yourself it's not real. Prove you're not weak. Rip the skin off her sweet little heart. And I'll release you. Without it, I'm disappointed. And if I'm disappointed, I swear on your pathetic life, the bank won't have to auction your land. I'll give it away."

I'm broken, hurt by Elenore's words, more so, because she's not bluffing. I know she'll do it. I sit on the edge of the bed. "Pick someone else. Anyone else, and I'll do it—I'll break her. Flog me, do what you will. But it can't be Jo. I don't wanna hurt her." My chest is sore, bruised, as if sandpaper scrapes across it.

Elenore sneers at my confession. "Break her or I will. Do it your way and it'll be clean, gentle-like, skipping the incestuous details regarding Margo. But if you leave it for me to do it my way? Well—" She reaches into her coat pocket, pulls out a lip balm, and applies it, knowing she doesn't have to finish her sentence for me. "Break her."

41

JOSEPHINE

Dim lights flicker on and off in the tunnel, adding little light to darkness. But it doesn't matter. The person covering my mouth is unseen, hooded by their leather coat. Their glove presses into my nose. It smells like dry leaves and pine needles. I grab the assailant's wrist using both hands, tugging downward—

I move my head side to side, try to break free. It doesn't work, so I stop moving, fake calm, and hope by chance someone enters this tunnel, someone who'll help.

"Don't scream," they say. It's a woman. She continues, "Make you a deal, kid. I'll move my hand away. You promise not to scream." The glove's pressure loosens. "Can you do that? Promise not to scream?"

I nod, signaling I understand and agree. But I don't. My lips quiver behind her glove. I'm not armed. Screaming's my only weapon.

The woman uncovers my mouth. With narrow eyes, I part my lips. Sensing I won't keep my word, the woman shakes her head beneath her leather hoodie, then covers my mouth again. "I asked you not to do that. If I wanted to hurt you, don't you think I would've done that by now? I just wanna talk. Can we talk, Josephine?"

She said my name.

My mind races. Who the hell is this woman? How she knows my name is beyond me. Kyra? Perhaps this woman heard Kyra calling my name in the tunnel. But Kyra called me Jo—she'd never call me Josephine. So, who is this woman—how's she know me?

The woman coughs, clears gunk out of her throat, spits it to the cement. It's dark in the tunnel, but flickering light shines on the spit—it's dark, as though there's blood in it, a lot of it. I'm not sure why but part of me worries about her— wonders what's wrong with her. Then I ponder what's wrong with me, that I'd worry about this stranger holding me captive.

The woman sighs. "I'm not gonna hurt you."

I inhale and exhale inside her leather glove. Panting, I shake my head no. The woman grabs my shoulders, turns me around. I glare, so she knows I don't trust her.

"Listen, this isn't how I wanted to tell you this. But if I tell you who I am, how I know you . . . will you hear me out after?" There's honesty in the woman's voice; she means what she says.

I nod in agreement. Anything to get away. There's nothing worse than being in a dark tunnel in the middle of the night when no one is looking for you.

She doesn't move the palm covering my mouth. But she makes a fake gun with her free hand. Coughing, she pushes her index and middle finger into my forehead, flexing her thumb like it's the hammer on a pistol. *"Click, click-click,"* she says, mimicking gun sounds. "So, what of it, girl? Gimme the chicken," she says in a raspy voice. "Gimme the chicken! Gimme the chicken! Gimme the chicken!" Every time she says the word *gimme*, the pressure of her palm against my lips increases.

Eyes wide, I gasp. But I don't scream. It's the jig from the alley—the one who held me gunpoint. I'm a little terrified—but more shocked—that she's alive. I'd assumed she died long ago.

I take both hands, place them over the glove covering my mouth, and gently move her hand down my mouth, chin. The woman moves her fingers away from my forehead, backs away from me.

"You're . . . you're her. The jig . . . I was nine . . . the woman with dreads in

Moats Alley. It's you, isn't it?" I say, stuttering, tripping over words, dreading her answer. But I gotta know, need to know.

She coughs harder and harder; between coughs she manages to speak, but her coughing fit makes her hoarse. "It's me. Yes, I'm her. Or was her, once." She pushes back her hood. Long dreads escape it.

I swallow hard without taking my eyes off her. "It was you, wasn't it? . . . The cemetery, the park, following me?"

The jig nods. My muscles tense. I wanna move, but can't. And I can't concentrate on anything except the past, envisioning being nine . . . a gun pressed into my forehead, her gun; it's her. I watch the woman who plagued my nightmares walk out of the tunnel, enter the well-lit park, sit on a steel bench beneath a maple tree.

Moving slowly, I detach my back from the tunnel's curved wall, and follow the woman. When I reach her, I sit on the far end of the bench. She seems familiar. Not just from Moats Alley. But somewhere here, sometime recent.

The woman adjusts the big round shades covering her eyes. And suddenly, I remember where I've seen her. She was the woman in the iCom Technologies waiting room, when I saw Gaitlin earlier yesterday—she wore black shades and read a plastic surgery magazine.

In the light of the streetlamps, she looks different. She's had a rough life, but I see beauty. Where blisters once covered her mouth are smooth brown lips. Gone is the beige crust that once flooded her eyes. Plaque-filled teeth and infected gums remain only in my memory. Her gums are pink now—teeth white, shiny, and straight.

One by one, couples leave the park. Soon only the woman and I are here. Surrounded by trees, listening to froghoppers, leafhoppers, owls' hoots, and rattling cicadas.

The woman turns in my direction. "I'm Rashad." She flashes a tentative smile. It's odd she's smiling, because in nightmares she never did. And in real life, I never thought she could.

I nod. She should smile often—it's gentle, kind, and warm.

Rashad removes her leather gloves, revealing aged hands. Rashad's older, but can't be over fifty. Maybe younger. I can't tell. Despite abusing crack cocaine, she's aged well.

She wheezes. "Look at you. You look different this side of the mountain. Posture refined. New clothes. No ashes staining your cheekbones. This new life suits you well."

"You've changed too."

"Here." Rashad reaches out and drops a copper toke in my hand.

"You don't have'tuh give—"

"You're rich, I know. The suitcase with the black card."

"How'd you know about that?"

Rashad wipes her nose with a hankie and smiles. "How do you think?"

Goose bumps race up my spine. "I thought you were dead."

"I was." She lifts her spine, releases a painful moan. "That night in the alley, you saved me. My life was a series of dysfunctional events before that toke," she says, pitching her chin toward my hand.

"It's the same one?"

She nods. "Money's never been an issue for my family. My stepmother was the wealthiest woman in New Georgia. When she died, everything she owned my stepsister and I inherited. I didn't take the toke that night because I needed it—I accepted it as a reminder there's good in the world. Heartbreak machetes a heart—splits it wide open, leaving two parts. You gave me hope, Josephine." She looks at me with kindness in her eyes, but I see sadness too.

Rashad's spine doesn't curve like it did when I was a kid. It's upright now, poised, elegant. Her black clothes appear costly—so does she, rare and expensive. "There's a lot you want to know, I'm sure." She takes a napkin from her purse. "But where to start?"

"The beginning?" I trace her strong profile with my eyes.

Rashad nods. "See the trains in the distance?" She lifts her chin to the sky, cheeks raised, gazing at a train soaring past the edge of the park. "At thirteen, I designed the engines in all the trains you hear and see."

"How?" The glowing lights of the AerTrains swoosh through the city, crisscrossing through the buildings.

Rashad grins. "An internal combustion engine, a battery electric drive system, and one hell of a split transmission."

"What?" I say.

Rashad laughs.

I laugh. "How'd you go from designing an engine to being a jig?" I say, and as soon as do, I feel sorry for being direct . . . like I don't have a right to ask something so personal. But you can't get more personal than holding a gun to someone's head. And in that regard, no question is too personal between us.

Rashad lowers her eyes. Her face is full of shame, and something resembling regret. "My father remarried after my mother died of swine flu. I inherited a stepsister. Over time, she became very jealous of me. There was something wicked in her. Saw it in high school first. There was a boy—his name was Jerry Frazer. Everyone thought Jerry was the sweetest boy; he had the greatest smile," Rashad says, clearly back in the past. "I brought Jerry home. She told me she'd have him. Take him away from me. Nevertheless, I met her hate with kindness. Thinking niceness would change her."

"But why would she wanna do that?" Hate is brewing for Rashad's stepsister.

Feeling such contempt for someone I've never met, I can only imagine how Rashad feels about her.

"Resentment, maybe? Her own mother compared us . . . told her she was the lesser daughter. Not long after, my sister said she hated me. Said I wasn't the smart daughter. That like my engines, she liked science too. And she'd use it to ruin my life. Said she had a scientific formula to make Jerry break my heart. And nothing would stop her. Didn't believe her, of course."

"Did she do it?"

Rashad nods. "Two weeks later, Jerry left me for her. After that, it was a game to her, and every boy I dated, she turned against me. Made them want her. At twenty-one, I'd had enough. I left New Georgia for New New York. Met my husband, Holt, a year later. We married the following summer in June, had a child . . . a baby girl. Winter came; the baby died. And I had to come back home."

"After everything that happened with your sister, why come back?" I slouch forward, elbows over knees.

"My stepmother's funeral. Radius. Her lungs just wouldn't stop flooding. Couldn't last a day." She tears up, wipes her face.

I start to say something to her, something like "Sorry for your loss." But I don't. I hush. Such niceties never make me feel better when people pity me for having dead parents. People say those phrases when they're clueless over words to say when someone close to you dies. Real friends just listen, like Boah did when I'd wanna talk about my parents. Because real friends know all you need is an ear. And that just being there is enough.

Rashad continues, "I thought the years changed my sister. That she was different and I could trust Holt around her. One month after the funeral, Holt broke my heart. Said he was in love with my sister, that he was moving into my childhood home to be with her. Told me to return to New New York alone. A year later they had a daughter, named her after our mother. It hurt. But it took pain to realize it."

"Realize what?" I take her hand in mine.

"That no amount of kindness would ever change my sister. Love's a chess game to her. And hearts are plastic disposable pawns." A long line of silence stretches between us, and deep breaths follow.

I hunch my shoulders, wondering how Rashad's sister could be so cruel. Then I wonder what happened to Rashad's mother when she was little that made her treat her daughters that way.

She continues. "Holt's death, not long after, crushed me. I escaped back to New New York. Humph . . . spent several miserable years in the Big Apple. Tried to leave my family's fortune behind. Wanted to do it on my own. Worked hard to make ends meet. One day I got tired of being hurt. Wanted to feel something other than heartache. Got hooked on drugs. Ended up in the Ashes, met little you in an alley a year later." Rashad scoffs with a sad smile, holding back tears. "I was at my lowest when I met you. There you were, this little kid with a beat-up sketchbook and a big smile. And you were kind to me. Me! A jig holding a gun to your head. I knew the chicken was infected. I didn't care. I wanted to die. Didn't care who I had to take with me to do it. And with a gun to your head, you, this little coily-head kid, told me no, made me live. You made me love life again, Jo. I owe you my life." She weaves her fingers into mine.

I don't pull away.

Rashad and I sit together for hours. Talking sometimes—sometimes not. She cracks a joke, and we laugh and laugh until she reaches into a black purse and pulls out a tube of lotion, massages it between wrinkled fingers.

The wind blows, hard, over her brown hands, and I smell it again. The sweet scent I smelled in the alley with Reed, just before the woman shot him in the head—the same aroma that plagued my nightmares while I languished in bed. Vanilla.

"Rashad?"

"Yes, Jo?"

"During the riot . . . in the same alley where we met before . . . someone helped me. A woman. I never would've escaped, if she hadn't—" *Killed him*, I wanna say. But don't. "Was it you?"

Rashad places her index finger over her lips, shushing me. We stare at each other in silence. She answers my question, and I thank her, without either of us saying a word. Until Rashad coughs blood into a white napkin—red splatters of blood drops surrounding large blood clots.

"What's wrong with you?"

"Isn't it obvious? I'm dying."

"Of what?"

"It seems with or without that chicken of yours, Radius was my future."

That doesn't make sense because—"It doesn't exist here."

"I got it in the Ashes."

"It's not fatal anymore. Gaitlin. There's a cure." I reach for her hand, but Rashad swiftly lifts her hand to cough into it.

"I've been back just as long as you've been here. I was on the train. I know about the plumes. How do you think I've stayed alive this long? Gaitlin only prolonged the inevitable. The last injection gave two more months of life."

I shake my head no; Rashad's not listening. If I can get her to understand she doesn't have to die, we'll go see Gaitlin, he'll give her the cure, and she'll live. "He's perfected the serum. It's not too late. You can live."

"It'll serve someone else better. It's my time. I've had a good life."

I want Rashad to hope, to fight, to take Gaitlin's serum and live. But how do

I convince someone life's worth living when they've already decided to die?

Light rain hits my face.

"Rashad?"

She coughs. "Yes, Jo?"

"Something you said." She turns her head in my direction. I say, "I never saw you on the train ride over."

She looks away to stare at the green pasture before us. "Ah, but I was there. I saw you at the Lineup, too. I was so proud standing there. Proud to drive you over."

"Drive? You drive AerTrains?"

"I created the engine. Why not?" She smiles. "For the past ten years, every train leaving here bound for the Ashes, I engineered." She sighs. "But that time has passed now. I won't make the next supply run."

"You were at the Lineup?"

Rashad nods, withholding coughs. "Yes. After you were chosen, I went to your house, met Vye, saw the drawings on torn shirts on the wall."

Like a bolt of lightning, it hits me. I remember seeing her there. Rashad's the engineer I saw talking with Reed the day of the Lineup and the woman Vye mentioned visiting the house.

Rashad sighs, presses the side of her fist to her mouth, stifling more coughs, while clearing her raspy throat. "I saw you again on the train back to the Ashes, after the Gala. You were sad, full of tears, asked which train to take. Remember?"

I do. At the train station after the Gala, she was the woman in white. I couldn't place her then, but sitting beside her, it's clear as the moonlight gleaming on my red sneakers.

Rashad continues. "In some way or another I've been there your whole life. I paid Jules—"

"Bootleg Jules?"

She nods, laughing. "I paid him to give your aunt Vye the art magazines. I wanted you to be the prettiest girl at the Gala. I bought the dress. Asked Jules to give it to you for free."

"He traded the outfit for some of Vye's moonshine and pecan pie."

Rashad chokes on laughter, clears gunk. "He wouldn't be Jules if he didn't."

I laugh and then I'm silent. Queasy, feeling so dizzy I can't think straight. I can't fix this. Rashad's dying and there's nothing I can do, nothing she'll let me do. I wanna help her, get her the cure. But her mind is clearly set.

Rashad's iCom holographic keyboard appears above her wrist. On it, she keys 911. "Go." She coughs. "Leave me. I need to be alone now. An ambulance'll be here soon."

"I'm not leaving you."

"You must, Jo. I don't want you here when it happens."

I grab her hand. "I won't."

Rashad snatches her fingers away. "Go!"

"Alright." I stand. Water fills my eyes. I check my pockets for tissues that aren't there. I pull my hands out of pockets and the sketch of Rashad falls to pebbled ground. Rashad grabs it before I can retrieve it, before the water snatches the image away. "Don't look at it," I say.

Rashad opens the folded paper, gazes at it. "I like the eyes." Rashad refolds the sketch, hands it back. "I scared you."

"Just a bit."

"I scared myself," Rashad says. "Now go!"

Rashad holds her head down, hiding her face, hiding tears. I leave Rashad's side. I wanna look back, see Rashad once more, but I don't. To prevent myself from thinking, I run. Faster and faster, I run farther away. Leaving Rashad to die beneath the large maple. In two hours, the unique beauty of her face'll disappear. She'll look worse than the night I met her in Moats Alley. Inside her mouth, her tongue'll blacken, pink gums'll blister. Pulpy lesions will cover her limbs. Two hours after, she won't be able to eat, drink, speak. One by one her organs'll shut down. She'll sleep forever.

At Elenore's doorstep, I stare at Hugo Park, see the bridge in the distance, thinking about how Rashad's gone. She saved my life, and I never told her goodbye.

42

COVE

Knock. Knock. Knock . . .

"Cove?" Jo's at the door.

From my bed, I see her shadow under the door. I don't speak. If I speak to her, it'll break me more. I close my eyes, listen to her addictive voice call my name. It hurts to ignore her. But as much as it hurts, it's nothing compared to what's coming.

Heartbeats—mine. I listen to the rhythm. It pounds.

Lub-dub, lub-dub, lub-dub . . .

"Are you there?" She releases a heavy-hearted sigh, sniffles.

I get out of bed, walk to my bedroom door, and wrap my palm around the cool knob. I release the knob and back away from the door.

There's a light tap on the other side, as if right now, Jo's resting her head against the steel door. She sighs.

iCom chirps. I answer on accident, but say nothing. It's Edith.

Knock. Knock. Knock . . . Then silence and heartbeats.

Lub-dub, lub-dub, lub-dub . . .

"Hello?" Edith says in my ear. I don't respond.

Knock. Knock. Knock . . .

Lub-dub, lub-dub, lub-dub . . .

Edith dramatically clears her throat. "iCom's pinpointed your direct location, Cove. Who's knocking on your door?"

Knock. Knock. Knock . . .

Lub-dub, lub-dub, lub-dub . . .

No more knocking. Dead silence.

"Ahhh." Jo exhales, cries hard, sniffles again.

"Who's crying?" Edith says.

Staring at the light under the door, I wait for Jo's shadow to disappear.

I hang up on Edith.

43

JOSEPHINE

Out the window, across the street, ambulance lights, red, blue, and white, glare in Hugo Park. If Rashad's not dead, she will be soon. She had a rough life. Just thinking of how Rashad's sister treated her brings tears to my eyes. I wipe them away and feel more form in the corners of both eyes.

It's getting colder and colder these days. October and Fall Ball's around the corner. And when the corner appears, AerTrains will return to the Ashes to deliver winter supplies. I have less than two weeks to decide. Will I take the train with Gaitlin with thousands of bottles of plume serum, to cure Radius in the Ashes? Or should I attend Fall Ball and become the newest member of New Georgian society alongside Kyra and Rald? Maybe if I did both—became a citizen, then left the next morning for the Ashes—I could travel back and forth like Aurice and Gaitlin. But would Elenore let me spend all that time away? Could I really leave the Ashes again? My chest feels heavy, tight, warm. My whole life I've dreamed of belonging here. Between Gaitlin's serum, and my feelings for Cove, I know what's right, but I don't know what I want.

I walk to the closet, pull a wool sweater over my head, and flop onto the bed. Ten minutes ago, I laid my head against Cove's bedroom door, crying as I knocked. He's not home or he's sleeping. It's strange, but for a second, I thought I heard him breathing. Maybe it's in my head. Maybe watching Rashad fight Radius is messing with me—making me hear things, think absurdities, and sulk over all the people still dying of it in the Ashes.

Inside, my heart hurts—my chest feels heavy, like it's falling fast and hard off a skyscraper. I miss home. I'd give anything for Vye's tight hug. Or the comfort of sniffing one of her cinnamon pecan pies. Before I drift off, I think of images I want to sketch when I'm not so tired. The first is Vye's strong hands holding a steaming pie. The second is the roller coaster in the broke amusement park in the Ashes, and the third is my brown hand reaching for Cove's pale fingers.

The next day, at the crack of dawn, Cove knocks on my bedroom door. When I open the door, the skin around his eyes is wrinkled and his jaw clenched. I ask him, "What's wrong?"

Cove takes me in his arms and holds on tight, asks where I've been. Says he woke up after we fell asleep last night to an empty bed, says he was worried, is worried. That he looked and looked for me, says he searched the witch's house top to bottom, and couldn't find me, and asks, "Where did you go? Where have you been?"

I tell him it's a long story. That if he'd agree to hold me while I tell it, I won't give him the CliffsNotes version. Cove agrees, says, "Yes." He leads us to the balcony outside my bedroom. We lie horizontal on the white chaise longue, where light rain falls on our skin. I don't care about getting wet. It just feels good to lie here, be here. The gray sky lightens as I talk. With my head tucked under his chin, I tell Cove the story of the jig with the gun, what happened that night, the nightmares after, and what happened tonight. Tell him she was like a fairy godmother . . . saved me from Reed, gave me the black card. That she died of Radius on a bench, and that's why I knocked on his door.

Cove apologizes for his absence in my time of need. He releases a heavy sigh, says, "There's no place I'd rather be than with you. Life alters in many ways, but it'll never alter the way I feel for you. No matter what happens I'm here. You're safe with me, always. Remember that."

Cove kisses my nose, forehead, then bottom lip. I rest my head on his chest, and exhale deep. Deeper. Tonight's a bad night, but somehow, being this close to Cove, I feel more warm than chilly, more brave than fearful, and more hopeful than sad.

44

JOSEPHINE

It's been almost two weeks since Rashad died in Hugo Park. Her death makes me think about life. And I hate it, wish I could stop morbid thoughts, but her passing makes me think about all the people've loved and lost, too. Think about Boah. Vye. Neal. Jessup. But Rashad's death makes me think about other things too, like that it's possible for people to change. If we're alive, we're allowed to transition from one way of thinking to the next. I'm in a transition now.

For most of my time here, I've felt torn. I've kept one foot in the Ashes and the other in New Georgia. It's exhausting, but I've enjoyed my time here. Tried to allow myself to be here, to live here inside and out, and accept the opportunities given, love offered, and happiness received.

Happiness.

Love.

Cove . . . My Cove. Ever since the night Rashad died, Cove's been distant. When I call him, he doesn't answer. I guess he needs time to study. Or at least that's what he says when he finally does answer but can't talk long. And when that happens, Cove reassures he's excited about Fall Ball. Says he can't wait to dance and see my dress. I don't know, I wanna trust things are alright between us, but I can't help thinking something is wrong, off, or not being said.

I pull my head out of deep thoughts. Scan the room that was my first introduction to New Georgia inside Elenore's house. Nothing perfect anywhere. But maybe that's the point. It's not supposed to be. Maybe perfect is a wilting red rose. A flower with missing parts of itself. But missing petals doesn't make it less beautiful; it makes it unique. From now on, I'll be like the wilted rose, stop seeking perfection.

I sigh, think of tomorrow night. And thinking of tomorrow night draws my attention to the gold envelope resting at the center of my bed. A drone delivered it this morning.

This is the moment Hopefuls dream of. I picked it up in a hurry, then threw it on the bed, afraid to open it. Afraid of the words inside it. Avoided it all day.

I close my eyes, exhale, and take a seat next to the glossy envelope. I'm excited about what's inside. And I'm terrified, too. Once opened, one of two things will become reality. Reality one? I'll open the envelope and it'll be an invitation to Fall Ball. Which means I've shown that someone from the wrong side of the mountain has once again successfully prepared for New Georgia society. I'll attend the ball, get inducted, and live happily ever after in rich bliss with Cove. Reality number two is less celebratory, less fun. In this reality, instead of an invitation to attend Fall Ball, there'll be a rejection letter, with information on the next AerTrain back to the Ashes.

Elbows on knees, palms covering my face, I think about my future. This is it. Right here and now. I know what I want. I'll still miss Vye, Neal, even Jessup, but I wanna stay. I want my life in New Georgia. And I've never said it inside my head before, but as much as I wanted Boah when he was alive, I want Cove that way right now.

I rise from the bed, enter the walk-in closet, flip the switch, and gaze at the red Marie-Antoinette gown with pockets I bought while shopping with Aurice. I carry it into the room, lay the gown gently on the bed. I lie beside the dress, braids touching its softness, eyes gazing in wonder, admiring the dress's beautiful crimson fabric. I swallow hard. My heart races. I shiver. All at once, I'm fearful and amazed.

"All of this excitement could be for nothing. And I'll never get to wear you."

I think back to what Aunt Vye said before the Gala. Hear her voice in my head:

Change is scary. Just be yourself . . . you'll do fine. They're the lucky ones. No matter what happens tonight, remember that. And her voice again as she lifted my chin. *Don'tcha know how special yuh are? Yuh ma'd be proud. Dad, too.*

Remembering Vye's words calms insecure thoughts and steadies my racing heart.

I exhale some guts, dust away fear, grab the gold envelope, and open it. Swiftly, I rise to my feet. With both hands covering my smile, I jump around the room like a kangaroo. I spin around and around and around, and fall face up onto the cushy oval bed. I gaze into the skylight. Watch a red robin soar by.

I've made it. I've been accepted. And I think in Cove, I've found something that feels like love.

45

COVE

Sick to my stomach over it. The very thought of doing it burns the lining in my stomach. But it doesn't matter. The pain doesn't matter. I must do it. I must break Jo.

The alternative, not breaking her . . . is too a lot of things. Too revealing. Too vulnerable. Too much of the past. Too hurtful. For both of us. I don't want to treat her like I've treated the others. I don't want Elenore to hurt her more by revealing my past. I sigh. For me. Wish I could curl fingers inside Jo's small, pretty head like a bowling ball. Discover Jo's reaction to information Elenore will use as blackmail should I disobey her orders.

Elenore will tell Jo that Margo and I swiped each other's V-cards, about how I break innocent hearts for fun, and about Edith, everything about Edith, before I get a chance to explain. I've thought about telling Jo before Elenore gets to her. If I do that, I won't have to break Jo, or be afraid of what Elenore might or might not reveal. But then I put everything in Jo's hands. Humph. I comb my hair back with four fingers.

I adjust my Fall Ball tux, flick lint off my suit, thinking seriously about how I would confess my toxic past to Jo. "I took my stepsister's virginity and she took mine. I was trained not to love. And broke hearts. I was trained so well that sometimes I liked it. I also envy those I broke too. At least they weren't afraid of love, afraid to love."

I shake my head at the imagined conversation. I can't tell her that. Besides, if

I did, what would Jo say? How would she take it? "It's okay you plucked your sister, no biggie, Cove." Yeah, no, that truth will never be okay for someone like Jo. Pure Jo. I've spent days on end convincing her she can trust me. Told her she could trust me. That she was safe with me. But can anyone be safe hugging a hider, kissing a liar?

I need to play it cool tonight. Be cool. Calm. You've got this. "But you don't got this," I say in the hologram mirror. I make funny faces, mean faces; I punch through my translucent reflection. "You prick. You little shit. You fucking coward."

———————

It's a perfect night at Maple House. Cream drapes frame candlelit windows; iron heaters circulate a warm breeze carrying scents of baked turkey, mac and cheese, and dressing among the chattering crowd. On the ceiling, the enormous vintage clock's hour hand touches Roman numeral VIII. It's early. But the Fall Ball's masquerade is in full swing.

In every corner, attendees laugh—sipping everything from pink champagne to ginger ale in tall flute glasses—dressed in eighteenth-century formal fashions, holding masks over their greedy eyes, or strapped around their bobbing, blabbering heads. Rald, Kyra, and Jo are the centerpieces of it all, treated like trophies as they eagerly wait for the citizenship ceremony near the end of the ball.

An orchestra plays classical music in the corner next to the Reps' extravagant dinner table where Elenore sits. She stares at Jo and I as we sway with the sultry strings of the cellist's solo. I face Jo, and spin us around, leaving Elenore's sinister smirk behind my back.

God, Jo smells good. I press my palm into the small of her back, pull her close—closer. Her hair fumes coconut, there are hints of lemon on her shoulder, and the skin below her earlobe is a quirky bouquet of citrus, ginger, and lime.

Tonight, her hair's straight, not coily—it's parted down the middle, swooped back in a bun just above her neck. She's a far cry from the girl with three braids at the Gala.

With a slight smile, I . . . watch her. Follow slight variations of movements nestled inside her nose, lips, and chin muscles—sighing at the rise and fall of her cleavage. I flash a smile Jo's way so she can't see my hurt, can't tell I'm breaking. I've been flogged by the witch until she drew blood and didn't shed a tear. And yet here I am with the girl who's been nothing but gentle, and it's taking everything in me not to cry.

"You clean up nice, slowpoke." Jo adjusts the hankie tucked in my tailcoat's pocket.

"And you, you're fucking stunning."

She blushes, leans her forehead against my shoulder. "You feel good."

"I like you this close." I breathe her in. I wanna remember this moment. The way we are right now: happy, free, and safe in each other's arms—tuning out the world and all the monsters living in it.

Jo caresses my arm. "I feel you . . . the real you. I like you."

I never tell girls I like them. "I like you too much." I love you. I close my eyes, smile on her shoulder, and inhale her brown skin.

Through her red feathered mask, Jo looks at me with those big round brown eyes, and I want to stop what's coming next. I want to beat myself in the head with something that'll hurt like I'm about to hurt her.

Edith Fairmoth sits at a table with her frisky mother. Every so often, Vimberly combs Edith's straight hair with her fingernails. Edith swoons, blushing.

Unbeknownst to Jo, I nod at Edith, instructing her to come to the dance floor. She rises from her seat, saunters over, tucking red locks behind her left ear.

"Do you mind?" Edith says, glowering at Jo. "I'd like to dance with my date."

With narrowed eyes, Jo stops her feet, stares back and forth between me and Edith. She pins her gaze on my face. Our eyes meet. "What is this?"

I can't look at Jo. I'm silent. And it's deafening.

Jo pushes away from me.

Edith stares with an arched brow. "Will you tell her or not?"

"What's going on here, Cove?" Jo glares.

"Tell her!" Edith says. "You've hidden it long enough. I've been a good girl like you said. Haven't told a soul."

Jo lifts her mask, takes it off; her eyes are watery. "Tell me what?"

In the distance, sitting at a table with Kyra and Rald, Margo shakes her head in disapproval. She knows what's about to happen. Ever since she's gotten out of the hospital, she's been different. Like somehow, slitting her wrists got rid of every ounce of sinister blood pumping through her veins. We admitted her to the hospital a suicidal alkie. And when Gaitlin bought her home, she was a born-again saint. But who cares; Margo can judge all she wants—throw the book at me. It won't change anything. There's one logical choice here. And it must happen. Jo's my masterpiece.

"Fine. I'll tell her." Edith takes her mask off.

I grab Edith's wrist, hushing her. "Don't."

Jo takes my face in her hands and removes my white mask. "Nothing you say'll change how I feel. Just be honest."

I'm a broken asshole. My heart pounds.

Lub-dub, lub-dub, lub-dub, lub-dub . . .

Sucking my bottom lip into my mouth, I shake my head and sigh.

Edith huffs. "Enough of this. I heard you crying at his door that night. You're so pathetic. All you people over there are."

Jo's glare's so ruthless, it could kill stars. But she doesn't seem bothered by

Edith or the derogatory remark she just made. Jo's pissed at me. "Wait. You were home that night . . . in your room? You told her?"

I wanna tell Jo: Edith's lying. She didn't hear you cry, but I did. And yes, I told Edith. I didn't want to. I had to so this moment felt real, feels real. So Jo'd believe the lie—believe I didn't care about her tears that night. That I don't care about her feelings at all. It wasn't the truth then. It's not the truth now. But I gotta break Jo. Gotta do it my way. Elenore's way would rip Jo to shreds.

Edith giggles. "Of course he did, silly. Why wouldn't he when we're enga—"

"Edith!" I interrupt. I take a breath. "Jo—" I say. "Edith and I are to be married."

Tears trail down her cheeks. "What?" Jo releases my face, backs away. "Since when?"

I can't meet Jo's tearful glare. Those sweet eyes. The gentle dark irises I melt for, die for. "Since birth."

Jo punches my shoulder over and over. Then repeatedly socks my chest. Eyes spin to us from all over the room. "How could you?" Jo says. "To think, I almost slept with—" The hitting stops. She inhales deep. Exhales with closed eyes. She flips her lids open and sighs. "I'm tired. I'm so tired," Jo says, chin quivering, then leaks more tears as she stares at the small space separating Edith and me. "Okay."

"Dance with me?" Edith says. I nod, take her into my arms and sway.

Jo's feathered mask drops to the floor. She lifts the hem of her red gown, rushes across the ballroom floor, headed for the exit.

Edith rests her cheek on my shoulder. "God, Cove . . . I love you so much. Do you love me?"

I never tell girls *I love you*. "You're pleasant."

46

JOSEPHINE

I shove the ballroom doors open, speed walk down the wide, long hallway, trying every door. So far, every door's locked. There're three doors left.

Door one is locked.

Knob two won't twist. Will nothing go my way?

Gotta keep trying. Gotta get some place dark, unseen, and cry my eyes out.

Door three opens. I push it open, rush inside, and close the door behind me, resting my back against the hardwood door. I push my face into my hands, slide my spine down the door, until I'm sitting on the cool floor.

How could I be so stupid? It was there all along. Truth was slapping me in the face. I refused to see then, but now it all makes sense. Like how Elenore told Gaitlin she and Edith were going shopping for the dress. The countless visits Edith made to Elenore's house, and how Cove evaded calls whenever he was with me, and how he never answered questions regarding his relationship with Edith. And to top it all off, the night Rashad died, he heard me knocking like a sad idiot, but didn't answer because he was on the phone with Edith. I needed him, and he chose her.

Scents resembling acrylic and newspaper fill my nostrils. It's cold in here. I *brrrrr*, take my face out of my hands, and scan the room. It's dark, but enough porch light and moonlight pass through open-curtain windows, gifting bright light to view my surroundings.

Black-and-white snapshots of people like me, folks raised in bordering lands, are displayed. I whip my head around. Discover sketches created from pencil and charcoal—my medium. In the corner is a name: Aurice Henry.

I think of what Vye would feel about me coming home. I've made it here, finally living the dream. But I'm so hurt. I don't know what to do. Can't think straight. I've made it this far, but everything's telling me to head back to the Ashes. I feel for the letter I tucked inside my gown's pocket. The one Vye said not to open until Fall Ball. Spine nestled against cool wall, I unseal it.

I flip the letter open, pull the paper out, unfold it. A shiver rushes across the back of my neck. I drop the letter, watch it fall to wood floor.

It's a letter written in Boah's handwriting. I stare at the paper on the floor like it's growing arms. My skin is hot. I swallow, eyes outlining the letter left to right, right to left. "Boah's dead . . ."

I lift the letter off the floor and place it on my lap, stare at it like it's a foreign object. Wide-eyed, I stare at Boah's handwriting. "How is this possi—? When'd he . . . ?"

I take a deep breath, lift Boah's letter, open and read.

> *My Jo . . .*
>
>> *I ain't dead.*
>>
>> *And shit, that ain't a good way tuh start a letter . . . it ain't poetic, fancy, or even damn pretty, but it's duh truth, it's plain. Plain's duh only way I know how'duh be. Yuh can't feel it, but I'm in a lot of pain. And yuh can't see it, but I'm smiling knowing you're reading these words, right now.*

I'm breathing so fast, barely blinking. I can't think, can't feel my feet. I'm outside myself, not believing what's happening, what I'm seeing, feeling. I watched him die.

So, tell me, are yuh famous yet? I hope that made yuh smile . . . hope
yuh not still mad. I should have told you what was going on with Jules
and the water hole. Didn't mean to turn you away, treat you bad. I don't
know why I'm saying all this . . . none of it really matters . . . Thought I
didn't do enough to save yuh that night—that bastard-ass Reed hurt yuh
or worse . . . thought yuh were dead.

I pause at this. *I thought you were dead, too.*

Vye told me what happened tuh Reed. I shouldn't say this. It's wrong
duh think it, but for what he did to me, and what he did tuh yuh, Jo, I'm
glad he's dead. Two girls found his dead body in Moats Alley. They cut
him up, buried his body in seven holes in duh wastelands.

I wanna feel bad for Reed. But I don't. Does that make me a bad person? Have
I changed so much since the jig—Rashad—held me gunpoint? I spared her life
when she threatened mine, and here I am glad Reed's dead. I take a deep breath,
read more.

I wanna stop here. Not bring it up. But . . . ugh, Jo. I'm sorry yuh had
to see me that way. Must've scared yuh. But I'm sorrier. Watching Reed
over you, unable to stop him, help yuh . . . Spent days worrying, thinking
Reed carried yuh off and left yuh in some ditch for dead. Aurice visited
after it all happened, told Vye yuh were okay. Said he found yuh in Moats
Alley hardly breathing, next to me . . . said he thought I was dead. If it
weren't for Neal, I would be. Ah, yuh'd be proud of him, Jo . . . what
happened to Neal that night, at the hanging tree, changed him. He keeps
watch over me, makes Healer Marie's sacred plant blue tea.

I stop at this . . . Cops never caught Neal. I'm not shocked Neal's alive; I knew
cops wouldn't find him in the mountains. I'm surprised he risked being caught to
save Boah. My eyes water over Boah's kind words about Neal. I read on . . .

Aurice told us that yuh were okay, healing in New Georgia. He said he'd deliver a letter to yuh. If yuh reading this, he kept his promise.

Wait, Aurice knew Boah was alive this whole time. He knew how sad I was, thinking Boah was dead. Why didn't he tell me? Why did he have Gaitlin pass me the letters?

And before you go getting all, you know, like you know yuh do. Don't hold Aurice's silence against him. Made him promise not to tell yuh I was alive, Vye did, too. We didn't want you tuh come home and miss out on yuh life there.

Vye says hello, wonders how yuh are. Wonders if her first letter surprised yuh, made you cry. I suppose I'll wonder if this letter does the same. Jessup says smile and see yuh later gator. And Healer Marie said had yuh not gotten Jessup tuh her when you did, he would've died. Yuh did good, Jo. Yuh saved his life. But then again yuh always do. Being yuh friend saved mine.

I can't write much anything else on it. Hard duh think about that night. Harder tuh write about. Don't think I'll read this after writing it. Wanna forget that night ever happened. Move on. Yuh should, too.

Vye's beside me right now, rolling eyes, saying dis letter's too long so I must be lying 'bout something. Says Aurice and the woman who stopped by earlier are leaving soon and we gotta give them our letters . . . But look, I didn't wanna get into this, but something's brewing in the Ashes, Jo. Good things. Beautiful things.

Until,

Boah

I don't know everything I feel; I just know I'm happy, lighter. Heart pumps calm pulses. But calm doesn't last long. I'm here, not there where Boah is. Under a wrinkled forehead, my eyes shift left to right. And slowly, the ache in my chest returns. I think about Cove, look down at Boah's words, think of Cove again, then rinse and repeat these cycling thoughts.

Boah's last words are troubling. *Something's brewing in the Ashes.* Could I be overthinking it? Boah also said they were *good things, beautiful things.* My eyes water again. Maybe the riot got so bad, it made the violence stop. Maybe good came out of bad.

"Beautiful, aren't they?" Elenore speaks and muscles in my face tighten.

I straighten my spine. I stuff the letter into my gown's pocket. Wipe tears. "Sorry. I . . . I'll find another room." How long has she been here?

"Nonsense. I come here to quiet the mind. Seems we had the same plan." Elenore grabs a box of tissues from the side table, the one next to the chaise longue in the middle of the room—the only piece of furniture in here. "Tissue?"

"No, thank you. No more tears. They're dry."

Elenore sets the tissues back on the side table, then walks to the wall of black-and-white snapshots of border people. "This one . . ." she says, referring to a photograph of an old black man, smoking a pipe, wearing a dark fedora and red shoes.

I step toward the photo, nod. "He's so tal—"

"Talented, yes. Had it not been for my sister, Aurice would've never made it past the Lineup that year." She touches the center of the photograph as if she's reminiscing. "Hmm, how she loved his work, loved him." She removes her hand from the photo. "But I discovered his talent. Made him what he is today."

"How so?"

Elenore pulls photos from her purse. "Aurice took these too."

They're more photos of the Ashes, but these are different. My throat feels dry, sore, like I'm gonna choke, then water fills my eyes. In the pictures, cops surround a girl; their faces are mean, eyes full of anger. I flip through the photos until the last one presents itself. A photo of the girl dead in the street, her baby crying in her lifeless arms.

"You could draw this, show the pain of this girl. Be the voice of the Ashes through your art. I'll make sure it happens. Make you famous. More famous than Aurice."

"When were these taken? Where?"

"During the Gala. Suffering's beautiful captured in photos, don't you agree? Dreadful about that riot . . . and what happened to you, of course. But that girl. I don't blame the authorities. They were doing their job, quite well I'd say; caught a little thief."

My jaws clench. "Hope."

"Pardon?"

"Her name was Hope."

"I'm surprised you know the name of such a troublemaker."

"We remember names of the fallen in the Ashes."

Elenore turns, shrugs with a hint of a smile. "Right."

"Hope's death was senseless. They killed her for no reason."

"Cops caught a thief."

"It was a loaf of bread. She was a teenage mother, with a three-month-old son, starving."

"Cancer, caused by sun or cigarettes, is still cancer. She was a thief who let a loaf of bread take her life." Elenore shows the photo of Hope's little boy crying. "Look at those cute little red shoes."

I turn away. Elenore continues, "Do you know why you people are only allowed to wear red shoes?"

I know the answer, but I won't give it. Back facing Elenore, I head for the door. The holographic clock reads eleven p.m. The first AerTrain since the Gala leaves New Georgia in five hours. Now I know I'll be on it.

"Unfair, isn't it?" Elenore says. I stop walking. "Your ancestors were once kings and queens, dictating over my ancestors. And now, present and future, generations of my descendants'll build houses, offices, and urban parks over the brittle bones of your failed people. But it doesn't have to be that way for your offspring. Red shoes mark blood spilled over greed."

I turn to face her. "And now your people do the same. Confine generations of people to suffer like dogs." I press my fingernails into my palms. I open my mouth. "Why do you hate us?"

She says, "Dogs are cleaner. More useful." Elenore removes her mask. Her eyes are sharp blue, cold, empty. Her gaze feels like paper cuts. "Your behavior is surprising, Jo. So much so, I don't think I can help you. Artists must see life from all sides, even opposition. You see things in black and white. Gray is a color, too."

I can't control my hands; they're shaking. I can't feel my heart; it's fallen. My throat is tight. I'll never fit in here. I don't belong here. Maybe Cove isn't who I thought he was, is. Nothing's what I thought it'd be. I shouldn't be in the place of my dreams, unhappy, with a broken heart calling for home. But I can't let go of the question. For some reason, I need to know why Elenore's so hateful. I need to know, so I ask again, "Why do you hate us?"

Elenore ignores my question, rubs an eyebrow. With cold eyes, she says, "Cove's not an option anymore, never was. He'll be married soon. But you're beautiful, for a black girl. There will be others. More suitable boys. Ones not as damaged as Cove. He's lost, you see. Like me. Like Margo. Three lost souls; together we're found. Shame things turned as they did. I saw so much potential. Now the only art you'll make'll be scribbled on paper you'll hang on tattered walls of the shack you inherit in the Ashes. It's where you belong. And that's where you'll live and die. Over there, in that shack. That is . . . if your home isn't ashes by now."

My face feels like fire; my throat burns. "You're manipulative. Toxic. You ruin things. Beautiful things. You ruin them. With your selfishness to always have control. Cove's not a lost cause. He's different, damaged, but not beyond repair. You're the reason he's this way. But there's a light inside him; I saw it."

Elenore clenches her jaw.

I shake my head. "You haven't won."

Elenore saunters in my direction. "You naive and thoughtless child. Like God created Adam and Eve, Cove's made in my image. You're a magician's trick. Poof. A game. A light-skinned black Barbie with a big thumping heart I wanted to crush. I cherry-picked you at first sight. You and all your true-love speak. Cove courted you as I instructed. Slept with you, broke it off, and stepped on your heart at my command. He's marrying a girl he can't stand for me. If that isn't a stunning victory with a gold metal prize, I don't know what is. You're Cove's tragically beautiful masterpiece. Your broken heart belongs to him. His belongs to me."

"You're wrong. He's nothing like you," I say. "He could've, but he didn't."

She walks over to view an oil painting, depicting a black half human, half boar, stabbing a half-naked pale girl in the chest with a pitchfork. Somehow, the girl sleeps peacefully. "He didn't what?"

It hurts to say it; to admit to Elenore that—"I'm still a virgin." The words sting my tongue because I wish they weren't true. I wish I wasn't.

Elenore's cheeks turn red. She grinds her teeth.

Slowly, I walk toward her, closing the gap between us. "If misery's all you live for, I can't hate or dislike you for it. I pity you. For what's sadder than a person devoid of empathy and love? Nothing."

Elenore flashes a side smile. She reaches out to me, tucks strands of hair behind my ear. "My heart was once as big as yours. Thumping and beating and more thumping. But time has taught me more than your little years have allowed.

Love is a feast of thorns and ashes, my dear. *Chew* its thorns, it'll *cut* your throat. Swallow it whole, it'll burn you from the inside out—it consumes souls, leaving trails of ashes. We're the same, Josephine. Destined to be consumed."

I swipe Elenore's hand out of my hair, back away from her. Watching her cruel face, I close the door to the large art room, turn around, crashing into a tall white man in a suit. Papers in hands fly over our heads, falling to wood floors like white feathers. "I'm so sorry," I say. "I'll help."

"Josephine! Thanks, but it's really not—" The man gives in when I bend down beside him.

Classical music from the ballroom plays as we gather scattered papers. On a fallen sheet, Cove's full name's printed in all caps.

The man's iCom chirps. "Greer here." He stands, rushes to the front door. "Going outside. One sec."

I don't know how I feel about Cove, but my eyes are still greedy. On borrowed time, I read the document with Cove's name on it. Financial papers. Maybe the man is a banker or accountant. At the end of January, land belonging to Cove's mother will revert to the bank and be sold at auction. Three more papers outline arrear payments unmade by Cove's legal guardian: Elenore Wells. Sometimes when you sign contracts you can't trust the person drying the ink.

Greer walks back inside. I hand him the three folders. "Sorry about that. My little girl's mischievous." He laughs. "She put gum in my wife's hair." Greer laughs but stops soon after. "What's wrong?"

I glance up; our eyes meet. "You work at the bank, sir?"

Greer chuckles. "Sure do, Josephine. I handled that black card of yours," he says conspiratorially. He narrows his eyes. "Why d'you ask?"

I inhale. I don't know where to start. "Can we talk?"

338

47

COVE

Up on the roof, I swing my legs over the edge and peer at the blue mountains in the distance. It's winter. Snow is allergic to New Georgia, but I wonder if it visits the Ashes. An angry breeze hits my face. I inhale the air, take in its aroma of pine needles, sun, and coffee. I breathe into the white crop top Jo left behind four months ago. It still smells like the coconut oil in her hair.

Across Elenore's lawn, the brick road that leads to Hugo Park is full of locals attending the regional meetup to debate the statewide curfew effective tonight. No one living inside the border travels outside their city anymore. Cops swear everything's under control. It's all lies. Untruths to keep New Georgia citizens calm. But it's too late. There's fear in the rich—fear I've never seen. Their fright reads like pages of a bestselling thriller.

Frequently, investigative journalists report stories involving the mysterious disappearance of citizens captured and held hostage by border people. Captors aren't interested in ransoms or frivolous demands. Taken folks just disappear. Never heard from again.

Walls inside schools, banks, grocery stores, AerTrains, and turbos display holographic photographs of the missing. Each hologram shows the Taken's full name, age, height, weight, hair color, and eye pigment next to their last known photo.

Two months ago, Edith and I married in a quiet ceremony in the middle of the forest. Peach and gray were the colors—Elenore's choice. I detest peach. It's one of those in-between tints, hiding between stronger colors. I take deep breaths, inhale cool winds, thinking of Margo—she's missing. The last time I saw her was after Fall Ball. If I close my eyes tight, I can hear her yelling her last words to Elenore.

"All of this sick fascination with breaking hearts. Now you've passed this sickness, this horror, on to me. Who ruined you? Huh? Who broke you?!" Margo'd said, eyes full of tears.

Elenore humphed. "My mother." Elenore held the brown leather diary, extended her arm, offering it to Margo.

Margo rejected her offer, rolled her eyes, turned her back to Elenore, and left the house—never seen since.

Elenore's convinced she ran away to New New York. In her mind, Margo burns her money card in the Big Apple by day and parties by night. More lies. I know my sister. We've shared too much. She'd never leave without saying goodbye. Larry hasn't seen Margo either, but he doesn't miss her—he misses Kyra. And he's been a blabbering nutcase ever since Kyra boarded an AerTrain last week to the Ashes. Kyra told Larry the love of her life was across the mountain—that her heart wasn't big enough for two people.

James doesn't come around much. But last night, he iCom'd asking if I'd heard any news about Margo. I told him the same thing I tell everyone: "Margo doesn't want to be found."

Last night in bed, Edith wrapped her arm around my waist. She kissed my chest. Asked if I thought Margo was one of the Taken. I joked and said, "If she is, they won't keep her bratty ass long." I laughed. And it was a real laugh, followed by happy tears, because despite missing my sister, I'm glad she escaped the witch who tormented us. And wherever Margo is, I have a feeling she's doing alright.

Humor feels good. It won't change all the shitty shit I've done, or the state of the world, but it feels good to smile and really laugh, just be—be anything other than afraid of the uncertainty of gullible life.

Below, Greer Jr. pulls his black SUV into the driveway and steps outside his vehicle. An hour ago, he iCom'd saying he'd be over in ten minutes. I wave from the roof. He waves downward, asking me to climb down.

On ground level, Greer Jr. pats my shoulder. "Where's the business-casual look? Don't think've seen you in jeans and a T-shirt."

"We'll see how it goes."

He nods. "How are my favorite newlyweds?"

I take a deep breath. "Adjusting."

"That's what it's all about."

"What's that?" I say.

"Marriage," he says. "It's one big change with a few kisses along the way. Now, hear me out, Cove. It's not always easy for Vera and me. We work at love. And marriage, well, marriage is hard, son. It's manual labor. It's daily trying harder than you did the day before. Almost like an occupation. And like most jobs, some days you don't want to drive to the office. But when the check hits the bank, you're proud of yourself. And realize it's worthwhile."

I nod, staring at the white pages in the black folder clasped in his hand.

In three hours, Plum Orchard becomes the property of New Georgia Trust. And next week, it'll be the prized possession of the highest bidder.

"Ride with me?" Greer asks.

One hour into the drive, Greer asks about Margo, if we've heard anything, gotten any clues.

I scoff. "Elenore thinks she's in NNYC."

"How is Elenore?"

"No change."

"Still having trouble with her memory?"

I shake my head. "It's been weeks. Just mumbles."

Last October, after the Fall Ball, Elenore learned her stepsister, a black woman named Rashad, died. I remember reading her name in the brown leather journal, wondering about the sister we thought was dead. The coroner asked Elenore to identify the body of a woman who listed Elenore her next of kin on her do-not-resuscitate papers.

After identifying Rashad's body, Elenore had a nervous breakdown. Edith and I drove her to the hospital. She spent three weeks dreaming and screaming, two weeks bathless, and one month starving herself so she'd resemble death.

Elenore eats and showers now, but she's eerily different. Day and night, she sits behind her white vanity, crying silently while watching her wrinkled hands shake.

I recognize the route to Plum Orchard long before Greer stops the car outside the orchard's tall vintage iron fence. He hands me three black folders. "Read nothing."

"Don't read?"

He rubs his thick mustache. "Just open the first folder. Look to the bottom of the first page. Sign and date."

I narrow my eyes at him.

"Trust me," he says, smiling.

Greer Jr.'s honest, always has been. I think back to last year when Elenore tried to swindle money from the trust fund. Greer Jr. told Elenore no.

I open the folder.

Greer Jr. places his hand over the black folder, closing it. "Wait! First, I need a toke."

"A toke?" I pat down my jean pockets. "Who carries pennies?"

He digs into his pants pocket, pulls the copper coin out. "I do. Take it."

Confused, I take the cold metal in my hand.

"Now hand it back," he says.

I drop the toke in the center of his palm. I stare at the hologram of his little girl displayed next to the glove compartment. She looks spoiled—black pigtails, braces, smiling, in a rainbow tee, holding a black unicorn figurine.

Greer Jr. makes a fist around the dingy coin. "Now you can open and sign."

I release a heavy sigh, open the top folder, sign my name the dotted line, and date it: 1/24/71.

Greer Jr. reaches into the glove compartment, grabs a red skeleton key, places it in my hand. "It's yours." He nods toward Plum Orchard.

"I don't understand. What about the arrears—taxes?"

He shrugs, nods. "Paid in full."

"My inheritance?" I say.

He shakes his head. "No."

"Then how?"

"A private, very generous donor." Greer Jr. clears his throat. "Private." He inhales, then exhales, adjusting his brown bow tie. "Red clay."

"What about it?"

"Per the donor's request, it's the only information allowed. Red clay."

I think back to that night on the Savannah River with Jo. The night we painted each other's faces with red dirt from the Ashes.

"It was Jo, wasn't it?" I say, but Greer's silent. "She used her money, didn't she?"

Greer Jr. shakes his head, showing he's not budging. "Gotta pick my little girl up from day care. She's placed purple unicorn snot in her teacher's hair."

"Unicorn snot?"

343

"Purple bubble gum," he chuckles. "Well, you'd better get going; someone's inside waiting for you."

I open the car door. "Wait, was it Jo?"

Greer Jr. puts the key in the ignition, turns it clockwise. The engine roars. "Red clay."

Inside Plum Orchard, it's how I remember from childhood. The long entryway lined with plum trees, with feathery white mums alongside plush understory. I stop in the middle of the dirt road, close my eyes and inhale, take it all in.

If heaven exists beyond the clouds, I imagine my parents are smiling—happy their son's a little like the scrawny kid they loved; standing on the land where they fell in love. Jo comes to mind. In retrospect, I wish I'd figured out a way to trap her giggle in a bottle, bundle her smiles in plastic bags, and tuck her affection deep inside my coat pocket.

Edith runs toward me. She jumps into my arms, wraps her legs around my waist.

I wrap my arm around her back. "Did you do this?"

"Do what?"

"Red clay?"

"Red what?"

"Nothing." It wasn't her. I knew before I tested her; it was Jo. "This marriage is not ideal," I say into her ear. "But I wanna be happy. I wanna be happy. Don't you?"

"I'm not happy." Edith slides off me. When her feet meet brown soil, I gently release her waist.

Me either. I nod. "We should talk."

Edith and I stroll through Plum Orchard like the friends we've been. She tells me about James. How he's the only person she's ever loved. That she pursued me in an attempt to make James jealous after she'd caught him and Larry in bed together the night before the Gala. Edith blushes when speaking about the night I took her virginity. Said it didn't hurt as much as she thought it would. Says she enjoyed it, but it never would've happened if she wasn't pissed at James.

Edith sighs, says it's my turn. That whatever we share stays between us. She laughs and says, "I won't tell anyone if you cry, Cove."

I laugh, shake my head, feel my face go red. Seconds later, I tell her how I feel—tell her about Jo. I tell her about how, even at the Lineup, my chest got tight, and my heart hit the floor when I first heard Jo's voice; say:

"All I know is when you feel a love like that, all you want to do is reach out, grab it, never let it go. You want to forget every past fuckup, only think of what you could've had, and kick yourself silly over the stupid shit and stupid people you let impede it. You think of the moments wasted not holding that love, moments not had. You think of their smile and how you'd mason jar their laughter just to hear it. How life ends and begins in their stare. And how parades march to the melody of them voicing your name. You want their skin close, their hand woven between your fingers. And you'd do and say just about anything to fucking kiss them, hold them. You'd be the little spoon because them holding you doesn't make you feel small, it makes you feel big. That kind of love says, here is my heart, eat it! Go ahead, eat it! Rip it out. Hold it, please. Digest it, take me in. All of me. Because I'm nothing unless consumed by you. A part of you."

"Does she know?"

"Know what?"

"Come on, we're being honest. Does she know you still feel that way?"

I shrug.

What I feel for Jo won't go away. It won't be re-created or recycled like old pet

345

names given to new entanglements. I'm the Hopeful now, hoping my hands meet her face once more. Hoping we'll stand face-to-face again. Her face in my hands, my lips near her mouth. And yet, I can't wipe the coward away. The coward I was for not standing up to Elenore and trusting in Jo to see the good in me. I'll always wonder—had I just been honest with Jo, would she have loved me imperfectly?—with imperfections?

Edith sighs, gives me a look of disapproval, much like the look I used to give her. "Does Jo know you love her?"

I feel it inside, rising. Eyes feel tight; I blink, cheeks are wet. Fuck. I never tell girls *I love you*. I love Jo. "She doesn't know."

"Well . . ." Chin up, Edith smirks, gazes at the mountains visible over the plum trees. "What are you gonna do about it?"

There's no easy answer. So, I don't give her one. Truth is, without question, I know what I want. I sigh, humph. I look into the warm sunny sky, gaze at blue mountains in the distance, and watch an AerTrain head toward the Ashes.

48

JOSEPHINE

It's dark in the Ashes. But last night's moon smiles hard over snowcapped trees, skeletal bushes, cracked streets, and jigs using cardboard for sheets in our cold streets. I take my head out the window and stare at its base, where a cockroach flaps, planning its next move. Didn't seal the window last night after Boah's peace rally. Knees pressed into the floor mattress, I peer out the window, glare at the bug, then back at the window. I think of catching it, but don't. Why should I? The Ashes is its home just as much as it's mine.

Vye snores.

Laying my back against the stained mattress, I lift the green curtain separating us to look at her brown face. Vye smiles when she sleeps. She seems so peaceful it's hard imagining the mess she is when awake. Three days after I read Vye's first letter in New Georgia, Neal was dragged out of bed by cops, killed, and strung up on the hanging tree.

I asked Vye why she or Boah didn't tell me about Neal—she said, "Yuh got yuh mother's temper. Had yuh known, I know what you'd've done. And whatcha thinking of doing now—" She paused, placed both hands gently on either side of my face, and continued speaking with red eyes and watery pupils. "Yuh my niece, but I see yuh as a daughter, my baby girl. Didn't wanna to lose another child the same way."

We still divide our sleeping space in three. Vye hasn't moved Neal's floor mattress. And I don't think she ever will. The stained bed's the way he left it.

Lopsided, unmade, with an army cap tucked beneath his thin pillow. Vye secretly hopes he'll strut right through the door, smiling, throwing bad jokes. Can't blame her. I wish he'd come home, too. I'd do just about anything to hear Neal call me a butthead again.

I check the time. It's almost time to go. We gotta get up, get dressed, and head to the water hole. I tap Vye's big toe.

Vye yawns. "What time is it?"

"Five o'clock."

"Boil enough for me, will yuh?"

"Okay." I tiptoe past Vye, stepping over red sneakers, head to the kitchenette to boil water for washing up.

Outside, fog exits our mouths walking to the meetup point. It's so cold out here, I can't feel my legs. I doubt Vye can either. But we keep walking. Tugging thin coats close to shivering bodies, looking up at the dark sky, wishing the sun was there.

It's been about four months since Gaitlin and I rode the AerTrain through the mountains back to the Ashes. Three months since anyone died of Radius. Plume serum works.

At first, folks were skeptical—suspicious of Gaitlin's true intentions—wondered why a doctor from New Georgia cared so much. To ease their worry, I'd stick my hand in Morones's cage. He bit my wrist and gave me Radius. Once physical symptoms of the disease presented themselves, people watched Gaitlin inject serum in my arm. Twenty-four hours later, they witnessed for themselves the miracle of the plumes. One by one, those infected with Radius received the serum. And like me, twenty-four hours later, they woke Radius-free.

We reach the water hole one hour before takeoff, just as Boah instructed late last night. In the past, whenever folks'd come here, there'd be kids coupled up on rotted couches, chairs, or matted together sucking tongues in a corner, while pot and moonshine users congregated in the middle of the room— smoking and drinking around trash burning in the green metal trash can. Not tonight. And not anymore. Boah's turned the infamous make-out point into our new headquarters.

Last meeting, Boah explained if we're gunna to take back freedoms, we've gotta start with a new name . . . a new mission. He stood before the crowd of border kids and a few adults from loads of neighboring New United States and said we can't use the phrase Revolt Rebels anymore, 'cause we're not rebels. He said Revolt Rebels hurt folks and we're not doing that—that we're different, that we just wanna make life better without pushing others down below us. Boah ended his speech with something John Ready said before the Lineup. He said, "We must be irrepressible."

White paint matted to my fingertips makes me smile. I look around the water hole. OldTimers, men, women, and children of every race sport black shirts with #IRREPRESSED painted in white in the center. Art feels good when it's for me. For so long it was something created to feel closer to my parents. To remember them outside bullets that claimed their sadness. But now sketching is my gift to me, another way to see the world and all the people in it. Still, I wish my parents were here to see all this. Wonder if they saw all the hope gathered in this space when they were alive, if they'd choose life or death. If they'd choose me. I'll never know.

In dim corners, folks discuss deadly outcomes with serious faces. Outside, kids stand in two-inch snow, warming stiff fingers with warm lava rocks. Every so often they dap, fist-bump, and brag how they pieced together an old freight train using scrap metal from the broke amusement park.

This coat's not warm enough; my hands are freezing. I'd stick them into my pockets, but they have holes cold air seeps through. In appearance, the inside of this old warehouse is the same. Cracks in the ceiling are huge—so are the holes in the tin walls. It must've rained sleet overnight—I can tell. In every direction, small patches of black ice glisten motionless, as if it sinisterly waits for passersby to make a mistake, trip, and fall.

Moonlight sneaking through holes in this oval warehouse gives a little light, but the trash burning in the green tin can in the middle of the room is the best source of warmth and light.

In the front room, fifteen to twenty kids gather around Boah. They're huddled over a small 3D model replica of the Ashes, New Georgia, and the mountain dividing us, built using matches, toothpicks, and Popsicle sticks—talking about tonight's plan, plotting our near and distant futures.

Boah catches me staring. He leaves the group with two tin cups of hot water, walks over. When he reaches me, he gives me the cup. "Look at us. I'm proud of you." His smile is gentle, reassuring. "Who'd ever believe this would happen?"

"You." And it's true.

Two years ago, when randos burned his family's sacred Siksika gathering grounds, Boah didn't get mad. He got hope. While I was in New Georgia, Boah, and Jessup, and John Ready traveled across New America. They stopped in borderlands, talked with border people. Raising awareness of the injustices and crimes committed in outer regions. Their tireless efforts created irrepressible groups all over NUSA rallying for hope, calling for change.

For months after I returned, I was skeptical—didn't believe. No matter how cruel some folks were, couldn't see myself causing harm to people I'd spent months with in New Georgia. Good people like Greer, Aurice, Cove. Folks who welcomed me with open arms after my attack. But month after month, I watched the number of Irrepressibles grow in insurmountable numbers. Each person had different issues with the government. Sometimes needs were basic. Just last week, a five-year-old white kid walked up to me. Scratching her bald head, she said, "Do you have any spare shoes? These shoes talk." The holes at the top of her shoes were so big, I saw holes in her white socks. Her toes were frostbitten.

Until Boah formed the Irrepressible group, I'd thought it impossible for poor folks to rise. Like many times before, I was wrong. But I've changed. I belong here in the Ashes beside my people, reassembling trains next to Boah and others, unafraid to fight and use our voices.

The night Gaitlin and I arrived, every cop was in the hole, starving—uniforms soaking in piss and shit, yelling for food and drink from their individual caged holes in the ground—dying of Radius. Several kids begged Boah to string up the cops, hang 'em. But Boah released them after what I said. "If we do this, we're no better than them. We might as wall strip 'em naked and wear their uniforms."

Boah folded his arms across his chest. "Trade Trains didn't come for months. Whatdah you suggest? Too many want 'em dead. And the ones that don't aren't good with dirty cops walking 'round free."

"Send them to Saven."

"Did you hear me? No Trade Trains for—"

I took his arm in my hand, tugged it. "By foot."

Boah set the cops free. Gaitlin cured their Radius. Excluding trustful Jessup, we packed the cops' backpacks with bread, water, and fish slices and sent them into the mountains to survive on their own.

Boah nudges my shoulder, bringing me back to the present. He directs my attention to Kyra and Margo. They're smooched together in a corner, trying to stay warm. I smile at them. They smile back.

I love seeing them together. "They're happy." I sip hot water.

"Me too." He smiles.

"Bo! We need you," Stella says. Stella's from the Rot—borderlands outside New Oregon.

I smirk. "She's calling you Bo now?"

Boah shakes his head, chuckling. "You're so annoying."

"Hmm, that's interesting coming from somebody so annoying."

He bumps my shoulder playfully. "Be right back?"

I nod, watch him join Stella and the others gathered around the 3D model.

I look up. Stars shine brightly through imperfections in the roof. It's cold outside—I know. But I wanna see the sky.

Two hours later, we're all outside. I stand behind the water hole, staring at the forty-two-cart freight train that's fired up and ready to go.

One by one, we board the freight, and listen to its iron wheels clunk across the mountain.

I lift my chin to lemon skies. For four hours, we'll ride toward New Georgia, signs high. Scanning faces of OldTimers and kids inside my cart, I see we all have the same dream. I smile at Vye and Jessup; they smile back.

We're sleepy, hungry, thirsty, and tired, but full of hope. We'll not submit. We'll conquer state after state, via freight train—cross mountains, swim rivers, and climb walls to bring change. We're no longer Hopefuls. We're not Revolt Rebels. We're the Irrepressibles. No longer controlled by laws passed down by Reps. Anti-silence in the hands of injustice. We deserve more. If more's not given, we'll take it. We won't be cruel like the RR's in 2030. We'll be different. We are different. We don't want rich folks to starve. But we don't wanna starve either. Don't wanna freeze to death. We want better. Our minds are no longer plagued with fear of disease. We crave knowledge. We want freedom. It's why we ride. And'll continue to ride.

I stick my head out the moving cart. In the distance, I see the old roller coaster. Boah grabs my hand, then sticks his head out too.

"It's happening now."

I nod. "There it is."

We lift our chins to the red sun. Allow its rays to warm our frozen cheeks and noses. I close my eyes and sigh. This feels right. It's strange, but for the first time in my life, I don't need *Great Expectations* and *Little Women*. Though they're beautiful tales, I prefer my story. It was hard leaving New Georgia behind, but in doing so, I realized that everything I thought I wanted, I already had.

Wealth lives in the heart of my people and our fight for survival. Unity exists in the stories of my childhood. Vye, Rashad, Neal, Boah, Jessup, Tessa, Kyra, Hothead Frank, Cove, Elenore, even Reed all had parts to play. They're forever unfinished chapters in my book—pages that shape, strengthen, and help me grow. And love, well, it's always been the brown palm holding my hand right now.

"Jo?" Boah says.

"Yeah?" I hear him smiling, feel him staring at my profile. With eyes closed, I imagine sketching his brown eyes. It's imperfectly perfect.

"I like you."

I flip my lids open, take warm sun into my eyes, and smile.

Author's Note

While *Monarch Rising* is a work of fiction, nonfictional elements of my childhood are weaved into the backbone of its story. Many of the fictional details in Jo's and Cove's character arcs are true—their personalities, backgrounds, and experiences are fragments of my own.

I grew up in the projects in East Georgia with a single mom—she worked while putting herself through college. Years later, she met my stepfather, a kind but stern ex-military man battling drug and alcohol addictions. And as a young adult, I discovered my bio father was ex-military and suffered from depression, poverty, PTSD, and schizophrenia.

Though tough to experience, these stories shaped my life, speech, writing . . . this book. I wouldn't be me without hard stories.

Writer James Baldwin once said, "Anyone who has ever struggled with poverty knows how extremely expensive it is to be poor." In writing this manuscript, I wanted to re-create the poor humans' struggle—to shine a light on underrepresented youth living in forgotten places—neighborhoods diversified with cool kids laughing, running, living, struggling, hoping for change.

Thanks for reading. Thanks for inviting these pages into your mind, heart, and world.

Metta,

Harper

Acknowledgments

Tremendous emotional, editorial, and creative support goes into writing a book; it's tough. I, like many others, didn't grasp how tough publishing truly is until undergoing the rigorous process. Below are some of the people who helped. I'll thank them below and I'll thank them now:

Harper releases a warm-hearted sigh. "Thank you very fucking much."

I'd like to thank my talented literary agent, Andrea Morrison. Working with you is magic. You champion my creative ideas and projects in a way I never dreamed possible. You brought back the joy of writing. I love brainstorming via Zoom and emailing work I'm excited about. I'm grateful for your professionalism, work ethic, kindness, and patience—I look forward to things to come. So lucky you're on my team.

I'd like to thank Genevieve Gagne-Hawes and Amy Berkower at Writers House, who read this novel years ago—your kind and straightforward constructive feedback helped this manuscript become what it is today.

To my editor Olivia Valcarce, I'm insanely grateful for you. You selected my book baby in the Lineup and now it's all grown up at the Gala. Working with you is cool, tough in good ways, teaching, exhilarating, and feels like freedom. Hope you had as much fun as I did. You changed my life.

To Scholastic, thanks for making my five-year-old self happy. I remember attending Scholastic Book Fairs as a dreamy-eyed kid. As an adult, I'm proud my debut book is with my childhood dream publisher. I'd like to thank the other talented folks on my publishing team who made this book possible, including David Levithan, Aimee Friedman, Rachel Feld, Shannon Pender, Daniela Escobar, and Melissa Schirmer.

To Mum . . . thanks for your love of writing . . . for putting pencil to paper on the day I was born (for reciting the first poem). You're the first writer I met. You taught me (while young) to love my brown skin. You encouraged and supported writing dreams. And when I came out, you challenged me not to hide, to be brave and tell Grandma. There aren't enough words to express my love.

To my grandparents: Hattie Virginia Jones (my real-life Aunt Vye) and Ernest Lee Jones Sr.—there's a hole in my heart filled only by memories of your love.

To my family—you know who you are—to the moon and back, I thank you.

Massive thanks to friends and writers who read my book—those who inspired, blurbed, supported, encouraged, or showed up to hold space during hard times: Tashamee Trotter, Casey R. Kelley (moon and back, honey boo), Sona Charaipotra, Shaun David Hutchinson, Alexa Martin, Liz Lawson, Beth Revis, Danielle Poulin, Kass Morgan, Kim Van Alkemade, Anna Berntsen, Alexandra Harper, Anita Howard, Taj McCoy, Debbie Rigaud, Christina Hammonds, J.A.M. Aiwuyor, Georgette Wilder, Aislinn Sarnacki, Jillian Smith, Debra Jones, Jennifer DeRosa, Emily Wibberley, Trish Lawrence, Therese Walsh, Kelly Coon, Chelsea Danielle, Suzanne Park, Irina Fabre, AJ Oakes, Ariel Vanece, Ellen O'Clover, Judy I. Lin, Cin Fabre, justin a. reynolds, Raquel Henry, Jenna Evans, Ari Tison, Ty Chapman, Andre, Kei, Noella Wells.

If unmentioned, know your time, compassion, efforts, panel discussions, and real life and online friendships are important. To aspiring writers, you've read it before, but I'll type it again: Don't quit. Keep dreaming. Keep writing. Keep querying. Speaking of querying, I'd like to thank literary agents I queried; the ones who read my book, loved it, offered constructive criticism, shaped it, and responded with kind, encouraging words. #KindRejectionsMatter.

Lastly, this book started as a dream. In the dream, a young girl walked toward a forbidden bridge where a boy stood amazed, staring at her. The boy feared love.

The girl craved it. In real life, being nonbinary, I was both the boy and girl in the dream, intensely battling a hate relationship with the concept of love; I wrote the first draft in three months. And now, a little over four years later, it's in your hands. Thank you for reading—I hope glimmers of your identity are in these pages, hope some parts made you smile. I even hope it made you almost cry. And to my Queer/ LGBTQIA+ Nonbinary (trans and non-trans), genderless kids and adult humans, in all the ways you present, in all the ways you love, you're seen, you're loved.

About the Author

Harper Glenn is an author of fiction. In addition to creating literary works that unveil the psychological, sociological, and economic disparities in poverty-stricken regions around the world, they love vintage books, anatomy, and old cemeteries. Though born and raised in Georgia, Harper resides in Washington State.

Connect online:

harperwrites.com

🐦 @harpwrites

📷 @harperglennwriter